P9-DCX-499

Praise for *The Shadow King*

NAMED A BEST BOOK OF 2019 BY
Time, *New York Times Book Review*, *Elle*, Barnes & Noble,
Los Angeles Times, *Literary Hub*, *Real Simple*,
Times Literary Supplement, *Library Journal*, and *BookPage*.

"Lyrical, remarkable. . . . The reader feels . . . in the steady hands of a master. . . . Hirut [is] as indelible and compelling a hero as any I've read in years."   —Namwali Serpell, *New York Times Book Review*

"A sprawling, unforgettable epic from an immensely talented author who's unafraid to take risks. . . . [R]endered all the more effective by [Maaza] Mengiste's gift at creating memorable characters. . . . The star of the novel, however, is Mengiste's gorgeous writing, which makes *The Shadow King* nearly impossible to put down. Mengiste has a real gift for language; her writing is powerful but never florid, gripping the reader and refusing to let go. And this, combined with her excellent sense of pacing, makes the book one of the most beautiful novels of the year. It's a brave, stunning call for the world to remember all who we've lost to senseless violence."   —Michael Schaub, NPR

"In haunting and beautiful prose, Mengiste shines a light on those whose lives are not often heralded."   —*Newsweek*

"Ambitious and illuminating."   —Elizabeth Sile, *Real Simple*

"A beautiful and thoughtful epic."
    —Francesca Capossela, *Los Angeles Review of Books*

"Stunning. . . . [Mengiste] produced a work of fiction that is epic in reach, with brilliant borrowings from the forms of classic tragedy. . . . The book is impossible to put down or put out of mind."
    —*BookPage*, starred review

"*The Shadow King* exposes a brutal chapter in Ethiopia's history and urges readers to listen for the untold stories of war, especially those of women." —Katie Noah Gibson, *Shelf Awareness*

"Monumental. . . . Mengiste's extraordinary characters—shrewd Kidane, militant Aster, the enigmatic cook, narcissistic Italian commander Fucelli, conflicted photographer Ettore, elusive prostitute Fifi, even haunted Selassie—epitomize the impossibly intricate ties between humanity and monstrosity, and the unthinkable, immeasurable cost of survival." —*Booklist*, starred review

"Mengiste again brings heart and authenticity to a slice of Ethiopian history. . . . [She] breaks new ground in this evocative, mesmerizing account of the role of women during wartime—not just as caregivers, but as warriors defending their country." —*Publishers Weekly*, starred review

"Fascinating and tension-filled. . . . Descriptions of the fog of battle are exquisite and horrific, all the more remarkable for being told from a woman's point of view. Highly recommended." —*Library Journal*, starred review

"Mengiste is a master of characterization. . . . A memorable portrait of a people at war—a war that has long demanded recounting from an Ethiopian point of view." —*Kirkus Reviews*

"A brilliant novel, lyrically lifting history towards myth. It's also compulsively readable. I devoured it in two days." —Salman Rushdie, author of *Quichotte*

"*The Shadow King* is a beautiful and devastating work; of women holding together a world ripping itself apart. They will slip into your dreams and overtake your memories." —Marlon James, author of *Black Leopard, Red Wolf*

"With epic sweep and dignity, Mengiste has lifted this struggle into legend, along with the women who fought in it. Beautiful, horrifying, elegant, and haunted, *The Shadow King* is a modern classic."
　　—Andrew Sean Greer, Pulitzer Prize–winning author of *Less*

"*The Shadow King* is a novel about war and history, both epic in scope and intimate in detail. . . . Maaza Mengiste has a gift for rendering everyone in this story, resister and invader alike, with great nuance and complexity, leaving us with no room for easy judgment. A wonderful book."
　　—Laila Lalami, author of *The Other Americans*

"One of the most affecting accounts of the terror of war I have ever read, all the more so for the being cloaked in the language of beauty, such that the words and their meaning burn through the senses. *The Shadow King* is a work borne of rage, a rage made magnificent for its compassion and the story it tells us—that in war there are no winners."　　—Aminatta Forna, author of *Happiness*

"Maaza Mengiste has given us a powerful tale of a woman warrior—not some mythical superhero, but a girl who holds on to the memory of her parents and her father's gun and longs to do battle to avenge their loss. Reminiscent of Maxine Hong Kingston's *Woman Warrior* and Marlon James's *The Book of Night Women*, this is a compelling story of female empowerment and an epic one at that."
　　—Mary Morris, author of *Gateway to the Moon*

ALSO BY MAAZA MENGISTE

Beneath the Lion's Gaze

THE
SHADOW KING

A NOVEL

MAAZA MENGISTE

W. W. NORTON & COMPANY
Independent Publishers Since 1923

The Shadow King is a work of fiction. Names, characters, places, and incidents are the product of the author's imagination or are used fictitiously. Any resemblance to actual events, locales, or persons, living or dead, is entirely coincidental.

Copyright © 2019 by Maaza Mengiste

All rights reserved
Printed in the United States of America
First published as a Norton paperback 2020

For information about permission to reproduce selections from this book, write to Permissions, W. W. Norton & Company, Inc., 500 Fifth Avenue, New York, NY 10110

For information about special discounts for bulk purchases, please contact W. W. Norton Special Sales at specialsales@wwnorton.com or 800-233-4830

Manufacturing by LSC Communications, Harrisonburg
Book design by Chris Welch Design
Production manager: Julia Druskin

Library of Congress Cataloging-in-Publication Data

Names: Mengiste, Maaza, author.
Title: The shadow king : a novel / Maaza Mengiste.
Description: First edition. | New York : W. W. Norton & Company, [2019]
Identifiers: LCCN 2019020502 | ISBN 9780393083569 (hardcover)
Subjects: LCSH: World War, 1939–1945—Women—Fiction. |
World War, 1939–1945—Campaigns—Ethiopia—Fiction. |
GSAFD: Historical fiction | War stories
Classification: LCC PS3613.E488 S53 2019 | DDC 813/.6—dc23
LC record available at https://lccn.loc.gov/2019020502

ISBN 978-0-393-35851-3 pbk.

W. W. Norton & Company, Inc., 500 Fifth Avenue, New York, N.Y. 10110
www.wwnorton.com

W. W. Norton & Company Ltd., 15 Carlisle Street, London W1D 3BS

4 5 6 7 8 9 0

To my mother
for your love, for everything

To my father
for never leaving me, even though you are gone

&

To Marco
without whom none of this would have been possible

. . . hereafter we shall be made into things of song for
the men of the future. —*THE ILIAD* BY HOMER,
TRANSLATED BY RICHMOND LATTIMORE

Woe to the land shadowing with wings, which is
beyond the rivers of Ethiopia. —ISAIAH 18:1

—what god hurls you on, stroke on stroke
    to the long dying fall?
Why the horror clashing through your music,
    terror struck to song?—
. . . Where do your words of god and grief begin?
—*AGAMEMNON* BY AESCHYLUS,
TRANSLATED BY ROBERT FAGLES

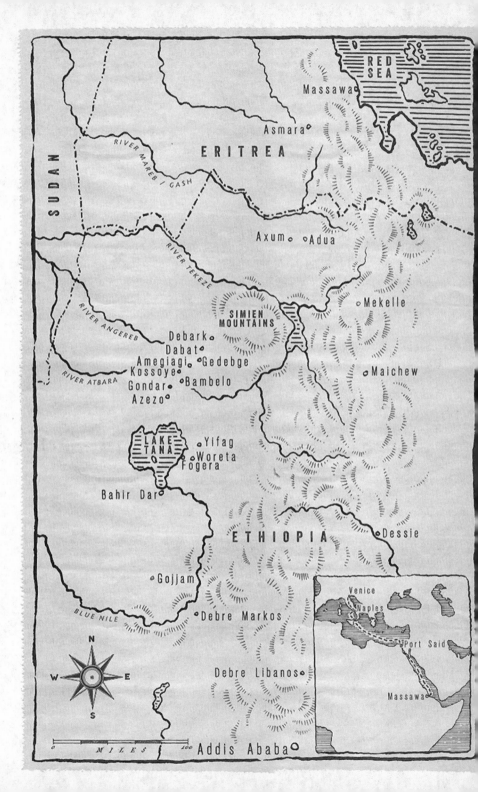

THE
SHADOW KING

PROLOGUE
WAITING

1974

SHE DOES NOT WANT TO REMEMBER BUT SHE IS HERE AND MEMORY IS gathering bones. She has come by foot and by bus to Addis Ababa, across terrain she has chosen to forget for nearly forty years. She is two days early but she will wait for him, seated on the ground in this corner of the train station, the metal box on her lap, her back pressed against the wall, rigid as a sentinel. She has put on the dress she does not wear every day. Her hair is neatly braided and sleek and she has been careful to hide the long scar that puckers at the base of her neck and trails over her shoulder like a broken necklace.

In the box are his letters, *le lettere, ho sepolto le mie lettere, è il mio segreto, Hirut, anche il tuo segreto. Segreto, secret, meestir. You must keep them for me until I see you again. Now go. Vatene. Hurry before they catch you.*

There are newspaper clippings with dates spanning the course of the war between her country and his. She knows he has arranged them from the start, 1935, to nearly the end, 1941.

In the box are photographs of her, those he took on Fucelli's orders and labeled in his own neat handwriting: *una bella ragazza. Una soldata feroce.* And those he took of his own free will, mementos scavenged from the life of the frightened young woman she was in that prison, behind that barbed-wire fence, trapped in terrifying nights that she could not free herself from.

Inside the box are the many dead that insist on resurrection.

She has traveled for five days to get to this place. She has pushed

her way through checkpoints and nervous soldiers, past frightened
villagers whispering of a coming revolution, and violent student protests. She has watched while a parade of young women, raising fists and
rifles, marched past the bus taking her to Bahir Dar. They stared at her,
an aging woman in her long drab dress, as if they did not know those
who came before them. As if this were the first time a woman carried
a gun. As if the ground beneath their feet had not been won by some
of the greatest fighters Ethiopia had ever known, women named Aster,
Nardos, Abebech, Tsedale, Aziza, Hanna, Meaza, Aynadis, Debru,
Yodit, Ililta, Abeba, Kidist, Belaynesh, Meskerem, Nunu, Tigist,
Tsehai, Beza, Saba, and a woman simply called the cook. Hirut mur-
mured the names of those women as the students marched past, each
utterance hurling her back in time until she was once again on ragged
terrain, choking in fumes and gunpowder, suffocating in the pungent
stench of poison.

She was brought back to the bus, to the present, only after one old
man grabbed her by the arm as he took a seat next to her: *If Mussoloni
couldn't get rid of the emperor, what do these students think they are doing?*
Hirut shook her head. She shakes her head now. She has come this far
to return this box, to rid herself of the horror that staggers back unbid-
den. She has come to give up the ghosts and drive them away. She has
no time for questions. She has no time to correct an old man's pronunciation. One name always drags with it another: nothing travels alone.

From outside, a fist of sunlight bears through the dusty window of
the Addis Ababa train station. It bathes her head in warmth and settles
on her feet. A breeze unfurls into the room. Hirut looks up and sees a
young woman dressed in *ferenj* clothes push through the door, clutching a worn suitcase. The city rises behind her. Hirut sees the long dirt
road that leads back to the city center. She sees three women balancing
bundles of firewood. There, just beyond the roundabout is a procession
of priests where once, in 1941, there had been warriors and she, one of
them. The flat metal box, the length of her forearm, grows cool on her

lap, lies as heavy as a dying body against her stomach. She shifts and traces the edges of the metal, rigid and sharp, rusting with age.

Somewhere tucked into the crevice of this city, Ettore is waiting two days to see her. He is sitting at his desk in the dim glow of a small office, hunched over one of his photos. Or, he is sitting in a chair drenched in the same light that tugs at her feet, staring toward his Italia. He is counting time, too, both of them tipping toward the appointed day. Hirut stares at the sunlit vista pressing itself through the swinging doors. As they start to close, she holds her breath. Addis Ababa shrinks to a sliver and slips out of the room. Ettore slumps and falls back into darkness. When they finally shut, she is left alone again, clutching the box in this echoing chamber.

She feels the first threads of a familiar fear. I am Hirut, she reminds herself, daughter of Getey and Fasil, born on a blessed day of harvest, beloved wife and loving mother, a soldier. She releases a breath. It has taken so long to get here. It has taken almost forty years of another life to begin to remember who she had once been. The journey back began like this: with a letter, the first she has ever received:

Cara Hirut, They tell me that I have finally found you. They tell me you married and live in a place too small for maps. This messenger says he knows your village. He says he will deliver this to you and bring me back your message. Please come to Addis. Hurry. There is unrest here and I must leave. I have no place to go but Italy. Tell me when to meet you at the station. Be careful, they have risen against the emperor. Please come. Bring the box. Ettore.

It is dated with the *ferenj* date: 23 April 1974.

The doors open again and this time, it is one of those soldiers she has seen scattered along the path to this city. A young man who lets noise tumble in over his shoulder. He is carrying a new rifle slung on his back carelessly. His uniform is unpatched and untorn. It is free of dirt and

suited for his size. He is too eager-eyed to have ever held a dying compatriot, too sharp with his movements to have ever known real fatigue.

"Land to the tiller! Revolutionary Ethiopia!" he shouts, and the air
in the station flees the room. He lifts his gun with a child's clumsiness,
aware of being observed. He points to the photograph of Emperor Haile
Selassie just above the entrance. "Down with the emperor!" he shouts,
swinging his gun from the wall to the back of the nervous station.

The waiting room is crowded, full of those who want to leave the
roiling city. They breathe in and shrink away from this uniformed boy
straining toward manhood. Hirut looks at the picture of Emperor Haile
Selassie: a dignified, delicate-boned man stares into the camera, somber
and regal in his military uniform and medals. The soldier, too, glances
up, left with nothing to do but hear his own voice echo back. He shifts
awkwardly, then turns and races out the door.

The dead pulse beneath the lid. For so long, they have been rising
and crumbling in the face of her anger, giving way to the shame that
still stuns her into paralysis. She can hear them now telling her what she
already knows:

The real emperor of this country is on his farm tilling the tiny plot of
land next to hers. He has never worn a crown and lives alone and has no
enemies. He is a quiet man who once led a nation against a steel beast,
and she was his most trusted soldier: the proud guard of the Shadow
King. Tell them, Hirut. There is no time but now.

She can hear the dead growing louder: We must be heard. We must
be remembered. We must be known. We will not rest until we have
been mourned. She opens the box.

⇒

THERE ARE TWO bundles of pictures, each tied with the same delicate
blue string. He has written her name in loose-jointed handwriting on
one, the letters ballooning across the paper folded over the stack and
held in place by string. Hirut unties it and two photos slide out, sticking

together from age. One is of the French photographer who roamed the northern highlands taking photos, a thin slip of a man with a large camera. On the back of the picture it reads, Gondar, 1935. This is what we know of this man: He is a former draftsman from Albi, a failed painter with a slippery voice and small blue eyes. He holds no importance except what memory allows. But he is in the box, and he is one of the dead, and he insists on his right to be known. What we will say because we must: there is also a photograph of Hirut taken by this Frenchman. A portrait shot while he visited the home of Aster and Kidane and requested a picture of the servants to trade with other photographers or exchange for film. She turns away from it. She does not want to see her picture. She wants to close the box to shut us up. But it is here and this younger Hirut also refuses a quiet grave.

This is Hirut. This is her wide-open face and curious gaze. She has her mother's high forehead and her father's curved mouth. Her bright eyes are wary but calm, catching light in golden prisms. She leans into the space in front of her, a pretty girl with slender neck and sloping shoulders. Her expression is guarded, her posture peculiarly stiff, absent the natural elegance that she will not know for many years is hers. She looks away from the camera and struggles not to squint, her face turned to the biting sun. It is easy to see the sharp slope of her collarbone, the scarless neck that rises from the V collar of her dress. It is this picture that will preserve the unmarked expanse of skin that spreads across her shoulders and back. No other way to recall the unblemished body she once carried with the carelessness of a child. And look, in the background, so far away she is hard to see, there is Aster, pausing to watch, an elegant line cutting through light.

BOOK
1
INVASION

1935

▰

HIRUT HEARS ASTER SHOUTING HER NAME, CALLING FOR HER IN A voice threatening to break from strain. Hirut looks up from the slow burning fire she is tending in a corner of the courtyard. She is hunched into a stool, next to a pile of onions waiting to be peeled. The cook is behind her in the kitchen, chopping meat for the evening meal. Aster should be drinking her coffee in bed, tucked inside a soft blanket, perhaps looking out the window and gazing at her flowers. This should be a quiet morning. Hirut stiffens at the intrusion. Then Aster calls Hirut's name again, and this time, she is speaking so loudly, with such exertion, that the cook pauses her rapid slicing, the morning birds fall silent, and even the large tree just outside the gate seems to catch the breeze to hold itself still. For an instant, nothing moves.

What did I do? Hirut feels her hands shaking.

The cook leans out of the kitchen door, startled: She's in our room. She points toward the servants' quarters. What's she doing in there? Hurry, get up.

Hirut drops the twig she was using to shift charcoal and scrambles up. The thought forms: Aster is in the servants' quarters. She is in that small box of a room that Hirut shares with the cook, that place where they go at night to shed their usefulness and sleep. It is a room separated from the many-roomed house where Aster lives with her husband, Kidane. It is a space that is not a space, a room that is less than a

room. It is a dark hollow carved into endless tired nights. It is not meant
to be seen in daylight. It is not meant for someone like Aster.

She's in there? Hirut asks.

She's never gone in there before. The older woman is leaning out of
the doorway, her strong arms holding on to each side of the frame as she
stretches to look at the narrow path that extends toward the servants'
quarters, as if she is afraid to leave the safety of her kitchen. Did Kidane
come back?

Hirut shakes her head. Kidane took his horse and left before dawn.

So it's just us, the cook says. She was arguing with Kidane when I
was getting his things ready.

Hirut wants to tell the cook that Aster should, in fact, be in bed. She
should be lying still to ease the pain of her monthly bleeding. They
should be proceeding through their day as usual, working until the
dome of sky hangs heavy above them, weighted by thick stars.

Go on, go. The cook steps back into the kitchen, but she stares
intently at Hirut, the knife held limply in her hand. She can't start looking in our things, she adds. She adjusts the scarf on her head, pushes
back the few stray strands of gray hair poking out in front.

The cook is talking about the old rifle Hirut's father gave her just
before he died. Along with the dress she came with and the small necklace she is wearing, Hirut has nothing else that is hers in this world.

Everything's hidden, she says, because the cook seems unusually
nervous.

Aster calls her name again, insistence giving way to unrestrained
anger.

The cook bends as if pulled by that voice. Go! she shouts. And
answer her!

Hirut spins on her heels. I'm coming! She dashes to the servants'
quarters.

She stands at the door of the servants' quarters and she sees for the
first time how truly small it is, how dingy and shrunken the space she

has called home for almost a year. In the semidarkness of the cramped room, Aster, dressed in a lovely abesha chemise, feels too much for this space that is barely enough for anything. It is less than a box, it is an airless hole enclosed in mud and straw and dung. There is no proper door, no crisp windowpane. They sleep on flimsy mattresses they have to roll up so they can walk. There are only scraps of discarded blankets nailed over narrow openings, rags that trap dust and dark. It is a space made to fit two people who have been made to fit their lives around one woman and her husband. It was not built for someone used to fine clothes and fresh breezes wafting through silk curtains.

Where were you? Aster turns to her. Her short hair carves a perfect arc into the band of weak sun sliding through the window above her head. The tepid light brushes a warm glow across her smooth cheeks. She is standing in the only place where the sun can enter the room, through that tiny hole no wider than Hirut's head, dug out of the wall like an afterthought. Each morning, the cook hooks one side of the torn curtain onto a nail to air the room, and every night she unhooks it to close it.

Where's the necklace? Give me my necklace.

Hirut watches a feeble patch of sunlight stretch at Aster's feet as if it, too, were at the woman's command. Her head is down when Aster pushes through to Hirut's side of the room.

He's just trying to protect you. Aster lifts Hirut's mattress and lets it fall, wiping her hands on the corner of the dress that looks too white in the dim room. She picks up the small crate that Hirut and the cook use to store their few belongings and shakes out the meager contents. He said he lost it but I know it's here.

Aster drops the crate and peers down, one hand smoothing the front of her long abesha chemise. She is a graceful woman with soft flesh where Hirut has angles and bone. She is not much taller than Hirut, but on the uneven dirt floor, she appears large and imposing.

My mother gave that to me to give to my husband when I married.

I know he didn't just lose it. She narrows her eyes as she looks down at Hirut. He's hiding something.

Hirut hunches her shoulders the way the cook has taught her. She wants to say it is not her fault that Aster fights with her husband, Kidane. It is not Hirut's fault that he is kind to her, she cannot help that this makes Aster cry.

I don't know where it is, she says. She knows that in the early days of mourning for their only son, Aster threw away many things. She made a heap of her finest dresses and capes and even jewelry and set them on fire in the compound, pounding her chest as flames began to chew into the items. The cook said there were some things Aster still looked for, forgetting she burned them. I've never seen it, Hirut adds.

So you want me to believe Kidane threw it away? Then she laughs. Or do you want me to think he gave it to you himself?

Kidane is the one her mother used to call "brother" and "friend" and sometimes she even said, Hirut, he is like my son though we are not so far in age. I cared for him when his mother died. I carried him on my back when I was no more than a child myself. He and I, we grew up together. This is a man who has shown me kindness, and if I am ever gone, he will take care of you. And because he was so loved by her mother, Hirut came to this house after her parents' deaths already loving him. It is not her fault that he loves her, too, that he calls her Little One, and Little Sister, and Rutiye.

Do you know what we do to thieves? Aster asks. In the somber light of the room, it is hard to see the beauty she is always so proud to display: the bright eyes and high cheeks, the full lips and the slender neck that slopes down to shoulders that have not borne the breaking weight of water jugs and firewood. If I find it here, not even Kidane will be able to help you.

Hirut knows what happens to thieves. She has seen those pitiful boys and men begging in the mercato, their skinny bodies hobbled by a missing leg and hand, their eyes still wide from the shock of the cruel loss. A sourness seeps into the back of her throat.

Aster lifts Hirut's mattress. Then she is unrolling it and undoing the rope Hirut uses to cinch her gun in place. The cook said Aster would take it away if she saw it, but Hirut never thought that Aster could come into this place that was only for servants. She thought there were places that Aster did not go. Hirut cannot breathe as she watches the rope slip off the mattress. It has been so long since she has been home, so long since she has known what it was like to move without asking permission, to do what needed to be done rather than what was demanded. Once, she had been more than a servant. She had been someone unafraid to own what was rightly hers.

And then Aster says, What's this? She is still standing below the window, the blanket and gun dangling from her hand.

A stench that Hirut has never gotten used to wafts by. It comes from a short stack of stones near the entrance where, as a boy, Kidane learned to slaughter sheep for special occasions. Beneath those stones is a small shallow ditch where blood used to flow. That's what you smell, the cook said to her when she first arrived at the house. It's the rot of blood, you'll get used to it. Still in the room is the stink of old blood, of help-less animals, of the piss and excrement that seeped into dirt, instinct and fear working together.

Whose gun is this?

Hirut says, It's mine.

The rifle was Hirut's father's most prized possession. It was too big for the small crate so Hirut kept it tucked into the pile of straw and blan-kets that she uses as a mattress, all of it covered by a large sheet that she knots at the corners to keep intact. On those nights when she is at her most tired, she sleeps so she can feel the rifle by her side and pretend it is her mother's arm.

Aster holds the rifle to light. It's old, she says. She runs a finger over the five grooves in the barrel, marks that Hirut's father said helped him count the Italians he killed. Do you know how to use it? She weighs its heft, testing its balance. My father taught me, like he taught my brothers. She presses the butt against her shoulder, one hand steadying the barrel. Where did you get it?

From home, Hirut says.

Home: exactly five kilometers from this place that is also called Aster and Kidane's house. Five kilometers: a distance that Hirut will not comprehend until later, when she realizes that all things, even those things lost, can be put down on paper and measured. What she comprehends, standing at the threshold of her tiny room staring at Aster, is that even if she could run back at a fast sprint, it would not decrease the distance separating her from the plot of land that holds her parents' bones. She is far from home.

Home, she says again. My father gave it to me.

Then Hirut feels a hand on her shoulder. She turns around and it is Kidane, bathed in the bright afternoon light.

What are you doing here? Kidane's frame fills the door and blocks the light. A slender line of sweat trails down his neck, darkening his white tunic. The bottoms of his white jodhpurs are dusty; a leaf drags from the hem. What happened?

Ask her where she put the necklace.

Kidane searches Hirut's face, then he turns back to his wife. Where did you get that gun? He is surprised. The cook had it?

It's hers, Aster says. Then she coughs, her nose curling. It stinks in here. They don't clean themselves.

Give it back to her. It is spoken in the tone Kidane takes when he expects to be obeyed. It's not yours.

Aster's laugh cuts through the room. So you'll let her disobey the emperor's orders? According to your leader, this now belongs to the armies of Ethiopia.

Kidane wipes his neck with a handkerchief he shoves back into his pocket. He dusts off his jodhpurs. He seems to be thinking. Then he says, Little One, can I see it?

He waits until Hirut nods before he takes the gun from Aster. He holds it in both hands. He hefts it to his shoulder the same way Aster did, the same way Hirut's father showed Hirut how to do.

It's a Wujigra, he says. My father used one in the battle at Adua when we faced these Italians the first time. This must be at least forty years old, maybe closer to fifty. He raises it higher and looks down the barrel, points it out the door, into the courtyard as if he can see beyond it, through walls and past the gate, toward Hirut's old home all those kilometers away. Do you have bullets?

Hirut has memorized the contents of the crate that are scattered around Aster's feet: the cook's spare scarf, knotted around three Maria Theresa thalers and two blue buttons; the outgrown dress that Hirut came with; a piece of charcoal she uses for drawing; a broken ceramic plate with pink flowers that is the cook's; the chipped handle of a water jug that is also the cook's; and a bullet that is Hirut's.

Where are the bullets? Kidane lowers the gun. How many does she have?

There is only that single bullet. There has only ever been one bullet and it belongs to that gun and that gun belongs to her. Her father made her promise to keep the two separate until she was in real danger and then, my child, you hold it like I've taught you and you aim it at the heart like I've shown you and you must fear nothing except leaving your enemy alive.

I didn't even know she had this. Aster puts her hands on her waist, and in the semidark, Hirut can see her chin trembling, her gaze on Kidane shifting between tenderness and unease. What did you do with it?

Not now. Kidane's voice is a whisper. Little One. He clears his throat. This gun is important to me. Do you know a war is coming?

The war is all that the cook and the servants who meet at the mercato can talk about. They gather and whisper about freed slaves and liberation by the *ferenj* army. She shakes her head.

She's lying, Aster says. Look. She holds up a piece of paper.

It is one of those leaflets scattered everywhere in the mercato. She did not know the cook had it. She did not know it was something the cook was keeping hidden.

This was in the cook's blanket. These are the papers the Italians have been dropping from planes. I've been hearing about them. They're telling them they'll be free if they join the *ferenj* side.

Kidane takes the slip of paper and holds it toward the light. A lopsided drawing peeks through from the back. There is a scrawny beggar in chains kneeling in front of a large-headed man wearing a crown. Below it and beneath a series of words, the same beggar stands, his chains broken off, the emperor's shattered crown at his feet. The beggar, now with a slight paunch, is waving at a soldier, his arm stiffly raised, his smile jubilant.

These Italians want to start a revolt before they try to take our country, Aster says. Mussoloni wants these people to join his army.

But they can't read. Kidane is staring between the leaflet and the gun.

They can understand pictures. Aster flings aside the cook's blanket and searches again, shaking the mattress. Puffs of dust bloom around her. Now, what do you say to this one?

Hirutiye, Kidane says. I need this gun. We're going to war and we need all the weapons we can get. These Italians have many more than we do. He looks at her with those kind eyes of his, pleading with her in a way that gives her the courage to say:

My father gave it to me. He said to always keep it near me.

If we don't gather every weapon in this country, we'll lose before the war begins, Kidane says. He's not loosening his hold on the gun, he's not extending it to her. He still grips it firmly in both hands. The emperor himself told everyone to contribute their weapons. He said it himself, on the radio. We all have to do it. Even your father would do it if he were alive.

No. It's mine. She has looked into his eyes before: where there was kindness, there is now a sternness that is new to her, a reprimand veiled by something else she cannot understand. But all Hirut can think about is the day her father handed her the rifle when he was already sweating and shivering, his cheeks unnaturally gaunt. She will not give the gun away.

You'll get it back. I promise you, Kidane says. He is kind again, gentle.

Stop talking to her like she can reason, Aster says, reaching for the gun. Just take it.

She's a child. Kidane pulls the rifle away.

A child. Aster stops. A child. She leans toward Kidane. You think I don't realize you brought her here exactly one year after our son died? Her voice is low but it holds a bitterness that makes Kidane step back.

He places a hand on the doorframe and speaks slowly: Her parents died. I made a promise to Getey, she was like a sister to me.

Aster stares down at her hands, uncharacteristically hesitant. She came exactly one year after Tesfaye died, she says. Aster lifts her head and repeats it, more confident. You brought her here after the mourning period. So you could do what you pleased without gossip.

She came here the day they were buried. There was nowhere else for her to go. Kidane takes a deep breath as if to steady himself.

You brought her here to insult me. Aster places a hand very quickly on her stomach and drops it. You brought her here to try to teach me my place.

On their faces, identical grim expressions, as if they have fought like this before, as if both are tired but cannot help it.

The necklace isn't here, Kidane finally says. I lost it a long time ago. I told you.

And she's not a child anymore. Think of what you knew of me when I was her age.

Kidane looks at his wife, his face faltering around the twisting line of his mouth. He says it softly, so softly Hirut thinks she is the only one who can hear: She's Getey's daughter. Then he walks out of the room with her rifle and after one long look, Aster follows.

They were both in here? The cook leans against the wall and tugs at the collar of her worn dress. Beads of sweat roll down on her neck. She wipes the back of her hand across her chin and chest. Stop looking at me like that, she mutters.

Hirut sits in the middle of the room with her arms around her legs. She buries her face into the crevice of her folded arms.

She was still looking for that necklace? the cook asks. Now she is standing over Hirut, her feet in that wide stance of hers, and Hirut doesn't need to look up to know that her hands are on her waist and her chin juts out. She sets the crate upright, then stops at her unrolled mattress. What did they do in here?

Hirut looks up. The cook's round face looms above her.

The cook's mouth begins to tremble. Why's everything a mess? She spreads her arms wide, and turns in a slow, stunned circle. She sinks to her knees and slides her hand inside the straw filling and begins to slowly pull it out, scattering the clumps. No, she is saying.

Hirut watches her stupidly, reminded of a bird she once saw, aged and thick-bodied, fall out of a tree already dead.

Why didn't you call me? The cook's mattress lies depleted across her lap. My flyer. She starts to tip to one side before she rights herself. You let them take it. You couldn't think about anyone but yourself?

Hirut turns to her and sees her clenched jaw, the rigidity of her back. She cannot understand what the cook is talking about. You can get another one. She hears the bitterness creep into her voice. He took my rifle.

It's so simple for you, isn't it? the cook says.

Both sit in silence, staring around the messy room. Over the cook's head, a wavering strand of light flickers past floating dust. There is no pool of sun that collects at her feet, like Aster. No sunshine glimmers over her shoulders, drenching her in golden light, like Kidane. She is the cook: square and stout, in her drab dress and the same stained scarf, standing in a room that still holds all she owns.

I was younger than you when I came here. The cook says this in a voice that Hirut has to lean forward to hear. My father was killed by those people who came to steal us away to work in rich houses. I saw it. She speaks with a quiet anguish. You think you're better. She pauses. But I'm stronger.

I don't, Hirut says, keeping her voice low.

I'm too useful. The cook plants her hands on her stomach and slumps. She is lost in her thoughts, still whispering in that tone that scrapes against her chest. I wasn't always like this. Look at me. She extends her arms like wings, lifts her chin.

Hirut looks at the cook's hands, the bones that are lost in all the flesh, the burns that crater her skin, the callouses she knows line her palms and are rough to the touch. Today her short fingernails are tinged yellow from turmeric, on the back of her wrist a dot of awaze, the red pepper paste gleaming like fresh blood. She woke before dawn to pack Kidane's food for his trip to recruit villagers into the army. She stayed up all night preparing the meal and filling jugs of water. She is often the first to wake and the last to sleep, working with a persistence and steadiness that Hirut has never questioned. She never considered what the cook would be, if not this.

You don't think I had a family before this. The cook reads her mind. You think I was born with these scars.

She has never heard the cook speak about the life she led before this one.

Some of us came by force, the cook adds. This war will help us go back. Berhe and I could have gone home. But now. She stops. They know everything.

Berhe said I can leave when I want.

The cook's laugh is a brief, sad sound. He said the same to me when we came here.

My father gave me that gun. Hirut turns to the wall and blinks away the tears.

The cook slides to the ground and sits next to her. In the long silence, loneliness stretches between them and draws them close.

You didn't know Berhe when he was a young man, the cook finally says. He was so proud, so strong. She picks at her nails. They dragged his father behind a horse and that man still wouldn't surrender. He refused to give them his land, so they took it and his son.

Hirut thinks back to her father's stories of the war against the Italians, the same ones who lost long ago and now want to come back. Those *ferenjoch*?

The devil has always lived in this country to torment people like me. The cook quiets and stares out of the door, toward the courtyard. The day you came, she begins softly, Aster was burning her clothes. She burned the flowers in the garden too.

Hirut nods. She remembers the barren courtyard, the charred bushes and grass. And now she remembers something else: the day she arrived, Aster met her on the veranda dressed in black.

Get her out of my house, she said to Berhe.

This is Getey and Fasil's daughter, Berhe said. She buried both of them today, she has no one left, Kidane brought her.

And Aster lifted a trembling hand to her face. Berhe, she said, is this how he intends to do this?

Kidane didn't know what to do, the cook adds. When their little boy died he was a broken man, you wouldn't believe it. Then you came and something changed. The cook shoves a twig out of the door with her foot. You can blame her for many things, but don't blame Aster for everything.

EVERY DAY, HIRUT SEARCHES FOR HER RIFLE AS SHE CLEANS. SHE goes into the sitting room and lifts the sofa. She shakes out the curtains and the rug and shifts the radio to either side. She runs a flat palm under the dining table and lifts each of the four chairs and looks underneath. She begs the cook to help lift the bags of teff and check their weight, to knock on the side of the gourd with the injera mixture. She looks in the sack of potatoes and the bag of lentils. She rustles through the rosebushes in the courtyard and the piles of hay near the horse's pen. She unstacks then restacks Berhe's neat pile of firewood at the side of the stable. She peers into the water well outside of the compound. She crawls under the veranda. She refolds all of Aster's scarves and beautiful dresses in her cupboards. Though she is not allowed in Kidane's office, she sneaks in when he leaves for his war meetings, and sweeps. She cleans thoroughly and diligently until every room sparkles, until all the silver and copper centerpieces glow like a slow-burning fire.

Aster grows tense and watches her with careful eyes. Kidane gets up and walks out whenever she enters a room. Every night the cook says: But you've cleaned these rooms already, enough. She says: They've given it to one of Kidane's recruits. She says: Berhe, make her stop. But Berhe follows her quietly when she rechecks worn paths outside the compound, an infinite sadness on his weathered face. Then one day, weeks later, he stops her at the gate and gathers her in his arms and whispers into her ear: What is lost is gone, my child, what is lost makes room for something else. But still, she washes and dusts and polishes and sweeps and does it all again as if it had never been done, and with every new day, the dread builds:

The rifle has disappeared. It is as if it never existed. As if this life, in this house, is all that she has ever known, as if she has been no one else but this unloved girl. Soon, she will have to admit that it is nowhere. It has slipped into a crevice that can swallow girls just as easily as it devours guns. She feels herself disappearing, senses her bones softening and sliding in her skin. She wakes, feverish, convinced that invisible hands are dragging her away, and she, defenseless without a weapon, is too weak to face the enemy. I'm sorry, Abbaba, she says each night. She apologizes to her father then waits for sunlight to blaze its angry heat and burn the darkness away.

Aster's necklace: She finds it one day, tucked deep in the top drawer of Kidane's desk, that splendidly carved wooden desk now always piled high with maps and newspapers and a portrait of their son, little Tesfaye. Hirut jerks her hand out of the drawer, clutching it in her palm. It is a thick gold crucifix on a splendid chain, heavy and solid in her shaking hand. It slips out of her hold and clinks onto the floor like a bag of coins and when she snatches it up, heart pounding, something breathes in the room. She spins around: In front of her are the two chairs facing the desk, on the wall is the faded photograph of Kidane's father and another of the couple in younger days. There is the same heap of documents and newspapers that cover the surface of the desk and on top, a picture of truckloads of marching men in their abesha *libs*, and a picture of Emperor Haile Selassie peering accusingly at her. There is the same sword that leans in the same corner. Nothing has moved, but Hirut feels as if the walls are expanding and a hand stretching to snatch the necklace away, so she grips it even tighter and runs.

She buries it at the side of the stable, in a hole that she digs beneath Berhe's firewood. She continues to clean. She continues to look for the rifle. Hirut goes about her days mindful of being seen, of being observed, of being a curious spectacle in the house that still shines from her thorough work. It is at night that she lets the change take effect, lets her heart swell with triumph, and allows herself to smile. Quietly, she pats the place beside her where the rifle once lay then she shuts her eyes and dreams of a girl standing on a mountain, gazing at her fallen enemies with the gun in her hand, victorious.

AND THEN IT is nothing, nothing at all, to take again and keep on taking. The things she takes: a yellow bead, a swatch of red silk, a golden tassel, five rubber bands, six thalers, a broken pencil, a rusted pocketknife, a torn umbrella, a horseshoe, a small amber stone, a hand mirror, an incense burner, a delicate gold-rimmed coffee cup, an inkpad, a broken compass, a folded map, a leather-bound miniature Bible, two closed amulets, a palm-sized wooden cross, a green wool scarf, a segment of a delicate gold chain, a shiny blue stone, a fragment of soapstone, a silver-handled letter opener, a wine goblet, six matchboxes, two crushed cigarettes, an empty pillbox, a leather bracelet, a strapless watch, a horsehair fly swatter, a collapsible hand fan, an ashtray, a stack of stamped documents, two folded envelopes, a wooden cross pendant, a leather cross pendant, two silver chains, a scrap of black velvet, a spool of discarded cotton, a ball of green yarn, a bent miniature frame, a beaded necklace, a leather satchel, a glass tea cup, a gold-handled spoon, a hand-sized painting of Iyesus Cristos, a child's bracelet, a pince-nez, silver anklets, one gold earring, a black scarf with gold embroidery, binoculars, a plain black scarf, a pair of gold and ruby earrings, a matching bracelet, and a brilliant ruby ring.

She buries the items with the necklace late at night, unstacking the firewood noiselessly, then restacking it precisely. She is careful, reveling in the thrill of possession, made bold by the sudden freedom of theft. She is no longer afraid to pause at the radio while Kidane listens to announcements and speeches in a language she comes to understand is called French. She lingers in the corridor when he talks to Aster in his office. She hears new words: League of Nations, Mussolini, Britain, Mauser, artillery, steamships. She hears him giving his wife commands as if she were his servant: Get the supplies ready, bring us enough water for three days, don't waste time on the scarves, let the other women do the knitting, tell them to get ready, it's coming soon. Hirut shoves the unnecessary details aside while listening for the name of the rifle that belonged to her father and once belonged to her: Wujigra.

WUJIGRA: ALSO KNOWN AS FUSIL GRAS. ORIGIN: FRENCH. A BOLT-action, 11mm rifle designed to deliver a single lethal shot with consistent accuracy, a hardy gun able to withstand cold and rain, repeated and rapid firing. Watch how I do this, Hirut, sit still and pay attention. Her father loads the bullet cartridge by opening the chamber. He does this by pulling back on a small handle situated toward one side of the barrel. Hirut looks at the handle. It is shiny and smooth, a silver knob as round as a full moon. Do you see this? He raises his right hand. This is the hand all good soldiers use with this gun. Hirut makes her left hand into a fist. It is the hand she is most comfortable using. It is the hand her mother is starting to tie down. She looks and sees he is right: the handle of the Wujigra does not favor left-handed fighters. So when she becomes a soldier, she thinks that day with her father, she must shoot with her right, the hand that resists when she tries to make it do anything. The left hand, her mother says, is the hand the devil uses. It is the hand a thief uses, and you are not a *leyba*. It is the hand to use for things no one should see you do, Hirut. You do not eat with it. You do nothing with this hand except for the most secret things. Hirut is too young for secrets, she is too young to be aware there are some things that should stay tucked out of reach of knowledge.

Her father raises the rifle and presses the end into the muscle between his shoulder and his upper chest. You rest it here, he says, exactly where your head goes when you fall asleep on me. He smiles. He uses his right hand to pull the handle back. This unlocks the bolt, he says. She sees a cradle-shaped groove inside, mottled with age. This is where the bullet goes. Her father holds the bullet between two fingers. When the barrel is opened, he says, you insert it, like this, into the chamber. He slides the handle and it locks the bolt. He lifts the rifle and his voice changes. It grows deep and it wavers as he tells her, You look until you can see your enemy through this space. He taps a finger on a small metal point farther up on the barrel. He brings his finger to the base of the gun, where there is a resting place for it. This is the trigger, Hirut. He does not sound the same. He does not sound like her father. When he looks at her, it is as if he is not looking at her. His face is collapsing around the eyes and she sees that he pretends to squint to hide it. This, he says, you do not touch unless you are prepared. Prepared for what, she asks. He slips the bullet back into his pocket. Prepared to be something you are not.

KIDANE KEEPS SHOVING THE SAME PILE OF DOCUMENTS FROM ONE side of his desk to the other. He mumbles as he wipes his eyes, peering closer at a map while Hirut waits by the door, balancing the woolen scarves and a thick cape that he told her to bring. Just behind her and down the corridor, Aster is in their bedroom crying and calling for the cook, whole words shredded into incomprehensible sound. Today is the second anniversary of their son's death, this means it has been a whole year since Hirut's arrival and three months since her rifle disappeared. Out of habit and from nervous impulse, Hirut glances around the office to make sure her Wujigra is not there.

Kidane, come here. Aster's voice is a low thrum against the walls.

Kidane throws the map on the desk. Nardos didn't take her to church? he asks. He rubs his forehead and the thin line of his mouth draws tighter. Just like the day we married, he adds. She thinks that's how she can get her way, by crying like this.

He hunches over his papers, bowed by the weight of his wife's voice. Beneath the stubble gracing his neck, a thick vein swells against the neckline of his tunic.

Can I put this somewhere, Hirut asks, flexing her shoulders to ease the strain.

Just wait.

Kidane lifts up the map again and continues to pore over it. The dim glow of the kerosene lamp seeps through the fragile paper. The map's slender lines bisect and overlap then stop short at a brilliant blue patch that clings to the boundary separating land from sea. There is Kenya, contoured like a queen's face. Ethiopia's pointed crown brushes against the Red Sea. Over there, the Gulf of Aden. The Indian Ocean. Hirut leans forward and squints to get a better look. Kidane holds entire countries in that hand, the long nail of his little finger digs into the sands of the Sahara. She knows somewhere above Ethiopia is Egypt, and not far away, there is a place called Sudan. She learned them all in the last few months while cleaning unsupervised. She has been taking one map at a time to Berhe, who grudgingly helped her distinguish shapes after she promised to return everything undetected.

You want to see this? Kidane shakes the paper, startling her upright. He taps his forehead. Memorize the land for yourself, he says. Maps are what the foreigners use. We know our country. He throws the map back on the desk and mutters under his breath. They rely on useless pieces of paper to start a war, he adds.

Put the blankets there and sit down, Little One, he says. Set them on the floor, it's as clean as a plate. His smile lengthens the deep lines around his tired eyes.

Hirut lays the items down and stands awkwardly by the elaborately carved chair across from him.

Aster's voice drifts into the room, a steady moan broken by the cook's unintelligible words.

He winks. I won't tell her you didn't use the stool.

Hirut sits. The wood feels soft and supple beneath her legs, as if it were molding to her.

You think you've gotten used to anything she does, after all these years, then you realize you haven't, Kidane says. He grows serious. I keep thinking I'll see him around the corner. You've been here how long? He frowns and glances down at a newspaper. Since we started fearing the worst with these Italians. He nods to himself. You're so young to lose both parents, days apart. His mouth trembles. But look at you, so strong.

Hirut is too short to fit comfortably in the chair. She scoots up, tracing the sturdy legs with her toes, and braces herself. If he keeps talking about her parents she will have to unlock them from the tiny corner of her mind where she has put them so she does not cry.

Aster's okay? she asks.

Kidane points toward the bedroom. She's always felt things too much, that's her problem. He watches Hirut. That was my father's chair. Not made for girls, is it? You're so small.

She folds her hands on her lap then settles them on the contoured arms, dangling them the way she has seen Kidane do.

I need your help, Hirut, he says, growing serious. Even I have to leave my land, this house. All my farmers have to pick up their swords and guns now, they have to leave their homes, too. We all need to do our part for the war that's coming.

Behind him on the wall, there are pale outlines where his swords and shield used to hang. He has taken down the picture of him and Aster when they were younger. In its place is a photograph of Tesfaye cradled in his arms, a miniature of the father that holds him proudly. Both are dressed in splendid white tunics that blaze bright against the black backdrop.

My gun, she begins. Can I have it back?

Kidane pauses, then continues: I'm going to need you to do what Aster says. You'll follow us as soon as we're ready to march. You'll take care of my soldiers. The cook and Berhe are getting old. You're young and strong. His eyes slide from her face down to her neck. Sometimes you look so much like your mother, he adds. She was like a sister to me. You must miss her.

There is a tremor behind his words, something that unravels him from the inside. It is a weakening that expands enough for Hirut to dare to ask again:

Please let me have my rifle. Anger snaps through her and she bites her lip to keep the tears from falling. They gave it to me.

He falls back in his chair and stares up at the ceiling. You'll help the cook carry the food and water. My aunts did in the last war. Don't you want to help?

Aster calls for Kidane again.

Kidane flinches. If Aster isn't well you'll be in charge of making sure our supplies don't run out. The cook will be too busy with other things. He lays his hands on top of his papers. Little One is not so little anymore, he says quietly. Your mother would be proud.

Do you know what your mother said to me the last time I saw her? You were such a small girl then. Again, the eyes drifting from her face to her neck to linger on a spot that she can feel well up with heat.

Hirut leans forward, not trusting her voice. A slow flush spreads across her cheeks, traveling over her chest to settle in her stomach. She tries to imagine her mother talking to Kidane. She can imagine him as he is, full-bodied and distinct, but her mother is just a ghostly figure, delicate features rubbed away by time.

She said, "Be good to my daughter." Kidane clears his throat. She wanted me to watch over you. She put you in my care.

She did? Hirut aches to hear more.

She did, Kidane says. He watches her carefully.

Her mother's love, her father once said, could make a river unbend and flow her way. Your mother, he said, brings out the goodness in the world. This is why Hirut returns his stare and time stretches between them until even Aster's voice blends with the wind outside. It is not possible that he could love her mother as he did and remain unaltered. It is impossible that her mother could love him as a brother and leave him unaffected. This means he is like a brother to her, too. If she explains more about her rifle, then surely he will be good enough to give it back.

My father was very kind to your mother. Did you know that?

Hirut shakes her head. She traces a scratch on her knuckles; it is intersected by a burn she got from splattering oil. Gradually, her hands are becoming like the cook's.

My father was a good man. Kidane's voice wavers.

From down the hall, Aster's coughing filters into the office. It is a hacking sound that seems to drag itself out of her body and crouch in a corner of the room, a wounded animal. It continues, on and on.

He rises and strides to the door. He pauses, listening, before pushing it shut. Then he opens it slightly, leaving it ajar.

Do you know what a war is, Little One? He speaks with his back to her, his forehead pressed against the doorframe. Do you know what it means to hate? He slumps, overwhelmed by the roughness of Aster's cough. It is grating and painful and zigzags into a guttural moan.

No one knows war until they are in it. But I think you'd be a good soldier, like Tesfaye would have been.

He turns to her and comes to sit on the corner of the desk. He rests a warm hand on her shoulder and bends into her face. Aster's voice is now a shadow of itself, a dampened call of a name he is ignoring.

She waits for more memories about her mother.

When I was your age, your mother used to tell me, Stand straight like a soldier. Don't cry, little brother, you're a soldier. His breath is tinged in the sharp scent of the coffee she served him earlier. He leans closer. You'd have cared for Tesfaye the way your mother cared for me. I would have cared for you the way my father cared for your mother.

He sits back and clears his throat. Two years. Tesfaye. Then he stops and they listen.

Aster says, Kidane. And it is not the utterance but the voice: angry and plaintive, troubled and insistent, made hoarse by overuse. It winds through the hallway and soaks into the room. It seeps through wood and flings itself at glass. It strips meaning from sound and leaves only a weight that hovers just above their heads, buckled by sorrow.

It doesn't get easier, does it, Little One? You know, too. But you don't cry? I don't see you sad, you just work, sometimes too much.

Kidane lifts Hirut's chin and kisses her forehead. Up close, she sees the way the voice is undoing him in increments: the twitching nerve below the eye, the shaking hand, the trembling lips that he presses now against her cheeks then slides to her neck as if for steadiness. He breathes in with his head in the crook of her neck, moving so close she has to lean back, and his breath moistens her skin like steam. Behind them is his name in the voice of an angry woman. Just past his shoulder are the maps on the desk. And when she looks toward the door, seeking escape, there is the cook, stricken and shocked, her mouth opening and closing around a silent word. And then because he says her name, Hirut is forced to look at him.

The cook clears her throat and taps on the door.

What is it? He jerks away, surprised.

I can't do anything with her, the cook says, speaking hurriedly, her head down. She won't stop calling for you, it's one of her bad days.

Kidane slides off the desk and strides out of the room, brushing past the cook. When Hirut stands and turns again to the door, the cook is already gone. Alone in the office, listening to the rise and fall of Kidane and Aster's voices, Hirut recognizes for the first time that some memories should be barricaded by others, that those strong enough must hold the others at bay. And as she goes back to the kitchen to help the cook, the first thread of sourness curls inside of her, pungent like rot, so tiny that she chooses to mistake it for the distant smell of smoke.

Interlude

Haile Selassie sits quietly in his office. It is 2 September 1935 and the first strands of night have begun to seep into the day. He is in his favorite chair, hands tight around the arms, a stack of telegrams opened on his desk. The reports haven't changed: Ethiopia is on the brink of conflict; Italy's threats are growing shriller. The rainy season is over and with drier paths will surely come the invading Fascist army. What does His Majesty intend to do? Supplies needed. Port of Massawa filling with Italian ships. Troops gathering in Asmara, primed to charge toward our borders.

Haile Selassie is sweating. The high ceiling is bearing down. The ground is shifting up. Addis Ababa is roiling, and his people are gathering inside churches. He should be praying. He should be with his Council. He should be with his family, but all the emperor can do is lean forward in his chair and nod for his aide to unwrap the two reels that have just arrived. They are old news, but he wants to watch them. He wants to be engulfed in them. He wants to sit in the middle of this shrinking room and pick his way into this war coming at him with a locomotive force.

The aide holds up a circular metal container in each hand. One is in English, the other Italian, Your Majesty.

The emperor eyes him: He is dressed like a *ferenj*, in a pinstriped suit specially tailored for him. His thin mustache is meticulous. His eyes have the piercing gaze of the unafraid. The emperor can't remember his name, suddenly, but knows this young man's father and his father before him. He knows which village his wife comes from and the secret mistress he keeps in Debre Zeit. And he knows that throughout the screening, the young man will be obedient but aching to step outside to gossip.

Which one first, Your Majesty? his aide asks him again. One is from Luce. He names the Italian propaganda news service. I can translate either for you, he says.

He hears the echo of his old tutor, Father Samuel, quoting from Psalms: Your right hand will find out those who hate you. The one on your right, the emperor says. And turn off the volume.

The reels are last month's news. They will reveal nothing unexpected: Italian soldiers are sailing for Eritrea. Mussolini is declaring his right to colonize Ethiopia. The emperor's soldiers are simply farmers with old guns. Italy is better equipped. Italy has planes. Italy has the tacit agreement of the League of Nations in the form of inert silence. All of this the emperor already knows. But mail has slowed down while events have sped up and these latest reels are all he has to help him imagine what the next days and weeks might bring.

Haile Selassie hears a discreet cough from the hallway. On the other side of the locked door his advisers are impatient, waiting for him to beckon them in.

Begin, he says to the aide.

The aide slides the reel onto the projector. Haile Selassie hears the slap of the rolling film and the hiss of the electrical power snaking through the machine. Soon the room is washed in gray and he blinks slowly as a black screen rattles behind flecks of white then numbers spin into view.

He faces forward and grips his hands and watches. He pays attention to every detail. He sees the gushing waters of the Tsissat Falls and the hills of Gondar. He sees a map and an animated white line following the path of the Nile, snaking past Sudanese women wading through the great river, past Egyptian laborers constructing a dam, moving out of Ethiopia to disappear completely. Then he sees the tall lines of New York City and a group of American men around a table dominated by two large tusks. He pauses at the tusks.

The reportage recounts his coronation and there he is. Haile Selassie remembers this moment. He was proud. He was ready for what lay before him. Haile Selassie sees his younger self saluting the Duke of Gloucester as he steps off a train. Behind the duke are foreign dignitaries who have come to witness Ras Teferi Mekonnen become Emperor Haile Selassie.

And then the broadcaster slips past the years and it is 1935 again and there is Benito Mussolini: narrow-eyed and stern-jawed. There are his *soldati*, numerous as ants. There they are clambering onto a hulking ship. There is Benito on a white horse before a statue of Julius Caesar.

And the scene cuts and there is an older and more somber Haile Selassie in an office, sitting with his hands folded, a quiet dread resting behind his eyes as he nods and looks past the camera. Who was speaking to him? What question made him turn away like that? The film slides to black, throwing the office into darkness.

We are here. We are here, he whispers then thinks better: I am here.

Again, he says. Move the projector closer to the wall.

He wants the images to bleed across three walls. He wants them to his left and to his right: stereoscopic. He wants to tilt into this splitting world. He wants to gaze at the center until the periphery snaps into the middle at his behest. He wants to train himself to withstand disorientation and stay calm until the world melds itself back together.

The reel begins again.

The emperor shuts his eyes and listens to the whir of celluloid on metal. He understands the pieces of this impending war. He can take it apart and analyze each corroded segment of Mussolini's dream for an empire. He can see the small parts but he cannot comprehend the whole. He cannot see what more he can do.

Your Majesty? It's ended. Should I begin again?

He nods because he doesn't trust his voice. He inches his chair back and opens his eyes and lets the images collide.

Your Majesty, again?

The emperor cannot answer. He can only sit in this dark room and blink to shift the world into focus.

HIRUT PAUSES OVER THE TEFF SHE IS SIFTING ON THE VERANDA. Kidane and Berhe are near the stable, around the corner and out of view. They are speaking with an unstrained camaraderie, unaware of what is buried beneath the firewood steps from them. It has been weeks since she put the items there and she has been vigilant, so aware of Aster and Kidane's presence whenever they've stepped outside that she wonders if they can feel her sitting at their shoulder, swiveling her head with theirs, tucking herself inside their throats to listen for that first hint of a discovery: the sharp intake of breath, the sudden snap of neck. The men's voices drift. Then they walk out of the gate, a long burlap bag with two new rifles in both their arms. They are going to deliver more guns to Kidane's new army, young recruits he is training for the war that has not arrived. Hirut bends her head and continues sifting the teff, relieved.

She tosses the bowl filled with the grain, letting the wind blow away the chaff. Her eyes follow the rise and fall of her hands. Her heart slows to an even rhythm. All the noises of the world quiet to their normal, buzzing calm. She is so intent on her work again that, at first, she does not notice Aster at the window, watching her intently, her eyes moving with Hirut's, noting the way the girl stares and tips toward the stable. It is only when Hirut hears the tap-tap-tap that she looks up, startled to see the woman's hand pressed against the glass as if she wants to shatter it in her fist.

Later she will understand the impulse as an instinctive desire to escape: Hirut sets down the teff and gets to her feet. She is shaking already, her body responding to what words have yet to form. Aster walks out of the front door and stands beside her, following the path of her gaze. Aster steps down from the veranda, pauses to look up at Hirut, then pivots toward the stable. Hirut stares at Aster's back, at the woman's hands clenching at her side. They stand like that, one behind the other, both facing the stable, until Aster takes a step forward then another, and Hirut follows, guided by a fear stronger than the dread trying to root her in place.

Aster stops at the stable door. What's in here? She grinds her teeth over each word.

Hirut will say later that there was no other way for this to happen. There was nothing else for her to do but to confess and beg forgiveness. It was foolish to take those trinkets, the jewels, the discarded coins. It was foolish to imagine them hers. There is no place in this world where a girl like her can own the things she has buried in dirt for safekeeping. All along, she has known this, just as she has known she will never see her rifle again. Some people are meant to be owners of things. Others, only to set them in their rightful place and clean them. It is a thought she has known but chosen to ignore, hoping that by force she can make herself into something else.

Are you hiding something in here?

No, Hirut says.

Hirut waits for Aster to say more, but the woman stands there, unmoving.

Then where is it? I've seen you turning to look this way whenever someone gets near.

She recognizes the stiffening in Aster's back, the set jaw that tugs at the muscles in her neck. Aster is controlling her temper, waiting for the perfect moment to let it loose. Whether it will come is not the question.

Tell me what you've been doing. Her face is flushed. Tears collect in her eyes before she blinks them away.

Looking for my rifle.

The space between them stretches and it is as if they are groping for balance as the ground beneath them starts to shift.

You don't understand? The look she fixes on Hirut swims between loathing and frustration. It's not yours anymore.

Hirut wipes her eyes. She does not want to let this woman see how much she understands.

From the stable seeps the ripe odor of manure, the acrid sharpness of urine and straw. They both smell it at the same time, and when Aster turns her head, Hirut does the same and finds herself confronted with the edge of firewood poking out from the corner of the building. She looks away quickly and settles on the stable door but not before she meets Aster's gaze.

There are enough hidden things in my house, don't you think? Aster says it quietly but now it is easy to see she is trembling with rage. She is trying to contain it, every muscle tensed toward stillness. The effort bloats her face, tightens her mouth into a grim line.

I've seen you looking around in my bedroom, Aster continues. You go into his office and go through his papers. You can't even read. You think you can replace me?

From inside the stable, one of the couple's horses huffs loudly.

Hirut is watching Aster's mouth, waiting for the words that will break her resolve and push her to her knees. She can feel color rushing to her cheeks, pooling at the spot where Kidane planted his lips. She lifts her hand to flick the sensation away before Aster notices.

Who are you? Aster asks.

Hirut tugs at the collar of her dress and keeps her head down. She knows who she is, but she knows she is also lost.

I don't want anything, Hirut says. Just my rifle.

Aster raises her hand to strike her then stops herself. She takes Hirut's arm and digs her thumb into her elbow. You still think this world was built around you? she asks. You were born to fit into it. That's your fate.

It was your mother's. That gun belongs to Ethiopia. It's been given to someone who needs it for the war. Do you think you matter more than this country?

Aster yanks her to the side of the building, in front of the firewood. Now, show me.

Here is something: she likes to sing. She likes the sound of her voice cupped in melody and rolling out of her throat. It is her mother who taught her how a voice can tremble between two feelings without splitting. She sings to memorize, to pin fact onto rhythm and lodge it firmly in her head. When she creates songs she can change a happening, reverse its course of action and alter meaning, even make it forgotten. She has always understood the shifting terrains of truth. She knows that it is belief that makes a thing so.

So when Aster leads her to the side of the building, in front of the stack of firewood and says, Now, show me, Hirut thinks of a melody and lets it tumble up from her chest and settle just inside her throat, ready. An incantation to wipe this moment clean. And when she has no choice but to pick up the firewood, piece by piece, as Aster watches with a set mouth, Hirut begins to hum. As she removes one row after the other, keeping pace with the sad cadence of her wordless ballad, she starts to say her mother's name: Getey. She whispers it as she works, until nothing but the narrow mound of dirt rises to meet her gaze like an accusation. Then she and Aster stand before it, both struck mute, until Aster drops to her knees and crawls to the hole and starts to dig.

Hirut turns her back. Then she feels herself swaying. Her body starts to fold into itself and not even her mother's name is strong enough to keep her upright. She puts her head on the ground, against her knees, and shields her skull with her hands and waits, moaning in rising hysteria: *Emama, Emaye*, help me.

What Aster finds: two crushed cigarettes, a broken pencil, a leather satchel, an empty pillbox, a stack of stamped documents, a leather bracelet, an ashtray, a strapless watch, an ink pad and a broken compass, a small amber stone, a horsehair fly swatter, a rusted pocketknife, a collapsible hand fan, two folded envelopes, a wooden cross pendant, two closed amulets, two silver chains wrapped around a silver-handled letter opener, a leather cross pendant, six matchboxes, a scrap of black velvet, a blue rock, a gold-handled spoon, a chipped piece of sandstone, a knot of discarded cotton, one fake gold earring, a scratched teacup, small binoculars, and her necklace.

There are words spoken in this moment, but later, Hirut will not remember if it was Aster or she clinging to the torn edge of a broken thought: Emaye, Emaye, why didn't you tell me? Why didn't you tell me it would be like this?

Aster dangles the necklace above Hirut's head. She cannot seem to comprehend what it is she is holding. Her face is contorted, features crumbling then gathering then falling again. She is shaking her head and saying, What right did she have? What right did she have? Then she looks down at Hirut and that is when Hirut realizes she has lifted her head to look upon this new version of Aster: collapsing and enraged, stunned into dizzying confusion, bowed beneath an invisible force that Hirut can feel but cannot grasp.

Sit up.

Hirut obeys without thinking. She finds herself on her knees, eye-level with Aster, reaching out to take the necklace so she can hide the evidence of her deepening shame. Aster is whispering: What right did she have, when she grabs Hirut by her hair and slaps her hard across the face.

The blow comes as a relief to Hirut. It is something to do: to be hit. It is somewhere to go: to be in pain. She welcomes the distraction from the tremor she feels seeping out of Aster and sinking into her own skin. She is crying as she braces herself for the shout because she knows that Aster, too, uses her voice, that she knows how to hurl it like a stone from a slingshot and buckle a grown man's knees. With her neck twisted awkwardly, Hirut grasps her hair at the roots to keep Aster from pulling chunks out. Already a section of her scalp burns raw. Then she shuts her eyes, stiffens her back, and waits for another hit. She braces for the fist to grind into her jaw and snap her teeth together. Her ears will ring from the slip of jawbone before it slides back in place, and it will be bruised but not broken. Hirut tilts toward the coming blow, a tiny kernel of triumph pressing through the dread. No matter what she does, Aster cannot untake the necklace. She cannot unbury it. She cannot force Kidane not to stick it so far inside an overstuffed drawer that he forgets where it is. She can do nothing but strike, each hit an impotent replacement for the fury she would rather direct at her husband.

Then: from somewhere far away she hears a snap, then the crisp crack of pliant leather. The thought is a slender beam of light sailing across a dark sky: Aster has unhooked the horsewhip, the one that Kidane rarely uses on the horses, Buna and Adua. It has hung on a crooked nail on the side of the building for as long as she has been in this place. It hangs just above the firewood. Now it is in Aster's hand and it is not the wind but this whip slicing through her.

Please, Hirut says. She turns over to shield her back from another blow.

The tip of the whip catches her on her shoulder and craters the skin on her collarbone. The cut is a split wound filling with blood, arching down one side of her throat like a broken necklace. A warm, wet shield spreads across her dress and she knows she is bleeding badly. Hirut breaks into a sweat and feels a dark curtain drop inside her head. For a moment, there are no words. There is no sound. There is only the deliberate, clawing weight bearing across her spine and shoulders, pounding its way through skin and bone. She wants to cry out but Aster is still hitting and there is no voice strong enough to climb out of this abyss. No sound deep enough to burrow beneath it. Slowly, she feels the cuts and gashes, the burn of open wounds. She is splitting into pieces.

She hears the cook: Aster. Asty. *Emebet.* Not like this.

Get out of here, Aster says as she kicks Hirut in the stomach.

Hirut rolls onto her back, coughing to breathe. Help me.

The punch lands in the center of her chest and Hirut curls breathless around the new pain, propelled by dumbfounded shock. Now she is afraid. One eye is sliding shut. She can see the corner of a swollen lip. She swings her head in the cook's direction, made nauseous by the momentum, and sees the cook is shaking her head, flat-eyed with a quivering chin. Hirut can hear a voice she knows is hers calling for her mother, calling for Kidane, calling for her father. And when she turns to beg Aster to stop, please stop, she will leave, she will go and die and never come back, she sees Aster fall to her knees and throw the necklace next to Hirut's head where it lands in a heap like a wounded animal.

For a moment, the world spins in an unnatural quiet. There is just Aster pressing her face on the ground, sliding toward her. Hirut notes the frantic sorrow in her eyes, the way her mouth is chewing words to spit them out. Dust blooms as Aster drags herself over dirt as if she has forgotten the use of her legs, as if her body cannot contain the full weight of her fury. Then there is nothing except a finger's width of dusty air to mark the distance between the two of them. Silence extends until Hirut can hear the ringing in her own ears. Then: It was for nothing? Aster shouts as she shakes Hirut by the shoulder. Was it for nothing?

Chorus

We see the young Aster. We see the way she creeps up the stairs with a chorus of women ululating at her back. She is gripping the railing for strength, dragging her leaden body over the steps. Her childish heart, wild with fear, shivers visibly in her chest. We can hear the men laugh in the hall below. We can hear the scrape of heavy chairs resounding through the great house. A bright kerosene lamp swings from a long nail on the landing in front of her. Shadows scamper across the walls and what can she do but recoil and look at her mother? She is young, after all. She is just a girl, so when they tell her, Go on, Aster, and walk to your new husband, what can Aster do but walk?

At the top step is the cook, her arms open to take her and pull her toward the bedroom. She does not know that we are there. She cannot see how her glorious abesha chemise glows in the dark, dark stairwell. There's no way out but through it, we tell her. There's no escape but what you make from the inside. We are whispering but she cannot hear. We are offering the advice all mothers give to daughters leaving girl-hood behind. She stumbles and pauses at the last step. She opens her mouth to plead again. This girl so hard to bring to tears is on the verge of collapse. The cook shakes her head and puts a finger to her lips and motions her on.

Don't be afraid, Asty, the cook says. He's wearing the necklace you gave him. It's a good sign. Go, *emebet*, don't worry, he'll be gentle.

But Aster cannot hear. She is suspended above the celebratory

voices, trapped by a curdling rage that she mistakes for fear. Past that
door is the bedroom. Inside that bedroom is Kidane. When she steps
in, she must do it without the cook or her mother. She must go in as
the wife of a man she hardly knows. They will be alone to do what it is
that husbands and wives do when they close the door behind them and
grow deathly quiet. There is no choice but forward. No other way but
through it: we say it again.

At the landing, the cook draws her close in an embrace. Lie down on
the bed and open your legs and close your eyes. In the morning I'll be
here waiting. I'll bathe you myself if you want. She kisses Aster on each
cheek, pats her hair, and adjusts the folds of her dress. You're beautiful,
she says.

The cook's swollen eye has almost healed, the cuts on her mouth are
now tiny scabs. Neither of them has spoken of the night Aster's father
caught them trying to run away. It is an erased memory, burned and
crushed to ash. When the wounds are gone, there will be no proof that
Aster and the cook once made a pact to leave together and never look
back. The cook speaks to her now as if Aster did not break her promise
to confess it was her idea. She looks at her tenderly, as if Aster took the
full weight of the blame herself, as if it were Aster who felt her father's
fists sink into her stomach and blast into her jaw.

Aster clings to the cook, burying her head in her shoulder. Come
with me, just through the door.

The expression that flashes across the cook's face is a glance of hard
light. We all have to do things we don't want, she says.

They walk to the bedroom and the cook steps away. Aster places
her hand on the door and pushes it open because there is no way but
through it, because there is nothing else to do, because there has never
been anything left to do but walk where she is supposed to walk. She
slips in and presses her back to the wall, her body pulsing, an unopened
wound. She still imagines escape. She cannot see her mother at the bottom of the staircase ready to catch her if she comes running down. The

cook, too, gazes at that bedroom door, her jaw tight as she tries to hide that smile she cannot fully wipe clean.

In the great hall below, the air has grown thick with musk and smoke. The men have shut all the windows, their impatience flattening their eyes. They are waiting for one sound: for a girl's startled cry, for the first signs of a man become free. Aster's mother is waiting, too, while she trembles like the young girl she used to be. She reaches for the cook's hand but the cook pulls away. She is tracing her steps back to that road she once hoped led to freedom. She is cursing anew the hard fists that brought her down. There is no way out but through it, she murmurs. There is no escape but what you make from inside.

The bed is made of sturdy wood and thick slats of leather. It is immense. It is monstrously large. It is much too big for a girl like her. And there he is, an eager man pivoting in the light splashing into the room, his white clothes shimmering, the seams bright as teeth. He is wearing the necklace she gave him. It hangs loose in the bend of his body, the rich gold catching sparks of light. Aster yanks on the door to get out but it has shut and locked without her help.

Come, he murmurs. He sits down carefully on the bed so not to disturb the crisp white sheet. He takes off the necklace and holds it out. Let's see how this fits you, Little One. He pats the bed and shifts over. Here.

Aster pounds on the door and pulls on it again. Please, she says.

Go, the cook hisses from the corridor.

Lijé, we'll be here when you wake. Her mother's voice is so small it can fit into the crevice between the wall and the door. This is nothing. Remember what I told you.

Aster, Kidane says. The necklace lies crumbled in the center of his palm. I'm very proud to have you as my wife. I know you're scared, but it's okay. You'll get used to it.

Only we know that he is unsure of what to do with the girl. He has heard the men talk but there has been no one to ask about one so small.

There has been nothing to do but walk with fake pride toward this bed-room and hold his hand out and say, Come. He has filled himself with drink and song. He has held his father tight. He has smiled and nodded and sat in church next to this Aster with a heart beating frantically in his chest. He is confused but he is not frightened. He is worried but he is not cautious. He is exactly as he says: eager.

Let me go home, she says. I'll come back tomorrow.

He looks at her lithe figure, the slender neck, the small wrists. He notes the tears she is blinking away. And as he sees the shivering body and the quaking shoulders, his nervousness quiets. He begins to under-stand the stories of those men who gathered around him in recent weeks. You will feel old then you will feel young: that is what they said to him. You must be strong, they added, don't give up. She will bear you sons who will be like their father, so decide what kind of man will you be from the first night. As Kidane sits on the bed, we can hear his breathing quicken. We can see the sheen of sweat. We can see him tremble and we know that he will do what has been done by those he has called his fathers.

Get away from the door. Do it now. His breathing is slower. His body is tensing. The looseness is draining out of his bones. He is seated but he is starting to ripple with strength, grow sleek and reptilian, stiff.

The floorboard creaks in the hall. The stairs groan and she knows that the women are gone. She smells the mingling odors of sweat and tej inside the hot room. It stinks of old butter and dried leather and sweet incense. Aster drops her head and clings to the wall. She cannot move. Her body has become like stone.

Kidane rises from the bed and lays the necklace on the sheets. He pulls off his shirt then stands before her, arms at his side.

Look at me, he says.

His bare chest expands, tight flesh pushing against rough skin. Taut muscles stretch like ropes over his shoulders and down his back. His arms knot with a definition she has noticed in only the strongest of her cousins. His body fills the room and saps the air and even though he does not move, she can feel his heat pressing into her. Aster wraps her arms around herself and puts her head down.

Look at me, he says again.

He puts on the necklace. The thick gold chain glistens against his skin. He kisses the pendant and looks at the back, where her mother insisted the goldsmith carve Kidane's name.

This will be for our son one day, he says. He smiles.

He pulls down his trousers and soon he is wearing nothing. Aster draws back from the sight. Between his legs is a triangle of hair, coarse and thick and threatening. He is bristling with hard flesh, draped in the room's dizzying smells.

He keeps his arms at his side. Don't turn from me, he says. His voice quivers. He takes a step.

We can only watch as Aster sinks to the floor and covers her face. She has promised the cook she will not cry but the tears are shaking loose. Her body slides flat onto the floor and in her mind is a growing space waiting to devour the memory of all that will unfold tonight. That, too, is a way, we remind her. That, too, is an escape.

Aster begins to tremble, the shaking uncontrollable, the convulsions so powerful that she cannot hear Kidane's steps until he is bending over her, wrapping his arms around her, lifting her to her feet, pressing her to his warm skin, to his knotted body, to his thickness and the necklace that cuts into her cheek like a knife. He is carrying her to the bed and there is nothing, nothing that she can do to pull herself back to safety.

He settles her easily in the middle of the bed. She cannot hear it but downstairs in the corner of that great and cavernous house, her mother weeps while the cook looks up as if she can see through wood. Aster tries to curl into herself, but Kidane grabs her hands and brings them to his chest and she feels his quickening heartbeat and the slickness of his sweat. She pulls away, letting a small whimper escape. Kidane takes off the necklace and puts it on her, laughing softly as it flops below her chest and grazes her stomach.

You're so small, he says.

Then he is twisting her to face him, pulling her hands to his face and kissing her fingers and when Aster tries to stand on the bed to run away, tripping on the hem of her dress, he yanks her down and flattens his closed mouth onto hers, pressing until her lips start to tear against her teeth.

She manages to turn her head. Let me go, she says.

Beyond the door, the world has fallen silent. The windows are shuttered. There is just the two of them, and there is nowhere to go. She strains to get out of his hold, a growing anger mingling with terror.

He jerks her forward and throws her off balance, then slams her on her back and presses an arm against her chest. It is effortless, so easy that he gasps.

It's better if you relax, he says. He pushes his mouth to her ear. It's okay, he says.

She brings her legs together and presses them flat on the bed. She does the opposite of what the cook told her because it is unnatural the other way. It is unnatural and cowardly to lift your legs and wait for this man. It is more natural, she is realizing, to resist. There is no way but this way, she will tell the cook. There's no way but to fight.

Close your eyes, he whispers, against her cheek. Close your eyes and pretend I am that servant of yours helping you change. Close your eyes. His voice is gentle, soothing.

Somehow he raises the hem of her dress and draws the skirt over her knees. The large hand that he plants on her thigh is a foreign object. It is a block of wood, a chunk of metal, a stone, inhuman and cold. She no longer recognizes what it is. It is just a mass resting on her leg, creating a strange sensation that feels like the start of a bruise. He moves deftly, strong hands working quickly while his shoulders pin her down, and then he is tugging one arm and the next out of the dress and before

Aster can find a way to slide out of his hold, he is flinging it behind her and stretching on top of her while one hand follows the curve of the chain from her neck, down to her breasts, to her ribs, and he flattens his palm on her stomach and the heat sears her skin like a burn.

I'll be gentle, Kidane says. It won't hurt.

Aster makes herself like iron. She imagines herself steel and locks every bone in place. She refuses to look at him. She refuses to listen. She won't move until morning comes and she is free. Then she will go home and face her father's beatings. She will dare him to bring her back here alive.

This man is still speaking, talking in that low voice meant to soothe her then catch her unaware but she is looking at the wall and on that wall hangs a sword and she is close enough to jump up and grab it and slice his throat in one easy stroke. She has practiced this with the cook many times, using rodents and chickens, planning for their escape. She will kill him if he puts his hands between her legs like the cook told her he would. She will kill him and spill his blood on this bed. Aster counts the steps to the sword and imagines the single leap back.

Kidane smiles and pinches her cheek, mistaking her silence for agreement. You're spoiled, he says, his voice is soft. He stares at her chest, his eyes shining. You're not a girl anymore, he says. Then he is pushing her legs apart with his knee, balancing himself between them.

When she opens her mouth to scream, his hand flicks against her teeth, the hit so stunning that it leaves her dizzy, the pain blooming rapidly across her jaw.

Stop moving, he says. Stop and it won't hurt. I promise. Again that voice trembling in the dark as if he is the one afraid. I promise, he repeats. I promise, he says again as he places his full weight against her.

And it is just skin on skin now, flesh against flesh, and though she knows it is futile, Aster tries to push herself off the mattress but he is leaden and thick on top of her, suffocating.

There is this: her mother told her when it was time, she would know what to do. But there is also this: the cook told her when it was time, there was nothing she could do. Take it, the cook said. Take whatever comes and wake up in the morning and live. And then Kidane jerks roughly as if he wants to punish her with his hips. He thrusts himself at her and at first, Aster does not know what he is doing. She cannot tell what it is he is searching for with his fingers and that part of him that she will break with the sword as soon as she gets a chance. And while she is wondering and swirling in numbing confusion, the pain slams itself behind her eyes and knocks her breathless, and she feels herself splitting. Aster opens her mouth to scream and this time, Kidane does not hit her, this time it is as if she is not even there even though she is the weight against which he is balancing as if he might drown while he gasps.

Her mind grows nimble in the pain and she feels herself leave this stinking room and this sweaty man and soon she is hovering over herself, staring down at the girl reaching for the sword to split this man in half then make her way home.

And then.

She is lost and disappearing.

SHE DRAGS HIRUT INTO THE STABLE AND WARNS THE COOK NOT TO unlock the door. Hirut lies curled where she is left, the pain a heated blade pressing against bone. After the first few hours, she steps outside of herself and watches, mesmerized, as a small pool of blood thickens at her neck. It begins to seam into the raised wound that stretches over her shoulder and onto her chest. When she grows bored, she leaves herself behind and wanders out of the stable and sneaks into Kidane's office. She shuffles through the newspapers on his desk, gazes past the picture of Emperor Haile Selassie that he has cut out and set aside, then settles herself in his chair and pretends to read. She sees rows and rows of marching *ferenjoch* and a ship overflowing with uniformed men. She sees them waving to her with their rifles jutting into the sky. She sees gaping mouths that stretch and envelop her and she knows she is sinking into the mouth of the beast, and she will keep falling if she doesn't move. She gets up and slides through the corridor then to the veranda and keeps walking, reveling in her unhindered freedom.

At the threshold of the compound, she stops at the gate to listen to the trees beckoning her onward. Home, they say. Go home. Kidane's horse, Adua, mourns for her in the stable. Aster's horse, Buna, shakes its head angrily. The owls have gathered on the roof to say goodbye. Even the wind has bent to wrap itself around her shoulders and cool the fire. And Hirut knows she must go home. She must find the path and walk until she is back in her mother's arms, waiting for her father to return from the fields. They are scared and she is lonely and she does not know why she has been away for so long. One day when she is strong enough she will nurse the bruise spreading across the middle of her chest. For now, she will let it roam, let it snag at rib bone and press at her lungs because she needs to be home. Hirut opens the gate and steps into the thick well of darkness.

Here she stands in the center of this chamber where there is only the dark and only these wounds and only pain offers a treacherous light into her head. Inside her head there are words that stumble free of meaning and nothing to hold them in place except the sound of her own name gathering strength in its repetition: I am Hirut daughter of Getey and Fasil, born in a blessed year of harvest. She is Hirut surrounded by dark-ness thick as flesh, and she the pulsing wound at the center. She is a feeble light slanting into the room through a crack in the wall. She is the light chewed up at the threshold of the wound. She is the pain puls-ing alone in this black chamber where there is only this, only the dark, only the wound that will not stop shivering like a damaged heart. Inside her head is the memory of light cracking like a whip above her head. Above the head of the girl who used to be Hirut daughter of Getey and Fasil, born in a blessed year of harvest. Above the girl who no longer has a head, who no longer has words, who no longer has memory, who no longer has a name, who is only a remembrance sinking into the dark hole of the forgotten.

A SLENDER CRACK in the wall slants light into the stable. Then dusk slips between clouds to hover low in the trees. The gate to the compound creaks open. Footsteps and the lively voices of men. Firewood shifts and settles in place. Kidane is speaking. Someone answers: Yes, Gashe. Yes, Dejazmach Kidane. Hirut tries to sit up inside this box that pins her heavy body in place. A cold breeze crawls like an insect down her neck and traces the edge of the bruise on her chest. The bruise is expanding like spilled water. It is a tender wound cracking open beneath her skin. It is governed by time, by minutes and hours and days that Hirut can no longer recall. She has been here forever. She has just arrived. She struggles to sit up, to lean her head against the wall and let her eyes peer past the swelling of tender skin to peek between the slats.

He is on the veranda and a hesitant light sags against the shamma he wears every day. He has on a belt as thick as a waistband. He stands next to a younger man with a rifle slung across his back. The cook is calling them to their meal: Gash Kidane, Aklilu, come eat. Kidane says the name that belongs to his wife. She's tired, says the cook. And neither of them speaks the name of the girl wandering lost inside the dark, tumbling backward and falling down.

Later, the door swings wide. Gray morning light floods the stable and a snap of wind rushes in. The cook pokes her head in and snaps her fingers, motioning her to get up. You didn't sleep next to Adua and Buna? She shakes her head, frowning. Come on, we've got guests and she said to help. Hurry, I'm afraid she'll come and check. Then the cook spins around and walks back to her kitchen.

Hirut struggles to her feet and stumbles out of the stable, unbalanced and blinded by the sun. The wind glides cruelly against her cuts. Fresh air is a sharp, cold burst in her nose. Berhe's whistling rattles against her aching head, and the chair scraping in Kidane's office grates roughly down her spine. Near the front door is a pile of swords on a burlap sack. Large baskets rest against the veranda steps. Blankets and scarves she has never seen before are drying across a new clothesline erected next to the fence. A new pile of firewood leans next to those already at the stable. The world has become something else since she left it.

The cook calls for her and Hirut finds her bent over her knife just outside of the kitchen, a cutting board balanced on her lap. She is slicing chunks of meat into smaller pieces, vigorously tearing off bits of fat. The blade hits the board with a jarring persistency, the sound throwing itself through the quiet courtyard.

Get a fire started for the wot. The cook points to the stack of fire-wood and charcoal in front of her then quickly resumes her work.

Hirut knows the cook is watching her from through lowered eyelids. I need help.

When the cook looks up, they lock eyes and the pain in her chest is so intense that Hirut lets her mouth tremble, and her legs relax beneath the great weight of her sadness. She would have let herself fall but the cook shakes her head, still bent over her work, and whispers: Don't you dare let her see you cry.

Over the cook's bent head, Kidane's figure is silhouetted through his office window: he is standing over his desk, looking down at his papers. Berhe balances the burlap sack of swords in his arms, grim with effort as he rounds the corner from the front of the house into the court-yard. Two young men stand up from the far corner where they were sitting and help Berhe set the sack down next to Aster's flowers. Aster is nowhere to be seen.

Are you deaf? Get the gulicha ready, we have a lot of food to make and more men are coming. The cook still does not look up.

The two men shift toward her briefly as she drags the clay oven closer to the kitchen, then they go back to inspecting the guns. The courtyard sinks back into its unnatural silence as Hirut lowers onto her sore knees and settles firewood into the clay oven's base. She lights it and blows. Every breath stirs the odors clinging to her: fear and manure, old straw and dried blood, all those smells she had once thought belonged only to the very poor. She fans the growing flames and tries to swallow her humiliation. The strangers are glancing at her again, their eyes full of knowing pity, like she is one of those who begs on church steps and in the mercato, pleading for mercy that does not come. For a moment, she is afraid of stirring the firewood more, afraid of smelling herself and pushing the odor toward the men, then Berhe drops the sword he is pol-ishing and the two men shoot to their feet, and Kidane turns from his desk near the window and all of them turn toward the knock at the gate.

I'll get them, Berhe says at the same time that Kidane shouts into the courtyard:

They're here! Bring water, they'll be thirsty. We'll eat after I'm done.

———

THEY ARE A WALL: men hardened by the uncertainties of a peasant's existence, callused feet cracked like old leather, wrinkles deepened by the sun. Across their arms and shoulders, down their legs and chests, they bear the evidence of crushing labor. They have names that she will not memorize until later, but what she sees of them, she recognizes. They carry the familiar scars of village life: the poorly grafted broken bone, the cratered marks of childhood disease, the raised knot of an old burn. They are young and old at the same time, weary and alert, straight and bent: ferocious. They stand in front of Kidane at the bottom of the veranda and watch him with awestruck eyes.

There are six of them, wiry men with determined faces. They are dressed in old jodhpurs and tunics darkened by wear. They do not smile, even after Kidane's face softens when he looks at them and nods. They do not break their sternness when he lays his hand on one man's shoulder then the next. It is hard for Hirut not to stare at their fearsome expressions, the burning anger that shades their eyes. They are slender but muscular with broad feet and wide shoulders. One has an earring made of a black stone. Another has a scar near his jaw. The shortest one carries a curved sword at his waist. The tallest, a rifle with a bayonet. None of them would ever bend and cower beneath a whip.

The photo of this moment does not exist. There is only this remembrance molded by Hirut, a thought collecting weight with each backward glance. For weeks, she and the cook will speak of it in the sparest terms: of strength and valor, of patriotism and pride and complete obedience. Only later will she look again and see what she could not see. Here, Kidane is a different man from the one who stood in front of Hirut and trembled at the sound of his angry wife. Different from the one who bent to kiss her cheek. Back then, he was bowed by the absence of many things: a living son, a content wife, a quiet home. Here, he claims what cannot be seen: a loyalty that has presented itself fully formed and unshakable, an adoration that borders on fear. The men watch his every move through half-lidded stares, his station a weight that keeps their heads tilted to the ground.

Will you die for your country? Kidane asks a man who steps forward and introduces himself as Seifu. Kidane paces around him, the others stepping back to make way. Will you follow me into battle and run past me if I fall?

The sun is a sheet of light behind them, dropping evenly into the valley below. The sky, a clear and vivid blue that holds up the lingering moon, a faint and ghostly intruder on this day.

Hirut is caught by the expression on Seifu's sharp-boned face. He is confident, unbowed by Kidane's physical closeness.

I said, Will you die for Ethiopia? Kidane leans in to speak into the man's ear.

First I'll kill. Seifu's answer draws the men more upright.

Then there is Amha, shorter than the rest, barrel-chested with a sly smile.

What do you know better than anyone else, soldier? Kidane leans into his ear.

I know the caves in this area into Keren, Amha says. I know every place we can hide and ambush. I know more than a *shifta*, I can outmaneuver any *banda*. I can watch a man die then sit down to eat.

The sword he carries is so sharp that the cook leans forward and exclaims with envy. He clasps the handle and slices through the breeze with the curved blade. And this, he says. A slender finger traces a row of delicate letters etched along the edge. A prayer for the dead.

Eskinder knows the mountains and their secrets. Yasin is as light as a *ferenj* and can speak the language of the Italians and of the villagers in the surrounding areas. Hirut sees Kidane smile when he asks, French?

And the man nods and replies, Yes, that too. Hailu can identify poisonous plants and those they can crush for medicine. And then there is the one with the scar on his shoulder and the intelligent eyes, the same one who looked at her and then turned away, his face full of revulsion and pity.

I'm the greatest sniper you'll ever meet, he says. No man can stop me, Dejazmach Kidane. No bullet will ever kill me.

That's Aklilu, you've seen his mother in the mercato, so proud of him. The cook is whispering. These are his special guards, sons of relatives some of them, she continues. If he had a son who was old enough, he'd be there.

After he goes down the row, Kidane closes his eyes and lifts his face to the sun. My name is Kidane, son of Checole, the greatest son of the greatest warrior named Lemma, he says. I carry the name of his father, the bravest man who ever lived. My blood is not afraid to leave my body and soak into this soil that is also mine. I'm giving you this oath today: from now on, I'll act as your shield in battle. You must lead the rest of my army in the same way. I'll protect you with my life, I swear that to each of you right now. You've each become my sons, my own flesh and blood. To lose any of you is to lose part of myself.

The cook's mouth hardens. His father gave this same speech when Kidane was a boy, she says. She points toward the stable. They were standing right there, armies of men in the compound and on the road and down the hill. Everywhere.

You were here? Hirut asks.

The cook throws her a sharp look and shakes her head. Of course not, Berhe told me. Before Kidane's father marched to fight in Adua, Kidane took his father's sword and cut his hand. Just a young boy, but he'd been trained like a warrior. She holds out her hand, palm down. He let his blood drip down then he rubbed the dirt onto his father's feet. A tradition in their family. When men went to battle, the son spilled blood before the father. She nods and looks toward Berhe, watching her from the stable. A secret understanding crosses the distance between them.

You'll go to your villages and return with an accurate count of all the weapons your people have, Kidane says. Pick the men you can trust to serve under you and take them to Kossoye, where you met me. I don't want a large army like the others are putting together. We'll be small and flexible, but powerful.

A murmur of approval rises from the group.

Dejazmach Kidane, we already brought all our weapons to you. It is Aklilu, speaking with his eyes lowered in deference. We're short of ammunition and rifles. He dares to meet Kidane's gaze. We can't use our fathers' guns.

Aklilu from Gojjam, son of my younger cousin, born in Dega Damot, Kidane says. Show respect when you speak to me. He folds his arms across his chest. You're the one that villagers talk about. The horseman with the aim of a sniper. But still, just the son of my cousin.

Aklilu bows then straightens, careful to keep his eyes averted. They are almost the same height, though Aklilu is taller. He is taut energy next to Kidane's mature strength.

You're worried that I can't lead you to victory?

I have complete faith in you, Dejazmach. Aklilu bows again. It's my rifle I don't trust.

Kidane narrows his eyes. You sound like your father. Mehari should have taught you to obey your commander. The weapons will come, he adds.

Aklilu waits for Kidane to continue, his expression shifting back to a remote sternness.

Kidane nods kindly to Berhe, who is holding a sack and extending it toward the men. Get some water, he tells his men. Berhe has cups for you. Then we'll eat. Meet me in the courtyard.

And here is where history falters. According to popular song, Kidane is interrupted by Aster, who appears like a ghost next to her husband.

The story goes that on the day the great Kidane mobilized his men, a lone figure rose up from her bed to heed his call to fight. They say the sight of those men gathered around her beloved husband pulled Aster back from her untended sorrows and carried her from the bedroom to the veranda to stand at her husband's side, clothed for war in his cape and lion's mane headdress. But Aster does not rise from her bed and walk to her husband while dressed in his clothes. She does not take her husband's hand and pledge her allegiance. She does not ask to be forgiven for her unfettered grief and anger. She does not swear to die at his feet if he should fall defending their country. She does not, in fact, touch her womb and declare more sons for Kidane's army.

No: Aster stands up from her bed, dressed in black, and makes her way to her husband's office. She moves, uncaped and unapologetic, out of the land of the aggrieved because she remembers what he does not: that this is her late son's birthday. And she, before Tesfaye's last breath, had made a mother's promise that she would leave him only when he was old enough to understand abandonment. And legend will never tell that Aster also realizes that all she once loved is truly gone.

The Aster of those famous songs will come later, but even then, she will be a legend molded by her own devices. For now, it is 27 Nehas 1927, also called 2 September in the year that is both 1935, and also Anno XIII. So many ways to mark the month and year when Aster walks into Kidane's office, sits down at his desk, and finds herself staring at a newspaper account of a woman they call Maria Uva, an Italian who lives near Port Said. While her husband draws himself into the circle of men and begins to speak to them of his father's feats, Aster is leaning to get a better look at the picture of this *ferenj* woman who is shouting while waving a flag like a declaration of war. Aster stares at the photo, at the arrogant woman's openmouthed glee, at that flag whipping freely in the wind, and by the time she lifts her head, Aster knows that she must make herself anew and meet this proclamation with one of her own.

In fact, the famous Maria Uva is not shouting, but singing. And the war that will come will not be declared by her. In the instant of the photograph, published 30 August 1935, Anno XIII, she is launching into the chorus of "Giovinezza" while the *Cleopatra* eases its way into Port Said. The tricolored Italian flag is indeed behind her. In the ship in front of her, two thousand soldiers are screaming her name. The light in her eyes could be gleeful devotion, or more likely, a consequence of the sun's sharp angle. But it is late afternoon and overworked journalists, frantic to fill word quotas and pass censorship before the day ends, report every movement of this *ragazza del canale di Suez, la madonnina del legionario* in the glorious terms of a seafaring goddess.

It is also the fourth day of the *Cleopatra*'s weeklong journey to Massawa. The soldati have traveled in units from Rome and Venice, from Florence and Puglia to embark on their great African adventure at the port of Naples. We know Ettore is there, though there is no way for Aster to know that as she sits in Kidane's office and stares at Maria Uva. Hirut understands the coincidence, sitting in the train station in Addis Ababa with the opened box on her lap, staring down at the same picture of Maria Uva. She remembers that day when Aster slipped out of Kidane's office and brought the photo of that woman to the kitchen and said to the cook: We women won't sit by while they march into our homes. This part, at least, the songs have gotten right.

The *Cleopatra*: a steamer built nearly 100 meters long and 14 meters wide. A giant chunk of metal extending 5 meters from the surface of the sea to its deck. It is a heavy mass that rises out of the water like a fortress wall. It should have been impossible for a woman's voice to travel across shoreline and water and then up, past that great steel hulk. I don't know how she did it, Ettore once said to Hirut. We could hear her, every one of us, and she sounded like an angel. This is why Hirut reaches into the box while sitting in that train station in Addis Ababa and takes out the picture and looks on the back.

La Cleopatra, it says. *Carissimi mi mancate. Caro Papa, cara Mamma, sono in Africa.* My dear ones, I miss you; dear Papa, dear Mamma, I'm in Africa. The picture is fragile and yellowed, torn out long ago from a wilting newspaper and pasted on an unsent postcard. Hirut flips it over again: she can see him only because she knows what to look for: he is on deck, staring down at white-garbed men rowing earnestly through choppy water, their galabias flaring in the morning breeze. In the picture, he is there but he is not there. He is one of the indistinguishable specks that hold no resemblance to a human form. There is nothing in this photograph that hints at what awaits these men, these shapeless figures blunted by light. This is Maria Uva's moment and she is the center of the camera's gaze, Mussolini's beam of light casting herself across Africa's dark borders, ushering men toward greatness.

KIDANE COLLECTS HIS RIFLE AND BINOCULARS FROM HIS EMPTY office, orders Berhe to walk the horses and clean the stable, tells the cook he will be gone for some days then, without a word to his wife, who is back in their bedroom, he leaves with his men. A strange lull seeps into the day, slowing everything down, draping silence over the compound. This is why they all tip toward Aster when she opens the bedroom door, walks softly down the corridor, and steps out of the front door. She stands where Kidane stood on the veranda, an old cape across her shoulders, her black dress billowing beneath it. The unnatural quiet curves in her direction as she goes into the stable without so much as a glance toward the cook or Berhe. She walks out holding the reins of her horse, Buna. She goes to the gate and pauses, and all of the trees bend and the wind stills and the birds pivot to see what she will do next.

I'm not waiting like a servant for him to come back, she says.

The cook doesn't get up from her stool beside the footpath leading to the courtyard, near where Hirut has frozen in place, dirty trays in her shaking hands. The cook doesn't move. She is mesmerized by the woman at the gate turning slowly to look in her direction. They lock eyes and the cook shakes her head. Aster opens the gate just as Kidane did hours ago, then climbs on the mare, kicks its haunches, and gallops down the worn path that blooms into countless destinations. And then she is gone.

Berhe and the cook exchange glances, both of them struck dumb by the effortless departure. They are spellbound and disturbed by something Hirut does not understand. Berhe peers out of the gate. He stares at the dust rising behind the racing horse.

What happened? Hirut asks.

What did she say to you? The cook rises to her feet and strides to Berhe.

Berhe shakes his head, looking through the gate with his hands on his waist. What does that woman ever tell anyone? he says.

The next day they prepare each meal and set the table and brew coffee as if she will appear at any moment. As daylight slips into dusk, they stand in the sitting room and stare out the window toward the gate that Berhe keeps opening, searching for the cloud of dust that will announce her arrival. When she does not come back by late evening, they collect the tray, set it on the veranda, and the three of them eat while listening for galloping hooves.

Where'd she go? Hirut asks the second night in their room, but the cook glares at her then slips into bed.

Let her stay, the cook says. What's it matter? The cook wipes her face on her sleeve. And don't think I didn't see you and Kidane. She points an accusing finger at Hirut. You make her worse, you make her jealous and it's your fault.

I didn't do anything, Hirut says, but the cook has turned her back and she's lying down with the blanket over her head.

———

THE RUMORS: There is a madwoman on a wild horse blazing through the hills, she is stopping at every church and shouting into the heavens and calling wrathful angels down to Earth. She is a nun shifting into a hyena, an angry spirit screaming vengeance from the tops of barren trees. She is Empress Taitu resurrected to fight these *ferenjoch*. She is an unnamed ghost thrown down by the Almighty, come to curse our foreign enemies. The villagers gather around their wells, their water gourds forgotten, to spread the news about further sightings. They pause while washing and during prayers to search for plumes of dust rising from the horizon. There are the whispers that start to breed the truth: It is Aster, wife of Kidane, racing through our hills with that horse the color of gunpowder. It is she who is rupturing our nights with those shouts, dressed in black. She is calling to us, ordering us to get ready to fight.

The cook ignores the questions when they go to the mercato. She slides past the hands trying to pull her aside for a private conversation. She shrugs and shakes her head and covers the side of her face when her friends, those servants from other households, want to know if what their mistresses are saying is true, if what the gossip from the monthly gathering of their exclusive *mehaber* groups could possibly be right, if the call for these women to meet at the banks of the river does indeed come from the cook's Aster. Is it her? Is Aster calling the women to gather at the river tomorrow? What are these women planning?

She's not my Aster, is all that the cook says.

And then the day comes when Aster returns and the cook stands, speechless at the gate, a half-filled bag of spices from the mercato falling from her hand and spilling on the ground.

You, the cook shouts, and pushes past Hirut into the compound. It's you. Her voice has come unleashed, the anger finally finding its full release. She is pointing an accusatory finger at the parted curtains of the sitting room window where Aster is blocked in the bright glare of the glass.

Aster turns from the window, and soon the front door opens. She steps out in her black dress, her hair unbraided and unruly around her solemn face. She is covered with dust and in her eyes burns a hard intensity: shifting light on a river's surface.

You thought I'd never come back, Aster says. Where would I go? Then her mouth curls in that way that only Aster can do. You could have left, I gave you the chance.

The cook looks more tired than she has in the last seven days of Aster's absence. I've had enough, she says. She slumps at the bottom of the veranda, drained of energy and will. Just give me money and let me go.

When we came to this house—, Aster begins.

We came here in different ways, the cook says.

Not so different.

The cook turns as if she is seeing Hirut for the first time. Get out of here.

The stable door creaks open and Hirut rushes to Berhe, who slips an arm around her shoulder, and together, they watch the two women.

There's nothing to give you. He took it all without telling me, he took everything. You think you're special because you're tired? Aster speaks with a helpless anger. I just sold the rug my mother gave me to buy us guns. I'm not selling my wedding necklace for you. That's all that's left, she adds quietly.

The cook walks up the steps until she is directly in front of Aster. The two of them stare into each other's faces, gazing into what the years have done. You promised that as soon as you could, you'd give me what I needed. The cook's mouth trembles. Last year, you said next year. Then you said on Tesfaye's birthday. You've got Hirut and I'm tired. I want to find my family, I want to go home.

Aster takes the cook's hands, her voice softens. Things have changed, the war's coming. Everyone's mobilizing and you have no money, you've got nothing but me. Aster stares at her. She takes a breath. I need you.

The cook's shoulders deflate and her head lowers while Aster raises herself taller.

Tell the girl to meet me in the sitting room, Aster says. Berhe, I have some things for you to alter. Her tone is the soft, intimate tone she was using with the cook: the old Aster is back, confident of being heard and obeyed. Get the wooden chest that's in Kidane's office, she says, motioning to the cook. You know the one.

Aster smooths the front of her dress. And I'm hungry. Then she goes back through the front door and shuts it behind her.

＝

THERE ARE TWO NEW RIFLES leaning against the wall, their sleek metal and blond wood shinier than any piece of furniture. Hirut bends down and picks one up, looking quickly over her shoulder to confirm Aster is still in the kitchen talking to the cook. It is cold and heavy in her hands, sturdy as bone. She traces the long line of its barrel with a hesitant hand, stopping at the sight, going past the chamber. She flinches as she grazes the trigger, remembering her father's warnings, then she rests her palm on the smooth plane of wood and presses down. The stock feels as warm as skin. A memory: her father taps her chest the first day he lets her touch the rifle. This is life, he says. Then he settles his palm on the gun, This is death. Never underestimate either.

Hirut carefully sets the rifle down and it angles back into place as if propelled by its own will. It is a sound that she has heard before, that slow scrape across a wall, then silence. Hirut listens carefully, past Aster's voice, past the cook's footsteps, past the low hum of wind brushing against windowpane and she sees her father, Fasil, falling at a stranger's feet. She sees him wrap his arms around the man's legs as if begging for something he knows he has lost. She is standing at the doorway of their hut, half draped in the shadows falling across her back. Her mother, Getey, is behind her, shrouded in the darkness and crying softly. Hirut hears her name and turns around. Getey is holding the rifle and telling her to move. She is pointing it at that stranger's chest. She is breathing hard, air dragging itself out of her body and scraping inside. She is saying, Move, move, Hirut, so I can aim for Checole, stand next to me. Hirut turns back and sees Kidane take Checole's hands and say, Abbaba please. He is saying, Getey is gone now, Abbaye. He is saying, Let's go home. He is saying, Come with me Abbaba, and he is pulling his father along as he turns and says, I'm taking him home, Getey. It'll never happen again. Hirut's mother stops crying. She leans the gun against the wall and it scrapes its way to the ground. She crumbles to the floor and curls into herself. She stays like that even after Hirut comes to kneel beside her. She stays like that even when Hirut's father runs inside and says, What have you done? Getey stays like that while Fasil lifts the gun and looks out the door and stares at no one as he empties the weapon of its single bullet.

Hirut forces her shaking hands to still. This is a new memory that has slipped out of the place where things are kept forgotten. Why was her mother crying? What was her father doing? She braces herself on the back of the sofa and looks out the window. The first time she understood she would never see her mother again was when Aster said, You will listen to everything I say. Then she dragged the long nail of her little finger across Hirut's cheeks: You are less than the dirt in my nail.

Did you get the clothes like I asked? Aster is in the corridor, making her way into the sitting room.

Hirut hurries to the wooden chest and opens the latch.

Turn on the radio and drag the chest closer. Aster is still in that dusty black dress, but her skin has lost that pallid sheen that drew her features into a somber cast. She draws the curtains closed and gives a satisfied nod at the sight of the rifles. Then she settles on the sofa, her hands cupped delicately on her knees, and waits.

Behind Aster's head, the sun presses into the room through the closed curtains. It is a square box of light brightening the room, striking soft lines into Aster's curls and heightening the curves of her cheekbones. It catches on the gold necklace and skids across the room when Aster shifts. It glances across the radio then disappears.

Hirut turns the black knob and the radio hums and crackles, rebellious. She spins it until shrill trumpet music bursts from the speaker, making her jump back. Then she pulls the wooden chest closer to Aster and pauses. She once opened it without permission and rummaged through the clothes for her rifle.

A thin voice pushes through static. It is a rapid-fire speech welcoming listeners to the new Imperial Ethiopian Radio Station, broadcasting live from Akaki in Addis Ababa. The man sounds as if he has been running, as if he is shouting through a tin can.

They're going to announce the empress, Etege Menen, and Princess Tsehai, Aster says. Listen to her, listen to every word.

The radio crackles and a thick band of static blazes into the room before a trumpet bursts through with a long trilling note.

Aster stands up. Hand me the shirt that's in there.

Hirut knows the trunk's contents by what it lacks. She knows it by its dimensions. She knows now that it is too short to possibly hold what she once hoped it did, but back then, when she was foolish enough to believe that some things could be made to fit into any space, she had looked. Hirut swings the latch up and tugs the chest open. She pulls out what she knows is on top: a tunic. It is a white shirt of the finest cotton, so delicate along its collarless neckline and the edges of its long sleeves that it is almost see-through. It has been preserved unusually well, still striking in its brilliance, the material smooth as silk to the touch.

Aster lifts her dress over her head and drops it to the floor. She stands naked in the room surrounded by radio static, the sun a smooth bright square on her shoulders. She sweeps her fingers into her hair to raise the curls higher.

The trumpet blares into the room. There is a long pause, a chair drags across a floor, someone clears their throat, there is a whisper.

Not everyone has one of these, Aster adds, motioning to the radio.

She slips on the tunic.

It hangs below her knees. The shoulders droop. The sleeves swallow her hands and they dangle like a pair of bent wings. Hirut is struck by how small she really is, how delicately framed her muscles and flesh. It is only her anger that makes her feel so large and imposing.

Then a man's hurried, pitched voice:

Good evening, ladies and gentlemen, once more this is a live broadcast from Akaki in Addis Ababa. It is 13 September 1935. Our emperor Haile Selassie's wife, Empress Menen, speaks to her people tonight. We welcome those around the world who are listening. One, two, three.

Aster bows to the radio, her expression reverent. Take out the *suri*, she whispers.

The trousers are at the bottom, beneath a folded cape made of animal hide. She hands the *suri* to Aster, trying not to stare at the radio. Until now, it has been a place for leaders, a row of men's voices waiting inside the box for the knob to open the door and let them through. Aster slips the trousers on. Her slender calves and ankles slide through the narrow cut of the jodhpurs. It drags on the floor, layers of the finely woven cotton folding like clouds around her feet.

You didn't clean the rug today, Aster says. She frowns and folds the legs of the jodhpurs. She tucks in the ends of the long sleeves to stop at her wrists. She adjusts the tunic so its neckline falls straight in the center of her chest. Then she stands still.

A woman starts to speak: *We are grateful tonight for this opportunity to be heard by women throughout the world.*

It's her, Aster whispers. Quick, hand me the cape.

We want to thank the World Women's League. Our beloved daughter, Tsehai, will also translate our words in English.

Empress Menen pauses and in the background, past the static and the gentle throat-clearing, Hirut can hear another voice, younger, delicate, whispering. She imagines Princess Tsehai leaning in, saying something only a daughter could say to a mother. There is the sound of shuffling paper and movement then Princess Tsehai's voice as she introduces herself. Her voice is clear, at once shy and steady. She speaks her English with an elegant cadence that Hirut has heard on Aster and her friends: it is a mannerism that comes from a mouth unaccustomed to pleas. Hirut stares at the radio, at the large black knob and the jittery dial that is possessed by the princess's breaths. She is spellbound trying to decipher how it is possible to hear this woman and this girl so clearly from far away. They are closer than the echo of drums that ricochet through the hills when there is news. They are here, but they are not here.

We are confident that women everywhere have the same desire in maintaining world peace and love.

The radio's speaker is an arch of mesh, like a webbed sun. She is so close that she can feel the warm hum of it, can almost sense the empress and princess like two solid blocks of light spinning in a place where voices travel faster than flesh. Somewhere in there, past the wood and the mesh and the knob and the glass that holds the nervous dial in place, there is a royal woman who has moved outside of herself and become both vast and invisible, mighty as wind. Lost in thought, mesmerized and awestruck, it isn't until she feels Aster nudge her leg that Hirut turns around to see what has happened.

We all know that war destroys mankind, and in spite of their differences in race, creed, and religion, women all across the world despise war because its fruit is nothing but destruction.

Aster is dressed in the tunic and jodhpurs, the stained cape across her shoulders, a new rifle slung against her back. The aged cape falls in folds, hanging in such a way that Hirut can tell it was cured by the surest hands, expertly rubbed and oiled to lie close against a body and mold to its owner's shape. Aster shifts the new rifle from her left shoulder to her right while her legs stay firm and strong beneath her. She is resplendent. She is a fearsome and shocking figure, something both familiar and foreign, frightening and incomprehensible. A woman dressed as a warrior, looking as fierce as any man.

War kills our husbands, our brothers, and our children. It destroys our homes, and scatters our families.

While the empress continues to speak through her daughter, Hirut glances from the radio to this woman, from her small feet to her proud head, from the necklace that lies over the cape to her beautiful face, from the cape to the sleek rifle.

At this hour and in such a tragic and sad period, when aggressors are planning to bring a heavy war into our lives, we would like to bring this to the attention of all women through the world, that it is their duty to voice and express solidarity against such acts.

Aster strides purposefully into the center of the room. She is a perfect weight balancing an unruly world and grinding it back into place as she lifts a hand to her forehead, and salutes.

ETTORE NAVARRA'S FIRST SIGHTING OF ERITREA: THE PORT OF Massawa, the stunning architecture that echoes the Ottoman influences of his own Venice. From the Red Sea, the city rises out of the sweltering horizon, a shimmering patch of white arches and red dust pushing through fumes and salt. The port itself is an overcrowded slab of sand pressing into the Red Sea, its pier groaning from the endless procession of ships and soldiers. On the deck of the *Cleopatra*, Ettore Navarra can see that the *Liguria* is backed in stern-first, next to the *Gange*. He winces as another ship bellows in protest in its advance. So many days on quiet waves, then this: noisy steamers fighting for space, braying donkeys suspended above the crowded pier, crates of artillery scraping loudly across planks. Vessel upon vessel dotting the sea that unrolls and twists behind him as if Massawa were the site of a great and ancient Spartan clash.

As Ettore waits for the ship to anchor, he takes out his camera and begins to focus on the pier. Behind him, men are jostling for space near the railing. He can hear Fofi and Mario shouting his name, trying to get him to turn, but he is transfixed by the scene in front of him: all the white of this port city's buildings, the tall and slender palm trees, the mountains of crates and barrels, the black men in turbans and shorts hauling supplies off ships, the cawing seagulls rushing toward a breeze.

Ettore shuts his eyes and thinks of home, of his father's graying head

bent over his books at his desk, his back to the window overlooking the
Venice lagoon, their home surrounded by canals. The impending war
brought with it one of the only moments in Ettore's life when his father
spoke to him with open agitation and worry. In the dim light of Leo
Navarra's study, Ettore saw both caution and disapproval in his face.

Leo said this: Not many are born when they should be. How I hope
this time is meant for you.

Ettore understood even then that this was not an admission as much
as it was an untelling, his father's way of moving around what he could
not say about those who were unlucky and those who were not born
when they should have been. And it was said in his father's accent: thick
from words crushed in the back of his throat. When they are in public, Leo enunciates every syllable and softens consonants unnecessarily.
But at home, Leo is a different man, and on that day, he released his
tongue and let it slide freely between accents while speaking from the
high perch of his intelligence, troubled and impatient, yet still elusive.

It is Leo's most distinctive characteristic, his way of building silence
while seeming to strip it down. His father has a way of speaking so that
meaning pulses at a different frequency, nearly inaudible. Standing on
deck, feeling the weight of the camera in his hand, Ettore realizes again
that he has spent all his years since he was a child trying to capture what
cannot be spoken, to manifest visually a world both trapped in darkness
and defined by it.

━

THIS, OF COURSE, he will never say to Hirut, not even in the days when
they are thrown together in the mountains of the Simien valley, one a
prisoner of the other. There is a photograph he shows her instead of
his parents on their wedding day, his father stoic and rigid, his mother
shy and happy. When she tries out the new word he's saying to her:
morire, he simply nods his head and repeats it. To die: *morire*. I die.
You die. We die. They die. To be dying. She says to him in Amharic,

Innateinna abbate motewal. My mother and father have died. *Memot.* To die. She says it again and he points to the photograph and points to his heart. On that mountain, staring at her through the barbed-wire fence, still fumbling through the Amharic that Colonel Fucelli has insisted he learn, he does not hear what she says. He thinks *morire* is a verb she does not fully understand without crude gestures. So he points to the sky instead, and when she looks up, they watch a blackbird slide its way into large clouds.

ASTER AND KIDANE ARGUE IN THE COURTYARD. IT IS NOT YET DAWN, and Aster is dressed in Kidane's tunic and jodhpurs. Across her shoulders, the cape ripples in thick folds to hang below her knees. She is stubborn and straight-backed confronting Kidane with his sagging shoulders and bloodshot eyes. Their loud voices erupted not long after he returned late in the night, his presence dragging the cook and Hirut out of bed to serve a late meal. The cook sits beside her now, lazily raking through a bowl of lentils while listening to the escalating tensions between the couple.

Take it off, he says. I told you that when I walked in.

It's my right.

It's my father's cape. You can't see his blood on it? Kidane's mud-flecked shamma slides off one shoulder. I don't have time for this, he says, I haven't slept in days. And now this. He reaches for the clasp at the throat of the cape to take it off his wife. Give it to me.

I know whose it is, Aster says.

Berhe has tailored Kidane's clothes for her. Beneath the cape, the tunic has been altered to fit across her slender shoulders, the sleeves have been shortened, and the seams and the hemline taken in. He has adjusted the trousers to curve against her calves before blossoming gently at the thighs, and now it cinches nicely around Aster's small waist. The outfit molds to her figure gracefully, hinting at the soft lines of her body.

The cook puts down the bowl and wipes her hands on her dress.

How long can they do this, she whispers, looking up at the tense couple. There's so much to do.

They have already taken all the spices, beans, and grains out of storage and separated them into smaller bags. They have filled baskets with powders and leaves for infections and wounds. They have arranged the scarves and blankets brought by neighbors into loads light enough to carry. They have filled countless jugs of water for the march. The cook has made enough food to feed a large wedding party, but that will only last a few days. They have worked continually, but there are still decisions to be made over what remains behind and what Aster must resign to being stolen by bandits or the Italians.

It's my father's, Kidane repeats. You've already ruined my shirt and trousers. Take off the cape.

She has worn those clothes for the last five days, removing them only at night when she returned from wherever she went, keeping the cape at her feet while she slept in her black dress. It is difficult for Hirut to see clearly in the dark, but she knows that Aster has drawn kohl around her eyes as she has done each morning before leaving, and she knows that the woman has braided her growing hair into tight, flat rows.

I'm keeping it. I've earned the right, she says.

Kidane's laugh is mocking. The right? Who gives you the right to take what's mine? He runs his hands through his disheveled hair and drops to his haunches, his arms draped over his knees. He sits like that, staring at the garden in frustrated silence.

I have a right, Kidane. She looks down at him. Who do you think has been getting these supplies ready for your men? Who's getting the scarves and blankets and water for you? She stops and swallows. I've been earning this for a long, long time.

It has been raining and the air is damp. It holds Aster's last words suspended in the space between the couple like broken leaves in search of rest.

What has she earned more than the rest of us? The cook mutters under her breath. Who's doing all the work?

My father bled on that cape and you're mocking his sacrifice for this country. Kidane shoots to his feet and points in her face. He is furious, dangerously close to lunging at her.

I have bled when I shouldn't, she says. She takes a step closer to him as if she wants to push her head against his chest. She is speaking in that steady, quiet tone she has used since she put on the clothes. It is the same tone she used when ordering Berhe to open the gate so she could leave before dawn yesterday. The same softness with which she spoke to the cook when, coming back, she said, Why don't you ever sit with me and eat, like we did as girls? To Kidane, she adds, Did you think I'd let you forget?

She never sees anyone but herself. The cook pushes a fist into the beans. Things don't change just because she wants them to.

Kidane shakes his head. They say you were in the mountains with Buna, that you're trying to mobilize on your own. He bends so their faces are close. You can't be that foolish, can you?

He looks both worn out and predatory beneath the light falling against the window to reflect back on his face.

Aster contemplates this man in front of her. Finally, she speaks: I've been doing what Empress Menen asked of me and every other woman in this country. Shouldn't we be doing something too? Or is this only your country? I got two new guns for you. The cook made extra medicines. Other women are bringing more donkeys and baskets. Isn't that what you need?

New guns? From where?

The Mauser, my gun that I came with when I married you, Aster says. Where is it? My father taught me to shoot with that gun. My mother made bullets for it in the last war. Give it to me.

The cook shakes her head and laughs softly. You see, she says to Hirut, he did it to her first.

Kidane raises a hand to strike her. I haven't beat you in a long time, he says, but I'll do it now.

She grabs his hand and flattens his palm to her cheek. Do it, she says, her voice growing louder. I've earned this cape, you can't tell me I haven't, you can't tell me you've forgotten everything, you can't tell me those things didn't happen. I've earned this, that's why you're still in my bed, that's why you love me, that's why you keep coming back after all those others you think I don't know about, because you know who you married. And you haven't even asked me about our son's grave. I went there, and I slept on his grave for three days without you, alone. You couldn't even remember it was his birthday, his second. Just like you couldn't even make it back from one of your precious meetings with the emperor to see him die. I was the one who went to the church alone, on my knees, begging God for him to live. Just like I was alone the day he died. I've earned this cape, I'm not giving it back. Hit me. Go ahead and see what I'll do.

She stops, breathless, draped in that deep blue shade of early dawn.

Kidane cups her face in his hands and raises it toward his. He speaks low but the voice carries: You can cry about the past but those Italians are near the border. Dress up like a soldier all you want, but it doesn't change anything. You'll serve my men like the cook serves you. You'll be an example to the other women. You'll follow my orders. You'll carry my wounded and bury my dead. You'll take care of those men who trust me to lead them, those men who'll die for me. You'll go out there and do it again and again until I say you can stop. Everything I owe to anyone, everything, goes to my men. From now on, until the day I die.

Kidane drops his hands, spins on his heels, and walks into the house. Soon, the light comes on in his office.

⌕

THE FIGURE APPEARS first as a dot between the two lines of the horizon, a twist of wind and dust that slides across the valley. There is nothing in what Hirut sees that speaks of a man running so hard his heart might burst. There is nothing that speaks of bone and flesh and all those things that weld a body to the earth. And so Hirut, filling jugs of water at the well, only watches, curious, while he comes closer.

By the time he gets to her, he is breathing too hard to speak. He taps his bony chest. Dejazmach Kidane, where is he? he asks. He has the gaunt, hungry look of a fervent priest. He bends over, coughs. Where is he?

He left this morning with his men, she says. They're training, she adds.

And then they hear the drums, deep, booming thuds ricocheting from valley to sky to mountain to sink between them, crackling with insistence. The drumming is syncopated, spaced in increments that tell Hirut they were relaying a message she has not yet learned to decode.

Go home, he says. If you see him before I do, tell him Worku's looking for him, it's urgent.

There comes another drumbeat, this one so loud it is a monstrous roar in a swirl of echoes.

There's raw panic in Worku's narrow face. Tell Weizero Aster and everyone else to get to the mountains. Go to the armies, they'll protect you. Find Kidane's men. Hurry. And don't forget to tell them you heard it from me. My name is Worku. Then he turns and rushes back up the hill and disappears.

She rushes back to the house, propelled by thunderous sound.

—

I HEARD IT, but I can't believe it. Is it true? Aster strides through the compound, still dressed in the cape and jodhpurs, moving into the stable, then the courtyard. We have to tell him, she shouts. We have to find a way to let him know. They're here! They've crossed the border!

Hirut stands in the courtyard watching Aster spin and call for her husband. In her head are the words she cannot dislodge: The war is here, the war is here, the foreigners are coming. Her heart hammers violently.

It's true? The cook dashes out of the kitchen, wiping her hands on her dress. She rushes to Hirut and shakes her. Is she right? Worku came?

Hirut nods, blinking back the sunlight. She passed frightened groups of boys and girls to get back here. She passed vendors hurrying from the mercato, children scampering back to their homes, women dropping their firewood and water gourds, plows and sticks, to race into their huts. She passed old men with spears and rifles running toward the mountains near Debark where Kidane is training his men. She passed young boys and girls skipping toward the river with their slingshots. When she burst into the compound, there was Berhe staring wide-eyed at the gate, a rusted spear in one hand, his walking stick in the other, ready to attack.

We have to go to him, Aster says as she takes the cook's arm. She looks around, sliding her hand down to grip the cook's. It's come, she says, intertwining their fingers. You'll stay. Her voice grows steadier. Her gaze on the other woman is firm now. You promised, do you remember that day? I need you here. Her face suddenly crumbles around a thought. They won't treat you well. Then she turns toward the stable. We have to pack up and leave now!

I'll get Buna ready but you can't ride her, the ground's too wet from the rain, Berhe says.

It's dry, Aster shouts over her shoulder as she races to go into Kidane's office. It's dry or else these *ferenjoch* wouldn't have been able to cross into our country. It's not wet. Get her ready.

And then the cook is dragging crates and bags onto the veranda, and Hirut is staggering under a large sack of grains she is taking out of the kitchen.

They crossed the border, Aster repeats, stunned. So the war is here.

Interlude

Time has collapsed and there is only this: an invasion. Haile Selassie reads the telegram again and stares into the stunned face of his adviser. He doesn't want to ask, How? He cannot bring himself to say, Like this? He can only look at the piece of paper and say, The Gash River was where Menelik marked the border with Eritrea forty years ago. This is what Italy remembers when it thinks of her defeat forty years ago. He thinks: My father took me to this river and pointed to it with pride and also reminded me that some called it the Mareb. I was once a small boy standing at its edge, looking down at its brown waters, bored. He looks up and he folds the telegram and creases its edges shut.

Leave us, he says.

He turns to face the window and watch the sun push darkness aside. He knows the Gash. He knows that it is an insignificant body of water that begins near Asmara and borders Ethiopia. It is 400 kilometers but it is not the Nile. It is not the Red Sea. It is not even a major tributary binding trade routes and merging cities. It is nothing. No more than a trickling stream in wet seasons. It is Emperor Menelik's forty-year-old demarcation separating Eritrea from Ethiopia. But it is just a feeble line, worth no more than the dirt around it. It is nothing, the emperor tells himself, trying to believe it as he watches dawn filter through this black night. It is nothing.

Just beyond the emperor's office door stands a guard who has pledged his life to protect him. His wife waits in their room, praying.

His advisers are in the conference room gathering information. He is alone, there is no one here. But it is 3 October 1935 and at five a.m. of this long day, Emilio De Bono entered Ethiopia by crossing the Gash River. It is now five twenty and his three columns have been marching on the emperor's land for twenty minutes. There are reports of planes dropping leaflets telling his people to rebel against him. Those leaflets say that his cousin, Iyasu, is the true emperor of Ethiopia. Those leaflets call him, Haile Selassie, an impostor and a lie. Across his country, his people are stepping out of their homes and gathering paper scattered like errant seeds. The war is here. It has crept in. It is marching toward him without so much as a formal declaration. The humiliation is a thick-boned, heavy-fleshed intruder. It holds him tight and he cannot breathe.

Photo

Half his uniformed body is cut out of the frame, so no one will ever know that in his disappeared hand, Ettore, too, holds a camera. The photojournalist includes, instead, the endless columns of other soldiers who march just behind Ettore, their eager faces beaming beneath their helmets. All are waving at the camera while squinting, the sun flaring in translucent bubbles over their heads. All have knapsacks and rifles, thick ammunition belts are strapped across their chests. They are the image of youth and earnestness, their cruelty still hidden by enthusiasm and patience, submerged by gleeful captions. On the back of the picture, Ettore has written his name in sturdy block letters, then: *l'invasione*. And the date: 3 ottobre 1935, XIII. In faint pencil, erased but not completely, he has written: *Guerra!*

The newspapers claim that one hundred thousand *ferenjoch* crossed the Mareb River in the predawn dark of 3 October 1935. That they marched in a three-column formation, infantrymen followed by mules, then construction workers, then lorries with supplies. The newspapers say that planes flew overhead and dropped leaflets telling villagers to surrender peacefully and be treated as allies. The newspapers say the soldiers marched to Axum and took the city without a single fired bullet. They like to say that all who led Ethiopia's armies were obedient to their emperor and let the *ferenj* invaders trespass further onto sovereign soil, a symbol of Italian aggression. They claim that after forty years of humiliation, Adua was finally, proudly, taken by the Italians on 5 October 1935 and the tiny, nondescript village welcomed the invaders with bowed heads and ululations.

This is the way it has been written, so this is the way it has been remembered. But what Hirut knows, sitting in that train station so many years later, shifting to move further into the shrinking afternoon light, is that when those carnivorous invaders crossed the Gash River to make their way toward Axum, the three-column formation separated, and the lines were broken and in between those spaces, Ethiopians stepped in and began to fight. Because what the newspapers and memory have failed to say is that you do not bring one hundred thousand men into a country in graceful strides. You do not send hundreds and hundreds of donkeys and lorries and laborers to follow them without incident. Because one hundred thousand men, however ravenous they might be for this beautiful land, can never total the numbers of Ethiopians intent on keeping their country free, regardless of mathematics.

KIDANE TEARS OUT THE ARTICLE WITH ITS BLAZING HEADLINE AND photograph from the front page and holds it closer. The picture depicts the Italian army as a single mass of camouflage and steel. The invasion it announces is a deliberate performance meant to be seen, meant to watched, meant to serve as visible proof of a braggart's strength. Kidane looks down the hill on the outskirts of Kossoye where he has based his camp, gazes toward a series of huts still tranquil in the early-morning fog. Ethiopia's men are fighters, but they are being told not to fight as these Italians cross the border onto soil Haile Selassie says is no-man's-land. They've been told by the emperor to let the enemy in so the world can see which country is the aggressor. Those are his orders, but in his father's war, the kind of war Kidane was trained to fight, the invaders would have been attacked immediately. They would have fallen beneath bullets and spears, their bones broken by the hands of vengeful men. There would have been no time for them to bomb the cities of Adua and Adigrat and kill women and children.

Kidane spits the dust collecting at the back of his throat. Nearly 300 kilometers separate him from the invaders, but the Italians will arrive quickly with their convoys and artillery unless they are stopped. Aklilu and his other men are already surveilling the area, practicing what they will need to do soon enough. They are shielded from view by large stones and shrubbery, by clusters of trees that dot these rocky slopes. Just below him, an old woman stoops over her walking stick, a hand on the shoulder of a young girl in a ragged shirt as long as a dress. There is no way to explain to someone like her that there is a large patch of land in this country that supposedly belongs to no one anymore, a strip of earth called no-man's-land that cannot be claimed by king or farmer, a ghostly region squeezed between two borders, opening a path to death, like a disease.

Kidane knows the Italians will declare their first victory in Adua, that city where they were first shamed during his father's generation. They will try to rewrite the memory of that day forty years ago, in 1896, when they were brought to their knees then forced to prostrate themselves before proud Ethiopian warriors. This is all for Adua, for that place that is more than a place. They have come to rewrite history, to alter memory, to resurrect their dead and refashion them as heroes.

Kidane looks again at the photograph. Sunlight blazes on a group of men just behind the front columns. They are *ascari*, those soldiers from Eritrea, Somalia, Libya, and even Ethiopia fighting for the Italians. Even in the slight blur of movement, it is easy to see their crisp new uniforms. Those new rifles and ammunition belts. Kidane stiffens. When the time comes, his men will be able to count on speed and their familiarity with the area surrounding Gondar. They can have faith in the benevolence of villagers. They can rely on the monks living in caves, can demand assistance from those hermits who have pledged a life free from human contact. But nothing except skill and surprise can help Kidane and his men against the *ascari* who know as much as they do about this terrain, who can force villagers and monks into submission, and can bend the same rain and fog in their direction. Aklilu approaches and motions behind him toward the narrow trail that brought them to this plateau. Kidane points in the opposite direction. Aklilu understands. They cannot use even the faintest semblance of a path. Every step they take from now on will have to be erased, their presence rendered invisible to an enemy as calculating as they.

IN KIDANE'S HANDS is a message from someone who calls themselves
Ferres, and this Ferres is telling him what he already knows, that Adua
has been taken. But it says that in Gedebge, only a day's march from
where he has settled his army, a convoy is scheduled to arrive in a few
days, and a unit of Italians will be setting up camp. Soon their well will
be poisoned. The message is telling him to prepare his men to ambush
the Italians there while they are in confusion. It is telling him to protect
three siblings who are planning to sneak into the new camp to pour poison into the water supply. It is telling him to attack the invaders as if this
were an order from the emperor himself. It is telling him to remember
this is war. Kidane looks up at the young messenger, just a skinny, long-
legged child with a gap between his large front teeth.

Who's this Ferres? Where did you get this? Kidane flips the message
over but there is no hint of its author or origin. It is just a scrap of paper.

The boy points down the hill. Biruk, the blind weaver, gave it to me,
he says. I was told to see him.

The blind weaver? The one who makes all those rugs? The famed
weaver trains other blind boys and men, then travels the highlands and
into Eritrea selling only to noble families. Aster bought one of his rugs
years ago. Kidane often sat on the thick wool holding his son, staring
at his father's sword and shield while repeating stories about those men
who came before him.

The boy nods.

And why you? The handwriting is strict and neat, the writing of a
bookish priest, someone who does nothing else but work on scraps of
paper barely the size of a boy's palm.

Everybody knows I'm the best runner in the area. The messenger
speaks with hurt pride.

Kidane looks down at the message again. The Italians have their
radios and telephones. He has this boy and this slip of paper. Kidane

looks over the boy's shoulder at Aklilu, who keeps glancing anxiously in his direction. Just below this plateau, Seifu and the rest of his men are waiting to hear what to do.

He has told each of his leaders to divide the recruits into groups of ten. They number nearly seventy. Not enough to fight an army, but large enough to ambush. Most carry old guns and spears, only a few have newer rifles, none of them have ammunition except what Aklilu has on his belt. They will do what he says because they have pledged their lives to him. He must guard them as possessively as he must guard this land until the time comes to risk everything.

Tell your weaver I said no, Kidane says, nodding to Aklilu and Seifu to dismiss them. Tell him these are not the emperor's orders. Go now. Be careful. He salutes the boy and turns to climb down the other side of the steep hill and check Adua's hooves for packed mud.

The ground is drying. There's nothing to slow the Italians down. The rainy season is over. A flock of birds drifts past, soaring languidly in the calm sky. At the base of the hill, he stares toward Gondar and Gojjam, toward the border of Eritrea and the Gash River, tries to imagine all the valleys and farmland between where he stands and where the Italians camp. At his back is the low rumble of his men marching toward their tents. Somewhere beyond where he can see is the flat-topped silhouette of the watchtower at Fort Baldessari. There, an Italian soldier is pacing on patrol, a speck of dark bleeding into the same spot of moonlight that falls across his horse now. Kidane adjusts his shamma and swings his hand through the threads of dust rising before him. He lets it sink against the feeble light of the clouded moon. It is useless to declare that even the smallest kernel of sand belongs to Ethiopia. He pets Adua's neck and lays his head against it.

Photo

The cook: a stout figure in a long abesha chemise bent over a large cooking pot. In her right hand is a stirring spoon. In her left she grasps the edge of the pot, tilts it slightly toward her bent legs. She crouches on the ground, the hem of her dress draping like a tent, the rough lines of her wide feet almost visible beneath the cotton. She squints against the harsh sun and her neck angles as if she means to get away from the photographer's gaze. She is hunched as if trapped. She is frowning in the way that only she knows how to do, in the way that only those who know her can interpret: her mouth is a straight line, her eyes are lowered, her chin juts as if daring to be hit. She grips her spoon too low on the handle and it is this that hints to Hirut the true extent of her turmoil as the camera points her way.

There are men sitting on their haunches behind her, their short hair just starting to spike with growing curls. They are like a mountain range rising over the cook's shoulders. From the length of their hair, the war is no more than a few weeks old, they have yet to approach the worst of it. There is Yasin, without the scar he will get near his eye. There is Eskinder, still with supple, unburnt skin. Next to them is Seifu and his son, Tariku. Seifu is turned away slightly, still defiant without a hint of the sorrow that will come. He is the only one who is looking at the cook, who turns in her direction with a sympathetic gaze. He has dropped his menacing air long enough to glance at her with a father's protectiveness. Just behind him is Aklilu, leaning forward while the others are straight-backed. He is unafraid to show his disdain, unashamed of his curiosity. The same light that dwarfs the cook draws the eye in his direction. He stares as if he wants to charge, as if he understands the camera's weakness. As if he already knows the difference between what one sees and what is true. He is the only one whose mouth turns up on one side in both a smile and in mockery.

On the back is a photographer's stamp that has faded over the years. There were several photographers roaming their area, shooting pictures and trading them with one another. Ettore has written: *Una schiava abissina*, an Abyssinian slave, but this is not one of his. He has never been near the cook and Aklilu and Tariku and Seifu at the same time. He has never been allowed the privilege of standing in front of those great fighters in complete and unquestioned safety. He would not have taken that photo and walked away alive.

HIRUT IS CLOSE ENOUGH TO SEE THE BOY RACING ACROSS THE SPINE of the mountain, his heels flying, that chest a swell of bony ribs and heavy air. In the ebbing night, he comes first as sound: the snap of a branch, a scrape of foot on stone, a hiss curving against the soft orange light. He is a fleeting mirage speeding over rough hills, swiveling to avoid steep drops, shallow gasps stalling in the thick breeze.

Kidane's not far, Aster says. That's a messenger heading toward Kossoye, she adds.

Now Aster will hurry toward the back of the line as she's done for the last two days of their march. She will encourage the women carrying water and blankets to quicken their steps. She might even shoulder a heavy stack of firewood herself. She will coax them all to move at this rapid pace that is leaving them drenched in sweat, huddled together when they sleep, too tired to do more than murmur a prayer, then shut their eyes to the bright sun.

They have walked at night to avoid the planes that have begun to ride the crests of mountains and dip into valleys. They have hidden in caves and tucked themselves at the base of tall boulders and dense trees. They have done their best to hide from those glinting large windows as frightening as the open eyes of Satan. Aster has told them not to fear. She has urged them to be brave. The land will protect us, she has said to them repeatedly, Every stone will come to our service, every river will flow in our direction. Keep walking, sisters, raise your head and straighten your backs, move as our mothers once did when they, too, went to war.

They are close to fifty women, some of them the relatives and servants of those who have joined Kidane's army. They are young and old, several speaking more than one of the languages in the area surrounding Gondar and Gojjam. They have been stripped down to their most essential ability: to carry what cannot move on its own, to shoulder weight and drag it forward. They have done it without complaint, heeding Aster's instructions as if they cannot imagine doing anything else. It is the cook who has been unable to keep her thoughts to herself.

These slaves don't realize they don't have to do this? she has asked in an angry voice that refused to whisper. We don't have to do anything we don't want to anymore. Let's leave, she said again and again. But the faces that stared back at her were startled rather than furious, resigned rather than uplifted by her continual urgings to walk down the hill and never return.

Berhe is the only grown man with them. He carries the cook's crate of medicine and bandages, trying to hide his rattling breaths beneath periodic coughs. Close at their heels are the women with stretchers and blankets, wool scarves and food supplies. They are the ones who will carry the wounded, bury the dead, and feed Kidane's army. Farther back, behind the children too young to join the army, there are those taking up the loads that drop along the way, carrying spears and shields and serving as their guards, those who stubbornly insist they will fight with Aster when she joins the men in battle.

Aster motions toward the women in the back. We have to reach them before daylight, she says. She turns to Hirut. Go see what's above.

Hirut moves ahead, climbing as fast as she can, cautious of any noise. By the final curve around the mountain, there is the dense odor of a dying fire. Hirut stops. Footsteps behind her pause. Silence trickles in. She turns, surprised to find Aster pushing past her. She did not hear the woman during the entire climb up.

Wait here, Aster whispers.

Hirut is quiet enough to hear the noises that bloom only at night, still enough to feel the snap of a cool breeze against her skin: the dampness is dissipating, the dry winds are rising. It is the season after the heavy rains, after the muddy roads and saturated paths that kept the enemy at bay all these months. Hirut feels the chill scrape against the back of her neck and slide down her arm. She shivers. And it is that shiver that rumor will mistake for an answer when Kidane calls out: Who's there?

Kidane steps out from the shadowed dark and he holds out his hand with a look that could be relief, that could be confusion, that could be, as some will later claim, even love.

Little One, he says. You're their leader now?

Hirut does not call him by his military title, *Dejazmach*, nor does she use the polite form of address, *Gash*, and she doesn't let the even more formal *Ato* escape when she looks up at him. She is so glad to have found relief from the frightening march full of sharp cliffs and dangerous planes that she lets slip from her mouth what her mother has called him since she was a child.

Kidu, she says, and when he smiles, she grabs his hand and takes that fateful step toward him. It is all so natural, so simply done, that neither of them notices Aster rushing back.

You're here. Aster's voice catches at the end.

Kidane pulls away from Hirut and looks at the approaching women, the numbers of them, the way they gather around the hill in absolute stillness. In the dark, their long white dresses pulse a soft, creamy paleness.

I need to find a place for them, Kidane says. I was worried about you, he adds. He envelops Aster in a quick embrace. She lifts her face and he lowers his and Hirut turns her head in embarrassment.

The cook walks to him. I'm leaving, she says. She takes a deep breath. I've had enough. Tell her. I kept my promise, she adds.

Hirut smells the warm musk drifting from the other woman, carrying the scents of turmeric and garlic and a pungent sweetness that Hirut suspects might be Aster's old perfume, a bottle that went missing weeks ago. Hirut looks at the cook quickly and as if reading her thoughts, the cook averts her face. Berhe moves next to Hirut, frowning.

Aster cannot hide her surprise. What did she say? she asks. She turns to the other women. Go find your places for the night, the camp's just ahead. Then she focuses again on the cook. What did she just say?

Kidane puts an arm around the cook's shoulder. I know how she is, he says. But this isn't the right time.

The cook pulls away from him. I've paid more than I should for her mistakes. She speaks to him with her back to Aster. You'll see what she'll do, you'll see what she'll do to this one next. The cook motions to Hirut.

She wants to forget but I saved her, Aster says, talking past the cook's shoulder. She keeps trying to forget.

The cook says softly, I shouldn't have been there in the first place.

And what choice did I have?

As if no one else has suffered worse. The cook folds her arms and stares at Kidane. I'm leaving.

You're staying, Aster says.

Berhe takes the cook's hand and raises it to his cheek. The gesture deflates the cook's anger. She blinks rapidly to stop the tears. Her eyes are wet, filled with an anguish Hirut has never seen before.

Over there. Berhe motions around the bend. Come on, and you can't leave without me anyway.

I'm leaving and you're going too, the cook says, but she follows him.

Hirut, Kidane says, go help the other women. He pulls Aster close and they begin speaking in quick, urgent tones.

Hirut goes to find Berhe and the cook, and sees them sitting on a large stone, their backs to her. They are leaning toward each other, the cook's hand still in his, talking quietly. She clears her throat and calls out to them, but they pretend not to hear. Hirut stands by herself, looking at their silhouettes. Then she goes to find the others in the camp.

Chorus

They dragged the cook by the hair down the dirt road. This is all she will let us say: that they dragged her by the hair while young Aster sobbed on her knees and begged her father to stop, please stop, it's not her fault, it was my idea, please stop. We can add this: that the cook was dragged by her hair down the road in the night because she listened to a young girl's desperation, she understood it, she knew what it meant to be taken from home and brought to a family and made to live there. She knew the slow death it was, and though young Aster was the daughter of the man who bought the cook and demanded certain things from her, she would help Aster escape the marriage she was destined from childhood to enter, she would take her somewhere far away and take herself from this place as well. They would both be free.

But the cook did not understand that when two are in the wrong, it is sometimes only one who is punished, it is sometimes that one who will drop to the ground on that road lit only by a sad moon and bear witness to the fury of one man who represents many. The cook hears Aster pleading and she hears Aster promising but she knows that Aster's punishment will come in another way: it will come in following the narrow road set for her. And she knows that after this night, this girl and she will never speak of this foolish hope they once shared, that they will be ashamed of it, because that hope is now lying in the middle of a lost road, battered beyond recognition. And she knows, too, that after this, they will be bound together by that shame, held in a pact so strong that no man will ever be able to break it. What they can do to a human body is wondrous, that is also what the cook is thinking as she is beaten until every thought drifts away: This body is wondrous even in its ugliness.

This is the other truth about that night they tried to run away: Aster could hear the cook crying out beneath the blows. She could hear her own name shouted like a curse into the night. There was her father's voice: Tell me where you two were going before I kill you. There were the cook's demands for him to stop, I've had enough, I'm going home, Aster, stop your father, come tell him, stop hiding. There was the cook folding her body into soil. There was the long road buckling beneath Aster's father's rage. Even terrified as she was, Aster could have stood between them and stopped her father but she did not. Instead, she chose to wait and witness how a grown man's fist drove into a woman's soft stomach. She wanted to understand the breaking point of a strong woman's will. She wanted to learn what it took to splinter a woman's pride with one's own hands. She wanted to calculate the price of rebellion. She would stand there and behold this woman who shouted then screamed then moaned then grew quiet and she would realize that never once did she hear this woman beg. Aster would discover that night the true measure of courage. She would vow to mimic it herself with a husband she did not yet know, and she would remind herself of her lineage and blood and her own inherent worth. Only after all of this would she grab her father's arm and plead for his forgiveness.

THE *FERENJ* STARES AT HIRUT FROM ACROSS THE FIRE PIT, HIS THIN face puckering at the mouth. He is chewing slowly on a leaf of khat while pushing his large sunglasses farther on top of his head. When they slip off, he tucks them into his shirt pocket and points to the tray of tea and bread Hirut carries. He shakes his head and pats his stomach. Hirut stares at him as Kidane motions for her to set down the tray. The two men face each other, a long black bag between them.

Take the guns out over there, where it's flat, Kidane says to the stranger, pointing several steps away. Then he speaks in the foreigner's language.

The *ferenj* says something, a long series of hisses leaving his stained lips.

Hirut cannot hide her fascination with his pallid skin, his blue eyes, the livid cuts that dot the back of his hands. He has been peeled of all color, left raw by sun and wind. The whites of his eyes, rimmed in red, blend too easily with his pupils.

Jacques doesn't want his weapons on the ground, he has to sell them, Kidane says to her. Let him have your netela.

Kidane has not been in camp since their arrival three days ago. While the women have organized supplies and cooked under Aster's command, he has been with his troops in the mountains just beyond this plateau, the moonlit clouds of dust in the valley the only hint of the training they were doing in the shelter of night. Since his return at dawn, all he has been able to talk about as he moved from one group of women to the next are Ethiopia's lack of guns and the Italian ships arriving in Massawa, loaded with ammunition and tanks. The war has begun, confrontations are escalating across the region, and all his men own are old Mausers and outdated Albins. What good is a rusted Beljig or Wujigra, he has cursed. What am I supposed to do with these useless spears and our lack of bullets? And now, here he is with a *ferenj*, looking even more exhausted than before, speaking with a hoarse voice, almost swaying while seated.

It's not going to be enough, Jacques, Kidane says quietly, becoming still. None of this is enough.

Hirut swallows her resentment as she slides the netela from around her shoulders and feels a brisk chill slap against her chest. Her ugly wound pulses in the cold, still red and painful-looking.

Jacques grins, nudging his chin at her as she lays the netela in front of him. He unties the long black bag to reveal a set of rifles. He darts a look toward Hirut then lays the guns on her netela. There are five new weapons, shinier and sleeker than anything Hirut has ever seen.

From somewhere, gunshots strike against the brightening morning sky. Hirut glances up but there is no sign of an army approaching, no rumble of planes or convoys. Jacques points at her and Kidane turns. She feels their eyes dip to her scar. She crosses her arms over her chest.

Jacques turns to spit and wipes his mouth with the back of his hand. It is a long, slow drag across his lips. He searches for something just past Hirut's shoulder.

The *ferenj* says something to Kidane, his teeth clamped down, his jaw tight.

Kidane shakes his head, slowly at first, then quickly. He is angry.

What's he saying? Aster looks between the two men. You know I don't know French.

The sun highlights the hints of henna in Aster's braided hair. It splashes a glow across her cheeks. Her eyes are liquid in the bright light.

Her full mouth curves into a frown. Jacques keeps stealing glances at her even as he points to Hirut.

Gunshots burst and echo against the horizon again. They all lean forward, startled, and stare in the direction of the sound.

Near Amegiagi, Aster says softly.

Closer to Bambelo, the foreigner says. He turns back to Kidane. Again, he points at Hirut.

Kidane picks up one of the guns. He weighs it in his hand and pretends to aim it. He sets it down gingerly. They're too expensive, he says. I used all my credit on the last batch, and he's gotten more expensive. Kidane shakes his head, and his glance toward Aster is confused, full of remorse.

The *ferenj* stares at the couple, both satisfied and curious. Then he leans in and whispers into Kidane's ear. He grabs his arm when Kidane tries to jerk away, and keeps talking, insistent and loud.

What's he saying? Aster asks.

Leave, now, Kidane says to her. Take the girl with you.

Aster stares at him, surprised.

Get out! Go! All of Kidane's exhaustion has given way to an explosive rage.

Jacques shuts his eyes and slips fresh leaves of khat into his mouth. He chews contentedly, sighing softly with his hands in his pockets. Hirut watches him, confused by his casual air, the disregard he shows for the argument happening because of him.

His eyes snap open, startling her, and he smiles. What's your name? he asks in Amharic. His intonation has the same hissing sound he uses when he speaks French. His accent is strange, the rhythm of the words soaked in spit. I'm Jacques Corat, he says. Do you like me? His mouth parts again in a grin, revealing more of his stained teeth.

Aster looks at him, puzzled. He wants the girl?

Hirut looks quickly at Kidane. When Aster holds out her hand, she takes it and grips it and moves closer to the woman.

Jacques gathers the netela by its ends and lifts the bundle of guns. His mouth swings into a lopsided smile, one cheek full of the leaf he's stuffed into it.

Kidane pushes between them and points toward the camp. He speaks in a soothing, coaxing voice. Jacques shakes his head.

Kidane turns to Aster: Get my father's cape. Bring it and the necklace.

Jacques shakes his head. I don't want an old cape, he says in perfect Amharic. I've got enough gold.

Over her shoulder, Hirut can hear the cook's heavy wheezing sliding around the bend, settling into the tense silence between them. Berhe is whistling, that same tune he always tries to perfect while he works. From beyond them, more gunshots: Kidane mutters a curse and Aster flinches. But they are frozen in place, like one of the newspaper photos in Kidane's office.

Go get the necklace, Kidane says again.

By now, the cook and Berhe have come closer and they stare, confused, at the foreigner.

I'm not giving it to this *ferenj*, Aster says.

The cook stares at the rifles. She looks from Jacques's face to Kidane's and when her eyes stop on Hirut, there is a knowing in them, a faint glint of disgust. The girl is useless, she says.

Aster opens her mouth but Jacques interrupts her. No girl is useless, he says. He winks at Hirut.

Take her and you'll just have another burden, the cook continues. She's not strong and she gets sick a lot. Look at her chest, are you blind?

Why don't you shut up, Aster says. She speaks through her teeth.

Then go get your precious necklace, the cook says. Go on, it wasn't meant for you to begin with, you didn't earn it.

The *ferenj* blinks slowly at the cook, his eyes red. He looks at Kidane. I've got ten more rifles. These peasant Italians will steal gold. Give me the girl. Fifteen rifles.

Kidane looks at Hirut, then Aster. He stares at his empty hands then looks back at the *ferenj*.

You'll come back, Jacques says to Hirut. I'll bring you back here, it's no problem. I move through this area often, two weeks, three weeks from now, we'll be back. He looks at Kidane and adds, Think of how many of your men you'll save with these guns. With these rifles, they'll kill Italians and take their rifles.

One week, Kidane says.

Jacques shakes his head. It's tougher to move easily these days, they're getting closer to Gondar. I promise I'll take care of her. She's a relative?

You wouldn't, Aster says softly to Kidane.

Hirut turns to the cook. Just over her shoulder, the grassy valley expands in the arc of sunlight spilling through feathery clouds. Not far away is a river, and she and the cook should have gone there together to get water.

I'll go, the cook says. Take me.

The *ferenj* looks at her and chuckles, then he keeps laughing. Never, he says.

The cook turns to Aster. I'm leaving, she says. It's time and I've had enough.

The *ferenj* stares at her, shocked. I don't want you. I'm taking her. He points at Hirut.

If you take me, you'll never go hungry or thirsty, the cook says. I'll make sure there's always food and if you're sick or can't get khat, I know what to give you. It's stronger and lasts longer. I'll find another woman to take care of your business with you, someone willing and experienced.

Now Jacques pauses. He feels inside his pocket for another leaf and slips it into his mouth. What is it? I get all the khat I need.

Not when these Italians come in, khat won't stay fresh long enough to reach you. I'll get you astenagir. I know how to make it stronger, I can mix it with other things, you can sell it.

Slowly, Jacques takes his sunglasses out of his shirt pocket with one hand and balances them on top of his head. He touches the rifles then arranges them on the netela again. He moves as if he has all the time and they will wait. Only the color rising from his neck betrays his tension.

I want to see it now, Jacques says. Before I leave or else we're done working together. I want enough for two weeks. Right now.

The cook nods, pride flickering across her face. Just wait, she says. And Berhe's leaving with me, he'll go back to his home. She nods to Kidane, holds Hirut's eyes in a long, unfathomable stare, then she turns and walks down the hill, moving quickly.

A Brief History of Jacques Corat

It is not as if his request were unusual, it is not as if he were asking a price that had not been met before, elsewhere. He had things to give and there were things to take and he wanted to be taking more than giving, aware that transactions are not by their nature inclined toward fairness. He knew what it meant to be taken: to be taken by his mother's hand from one house into another until a man who was not of his blood bent on callused knee and said, Boy, what I give to your mother is not what I will give to you, and even at twelve years old Jacques Corat was sure all doors to his life had shut right then and would remain so until he found his own way out. Nothing to ask for, nothing to give sir, is what he said. Over the man's shoulder, the boy would see his first sale item: a worn Charleville 1777, manufactured in Charleville, Ardennes, birthplace of one Arthur Rimbaud, poet and gunrunner. Here are things that Jacques, the man who would roam Ethiopia and Eritrea as Le Ferenj has been known to take in exchange for rifles: silver and gold, ivory and salt, slaves and horses, young girls and slight-boned boys, bundles of khat, and artifacts purportedly belonging to Rimbaud.

Jacques Le Ferenj keeps an old grainy photograph of Arthur Rimbaud in his front shirt pocket, left side. He takes the photo everywhere, even has it clutched in his aged hand on the straw-covered cot where he will breathe his last, splintered by an illness presumed to be dysentery. That photograph depicts poetry's enfant terrible standing beneath a palm tree looking into the camera, feet slightly apart, arms folded across his chest. It is hard to know which way the sun angles, hard to pinpoint the exact time of day. The photographic negative has been printed and flipped and printed again as if a life happening left-to-right and right-to-left is the same. Jacques's copy shows Rimbaud with left foot extended in a pose that Jacques has spent years trying to emulate. The Rimbaud of Jacques's photo lived in Ethiopia amongst people who understood the left hand as a sign of bad luck, the physical reminder of a terrifying left-handed warrior from the sixteenth century, Mohamed Gragne: Mohamed Left. But Rimbaud's left foot, stuck out in that photo, seems to depict a man who cared neither for superstitions nor for customs not his own. This is what Jacques admires. This is why he leaves home for Aden, just as Rimbaud did decades before. Each step he takes into new territory, he imagines himself as the great poet. He aches to be ruler of all he surveys. He imagines that everything has a price, particularly young native servants expendable in the homes where they work. Le Ferenj takes and gives, gives and takes, knowing the balance of things will one day come and he will never have to ask for anything again.

Le Ferenj, Jacques Corat, approximately thirty-nine years of age at the time of his brief encounter with Hirut. Father: deceased. Mother: Jacqueline Arnaud Corat Livin, seamstress. Last known stepfather: Charles Livin, farmer. Born in Bordeaux, that famous city of wines, Montaigne, Montesquieu, and that tremendously profitable harbor where ships sailed for the coast of Western Africa on the Triangular Trade. Triangle: a figure composed of three straight lines and three angles, not necessarily equal.

—

LE FERENJ. HIRUT will say it to herself repeatedly while staring at the pile of guns. And Le Ferenj, aware of distance and time and the corresponding decreases in profit, will turn toward the path the cook used, anxious to be on his way. They hear the fresh round of gunshots at the same time, and while Hirut jerks and looks up at the sky, Le Ferenj merely grins and shrugs, aware that every threat and each spent bullet is potential for another sale. Neither of them can guess that at that same instant, three siblings—two brothers and their older sister—are marching at gunpoint toward a large boulder they once climbed as young children, chased by Italians through kilometers of familiar terrain only to be caught close to home.

And while Jacques Corat may guess at the many causes of the noise, neither will ever imagine that the *soldato* who holds the camera to capture the siblings' terrified stares will one day point it in Hirut's direction and follow orders to shoot. How can Hirut know, either, that when she looks up and catches a slow wind floating between the trees, one boy, just a child, is pushing his face into that same mournful breeze while seeking salvation? Here: his sister's smile, offering him much-needed consolation. Here: his elder brother's hand taking his small palm to his lips. Here: the two brothers and their sister, walking in tight steps hampered by chain and rope. Here: the familiar boulder, now bloodstained, waiting for more.

Hirut will not hear the women of Amegiagi gather the young patriots' mother in their arms and weep so loudly that heaven bends. She will never know that there is a father of three dropping to his knees to beg Colonel Carlo Fucelli, famed butcher of Benghazi, to spare his children's corpses from the added indecency of the gallows. She will not hear Fucelli order both Italians and *ascari* to form a deadly row in front of the three prisoners. She will not see the surprise in a certain Ettore Navarra's eyes when the colonel again bypasses protocol and military ranking to say: Take another picture with that camera you always carry, *soldato*. She will not know that Ibrahim, a proud and trusted *ascaro* long in the service of Colonel Fucelli, stands stiffly next to his men while a muscle near his eye twitches like a leaf.

When Kidane and Aster, a few steps away and in private conversation, draw back at another round of scattering shots, they cannot guess at what distance and fate have shielded them from: the sight—both awful and awesome—of a spray of bullets striking three siblings who had failed in their valiant attempt to poison the invading Italians' well. And no one except the faithful *ascari* will ever know that on that wretched day, their leader, *Sciumbasci* Ibrahim ordered them not to shoot, that he commanded his *ascari* to disobey Colonel Fucelli's orders, that he staked his life on that disobedience and he swore to kill or die in their defense: he told his men to raise their rifles and aim, and when the order came to fire, they were to wait for a breath and let the first bullets come from the Italians themselves. We kill Ethiopian men, Ibrahim told his *ascari*, we will not kill their children while I lead you.

Let us pray.

THEY'VE BEEN SHOOTING AT OUR ARMIES FOR WEEKS NOW, ASTER says to Hirut as she points down to the crate of discharged bullet casings beside her. Her face is drawn, tense. We're high enough in the mountains that they can't reach us yet. She pauses. We have to be ready. One day we'll have real bullets, real guns, she adds. Did Getey teach you how to make gunpowder? she asks.

Hirut shakes her head and gathers a handful of the used casings.

They are standing near Aster's tent, waiting for more women with the powders and salt that Aster requested. Ahead, a group of villagers eases up the last few steps of the hill, each woman is stooped beneath a backbreaking load of firewood. Two of them wave before veering off to what used to be the cook's area. Several more are dragging burlap sacks toward where Aster stands, her arms folded, looking imperious in Kidane's father's cape. They have been arriving since dawn from surrounding villages, bringing casings and wood, scarves and food for the army. Hirut gazes at the hill then back at Aster. The camp has been in upheaval since the cook left, the disorder escalating amidst the neverending stream of deliveries. She has looked for signs of the cook's return every day since she left, but it has been four days now and even Aster has stopped glancing at the horizon while going about her tasks.

You'll have to learn how to make the bullets, Aster says. Find someone to teach you.

This is another one of the things the cook could have shown her.

Getey learned it from your grandmother, Aster says. They had to know it for the last war, in case the men ran out. Aster pats the front of the cape and tugs gently on the golden clasp. Some things you don't learn if your mother's not around, isn't that so?

These are used, Hirut says.

They've been picking these up from what the Italians leave behind, Aster says. We just need the casings. We'll give them back their killings. Aster shakes her head. I'll teach every woman how to make gunpowder. I'll teach all of you how to shoot a gun. You have to know how to run toward them unafraid.

ASTER IS A GLORIOUS figure astride her horse, Buna. She has loosened her braids and thick strands of hair fall against her neck and spread like a dark curtain around her sunlit face. She snaps the animal to a trot across the crest of the hill, her cape fanning around her figure, the golden clasp trapping flints of afternoon light.

Women! she shouts. Sisters, are you listening to me? Her voice rises into the sky: a blade slicing through the valley below, startling the women from their tasks, forcing them to lift their heads and turn in her direction. Sisters, are you ready for what's to come?

Ethiopia's gifted *azmari* will sing of this day for years: of how the women drop their baskets and their jugs. How they push away their looms and piles of wool. They rise to their feet nearly in unison, unaware of their own glory, and lift their faces toward Aster's voice. That they pause long enough to listen to the soft tap of distant gunfire is a detail that the songs will repeat again and again. The musicians will make of the women's frowns a forewarning of what's to come. The singers will use the women's gasps and exclamations as signs of their growing strength.

One *azmari* after the next will sing these words as they play their *masinqo*: that first battle cry was already forming in the women's throats. Aster knew she just needed a way to usher it out. The women were ready but did not know it. There were bullets to be made and gun-powder to mix and rifles to load and enemies to shoot.

Women! Those who can make bullets, come to me! Aster's voice car-ries across the valley before breaking into echoes and scattering into the horizon. She is one woman. She is many women. She is all the sound that exists in the world.

The women rush forward, breathless, their steps like the swoosh of leaves pushed by rough wind. Hirut sets down the dried leaves she is scooping into small medicine sacks, and watches: Aster descends grace-fully from her horse and leads the skittish animal to a nearby tree and ties the rope. As she strides back to the highest point of the hill, she is familiar and strange, someone Hirut has never seen before but has always known to exist.

Do you remember when we learned to shoot with our brothers and cousins? Aster opens her hand and a hush falls over the women. A few spent bullets rest in the center of her dusty palm, bent and singed by gunpowder. Hirut, come help me, she adds, looking across the heads of the crowd that has gathered at the top of the hill and spills down one side.

Hirut pushes her way through the group, the women so numerous it is difficult for most to see.

Aster continues: We were taught to run through hills and guard live-stock, just like the boys in our family. We shouldn't forget these things, she says. Our country needs us.

The thick silence expands and draws them into an intimate embrace. They lean forward, mesmerized. As Hirut approaches, Aster points behind her where a metal pot and a burlap sack sit. Hirut pulls both next to Aster's feet, surprised by their weight, then steps aside, unsure of this Aster, this woman who seems to shimmer in her cape.

Go on, Aster says to her, open it and bring me what's inside.

Hirut unties the sack and reaches inside.

A woman whispers from the back: Our country? She's saying it's our country? Look at how hard we work while she takes from us.

Hirut turns toward the woman. She is tall and angular, and clearly agitated. She shifts from foot to foot, her words tumbling out of her mouth in short, angry bursts. She cannot seem to stop talking: Follow her and you'll always beg for what she throws away. Let the Italians come, they're better than these greedy people. And look at her, who was her father? Who was her mother? She's part slave, look at her. At least I'm pure.

Hirut stiffens. No one has ever dared to say anything like that directly to Aster.

Anchee, you, stop this: another woman's voice floats above the stunned silence.

But it is too late: the effect is immediate on Aster. She flinches and brings her hands to her face, one fist still bunched around the bullet casings. A gasp escapes from her: the sharp breath of someone struck without warning. Her eyes are wide, unsure of what will happen next, because the truth of the woman's words are undeniable: Aster cannot boast the delicate beauty of Nardos or some of the other women. Her skin gleams in a rich shade darker than most, and her mouth turns up like a ripe flower, full and lush, threatening to overwhelm her face. Her round cheeks and sloping brows accentuate an elusive loveliness, but those lips are what bring the gaze again and again to her face. Hirut has seen her effect on those who first meet her: her commanding presence so jarring next to her unusual looks. Without her haughty air, Aster might appear common, nothing special at all, but she has inherited the arrogance of those born into noble households and it is a fire that burns inside of her, illuminating every feature. It is something the poor are not born with: that way of gliding into large homes and expansive fields as if the ground begged for their footsteps. Hirut smooths her hair and tucks loose strands back into her braids, and braces herself.

A soft murmur ripples through the crowd and what the songs will later say is true: when Aster looks across at the stunned women, wisps of clouds cover the bright sun like high-flung sheets. A faint shadow drapes the plateau then slips away to shoot a brilliant spot of sunlight against the woman's shoulders and that bloodstained cape. It is a heralding. It is a divine confirmation of her rights and her power. Every *azmari* will sing of this moment. From every *tej bet* and out of every hut and house and hotel, the singers' words will be the same: that a blast of sunlight, powerful as an exploding bomb, spread across her shoulders in a message from God.

Aster senses the change, though she is too angry at the woman's words to notice the uncanny sunlight. She straightens, proud again, and starts to speak in that quiet voice that knows it will be heard.

These aren't the days to pretend you're only a wife or a sister or a mother, she says. We're more than this.

This last line will be sung as an anthem and a refrain while musicians slide a bow across the strings of a lovely *masinqo*: We're more than this.

The women whisper it amongst themselves: We're more than this, we're more than this. They touch their faces, beautiful and plain alike, they press their palms against their breasts and on their stomachs and several plant a palm between their legs and laugh. We're more than this.

The woman with the angry outburst stands in the middle of the crowd, looking from one person to the next, her rage rendered futile by the combination of sun and cloud and Aster's magnetic pull on all of those around her.

We're more than this. We're more than this.

Aster shushes them and the noise drops immediately. She goes on, the smile she gives the woman who berated her pointed and cruel: When I missed during target practice, my father beat me, she says. I know it was the same for many of you.

Hirut thinks back to her own father's lessons about the Wujigra, the seriousness of his instructions, the relentless drills he put her through after a long day in the fields, forcing her to pretend to load, then aim, then pull the trigger while he whispered, Again, do it faster. There were times when he exploded in frustration and wished aloud for a son.

Our fathers were strict with us, but we learned to be strong, she adds. For a moment, her face twists. Aster opens the burlap sack and takes out a smaller sack, tightly knotted. She opens it and shakes out the powdery contents into her hand. She does this without acknowledging the woman who is still staring at her and shaking her head.

Aster reaches into the larger sack and brings out a handful of charcoal. She puts it into her palm too. Then she straightens, tall and proud again, and extends her hands. You'll know what I'm doing, Aster says, if you remember what our mothers and grandmothers told us.

Gunpowder, this is how they made bullets, she's making *kilis*, my mother showed me, my aunt taught me long ago: the women talk amongst themselves and it seems to Hirut that the longer they continue, the angrier the tall woman in the crowd gets. She is stiff with malice, unable to hide her distaste, unwilling to erase the look of contempt that curls her mouth up and narrows her eyes.

There are women who don't want to help us, Aster says. She points to the woman. This one refused to give me her sulfur earlier today, so I took it.

The crowd shakes its head, hissing in disapproval.

I have to feed my family, the woman shouts. Her voice is tight. It's not hers, she adds loudly. And who cares if you lose, all of you? She spits on the ground. Who wants your king? She thumps her chest and spits again. Let the Italians come.

Aster cannot hide her anger; her composure has left and there is no hint of the elegance with which she manages to do everything. She is stripped of reserve, and what Hirut sees is the part of Aster that beat her with a whip and left her in a stable. There it is, trembling in front of them all in the form of Aster.

Aster continues: This woman is like the rest of them, they'll divide our country so we lose and become slaves of the *ferenj*. They think these invaders come in fairness, she says. These fools don't understand what happens if we lose.

The two of them glare at each other, then the woman spits on the ground and turns to the other women: She's a thief, worse than a beggar. Let the *ferenjoch* come, I'll help them. Then she rushes away, and down the hill, her cries growing fainter with distance.

Any of you who want to leave, go, Aster says.

Two more women stand up and hurry away without looking back, their heads down. Aster is rigid, her face impassive again, the stern set of her mouth a defense against any sign of emotion. She takes a breath and tips the pail toward the rest of the women. It is half full with sulfur.

Who remembers what to do? she asks. Who remembers what it means to be more than what this world believes of us?

ANOTHER MESSAGE FROM FERRES, WRITTEN IN THE SAME CAREFUL, neat script as before. *Rossi. 3 columns. 1500 strong. Pushing through Debark to Bahir Dar. Will be attacked, reinforcements needed.*

None of this is new information. It is what the emperor's runners have relayed to the armies in the region. What's unusual is the unspoken directive that Ferres is giving. This messenger, a different boy, looks from Aklilu and Seifu back to Kidane, trying to gauge the importance of his message by their reaction.

Biruk gave this to you? Kidane asks.

The boy nods quickly. He's the weaver, the blind one.

Biruk? Seifu looks startled. My neighbor from Fogera? Seifu starts to say more, but Kidane raises his hand and shakes his head. He looks down at the messenger. Go, he says, be careful.

Faven's brother, Seifu says as soon as the messenger has disappeared. She was my good friend when we were children. She left for Asmara.

Fifi, Kidane says. She's called Fifi now.

Aster's voice rises from the bottom of the hill just in front of him. She has had groups of women working all through the night mixing gunpowder and making bullets. They've run out of used casings but she's sent women in threes and fours to scour the hillsides and villages in search of more. That she is doing all of this while

still wearing his father's cape is a detail that he cannot stop thinking about.

Kidane turns away from her direction, looks toward the horizon. If
the Italians get to Debark, he says, they'll get to Gondar and Bahir Dar
then head toward Addis Ababa. What he does not add: Gugsa, the man
governing Mekelle, has become Italy's celebrated collaborator. Many
of his men are said to be joining the *ferenj* army, weakening the northern front. To stop Rossi, however far away from Mekelle, is to stop the
momentum of Gugsa's betrayal. It is to stop another strategic advantage
the Italians need in order to keep moving toward Addis.

People are scared, Dejazmach, Aklilu says. He keeps his voice low,
his head down. We can't protect them with the guns we have, he adds.

The bones in Aklilu's face are sharply etched beneath his skin as he
turns. Kidane stares down at his own hands, the thick veins that press
up, knotted, whenever he moves. All of them have grown thinner,
but it's more pronounced in Aklilu. His already taut frame now molds
around leaner muscles, giving the impression that the younger man is
constructed out of bundles of unbreakable wire. He has heard several
of the men whispering in disbelief about the fact that Aklilu refuses to
eat until all of them are fed.

Distribute whatever guns we have, take the bullets the women
have made, divide them up. No one should have more than three,
Kidane says.

Dejazmach Kidane, three? Bullets? The shock is too great for Aklilu,
he cannot keep silent.

Kidane is already turning his back to them: there is a battle to
prepare for, supplies to give out, guns to distribute, men to measure
for courage.

My father always said it only takes one bullet to kill a man. I have one
extra gun, a Wujigra, I need to give it to a strong fighter, Kidane says
as he leaves. Select our best shooter. We won't take a large number with
us. We're reinforcements, not the whole fighting force.

———

KIDANE HOLDS THE OLD WUJIGRA in front of him, relishing the sturdy weight of it, the smooth marks where strong hands made slight grooves into polished wood. On the barrel are five scratches that track the number of men felled by this rifle. These marks—like scars—told their own stories about battles fought and survived. On his father's gun, too, had been these same slender lines dug into metal. They were meant to be signs of courage, badges of honor and patriotism, a way to remember the glories of war and victory. But his father once pulled out his old gun, a Mauser, and dragged his finger over the marks on the barrel, and said: These are the mothers I made weep, my son. These are the children I made fatherless.

But if you didn't shoot, Kidane had asked, gripped in a young boy's fear, they would have shot you?

His father had smiled at him. And so somewhere, a woman is always weeping, he had said. Then he had laughed, the sound bitter, full of an irony that Kidane did not understand back then.

Dejazmach Kidane, I've brought him. Hailu approaches his tent with his brother, Dawit, beside him, their long strides matching.

Dejazmach, Dawit says, Hailu told me you saved this one for me. Dawit looks up and flushes, pleased.

The brothers are a few years apart but they are nearly identical. Hailu, the elder, is slightly taller, with a more somber air that gives his good looks a gravity and refinement. Of the one hundred men who will go with him to Danakil, three-quarters have guns. Only a few of them have rifles that are relatively new. Aklilu has asked that Dawit have the Wujigra.

We'll face bandits bribed to fight for the *ferenj*, Kidane begins. They'll have weapons, and the *ascari* know this land. Be careful, he says, extending the Wujigra, letting the weapon slip from his hand into Dawit's.

For a moment, they hold the rifle between them, the young man's eagerness an electric charge that slides into Kidane and makes him smile. He watches as Dawit aims through the sight, weighs it in his hands and then, almost instinctively, finds the five lines.

It's known blood, Dawit says, nodding. He nudges Hailu affectionately. Our father always said that a gun that's tasted blood will want more. This one knows *ferenj* blood, he adds. We'll be good together.

Hailu frowns. Enough, he says.

My father always said, Kidane begins, smiling, that a gun will not keep you alive. It's only designed to kill. Be careful, listen to your brother.

I'll watch him, Hailu says. He's always been foolish ever since we were children.

My brother should be a doctor, Dawit says. He throws an arm around Hailu's shoulder, the gesture practiced and quick. He's the wise one, an old man already.

Go with God, Kidane says to them. He looks between the two, at their mutual affection and pride, and imagines himself with a son that might have lived, both of them bound by the dangers of war, but equally strong.

Aster is pacing back and forth in front of his tent when he returns from a final inspection of his troops. Grass stains mar the knees of her trousers—his trousers, the ones he kept for special occasions. Two swipes of charcoal rest on her cheekbones, and a thin film of dust coats the loose curls around her head. She looks sprightly, younger, more free than he has ever seen her.

I gave out all the bullets, she says. The villagers say there's a convoy heading to Mekelle, journalists, musicians, administrators from Asmara. They're celebrating that traitor Gugsa.

Kidane goes into his tent and lets her in. In the cramped tent that he uses for an office and sleeping, he is astonished, once more, by her appearance. Her hair is an outgrown, unruly bloom around her head. She is dressed like a man. She is speaking with new authority. He steadies himself.

Gugsa's throwing a party for top-ranked Italians. Mekelle's going to be full of them, Aster continues. They're taking photos, it'll be in the newspapers and on the radio. How humiliating for us. That man. Remember his wedding? She pauses, lost in the memory of Gugsa's wedding to Emperor Haile Selassie's daughter. Poor Zenebwork, she says. Poor girl to be with that wretched, spoiled, weak man.

The match was for the families, Kidane starts, then stops. It's an old argument between them, the disastrous match that should have established harmony between two tense houses.

It's always for the families, Aster spits out. She pauses, and for the first time she seems to be aware of him. You're not getting rest, she says. She reaches out to touch his face, then drops her hand when he pulls away.

What do you need? he asks. He sees again the seams on the shoulders of her tunic, the fine stitching that she ripped out during alteration. He knows for certain that she has other clothes, dresses that she chooses not to wear. Any news about the cook?

We've been training, she says, tugging at her sleeve. After meals, we go through drills, same ones my father taught me. Same ones your father taught you. We all know them. She stops and straightens. Let some of us go with you.

Through the canvas, the sun is a block of light pressing into the tent, illuminating the tin cup sitting on the upturned crate he uses for a desk. She rests her gaze on his blanket. She has been sleeping with her women in their area, as if it is an unspoken agreement between them. He has started to suspect that she is not allowing those with spouses or lovers in his army to share tents. She has told several of his men to stay out of the section she has claimed for her women, and that has separated those who would have met and begun to stay together in the tradition of men and women who march toward war: one following the other, one making the other comfortable, one serving as a surrogate wife without the emotional demands of a spouse. The camps are so divided now that he is sure this is one more thing that his men talk about when he is not there: that this woman, his wife, has come in and changed the way things have always been done when men go to war. But how to raise the issue with them without the glaring admission that his wife has kept herself separate from him, too?

Let me go with you, she says. Some of us are ready, we'll be your reinforcements. She takes his hand and doesn't let him pull away. She presses her lips to his palm, the pressure gentle and soft, so tender he feels his heart lean toward her, remembering those days when she was someone else, someone he could comprehend.

He stiffens and steps back. You'll meet us in the valley with fresh supplies, he responds. We'll carry the wounded there, Hirut will help Hailu. I've told you this before.

He wants to remind her she has never been in a war. She was not raised to anticipate assaults. She was not taught from an early age about the body's abilities to withstand force. She did not learn how to maneuver in the dark, through hills and rough mountains, all in the guise of boyhood games. She was instructed on how to shoot, yes, but what does she know about what to do if attacked?

Come back here with your women, he says. I'll talk to them before you leave.

She stares at him long enough for the resentment to wash across her face. She lets it slide between them like a curtain finally dropped into place. Then she nods and walks away.

Chorus

A black cloud, dense as iron, slides through the hills, easy as a blade. It threatens to shake the women loose from the hilltop, to dislodge those fragile bodies inclined to bend toward the dark form. It is ungodly made, fashioned by man, a beast spun from fire and steel. On the flat ridge of the mountain, the women wait for a whisper that carries on a gust of wind: We are more than this. We are more than this. They watch as their Aster, splendid in that cape, points down toward the cloud and signals: Wait, sisters, wait and listen. Then the clamor blooms. It fills the sky in the whirling dust that siphons past them and dims their vision. It knots and billows, contracts and expands, and from the cacophony comes the deep-throated boom of full-grown men. The women look from on high as the convoy passes, traveling with the grim weight of war, the song of men and beasts fading until it is no more than the distant cry of ghosts: *Faccetta nera, bell'abissina.*

THREE FLASHES OF LIGHT GLINT FROM ACROSS THE GORGE AS KIDANE tries to get his bearings. The signal comes again: three flashes. He has been seen by the other Ethiopian armies. From his pocket, Kidane withdraws a shard of glass. He stares across the gorge, but there is nothing to see. His trusted friend Bekafa's army is invisible. He twists the glass in his hand until it hits the sun, then he lets it flash once, then he waits. The march has taken two days with little rest, each step moving into more dangerous territory. His men should be tired but their energy is a dense, thick rope knotted around him, making his heart beat loudly in his chest. A whistle comes, two clear notes: this will be the signal to attack. His hands begin to tremble. It is difficult to lift his binoculars to his face. He focuses toward the dry riverbed. It is quiet, but it is a deception. The Italian forces are not far away. Already, he can make out the cloud of dust that rises weakly in the horizon.

Kidane adjusts the binoculars as if he can see through mountain and stone. Lookouts near Wolkefit Pass have reported a column of at least one thousand *ascari* led by a small group of *ferenj* officers. The men are in left- and right-flank formations, with a center column and an advance guard made up of five hundred mercenaries. They are approaching the outskirts of Debark. Kidane presses the binoculars against his eyes trying to get a better look, trying to bring them closer so he can squeeze these tiny figures in his hand and shake them off like unpleasant dirt. He cannot control the tremor that snakes through him.

He and Bekafa will have to attack while the Italians are in the gorge, unaware of their presence.

A flash of light: so quick that it is easy to miss, just a flicker of the sun ducking behind clouds. A signal to wait. Kidane puts down his field glasses and crouches low. His fighters are farther up, pressed flat against the ground, barely breathing, fully alert. His heart lurches again. He has brought them this far safely, and now he will do as his father showed him: he will spend the moments before battle emptying himself of everything but that singular task of eliminating his enemy. Every worry must be pushed deep into your muscles to make yourself stronger. Every fear has to be chewed and swallowed to harden your stomach into stone. Use yourself as a weapon and charge without hesitation. Close your eyes at night, Kidane my son, and practice this again and again. Kidane looks up, makes the sign of the cross. He touches the center of his chest where he is building his armor, then waits for the signal to launch the assault.

Voices float up from the approaching battalions, shouts volleying back and forth in Amharic, Arabic, Somali, Tigrinya, Italian. The advance column is marching faster than the left and right flanks. It is drawing ahead of the others. The Italian center battalion is lagging behind. They are all having a hard time staying together; the line has stretched and large gaps are forming. There is, beyond the gorge, in the direction the Italians have come, the bray of camels and the slow, grinding noise of a supply column still making its way. That means there are rear guards and they haven't caught up yet. That means the Italians have an advance guard and a rear guard that are dangerously disconnected from the center.

Kidane dares to lift his binoculars. He sweeps his gaze across the gorge and finds what he is looking for: the Italian commander. The officer stops his men to let the tail of the middle column catch up. Then the Italian raises his own binoculars and stares in Kidane's direction. Kidane freezes. He turns to warn his men to draw back, and sees

Aklilu has crawled almost next to him without a sound. Kidane holds his breath, sweat collecting on his forehead. He can feel the tightness in his chest. The officer strides to the edge of the gorge. He angles his binoculars up. Kidane tenses. The man knows something is amiss and it comes in the form of Aklilu's murderous gaze burrowing through grass and foliage to drill into the officer's chest like a bullet. It is impossible for the *ferenj* to see them, but a good soldier knows to look for those things he cannot see.

Bekafa's whistle: two sturdy notes, clear and loud—birdcalls needling through wind. The Italian tilts his head. He turns in a slow circle, one hand slowly rising as the whistle comes again: the same two notes. The Italian drops his hand and his shout is a shrill clarion call to battle. Kidane motions Aklilu, and Aklilu signals Seifu, and Seifu whistles for Amha, and Amha motions and his fighters are sliding on their bellies toward the left flank, and as Kidane raises his hand and brings it down in the midst of soaring birdcalls, Eskinder and Yasin and all his other soldiers obey and raise themselves up, giants birthed from stone, and race swiftly down the mountain, surefooted and white-clad, as the Italian officer in the gorge spins, screaming orders and curses as he watches these men, silent as phantoms, rise out of the earth.

First: a ringing in his ears, then the piercing clarity of stunned silence. The loud roar of an angry wind, then a bird's melodic call. There is his chest, heavy as a boulder, and his legs moving light as feathers. As Kidane rushes down the mountainside into the gorge, he feels it all crashing through him: the ecstasy and elation, the sway between catastrophe and calm. The world slides free from his grasp. A tunneled path opens in front of him and soon he is racing past the chaos toward a slender figure in the waning light. It is Dawit, hoisting the Wujigra that Kidane gave him, turning to look at him, both proud and disoriented, before pivoting to face the enemy again. Dawit shouts Hailu's name like a war cry and Kidane watches, mesmerized as Dawit aims with perfect precision and pulls the trigger.

Kidane braces for the thunderclap of a discharging bullet. There is nothing else but this, he thinks, there is no one else but this one. It is an old warrior's song, an ancient refrain sung before a battle, a father's lullaby to an adoring son. Then he locks eyes with Dawit, and hears clearly the horrified whisper: But it doesn't work? And then Dawit is grasping for him desperately, flailing in empty air while calling Kidane's name. His leg explodes into splintered flesh, bone rips out of place, and Dawit falls, splattered in his own blood.

There is nothing else but this: Kidane lifting his knife at Dawit's attacker, his own gun forgotten on his shoulder as he lunges forward before the *ascaro* has time to aim once more. There is no one else but this one, this *ascaro* straightening tall in the face of certain death, refusing to yield to the knife thrust with such ferocious strength into the center of his uniformed chest. And the two of them spiral in the momentary quiet: ethereal and warm.

Dejazmach. Dejazmach!

They are calling for him, his men who have followed him to this wretched place. They are asking for his help while he stands over this felled body and those eyes staring at him and reaching out in a gesture of love. What is there to do but drop to his knees and bring Dawit close and let him slump like a small boy against his chest? What is a father to do, but this?

Help me, Dawit says. Where's Hailu? Where's my brother?

Dejazmach!

He lets go of Dawit and staggers to his feet, his trousers stained in blood. He sees Aklilu stepping over a writhing body, two rifles slung over his shoulder. Shame chews through him but Kidane, whole and strong, fierce and unflagging, ignores the noise in his head and the ache in his jaw and screams his father's name until ahead of him, beside him, behind him, he sees Checole the great son of Lemma, the eldest son of the first and greatest Kidane. They are so close their flesh melds together and then his father steps into his bones and settles behind his eyes and Kidane, fortified and enraged, jumps into a tangle of fighting men while his father watches, proud.

And then comes the *tirumba*.

The horn blows and only those who know its language understand: Kidane feels his heart expand. His men pick up speed. His legs grow more nimble. His hands grip his new rifle, and as he flings himself on top of a stumbling Italian soldier, Kidane begins to laugh. He laughs and shouts his father's name. He laughs and shouts his own name. He laughs and calls Aklilu and Seifu and Eskinder and Amha and Yasin and as he shoots at a charging *ascaro*, the earth grows wide and he is running once more toward light as hot as the sun and when the horn sounds again, he knows it signals for more men, invisible until now, to descend on the Italian columns and suffocate them.

It isn't until later, staring at the field wet with blood, that the fear sets in, that he shivers in the sun, teeth chattering, and wants nothing but Aster's embrace. Kidane staggers back up the mountain, hurrying before Aklilu and Seifu look for him, and lies flat on the ground, on his back, and stares at the unmarred sky. Below, he hears Hailu's mournful voice breaking free of silence, weaving past wind to find his ear: Dawit! Kidane shuts his eyes. His father breathes into his ear, his mouth pressed close to his cheek: What did you think it took?

Interlude

Some cities hold blood, Haile Selassie thinks. They overflow with dead thoughts and the cries of terrified girls. Some places call out to trouble the dreams of grieving fathers. Emperor Haile Selassie shakes his head and pulls himself back to the present. He is outside in his garden, surrounded by bougainvillea bursting with color, facing a rosebush in shy bloom. His dog is chewing an old bone at his feet and ahead, little Mekonnen is chasing imaginary enemies while hurling invisible spears. If he turns his head even slightly, he will see her. Zenebwork. His late daughter. She is standing in her wedding dress, a girl decorated like a woman, trembling with her hands folded in front of her. If he looks, she will move. She will beckon him toward Mekelle and point at Gugsa and hiss the man's name and say: I begged you to save me, Abbaba.

Haile Selassie looks down to avoid her. In his hand is an Italian newspaper with a front-page photograph of Gugsa seated next to de Bono at a table, the two of them peering intently at a large map. The article below announces that Italian troops have entered Mekelle to applause and salutes, with Gugsa to greet them. Haile Selassie doesn't want to think of three years ago—not now – but he must, this much he owes his daughter, Zenebwork. He knows she is standing at the edge of his vision, just steps away from the rosebush she loved. She is shivering in fear, clasping her hands as if it is still 1932 and three years have not passed. As if even now he can stop the wedding he arranged for her, and send Gugsa back to Mekelle alone.

Leave me, he says underneath his breath.

Mekelle has fallen. That cursed city that witnessed his daughter's last moments has surrendered to Italy, and the man who had been her husband has embraced Ethiopia's enemy.

Go, he says.

But she doesn't want to go. He can tell by the breeze blowing across the rosebush. He can tell by the ringing stillness that follows. She is waiting for him to say more and she will not leave until he says it. In the year since her death in the home of Gugsa, she has learned patience. She has learned to sit through the night and come to him in sunshine. She has learned to hold her anger and smile. She has learned to be the fourteen-year-old girl she was before he wed her to a cruel man close to fifty.

It is almost eight hundred kilometers from Addis Ababa to Mekelle, imagine how long it takes by train. That was what he said as Menen pleaded with him to bring their daughter home. It was what he said as Zenebwork kept sending panicked messages to them. It is almost eight hundred kilometers. By the time we even get to the train station, she will be fine. She is just homesick, she is not used to being a wife. He should have flown to her. He should have boarded his plane and brought his army and stormed Gugsa's palace. He should have swept into her room and gathered her in his arms and banished Gugsa to prison after breaking his bones one by one.

I'm sorry, he says, because it is the only thing he knows to say to make her leave him alone. I'm sorry, lijé. I'm so sorry.

She begins to retreat grudgingly. He can feel her anger wafting past him, warm as a breath.

She will be with him to the end of his days, he knows this. She will be the reason that even in the best of moments, he will move with the weight of his regrets, that he will mumble apologies to an invisible intruder and start awake at night calling for a plane to Mekelle.

He reads the telegram again: Mekelle has fallen. Bekafa's ambush was a success with Kidane's help.

When Zenebwork died a year ago from causes they claimed came from childbirth, only two years after her wedding to Gugsa, he flew her body home from Mekelle for burial. Not one more day in that wretched city, he had promised a weeping Menen. She will not see another sunset in that coward's house. Gugsa had tried to insist on burying her in Mekelle. How close Haile Selassie had come to ordering the man killed. How close he had come to acting like the father of a dead daughter. His advisers had moved in to calm him down. Kill him and Zenebwork's life will be wasted. Kill him and the families remain divided. Kill him and reveal your weakness. Girls die from many causes: childbirth, illness, disease, men. She is but one child, look how many you have left. Mourn for her like an emperor. Crush Gugsa beneath the weight of his own arrogance. Smile at him but shower others with titles; never make him Ras. Praise others while never speaking his name. Grind him down in increments. Haile Selassie had listened to the advice, but he had not anticipated Gugsa's betrayal. The marriage should have permanently cemented the powerful families. His measured benevolence should have counted for something. He had thought Zenebwork's death would have forced Gugsa into an obligatory allegiance fueled by guilt. But he had been wrong and now he has lost even Mekelle, that city of ghostly daughters.

There's a message, Your Majesty, his aide says. The young man is at the door, leaning outside, unaware that a blade of sunlight cuts across the growing bloom of his curly hair.

Haile Selassie walks back inside, pretending patience and calm.

The aide ticks off a series of updates from the latest telegrams as they walk down the corridor to his office: they're finished with the ceremony at Mekelle. Seyoum's afraid Gugsa will cut communication lines, he'll keep calling for as long as he can.

Inside his office, Haile Selassie sits in his chair and folds his hands on his desk and continues to listen.

The aide turns a proud face to the emperor. Your Majesty, he says, Bekafa cut through columns near Debark, Kidane helped.

You told us already, the emperor says. Then Haile Selassie allows himself to think through what is being said. He ordered no one to move against the enemy in the gorge. He did not tell Kidane to take his men to reinforce Bekafa. He has to slide his hands beneath the desk to hide their shaking. He is losing control of his country in pieces, one region at a time.

The aide shakes his head, visibly disturbed, and brings a telegram so close to his face it brushes against his nose. He rubs the back of his neck. They're using poison? he asks. He lowers the paper to the desk carefully, as if it will explode. He is suddenly drawn, pale. Gas? he repeats. His voice shakes. There was a reconnaissance plane, or it says reconnaissance plane but it can't be because it dropped poison. Mussoloni's son was flying. They targeted civilians. Women and children. Rivers.

That's not correct, Haile Selassie says, even as a part of him is tumbling into that cruel revelation. Verify this and come back, he adds. He makes no mention of the aide's refusal to call the Italian by his proper name. Mussoloni: the deliberate mispronunciation has spread across the country, started by those who did not know better and continued by those who do. It is another sign of his people's rebellion, another sign that they are trying to fight in every way that they can.

As his aide walks out the door, caught between bafflement and horror, Haile Selassie presses himself against his desk and leans into the sturdy wood until he can almost push aside the thoughts of what it means to pour poison gas on human beings. He digs himself deeper against the slat of wood and the buttons on his jacket burrow into the bony curve of his sternum. A splinter of pain shoots into his head and briefly, there is nothing else to think about but that discomfort.

Photo

A slender line of lorries threading through the hills. Helmets dusty and pale in the glare of afternoon sun. A narrow road dug out of rock and dirt, clinging to the edge of a breathtaking drop shrouded in fog. It is all there in front of the tired, sunburnt Italians: the road to victory, the winding path toward certain glory. Indro Montanelli, Herbert Matthews, Evelyn Waugh will look through binoculars at that fragile route creeping steadily from Asmara closer to Addis Ababa and speak of the sun and the flies, of heat and altitude, of decrepit huts and unwashed natives. They will complain and scoff at the feeble offerings of Abyssinia. They will point toward Asmara, then Massawa, then across the Red Sea toward Rome and declare: There is no hope for this place but Il Duce, no dreams greater than those of Benito Mussolini. But old Ato Wolde and his beloved Weizero Nunush, stepping out of their small hut to gather eggs to sell to these *ferenj* soldiers, blasting through their village in endless convoys, will look toward those same hills, gesture toward that same sea, and proclaim: There is nothing that can come from this but blood and more blood.

KIDANE OPENS THE NEWSPAPER IN HIS HANDS AND SHUTS HIS EYES. He has only imagined a signaling light in the dawning horizon but still, the dread wraps around him again. Though the ambush is over, his heart beats louder, and he holds himself rigid as Aklilu and Seifu peer over his shoulder. Any unexpected sound might force him to his feet, ready to charge. Aklilu points to two of the pictures on the front page. In one, beaming Italian officers and soldiers stand around an awkward-looking Gugsa. In the other, a dignified Haile Selassie stares out from behind a desk. The weak campfire flings a tepid glow across the page.

What does it say? Aklilu asks.

Kidane glosses over the articles quickly. The French newspaper emphasizes the military fanfare and Gugsa's welcome, but a smaller article speaks of the bombing of nearby villages where women and children are reported killed. One line talks of an Ethiopian rebellion thwarted by Italians near Mekelle. Another line is reserved for what the paper calls a small skirmish near Debark that saw Italians retreat.

The sharp scent of gunpowder mingles with the campfire, floating like a dry patch down Kidane's throat. He coughs and for a second he sees him again: Dawit, glorious and fearless, charging at the enemy, that old Wujigra in his hands, his eyes ablaze with a hatred so pure that for a moment, the *ascaro* draws back before he lifts his weapon and aims. Kidane holds his breath until the memory passes: it grows clearer with each remembering.

There was a time when he would not have shied away from bearing witness to the pain he caused. Always look at the blood you spill, let this be training for later, hold her while she trembles so you can feel your own might. That had been his father's instructions on his wedding night. He had done as he was told. He had moved through that large bedroom like a man unconquered and unconquerable, and Aster had given in, then learned to meet his needs with love.

We have to leave men behind, Kidane says quietly.

We can't move Dawit, he won't last long as it is, Dejazmach, Aklilu says. He is visibly shocked. Hailu insists on taking him with us down the hill, he continues. I promised him we would.

Shadows scallop deep lines around Aklilu's mouth. The younger man has spent most of his day inside the caves, checking on injured men, sending some back with villagers and burying others. He still wears his bloodstained tunic with a streak across his chest that marks the failed path of a bayoneted rifle. He has circles beneath his eyes and his gauntness gives his handsome features the solemnity of a monk. The three days since the ambush have taken a greater toll on him than the battle itself. He seems to have aged years.

We move tomorrow, Kidane says. It's too dangerous to stay here, we have to leave the weakest behind. He feels the ache of a heart making room for new guilt. He shifts in his seat. What he has betrayed is bigger than this young soldier.

I'll talk to Hailu, Kidane says.

Aklilu stands up to feed the fire and for a moment, all his grief blazes before them, sharp as a wailer's lament.

—

HAILU IS A hunched figure cupped in darkness, sitting quietly by the dead campfire. He jumps to his feet when Kidane approaches. In the dimness of the dawning light, Kidane can make out his elegant and tall frame, his thick black curls growing into unruly strands. Behind him, the sky is opening, pulling back the layers of night to reveal the deep blue of the mountains.

Hirut's meeting us at the cave, Kidane says. She might have something the cook left behind.

Hailu's frown deepens and pulls at the gentle slopes of his face. I've got nothing to help him. He points to the basket at his feet and he clears his throat.

I'd like to see him, Kidane says.

For what?

Kidane is startled by Hailu's sharp tone.

Hailu picks up the basket and opens it. Inside are several small sacks knotted shut. Rolls of bandages are tucked between the bags. He drops the basket on the ground, nearly tipping the contents over.

I should know what to do, even the cook showed me new things before she left, Hailu says. He stares at Kidane defiantly. It shouldn't have happened, he says quietly. That rifle was old, he should never have had it.

Kidane nods, not trusting his voice. Then without another word, he brushes past the man and strides down the path to Dawit's cave.

Hirut leans against the boulder next to the cave, staring at the sun as it cracks through the shelter of fog. She is nearly nauseous from fatigue and the smell seeping from the cave: the unmistakable odor of the dying.

You haven't gone in to help him?

Hirut turns around. It is Hailu, followed at a distance by Kidane. A sickly dawn light reflects against the mountains and drapes the men.

Hailu brushes past her and goes in. Kidane presses his forehead against the rock at the entrance, his palms flat against it, so visibly shaken that Hirut backs away.

Hailu's voice slides out of the cave: Dejazmach, come in, he's awake.

Don't leave him by himself, Kidane says to her.

—

DAWIT IS A broken figure held together by stained bandages. He is stretched on a pile of blankets darkened with old blood. One leg is wrapped in layers of thick cotton, the bandage splotched with pale yellow medicine and the gleam of fresh blood. Hailu opens his basket. Dawit stirs, his eyes fluttering open then shutting quickly.

Get the turmeric, Hailu says to Hirut as he takes out a clump of dried leaves. Then he unwraps a tiny jar of honey from one of the rolls of bandages. He pours the honey onto the leaves in his hand then leans closer to Dawit.

I'm sorry, Hailu says. It's the only way.

Hirut has to turn her head and hold her breath. Turmeric did not work on her parents. Neither did the honey. Every leaf that the villagers tried, every mix made by that strange woman who traveled an entire day to help, every prayer the priests whispered then shouted then began to wail, every promise she made to her parents and then to God, none of it had worked. All of it was useless.

Dawit releases a weak breath and the curious gaze he turns toward Hirut soon swings to the entrance. His eyes widen. Dejazmach Kidane, Dawit says. He stiffens beneath a wave of pain.

Hirut turns to watch Kidane come inside, his head lowered. That's when she sees it: her Wujigra, her father's gun. There it is, leaning against the wall, tucked into the cave's dark shadows like a thief. Her stomach clenches, her forehead moistens with sweat, and she looks quickly at Hailu, but his eyes are locked onto Dawit's, full of tenderness.

Then Hailu turns to Kidane, stricken and angry, so furious that the rage distorts his features.

I've seen these injuries before, Kidane says softly. I've seen a bullet cut into the back of a man's head and come out through his mouth. My father taught me things, he adds. But this. He stops, all the anguish in his face twists him unrecognizable. But this. He lays a hand on Dawit's shoulder, staring down at the young man. I should have checked the gun, he says. I should have tested it before giving it to anyone.

It was mine, Hirut says quietly.

Kidane clears his throat. Dawit, brave soldier, he begins. Did you know they're singing about you today? Did you know they're talking about the way you charged at the Italian with that old gun? You were like fire, Kidane continues.

A loud sigh escapes from Dawit's mouth and the young man shuts his eyes, his breaths shallow and rough. Hailu nods to Kidane and points outside. He gestures for Hirut to collect the basket, then Hailu smooths Dawit's blanket beneath his chin and motions for them all to leave.

Hirut waits beside Dawit until they are both out of the cave. She waits until she hears Kidane walk away. Then Hirut reaches for her Wujigra. She clasps it tight and drags it out with her. As she stands and turns to go back to the camp, she finds herself staring at Hailu and Kidane. They are farther down the same path, looking at the rifle in her hands.

What are you? Kidane asks. What have you done? Beneath his anguish, beneath the defeat and fatigue, glows a bright and curdling rage.

Chorus

The girl: She does not see the doomed path that opens so easily before her. She cannot foresee what is only natural: that all of Kidane's guilt-ridden weight will pivot toward the open space her rebelliousness lays bare, and he will force his way in. What is this, he is saying as he drags her away from the cave and toward the center of the camp. What is this, we say, so she will turn and put that gun back where it belongs. But she cannot know that grief cradles at the breast of cruelty, and it hungers for more, and she is for the taking. There she is, hurtling forward in his grip, a cursed keeper of promises. She notes the disappearing fog and believes it is simply the wind. She ignores the blackbirds that soar above her head in broken formation. She simply moves toward that dead campfire with her old gun slung across her back, trapped by Kidane's momentum.

At the campfire pit: Aster, draped in a blanket waiting for her husband, her face hidden in its folds. Seifu and Aklilu, in their shamma, waiting obediently for their commander. She will not remember them. She will not recall the way Aster shrinks at the sight of her. There will be no memory of Seifu's troubled gaze or the shaking hand Aklilu has to hide by clenching both into fists. What she will note as she thinks back to that moment when she was still the same as she was born: the crooked path of pale sunlight falling across the leaning, flat-topped tree.

KIDANE PAUSES AT THE EDGE OF THE CAMPFIRE PIT AND RAISES A FIST, shuttering the morning light. His mouth moves but she cannot hear his words. There is only the bloated rage that contorts his face and shifts him into a stranger. She stumbles, her heart plummets. Her face flushes with heat as Kidane pulls her toward him, nearly throwing her to the ground. She knows, somehow, to bite back the cry of surprise. She understands that it is better to dig her teeth into her tongue than to make a noise, aware that everything she says will be meaningless with that Wujigra strapped across her back.

That gun is not yours! What have you done?

She shakes her head. Her thoughts are a single, unbroken thread of nothingness.

She does not expect the hard slap that seems to land on both sides of her face at once. There is no time to look for the hands that feel as if they are made of stone. In her head: two knives are sharpening against each other, the whir of metal against metal, the high-pitched screech of terror. Hirut opens her mouth to scream but she is breathless as she bends gracelessly into the unnatural momentum. When she collapses to the ground, it is with a muffled groan, her scream broken by the impact of her body.

Kidane drops down beside her. Then he is pushing his knee into her side, yanking at the strap of the rifle. He's a dying soldier, he says. What are you?

From somewhere, Aklilu's voice: Dejazmach Kidane, I'll take it back to Dawit and get her out of here.

There is Aster: Kidane!

For a moment, everything trembles in silence.

Aklilu's voice: Dejazmach, let's find Hailu and give him the gun.

Shut up! Kidane says.

She hears Kidane add: Leave, all of you. Now!

Then: departing footsteps.

But Kidane's rough hands are forcing her flat on her stomach and then Kidane is on top, his breath at her ear, his chest moving against her back, flesh expanding, fitting into the dips and curves of her figure, grinding her into the dirt until she can feel her ribs bend. She turns her head and sharp pebbles dig into her cheek and through the dense fog of her tear-filled eyes, her father shakes his head sadly.

Kidane whispers into her ear, What did you think? What did you expect?

His flesh hardens in the crevice between her legs and he pushes in, through her dress, and her mind slams into that space where meaning is absent, where nothing but confusion awaits.

It's that woman's fault, Kidane is saying. It's all her doing. All of this.

This: the body is blood and flesh, and always a blow away from falling apart. This soft stomach, this arched back, these kicking legs, the flailing arms, her marked flesh, all of it is a traitor. Then Kidane pushes himself off her. He jumps up and grabs the Wujigra and strides away. Hirut stays on her stomach, feels that spot between her legs where her dress digs in, tight like second skin, and begins to cry.

Interlude

Everything has its place, Teferi, and there are some like you who must learn this so they can lead. You are just a boy, Ras Teferi Mekonnen, but you are destined to be a king amongst kings. All men live and die by the will of God, there is no disorder in His world. Teferi, do you believe? Yes, Father. Yes, Father what? Yes, Father Samuel, I believe. And Ras Teferi Mekonnen, now grown into Emperor Haile Selassie, knows it to be true even now, even on this day when he is trapped on the edge of forgetfulness trying to find his way to safety. The Italians have intercepted his messages, they know where every one of his northern armies will attack. They know where his columns are stationed and they intend to find them. He should have never trusted the transmissions, should never have relied on manmade tools. Teferi, we are explaining Simonides again. Did you study your Quintilian? Memory is the gift of the divine. It is vast and labyrinthine. Imagine it a palace, a building with many rooms. Put details in each room. Give them their rightful place. Light a candle inside the room and illuminate it brightly. Nothing is ever gone. It is always just within reach. Father Samuel, I have forgotten where I put my son's picture. I cannot find it and we are at war.

Teferi, imagine Simonides in the banquet hall just before its collapse. He is preparing for his speech, like one day you will do. Imagine that moment he is called outside, just before the earthquake destroys the building. The relatives of the dead come to find him, the sole survivor, and what do they want? They want to find those they've lost,

Father Samuel. Do as he did, Teferi. Close your eyes and tell us every-thing you remember. But they are bombing my people, Father, they are throwing poison on the children. Women are dying. I have led them all into danger and I cannot find where I packed my son's picture.

First he is afraid, then he is staggered anew by the thought: he cannot remember where he put his favorite photograph of his son Mekonnen and him, the one that the American journalist George Steer gave him as a gift. The man had come to pay a visit and waited politely for him to finish a meeting. That day, Steer wore a gray shirt and dark-blue trou-sers and a pen stuck in the pocket of his blue jacket. Haile Selassie took the photograph, pleased, and thanked the man profusely. They sat and spoke for nearly thirty minutes about Italy, about Wal Wal, about the northern highlands and the southern front and defense. The man's socks were an elegant shade of gray with thin blue stripes. As soon as he could, Haile Selassie found a frame for the picture, then he set it on his desk. It stayed near his elbow, a photo so precious that he allowed no one to touch it. And now it is gone, as if it did not exist. As if the Italians snuck into his office and found that, too. Simonides reconstructed a collapsed building from memory. He looked at ruins and recognized their former glory. He found a way to resurrect the dead by remembering where they sat. He helped them find a way back to their grieving relatives. He called them to life by calling them by name.

Teferi, all we have is what we remember. All that's worthy of life is worthy of remembrance. Forget nothing. Haile Selassie stands in the corridor and gazes into his nearly empty office, the unsteadiness creeping up. He must leave Addis Ababa and go to his headquarters in Dessie. He will fight the war from there. The Italian advance into Addis Ababa has become undeniable and his head is thick with dread. His desk is clean. Cardboard boxes are piled next to the door. There are no more books on the shelves. Everything has been put into its rightful place, carefully marked and sealed. Just hours ago, at dawn, he stood in this office and slipped some of his last remaining items into one of these boxes, then he walked on a beam of light lying across the floor like it was carpet, and went up the stairs to rest. Now he cannot remember what each box contains. He cannot remember packing the picture away. He shuts his eyes and there is a lone figure of a man standing in rubble. Behind him, women and men, bent in half by grief, point to the fragments of bodies buried in dust and stone, and weep.

Simonides, he whispers. Simonides, he says. Haile Selassie touches the split in his chest held together by the sternum. It is there, in a place no human hand can reach that he feels himself fading away, rubbed out in increments by his enemies. It is a disappearance that begins like this: with forgetfulness and boxes.

A gentle cough behind him. Haile Selassie turns around and it is his aide, his hair unruly, the curls starting to fall into themselves. He is barefoot, still dressed in the same suit he has been wearing for two days, his tie unknotted and sloppy. He stands there holding a stack of files to his chest like a shield, his face drawn and dark circles beneath his eyes. Over his shoulder and down the hallway, light skips across the gramophone that a servant is packing with the utmost care.

The cars and trucks are nearly full, Your Majesty. I just confirmed with the driver. There's not a lot of room left.

The runners? Haile Selassie asks.

His aide nods. We're locating Kidane, he'll know they're planning to ambush him. We'll get to him before they do. Then the aide turns to stare at the servant packing the gramophone.

The emperor waits. He knows what the aide wants to say; the young man has found the most polite ways to repeat himself, and he won't be able to resist trying once more.

On the narrow table next to the servant, Haile Selassie sees the new box of needles he ordered from Djibouti. There is also a stack of 78s given to him by dignitaries as gifts: Wolfgang Amadeus Mozart and Edvard Grieg, the American Duke Ellington, the German Comedy Harmonists, a rare Japanese recording. These are records he has listened to once, maybe twice, more often as war became inevitable and defeat loomed. He has hoped that their unfamiliar tunes would help drown the repetitive vulgarities of "Faccetta Nera" and those other hateful Italian songs that detail skinning him alive.

Make sure they pack it, the emperor says. Move other bags out of the car to the trucks if there is no room.

The emperor can feel the aide's frustration. He cannot seem to understand why the gramophone must come. We are existing in a moment beyond reason, the emperor wants to say. We are now firmly in the irrational.

The aide sweeps a careful eye into his office and through the house. I'll make sure all the doors are securely locked.

Past the sloping valleys of his capital city, across rivers and dry savannah, Kidane is marching toward ambush. Haile Selassie can almost hear the shouts and cries that will soon echo through the hills. He has ordered the fastest runners in the country to speed to the north and find Kidane and his men. He has sent his drummers across the city, their urgent rhythms announcing new danger, beating so loudly that the sky grew dark with birds: the Italians will invade Addis Ababa soon, they will come in and burn the city and claim it as their own. His messengers have bypassed the rubble of bombed homes to raise the alarm: Jan Hoy, our emperor, the divinely appointed Haile Selassie, our guiding sun will himself lead his men against the devils, he calls every soldier of the north to gather strength and join him, God will lead the way. Arise, soldiers!

The emperor can outline Kidane's journey in his head. He thinks now of each village Kidane will pass. He knows every river he will wade through. He can imagine the kilometers of rough terrain. He knows the two mistresses who would weep at any news of Kidane's death. He knows which of the man's enemies would breathe sighs of relief. He has learned to store countless details in the palace of his memory. He has divided his men into separate rooms, giving their wives the bed, the children the windows, the mistresses the rugs. He has let each sharp detail claim a space in that room until he can see them all in place, rooted and immovable, waiting for a candle's illumination in order to step forward and be remembered. He has done it this way since he was Ras Teferi, the ritual now so rote it is automatic, faster than conscious thought.

From upstairs, a soft voice filters down. The emperor can hear his second youngest, Mekonnen, call for him: Abbaba. Abbaba. Are you gone?

I am here, *lijé*, he thinks. But there is a headquarters in Dessie and a battle in Maichew he must organize and more officers he must contact. There is no time to be this child's father. He hears his wife, Menen, call the boy. He looks up, aching for a glimpse of this beloved son, his father's namesake, subject of a picture now lost.

Then another voice drifts in, a memory resting in the corner of his mind. Zenebwork calling to him as a child: Abbaba. Abbaba, don't go. He turns his head so the servants do not see him flinch. He cannot leave her no matter where he goes. This is not an arrangement of his making, nor is it one of her choosing. It is the preordained balance between this world and the other. Between the living and dead.

I'm ready, Your Majesty. His aide clutches the reports that he has folded neatly. We can sit in the boardroom if you would like.

The aide says more but the emperor isn't paying attention. He is thinking back to his school days, to his teachers and their demand that he remember the smallest detail. He has an exceptional memory now for the minutiae of the intricate systems that the reports imply. It is his enemy he cannot memorize. He cannot form a mental image of this man his people insist on calling Mussoloni. He cannot see him clearly. His eyes fail him in this effort, so he doesn't know what else to do but listen. In the months since Benito gave his orders to invade, the emperor has done nothing but buy the music of the Italian people, sending his servants by train to Djibouti, Sudan, Somalia, Yemen, and Eritrea to collect the 78s and bring them back. Now there are three heavy boxes waiting to be moved with him, neatly catalogued.

The records, Haile Selassie begins.

The aide lifts his head. His shoulders fall. Behind him, the servant settling the gramophone in its crate pauses. The maid sweeping behind the curtains raises the broom off the ground. It is as if behind him, too, his children's chatter has stopped and only Zenebwork leans in, challenging and afraid.

Your Majesty?

We will listen starting this evening, before we depart, to the music of these Italians. Which one would you suggest? We have time for one, the emperor says.

The answer firm and swift: Giuseppe Verdi's opera *Aida*.

He thinks he feels Zenebwork slide from the rosebush into the open window. She is hunched in the corner to his left, shaking. *Aida*, he says. The story where the Ethiopian princess dies. He cannot keep his throat from closing.

WHEN KIDANE WAS A BOY, HIS FATHER WARNED HIM: BE CAREFUL OF the runner with the trembling legs. Measure the man's words and weigh his message. Stay calm and listen. Never let him see that you are bent by his words. Stand tall and motionless until he is gone. He will be watching your reactions. He will be gauging the danger ahead from the lines of your mouth. He will look for the tremor in your voice that will betray your distress. He will listen for the message you do not say aloud. Let him see nothing but certainty. Let him hear nothing but confidence. Be still, Kidane.

Finally alone, Kidane steps back into his tent and sinks onto his cot. The messenger, Worku, has left to relay his warning of a coming Italian ambush to another nearby camp. Kidane has been ordered by the emperor to preempt the attack and lead a charge against Carlo Fucelli. Dessie has been bombed and the emperor is soon moving to Maichew and will lead his army against a larger Italian army in one final battle. So many armies have fallen to bombs and mustard gas and heavy artillery. The northern front is disintegrating and Kidane is being ordered to join the offensive after this ambush. But there is almost certain defeat if they confront the Italians in face-to-face battle in Maichew.

The tent feels like it is shrinking; it is collapsing above his head.

The ambush on Fucelli, then a battle in Maichew: it will be a death sentence for many of his men. Kidane tries to calm down. From outside his tent float the gentle voices of women bringing water and firewood. There is the low, sly whir of the reconnaissance planes in the distance. Somewhere in the camp, Aster is organizing bandages and supplies as he told her to. Hirut is with her, subdued but finally obedient. Kidane digs into his small satchel next to his feet and pulls out a picture of his little Tesfaye, a clipping of Haile Selassie's picture, and the medal from Emperor Menelik to his father for his bravery in the war. Once his father returned home, he shied from contact with those who fought beside him, turning down invitations to dinners and weddings, declining attendance at funerals, and dropping out of his *mehaber* monthly gatherings. They're ghosts, he'd once said to Kidane. They forgot how to stay alive.

Was that Worku? It is Aster, speaking into the tent, her figure outlined through the canvas.

He can make out the hem of her dress through the tent flaps: she is not wearing his father's cape.

She steps inside without permission and stands in front of him with her hands crossed, her mouth in that narrow, anxious line he has come to hate over the years. What happened? she asks.

He starts to tell her this is none of her concern when he sees that just behind her, shrinking against the tent flaps outside, is Hirut. The girl's knees are slightly bent and pressed together and it is that simple, childish gesture that takes him back to only a few days ago when he found Hailu sitting at the campfire cradling the Wujigra, doubled over in grief so intense that his entire body seemed ready to split from unspent cries: this was the way he announced Dawit's death, and he has refused to mention his brother's name since.

The rage rises in Kidane again. There's no time for this, he says. Get things ready, we're moving against the Italians nearby.

Aster frowns and points at the girl. But she saw a convoy, she says. They're heading toward us. They're coming with tanks, they have trucks filled with supplies. They're getting ready for a big battle, she adds. You want to attack this camp instead of the convoy?

She waits for him to respond, and when he doesn't, she starts again, her voice conspiratorial.

We can help, she says. She pats her hair and clears her throat. I've already separated the women who want to fight from those who'll follow behind us. A good number on both sides. We can test the older guns for you, she adds softly.

He wants to reach out and strike her. It would be so easy to bring the angle of his hand down on her ear. There is that small indented place on her temple that he discovered years ago. It will leave her dizzy and awkward and send her to the ground in an ungainly heap. He has not done this in a long, long time. He has not turned his wrist and brought it down on his wife's forehead in this same way since Tesfaye died. He has felt some unspoken allegiance to her grief, an understanding of all the ways that loss can warp the spirit.

You'll follow behind us and tend to the wounded. Pack bandages and medicines, he says. Tell your women this is their way to fight. We'll leave from here at sundown.

—

KIDANE LOOKS DOWN at his feet. He feels as if he is gliding. Inside him are all the familiar emotions of battle: the eagerness and caution, the fear and the anticipation, and beneath it all, the freeing sensation of movement, of acceleration, of his body as an instrument of force. Dust collects in his eyes and he blinks to see past the tears. He extends his hands in front of him and stares at the shape they make in the falling night. They are strong, supple, capable of gripping a rifle and swinging a knife while leading his men in combat. This is his destiny, Kidane thinks as he listens for his army marching behind him. This is what all his days have led him toward. This is what awaits him at Maichew, once he has attacked this Italian camp and fulfilled the emperor's orders.

In Maichew, he will stand in daylight and face the enemy and fight until he dies. In Maichew, he will claim his inheritance, a promise passed down through blood. His father's mistake was that he stayed alive, Kidane sees this now with painful clarity. His father found a way to cheat destiny and he died a splintered man, a ghost made of bone and flesh. All Kidane has to do is attack this Fucelli's camp. It will harden his men and help them move toward that great defining conflict. His heart hammering, Kidane picks up speed, noting the quick jogs behind him, the huffs of breath as his troops struggle not to lag. Above them, a flock of dark-feathered birds scissor through the dim sky.

═

ASTER GATHERS THE women around her. Just below the hill, the men are readying for the ambush. The Italians are nearby, she says. Kidane's counting on us to help them stay strong and brave. Let no man retreat, run behind him and turn him around with mockery and song. Pick him up if he falls, drag his body away if he dies. Use your voice, use your arms and legs, turn your body into a weapon the Italians will never forget. It will not be the same as fighting, she repeats to them again and again, but it will help ready you for the front lines in the next battle. It will prepare you to look at dying men without collapsing at the thought.

Hirut stares at Aster and refuses to look away. It is as if the rest of the world has fallen aside and there is just the two of them on the hill that tumbles down into the Italian camp. There is no room for any thought that does not begin in that woman's eyes. Because Hirut remembers now that it is all Aster's fault that Kidane discovered her Wujigra. It is her fault that the gun is not in Hirut's possession now. It is her jealousy and suspicions that made it so, and all Kidane has been doing is following the unspoken commands of an angry woman. Hirut blinks, then blinks again, but still the spell is not broken. Frightened, Hirut hums and looks down and when she raises her chin, Aster nods to her as if they have made a pact that no one knows. Hirut turns away, humming to herself, and glances up and the bright sun catches and swirls on the wings of a flock of dark birds. She keeps gazing until the birds disappear, until there is nothing left but the heavens and when she blinks once more, the sky itself is drained of color: there are no clouds, no bright splashes of sun, no deep and pale blues. What remains is the sad, lonely shade of ash.

A DROP OF SUN ZIGZAGS THROUGH THE VALLEY TO SKID ALONG THE grass. It touches lightly on the patch of yellow flowers clustered on the side of the hill. It alights, graceful and quick, onto the tops of trees and disappears into a cloudless sky. Ibrahim tracks the elusive flicker: the planned ambush is now a battle and the Ethiopians have arrived. His *ascari* stiffen. When he raises his hand, his men draw upright and the movement shifts the Italians behind them into position. The valley swells with a thickening silence. Ibrahim looks toward Colonel Fucelli on the hill above. The colonel is a slender figure pressed into his binoculars, leaning toward them as if he might hurl himself into the fray. A flock of birds glides then dips in the bright expanse just beyond his head.

Sounds come from around the bend, floating on a breeze: the rumble of large engines, the snap of rocks beneath chained wheels. The tanks are rolling in. Ibrahim's men press forward. He has trained them well. He has lifted some with praise and broken others with discipline. He has molded them into a cohesive unit, and every one of them knows the enemy they face. They know what will happen if they are captured. He has left no doubts in their minds that it is better to die on the battlefield than to surrender to the Ethiopians.

Above them, high on a plateau, Colonel Carlo Fucelli watches through his binoculars, pressing his feet onto solid ground, denying his mind the luxury of fear. There is Ibrahim, turned toward the signal from the Abyssinian fighting force. The *ascari* are in a perfect line, their precision a testament to Ibrahim's endless drills. They exhibit none of the restlessness of earlier days. All hints of anxiety are gone. They stare ahead, immobile and alert, waiting for their leader, who waits for his leader, who waits for that crisp snap of light to manifest its human embodiment.

Kidane flattens himself to the ground as Amha sweeps reflected light across the valley again. It strikes against the clear blue sky, startling the blackbirds, their angry caws piercing through the steady heat. Kidane has seen the man demonstrate his technique to Aklilu and Seifu, but Kidane still cannot understand how he does it, how he gets the light to move in such unexpected ways across vast distances, at impossible angles. And now he surprised Kidane once more by insisting that he and Aklilu find a way to hide close to the Italian tanks while the rest wait for Kidane's signal to charge.

Amha had pleaded: If you let us go after the tanks, we'll eliminate their strongest weapons, the front lines will be stronger for it.

There had been none of the postures of deference from him, none of the deep bows or lowered eyes that others used when speaking to Kidane. There had simply been this urgent insistence, punctuated by Aklilu's silent but obvious agreement. Kidane had finally relented, trusting Amha's instinct. As soon as he gives the signal, Amha and Aklilu will hide in the hills behind the tanks.

Amha looks his way, and Kidane nods for them to head for the tanks. Then he listens. His order to attack will ricochet through the hills with the blast of the horn. A recent recruit, a slightly built man with the strange name of Minim, Nothing, will blow that thunderous instrument. Some of the men had grumbled about Minim's selection. Why would a mother name her child the word for nothing, they had asked. It's bad luck, they added. Aklilu, tell the *Dejazmach* what we're saying, tell him it frightens us, this Minim, this nothing, maybe he's a spy. Aklilu returned to Kidane and simply said, He was never made for war, but he's a good musician.

Above his head, the blackbirds slide into formation again, their squawks less shrill. Next to Kidane, Seifu is rigid, only his eyes, darting from one end of the valley to the other, give his tenseness away. They are all waiting for Kidane's signal, but he is waiting for Amha and Aklilu to get in place, and he is waiting for the women to settle at a safe distance behind them, away from artillery fire but close enough to reach the wounded who will surely fall. As soon as Aster is ready, she will let him know.

The sound punctures the tender base of his skull: a tap, no more than that. Carlo looks up, but the noise originates from beneath him, then inflates to either side of him, then shifts to hover just behind his hunched back and he feels a rolling momentum gather and he is standing on a pile of firewood staring down at his father's stern face: Aren't you a big boy, Carlo, aren't you too big to cry? Jump or I'll pull this log out of the stack, jump. And then the noise is everywhere and nowhere, primitive and controlled, strange and familiar. Lento, lentissimo, piano, pianissimo, he tells himself. But there is an electrical surge that is cutting into his resistance. It is softening his spine. The fear is gradual, wafting through him like a smell, old horrors flexing and straightening in the flimsy cage of his heart. He feels his throat tighten. His chest constricts. He stretches his mouth to form Ibrahim's name. He will say it if he has to.

Pause, he tells himself. Pick up the binoculars, put the strap on your neck. Check the map. Pausa. Lentamente. Tranquillo.

It quiets.

The horn disappears.

Stillness creeps back.

He listens again: nothing.

Pause. Breath. Then: a light. The first straining sounds of a horn's ferocious blast. The blare tearing a seam into the horizon. The sky shattering.

Carlo is almost toppled by the force of his arm rising up then dropping down. *Avanti, ragazzi!* Charge!

At Ibrahim's signal, the *ascari* stand and arch forward and then they are gone and running, and it does not matter that nothing stirs in the valley in front of them. It does not matter that they run headlong into a silent field. It does not matter that while the *soldati* advance swiftly behind them in the vast stretch of land, the Abyssinians seem to have disappeared. None of this means anything because Carlo is certain that soon, those twitching blades of grass will unleash grown men and all that is unseen will make its treachery known.

And then: noise. Ravenous and painful. Carlo leans into the pocket forming around him, hears his men shout his name and draw him into their fold. They hold him close, upright and balanced, with no other thought but total obedience. This is all they have been waiting for: for him to tell them what to do. Carlo steps back from the plateau, staggered by the power of it. This, he thinks, this is what it means. He raises his arm and brings it down and hurls his voice into the valley: Charge! He screams it though there is no way he can be heard. Charge! The war cries erupt, the *ascari* surge forward, the air thickens with dust and voice and horn, and soon the chaos no longer spins. It is his to control. It becomes exhilarating. And as the *ascari* dash across the field, he imagines the coming clash as colossal and symphonic, operatic and tragic. Carlo raises the binoculars back to his face and watches his battle unfold.

⟶

LOOK: A HEAP OF BURNT HUTS, Ibrahim, openmouthed and lionhearted, leading his men across the rubbled field. There he is, soaring over stone and thatch, nimble as a gazelle, racing through a valley still refusing to reveal the unearthly source of those war cries and bullets. Ibrahim, courageous son of Ahmed, wondrous-voiced, swift-footed tamer of horses, watch him sprint through this burnt land free of fear, propelled by those who run beside him, who look at their leader's proud face and bend into the wind to gain momentum. And where are those men, those ghostly spirits descended from the brave sons of Adua? Who throws that slender rod of arrowed wood that graces the dusty sky? Watch as it tucks so neatly into the throat of a startled *ascaro*. See Ibrahim signal his own command. See the *ascari* obey, how quickly they stop and aim and begin to shoot at unseen men. Zoom to their stunned faces. Those perfect arching spears. Their high-flung arms. That quivering beam of light curving through the field like a god's mocking defiance. See Fisseha fall, that last son of Samuel. See Girmay stumble, that only child of Mulu. See Habte drop to his knees, speared through lung and heart. Listen to the wind vibrate with spear and flung stone and hoarse shouts and agonized cries. And still Kidane's army is no more than an expectation, a weighted thought without substance and form, no more than air.

—

IT IS ALMOST TOO LATE when Ibrahim realizes what they have done. He is already rushing into those spears when he grasps that they have somehow been moving backward, uphill, through grass, invisible as air, while he and his men have been propelling themselves toward slaughter. Ibrahim shouts as he spins and hurls himself into the path of his men angling to push around him. He comes face-to-face with their eager terror and confusion. His heart stills then lurches at the sight and he vows to himself there will be no more days like this, when he finds himself surprised and unprepared. Ibrahim lifts his arm and points behind them and says again the only word solid enough to come out of his mouth: Back, back, go back! Pull back. He lifts his arm and there is Suleiman, refusing to stop, his startled eyes stuck on the hill, his mouth open, screaming something to him that Ibrahim cannot hear until he hears the *thuk* of pointed arrow breaking bone in its accelerating search for flesh. Ibrahim motions his men back, and this time, they are rushing toward safety, jumping over the bodies of their fallen, over the pools of blood, over the splintered spears, back to where they started.

And then Colonel Carlo Fucelli hears the tanks. There they are, crushing stone, snapping broken thatch, roaring with a fury surpassed only by his swelling grief. There are their pivoting muzzles turning toward the enemy, those cowardly men who shoot while hiding and continue to hurl spears. These tanks will blast through the tall grass, the thick boulders, the large stones that hide the Ethiopians. The tanks—his tanks—will crush their skulls and pulverize downed bodies. His tanks will be merciless and inhuman in their attack. There will be no fear of spear or bullet, no hesitation in that mechanical forward drive. Then another *ascaro* goes down just in front of Ibrahim as his men clear the field for the machines. Carlo zooms to the injured *ascaro*'s stunned face, the blood blossoming from his chest. Is this the flower of youth? Is this what they mean? He raises his arm again to aim the tanks. And yet. And still. Despite. The bullets do not stop. The spears do not waver. The *thuk thuk thuk* is a steady rhythm, orchestral, and Carlo stands in Abyssinia but he is also tumbling from a stack of firewood and he is hiding beneath his bed and all that has pursued him in those darkest terrors remains invisible to humble human sight.

Kidane stares at the approaching tank and repeats what he learned another lifetime ago about the machine: the hatch, the turret, the muzzle, the barrel, the mudguard, the side armor, the road wheel, the link. Beneath him, the earth trembles as if preparing for this latest violation. The grass bends and snaps in thick currents of fume and heat. Above his head, the wind whips dust and tiny pebbles that splatter back into his eyes and down his throat. They have done what they could while staying hidden. They have used the terrain to the best of their advantage. His men have defied his own expectations, done the impossible, and maintained a fight against unlikely odds. They have done all of this, but there is no more they can do. What comes for them now is beyond their strength. Quickly, he flashes his mirror, signaling retreat and through the grass, traveling along the damaged earth, he hears Seifu shout his order and the men begin their crawling ascent up the hill.

Carlo feels the familiar fire of his childhood nightmares, the brimstone hurled from the dark palms of demons. This noise, the dusty plume of splitting rock, the tremor of tree roots rising from the bowels of earth—all this he has known in his deepest terrors. Carlo presses his binoculars closer, blinks the haze of wetness from his eyes, and reminds himself: But I am here. And he thinks back, past the march to this valley to that point on that mountaintop close to the fort, where this country spread glorious before him, her lush valleys resplendent in sunshine. He thinks of serendipity and divine favor and destiny. He should have known it then, but he is certain of it now: his moment of greatness has begun and it has started like this: with a spectacle that confirms the true grimness of this world.

And then: a single human form, small as a child, crawling, stomach-on-rubble as all the noise of war lifts from the hot ground and shimmers like desert heat. And then there is another Abyssinian sliding across dirt, an apparition blinking into view. They are two come from nowhere, twin figures sprung from a darkening imagination, moving toward his tanks as the valley sinks beneath their war cries, as Ibrahim and the *ascari* retreat. But this is the miracle of man, Carlo thinks as he touches the scar on his chest. This is impossible and yet, this is the miracle of man: to withstand the blows, to rise beneath them unmoved and dry-eyed. That is man and yet there is this: two men scaling his tanks as if they were simply iron mountains. And look, how the child-like man raises his arm, sword held high, and screams at the hatch to the driver inside. See him pounding on the small door, his fury relentless, a clanging note in the valley suddenly empty of all sound. It is a voice that needs no language to express itself, and Carlo falls now to his knees, his arm up, but there is no crescendo, there is nothing but that voice splintering the sky and where are the bullets, where are my *ascari*, where is my Ibrahim, where have they gone because it is as if all has disappeared and muted itself in order to bear witness to the hatch creaking open, so obedient, and that head emerging into daylight and the sword swinging gracefully, so splendidly, so perfectly arched that the head has no choice but to follow.

See: thick red ribbons of blood. See: viscous sun curving against the belly of sky, and still, despite, and yet, there is nothing to do but watch as the next Abyssinian simply stands close to the mudguard, leans toward the tiny window, and shoots inside, and then they jump down and there is nothing, there is nothing left to report sir, my men tried their best but we were simply surrounded.

Then from somewhere, the tender voices of women.

Carlo gets back to his feet, stumbling for balance, binoculars up again. Zoom and focus, focus, focus because: those tanks, majestic felled beasts, because: they are steel and rubber and ammunition and man is a miracle but this leaves no room for woman or song. This is impossibility itself, he thinks as he looks down on the smoky field and spies a bloom of white dresses, skirts rippling in the wind. They are tumbling down the hill as if gravity were of no consequence, as if sharp stones and tender feet did not matter, as if a human figure could be propelled at improbable angles and still maintain such effortless grace. He sees them but does not believe. He hears them but cannot grasp. Where he is in this place amongst steel and rubber and bullets and blood will not allow for distortions and fissures. They are not women, he decides, but illusions. They are a mirage, a glimmer on this mountaintop overlooking the churning valley. What is real is the distant warble of planes that are coming. What is probable is the assault that will rain down from his sleek flying machines.

But: the voices persist. Carlo stands upright and puts down the binoculars and slowly tips forward and feels awareness flow over him cold and merciless, and he begins to comprehend that the body is wiser than he can even know. It is telling him to beware, to listen carefully, to look up, to scrutinize, because even a woman carries danger, and where she walks, there too is death.

And then Kidane rises from the grass, his heart a solid mass pressing

against his lungs, pushing bursts of air through his throat as Seifu stands
beside him and raises his arm and the soldiers unflatten themselves
and push to their feet. He trembles before the awesome vision of full-
blooded rage. As he gives the order, they rush toward the tanks, gather
Aklilu and Amha in their fold, and collect the rifles of the fallen. That
his men—two of his men—could bring the tanks to a halt is a thought
that Kidane feels more than comprehends at the moment. That they did
this with one sword and one bullet, he knows, will become a song that
will carve itself into a nation's eternal memory. He finds his momentum
by keeping his gaze on Aklilu's back, by matching him stride for stride.

From above them, as if raining from the sky, the women begin to
sing. Aklilu laughs and Kidane shouts for his men to move faster, keep
going, do not stop until we have won. Together, they race for the *ascari*,
aware only of their beating hearts, their uniform pace, the battle cries
that surge in violent waves from their women as they move, swift-
footed and proud, through the dust-veiled air.

Hirut sees Aster lift her arm: Louder, she shouts. Louder so they
can hear you. And it is all such a surge of body and breath and song
that Hirut has no thought but: Louder, louder, louder, and as she sings
of valor and enemies, she feels the walls of the sky slip away and the
cacophony soften to a rumble, and the valley opens before her, green
and lush, its beauty unbearable.

Later, she will not be able to say which happened first: whether she
heard the rattles of the planes or saw Beniam trying to pull himself
across dirt. It felt, she will say, like everything happened in silence,
and happened slowly, and happened all at once. She will pretend that it
was all too much, that memory blessed her with erasure. She will claim
to remember the trees and the flock of birds that still clung stubbornly
to the sky. She will say that there was nothing to witness until it was
upon her, until those planes dropped their poison and they had to flee to
avoid choking to death. She will repeat to any who ask that yes, she was
there on that day, but no, she did not see much. She will flit around that

first sighting of Beniam and talk instead of the sharp smell of straw that followed the planes. We ran on blistering feet, she will say, our throats collapsing around our screams. It hurt to open my eyes, I moved like the blind.

But: she sees the first puddles of blood-soaked earth, the stains that chew into the soles of her feet. She sees the edge of an arm, distended feet, a strangely angled head. Soon, she is forced to shift her gaze from the expansive landscape in front of her and stare down to avoid a fall. She will come upon Beniam in this way, as if he were a message thrown in her path to pick up. And from the corner of her eye, she will note how, here and there, other women drop to their knees while others still urge the rest onward, because, she will later say, we knew that there was no way but through it, there was no escape but to run toward battle, run toward the men, run toward those planes without thought.

Hirut sees Beniam's dark form and she hears the moan but she thinks: A tangle of cloth, dirty rags, blots of ink, chunks of mud, and she does not think anything else because how could there be a boy in front of her keeling to one side while trying foolishly to stand on legs that hang as so sloppily from the hipbone? What kind of logic allows for a boy to crumble in front of her with skinny hands flailing out for balance? She becomes angry. She gives in to fury, because there is no sense in his efforts. She wants to shout that it is a futile gesture and he should find another way to move out of her path. Then she sees the blood that is a small pool around him, thick as a blanket to lay atop, and Hirut thinks of Dawit and she thinks of Hailu and she knows that some must do what others cannot. So she bends and catches him as he collapses and they tumble together into the grass, limb entwined with bloody limb. And when those dark eyes find her and that mouth opens, Hirut leans into the slackening young face, her heart a series of tremors, and she peers into the flattening eyes to say to him, What are you?

Because there is no word for what is shivering in her arms while wasting breath to say, Beniam, I'm Beniam. There is no word for the blood that seems to seep into her own skin. There is no way to comprehend what is withering, nameless and nearly formless, in her arms. Then there is no air anymore, only a hot spray that splatters then chokes and then she cannot breathe and there is no longer singing or shouting but another sound she cannot hear past the wretchedness of this boy's pleas to save him. It is impossible, she thinks, to burn like this without fire, to choke like this in daylight. Impossible to be breathing and choking, to be alive and dying. So this next part she will practice forgetting every day that follows. She will not remember his screams for help, she will not recall his grasp on her hand. She will force herself to unremember, to go back and erase that moment when someone named Hirut got up and left a dying boy named Beniam, and ran.

BLACKBIRDS. THEN THE RIP and tear of childbirth, of stillbirth, of first nights, of a body come undone and splitting at the seams. The women hold their stomachs, bend to the ground, gaze up in wonder. Blackbirds, they think. Dust rising from the carnage below. Hirut looks past the thick air but it is only a plane. Only two. Three. So low. Then four. Five. Then they are birds in formation, flying so close to Aster's head she can see the grinning face inside, mouth open and gleeful.

And Aster looks down into the valley for Kidane but the air is singed with gunsmoke, bristling with heat, wet with a stinging liquid that wraps around her neck and sets fire to her eyes. Her feet stick to grass, melt into soil, burning bone loosens its way free of flesh. She drops to her knees and looks down at her hands, at the swelling blisters, and still she finds a way to take a breath and shout her husband's name and Ettore says, Father, there is this: that man is fragile. That wood and metal can easily puncture a young throat. That Icarus fell today, again and again and we who are left behind in the tower can only grope in the dark and aim at nothing. There is nothing to see, that is what I'm trying to say, Father. I cannot see the sun. It tricks my eyes and men are invisible and a vengeful chorus of women sings as we are told to stand. But it makes no sense what they are telling us, Father: to put on our gas masks and turn around and run.

He watches Abyssinians rush back up the hill with cries ballooning behind them, the tin roar of planes and static bearing on their heels. Then come the shots fired from those low-hanging planes, killing those already dying, killing those dropped to their knees with poison, killing those lucky enough to survive the initial battle, killing those risen like Lazarus. The lieutenant shouts his name. Mario calls for him to follow them. Fofi screams they will kill him. The *ascari* brush past him, startled eyes large behind those masks. Even Ibrahim tries to take his arm and pull him along. But Ettore stays, no more than minutes but it is a lifetime, it is an eternity. It is enough to see what it means to be a soldier. But it was not war, Father, this is also what I'm trying to say. This was a slaughter.

≈

THEY WILL SAY this did not happen. That their planes did not fly above Kidane's army and pour mustard gas across the fighters and rivers and land. They will deny the children dead, the women scorched, the waters poisoned, the men choked. But did you see the gas? reporters will ask Ettore. Did you see it drop from those planes? Then how do you know it happened? And when he points to his mask they will shake their heads and point to the sky and say, Those are two different things, my friend, we are here to report what you saw.

Chorus

Behold the emperor in the quiet bloom of despair. Behold him bent into the voice scaling the sky like a strange and desperate bird. There is the mournful curve of his back, the downward tilt of his crown-heavy head. On the sad mouth that age will tug into unswerving firmness moves the first sweep of an angry frown. That paralyzing thought: Kidane's army was massacred, so many brave lives lost. We are in the room as he settles the needle back onto the spinning record of *Aida* and guides it again to the start of the opera. We watch as he returns his hands, slender and graceful, against his chest in quiet supplication. Listen as the aria fills the empty chamber of the dimmed room, as a young girl whispers her love for a warrior who holds her father captive and has slain her people beneath his sword. Hear the chorus of slaves, the firm ground they offer this traitorous girl, the refuge they give to her blasphemous secrets. This emperor, growing old before his years, listens to the songs and shakes his head again: O Aida, foolish believer in torn loyalties, what new ways will you find to keep your own people enslaved, he whispers. Is it possible you do not know the duties of one born of royal blood?

THE PRIEST IS A YOUNG REDHEAD FROM MILAN WITH A NOSE LIKE A boxer and scars on his hands. He has broad shoulders and short legs and the steady stare of a playground bully. He has a piercing gaze that winds through the long line of soldiers waiting to make confessions and be blessed. He is probing and inquisitive, searching their faces with a growing frown, a sternness falling across his thick features. It has been only one day since the battle and his arrival has punctured the agitation of the night before, when all the men could do was gather close around the campfire and make feeble attempts at jokes and song.

Only Fofi was brave enough to voice what some of the others felt: Why didn't they let us fight? I was ready. He made the motion of lifting his rifle to aim in front of him.

The padre prays over a *soldato* who has buried his face in his hands, his shoulders shaking as he weeps. On the padre's face rests a beatific expression. His rough features convey serenity. His lips are moving, a hint of a smile tugs at the corners. Ettore feels the sweat building up on the back of his neck, pushing through layers of dust and grime to soak into the collar of his shirt. He can hear his father: And you let yourself get pushed into this? Haven't I taught you to question those who want to hide their brutal deeds behind some invisible god? The world was built by man, my son, we are made in our own crude image, there is no fate, there is no destiny, there is no divine will, there is only this: knowledge. Ettore finds himself shaking his head involuntarily and out of the corner of his eye, he sees with relief that a small number of *soldati* are gathering out of line, chatting easily. He moves to stand with them, aware of the stares at his back.

The mail arrives soon after the priest is done and a crowd quickly gathers around the truck. The men push and shove to get first in line, shouting their names to get the postman's attention, waving their hands in the air as if to catch whatever letter he might fling their way. Ettore waits at the edge of the circle trying not to worry that this will be another day without a letter from his father. The silence from Leo has stretched across the three letters his mother has sent. It has brought back memories of displeasing his father, of not answering a question right, of not doing what was expected, then watching his father calmly walk into his office and shut the door, silent, as Ettore begged to be let in so he could apologize, the door looming like an insurmountable wall between them.

How old had he been when his mother barged into the office and started shouting at her husband: You know nothing of regret? You remember nothing of remorse? What transpired in the look between them was part of another story that the two of them had locked him out of long ago. His father had gotten up from his desk, come around to him, and dropped to his knees, his eyes uncommonly soft. Without a word, he brought Ettore close and cupped the back of his small head in an unsteady hand.

I love you, my son, he had said.

Navarra! Navarra! Hurry up, take it! The postman flings an envelope toward Ettore while his name, Navarra, Navarra, ripples through the crowd.

Ettore grabs the letter and hastily steps away, eager to find a private place to read.

Fofi is pushing himself out of the throngs of men toward Ettore. He waves his letter into the air, jubilant. From Sandra! He kisses the letter and presses it to his cheek. Let's go over there. He points to a small group a few steps away sitting on the ground and reading their letters, taking turns trying to playfully peek over one another's shoulders.

You go on, he says. There's Mario, he points out. Mario sits apart from the group, holding a letter and looking stricken. You better see what's wrong, Ettore adds. Then he hurries to his tent, his hands shaking.

The letter he reads in his tent is a simple but loving note from his mother saying all the usual things: We are fine. We are proud of you. Nino sends his best, etc., etc. It has been filtered of information, stripped clean of any danger, written and rewritten to pass the censor's test. What Ettore will not know until much later, when it is too late to do anything with the knowledge but mourn, is that Leo, too, writes unsent letters to his son. He writes furiously and without rest for days on end, continuously. He sits in his office and flings open every locked drawer and empties them of their secret contents. While Gabriella cooks dinner, he pieces together his old life, traces his fingers down the seams of a past he has tried to keep intact and benign. He exposes the fissures in order to explain to a baffled son why it is that he has not been able to write.

This is what Gabriella is trying to tell Ettore when she mentions their map hanging in their kitchen. This is what she means when she says, Your father misses you. She means that Leo cannot do as she is doing. He cannot write those niceties that the post office claims are bolstering morale. Instead he writes down all that he could never say to his son while they shared the same house. He tells him about the man he was before Ettore was born, before he married Gabriella, before he learned to tame his tongue and clip his accent. He writes his soul onto those pages, his handwriting looping in expansive moments and shrinking during memories he would rather bury for dead. When he is done, he stands in front of Gabriella with a pile of letters in his trembling hands and says, I'm ready. Then they put the letters into a box they are saving for Ettore's return.

THE MOURNERS TURN their dresses inside out and rub dust across their faces. They pull at their hair and wail at the falling sun. They walk in slow circles around the bodies of the dead, beating their chests as they scream the names, their litany a slow dirge that threatens to tip them over and flatten them to the ground. As they go around the blanketed figures, Hirut forces herself to listen, dreading that name that will rise from their throats and bring Beniam forth to point at her with an accusing finger. They will work until every person has been mourned. They will repeat the names and utter the blessings, and curse the enemy that brought the men down. They will walk so many times around the corpses that a faint footpath will bloom in the grass. And then when they are done, those men still alive and able to move will give the bodies a burial. They will leave them in graves so poorly marked it will be as if they have vanished. They will rest in abandoned villages and near destroyed churches, a new set of inhabitants roaming lost on poisoned ground.

Hirut looks down at the basket of medicine in her hand. There are countless ways to put the living in the service of the dying and the dead, to pull a veil over the feebleness of every effort. It is easy to shield ourselves, she thinks as she watches the women continue to pray, from a fact that has always been so: that the dead are stronger. That they know no physical boundaries. They reside in the corners of every memory and rise up, again and again, to resist all our efforts to leave them behind and let them rest. How else to explain the tugging at her ankles, the grasping hands that keep insisting that she bend down and look him in the eye?

Over her shoulder, she can hear Aster call for more bandages, pain and discomfort evident in her voice. There are the murmurs of women preparing a meal out of meager supplies. She imagines she can hear Aklilu and Seifu's firm footsteps as they supervise the ongoing surveillance of this area. Hirut arches her sore back and checks the sky, listens for a fearsome rumble, listens for a boy's voice saying his own name again and again. There are rows of injured men and women waiting for her to return with her medicines. There are bandages to wrap and wounds to dress and plants to search for and save. There has been no rest since they escaped the planes the day before.

She has been moving at a dizzying pace, with hardly any food, her body threatening collapse in moments of stillness. She has applied crushed leaves and honey to almost every kind of wound and hoped silently that it would work. She has packed open sores with turmeric and ash and held trembling hands until the pain subsided. She has found herself rushing between one fallen body to the next, the burns and injuries mingling, the pleas melting into one another until every increment of time, even the smallest, bursts with her own ultimate helplessness.

She has done this with a thoroughness mistaken for devotion, repeating the act from patient to patient. She has let approving glances grow into appreciative whispers, and when those whispers formed into spoken praise by the other women, Hirut has simply nodded and continued to do as she was doing, hoping that it was adequate penance, fearing that no wound could be powerful enough to erase Beniam's young face from her mind.

Interlude

Every day since leaving Dessie and arriving in Maichew, Emperor Haile Selassie has abandoned his Bible and his prayers to listen to *Aida*. He has taken each song and played it three times, then again, winding the machine until his arm grew sore and his lower back ached from the bend into the mouth of the speaker. Every morning, he has woken up in this cave that is his temporary headquarters to play those tinny, rattling voices and decipher the clues sitting between the overwrought, ballooning notes. That no true Egyptian sounds like this is another small fact that the emperor has had to set aside in order to find what it is that Aida has managed to keep hidden.

Now Haile Selassie lowers the needle onto the 78 and waits for it to slide into the opening notes. This is not the best thing to do while his army readies for the offensive in Maichew. There are messages to convey and troops to inspect before dawn. There are supplies of artillery and mortars to distribute. He must gather his reserve troops and head to the mountains and have them wait until his men need the reinforcements. He must give more money to the people in this area, he must convince any who are unsure that he is their true king. He looks at the calendar, then down at the reports. There is still so much to do. And yet here he is, bending into the first orchestral sounds of *Aida*.

He will skip his evening prayers in order to listen before his advisers come to discuss the next day's plans. Because it was not until this morning, when confirmed reports of the poisoning and massacre of Kidane's army reached him, that he could finally accept Aida's real betrayal: the Ethiopian princess did not know the duties of a splintered heart. She could not fathom the burdens woven into her royal blood. It is an unforgiveable treachery. Her tormented innocence stops Haile Selassie short: it is as if she has forgotten rage and vengeance, as if she knows no other emotion except that childish, narrow-minded devotion to a man who enslaves and kills her own people.

And as news comes of the devastating losses suffered by Kidane near Debark, Haile Selassie thinks back to the Christmas Offensive and Ayalew and Imru's strategic attacks on Criniti's forces at Dembeguina Pass. He reminds himself of Kassa and Seyoum and Mulugeta's forces that pushed the Italians back to Axum. He considers the humiliation that left the enemy morally broken. He thinks of Desta gathering his troops to continue resisting enemy advances on the southern front. And the emperor stands in front of the record and feels his resolve grow: they do not expect an offensive, so that is what he will do. They have been weaned on lies set to music, so he will attack them with his army's battle cries. They imagine this country full of Aidas and desperate kings willing to leave their people in enemy hands. And he will show them this is a country full of soldiers and leaders who charge rather than retreat, who will die on their feet rather than bow to save their lives.

Caught in a moment of exhilaration so powerful that he trembles, Haile Selassie lifts the needle and takes the 78 off the turntable. He pushes the gramophone aside and holds the record in both hands. He stares at it: its sleek black vinyl, the neat and even grooves, the fading label with *Aida* then *Teatro alla Scala* in large block letters. Then he throws it across the room. It slaps gently against the wall of the cave and doesn't break. He marvels at it, at its stubborn strength, and slowly gathers himself again. He pats his uniform straight and picks up the record and slips it into its sleeve. He sets it next to his Bible, opening the book to the verse in Isaiah he has read daily since the start of this war: *Woe to the land shadowing with wings, which is beyond the rivers of Ethio-*

pia. Then he bows his head to pray for vengeance and the mighty rage of a thousand armies.

—

HE CALLS FOR his priests. He raises his head from prayer only long enough to answer questions and give orders and update maps and reports. He turns his advisers away and ignores their urgent pleas to do it now, Your Majesty, attack now, it's the only time. He writes letters to his wife and sends messages to his children. He dismisses the evidence of Italian fortifications. He confirms strategies and selects his commanders for his attacking columns. He orders preparations for a banquet in honor of Saint Giorgis's holy day. He feels the sacred might of the divine. He lies down at night filled with a deep, unshakeable faith. He dreams of King Dawit, and Goliath's head, and that single stone flung from the slingshot.

On the night before Giorgis's Day, Haile Selassie stands from his desk. He slips on his shoes. He flattens the collar of his shirt and cinches his belt. He winds the gramophone and turns up the volume then stands at attention. He listens to Aida: *O patria mia, O patria mia*. He hears the guttural screams of a million soldiers led by her father, Amonasro, breaking into the palace to take her back home. He hears the wind slapping against the palm trees and the crack of an overextended throat. He hears a hundred armed men charge into deafening noise. He hears the names of his beloved cities: Adua. Axum. Mekelle. Gondar. Harar. Dessie. Addis Ababa, they line up like dutiful soldiers and aim in his direction while shouting his name. Haile Selassie shuts his eyes.

Ora basta. Ora basta. Emperor Haile Selassie puts his hands on his waist and stands with his feet apart. He repeats Mussolini's words to himself, first in Italian, then in French, then in English, then in Amharic. *Ora basta*: Enough now. *Yibeqal.* We've had enough. Enough already. The meaning is unchanging. Haile Selassie listens: A true leader is not a stone lying immobile in a changing tide. A real king does not tuck into himself like a beast at night. This will not be a war between two immovable forces. This will be a contest between divine force and merciless greed.

Ad atti di guerra risponderemo con atti di guerra! To acts of war we will respond with acts of war! *Yetorin dirgitoch betornet dirgitoch inmelissalen!*

In the dim candlelight flickering in the cave, the emperor spies his shadow. He pivots in front of that billowing figure and juts out his jaw. He lowers his chin. He folds his arms across his chest and moves his head from side to side. He scowls and shifts from foot to foot. He is constant motion. He is uncoiling energy. He is aggression molded into human form. He practices saying in the dark what must be spoken in daylight: Now it begins. He says it again and again, arms folded, unfolded; feet apart, feet together; chest puffed, straight-backed; jaw tight. Now it begins.

THERE ARE OATHS THAT HOLD THIS WORLD TOGETHER, PROMISES that cannot be left undone or unfulfilled. There is the bond between a ruler and his people, between the people and the soil, between the soil and the sun, and the sun and the tiller. There is that unspoken vow that leads the river to the tree, and the tree to its sky, the sky to the bird that flies up toward new lands and other kings. But this bird: it pivots away from plumes of smoke while a small child looks down from a hilltop and stares at all that man has wrought. Because it is all laid bare: the burning cities and the mountains on fire, the ruins of homes and collapsing churches, the scorched fields, the boiling rivers, the poisoned soil and the fallen trees, the exploding bombs, the choking men, the fragmented bodies, and those uniformed columns slipping into the valley numerous and innumerable, their rifles discharging, their bayonets swinging, their voices lifted, *Giovinezza*, *Avanti*, *O patria mia*. In the upheaval and debris, the emperor charges and charges and charges and his soldiers rise up and crumble down and rise up again, and the poisonous rains continue to fall on a blistered earth and because there are oaths and promises and vows to keep, Haile Selassie's men continue to fight as hours pass and the blood-soaked sun slides slowly into the shelter of the horizon, and still the emperor and his army keep going, in death-defying conflict, until the order finally comes: Retreat. Retreat.

I N THE DEAD HEAT OF THE AFTERNOON SUN, WORKU RUNS, HIS FEET like wings, his heart a swollen ache growing in his chest. Somewhere beneath the blue stain of sky, the ground pulses with the steady echoes of a locomotive train carrying the emperor farther away from his people. What will Worku tell of first? The weeping soldiers standing in a row before their emperor, as straight as a knife's blade? Or the solemn royal grandchildren grasping their small suitcases and waiting obediently for their nanny's commands? Maybe it is the emperor's steps— so measured and slow—that he will mention first, the way they sliced through the distance between the royal car and the train, his heavy shoes scraping dirt? The emperor has left. Jan Hoy is gone. Teferi Mekonnen has boarded a train out of his country. Maybe that is what he will say first, breathing through burning lungs, speaking above the sighs of crestfallen angels: Our greatest warrior has left his people after the defeat in Maichew and the devastating massacre at Lake Ashangi. He is gone. He has left us.

BOOK
2
RESISTANCE

HIRUT AND AKLILU ARE TWO SLENDER SILHOUETTES ETCHED IN GRAY light, talking back and forth with the ease of old friends. Kidane catches the lilt of Hirut's voice filtering through the night and a lower answering reply by Aklilu. They shake blankets loose of leaves and dirt and lay them gently over the injured. They re-roll a shamma to make a better pillow for one woman. They check the bandages of another. They move down the row without a break in conversation. There is no tension in their rhythms, no nervousness in their gestures, there is none of the fear that Hirut exhibits when she is around him. And though he has assumed that Aklilu's behavior with him was both honest and comfortable, he sees now that the man has always approached him with a respectful but distant reserve, there has never been any real closeness between them.

Before Kidane was pulled into the allegiances of war, he and his friends loved each other like brothers. They were men who understood him without explanation. Childhood companions who knew what it meant to be trapped by duties and expectations, and who shouldered all of it by moving deeper into their familiar circles, taking advantage of privilege because it all came at such a high, invisible cost. Aklilu and Hirut cannot imagine any of this. They are simple people, tillers of land. They hold nothing dear except what is directly in front of them: food and water and basic survival, and this is why they cannot imagine that he watches from behind the tree where, just moments ago, he received the message from Worku: *The emperor's speech at the League of Nations has done nothing to stop the Italians. The League has broken its own promises. They have abandoned us to continue this war alone. Mussolini has declared victory but there was no formal surrender and Ethiopia will not give up. Do not wait for Britain or France, do not wait for the League. Ethiopia is still ours, Kidane. Fight.*

Kidane's chest aches. It is difficult to hold himself straight. Every part of him wants to curl into the gaping hole this new devastation has left behind: the emperor has deserted his people; he has gone to England and left them to fight or surrender alone. And his order to Kidane is to settle his camp permanently in the mountains surrounding Debark. He is to help protect this territory while the emperor gathers weapons and assistance from abroad and finds a way to oust these Italians. He is not to let Carlo Fucelli get a foothold in this area the Italians claim they already control. Fight and persevere. Have faith and rise toward battle.

This is the order left behind by Haile Selassie, and this is what it contains: the assumption of obedience and loyalty at any cost. Kidane stares at Hirut looking up and smiling at something Aklilu has said. She is still in the early sweep of womanhood. She is still untouched, still pliable, only a little older than Aster when he married her. For the first time, he sees the emperor's order for what it really is: a command from a man who has a son to one who does not. These are hasty instructions from a man who has a place to go to one who has left everything behind. A series of directives, hurled from the long echoing halls of European buildings, from a man who still claims his birthright to one who cannot even claim a child in his name. And Kidane understands that this is how a disappearance begins: with an order to move toward danger then continue on toward oblivion.

Chorus

Go back. Open the bedroom door and send young Aster down the stairs. Place the groom on his feet and draw him away from the bed. Wipe the sheet clean of the bride's blood. Shake it straight and flatten its wrinkles. Slide off that necklace and return it to the girl as she races to her mother. Fix what has been broken in her, mend it shut again. Clothe him in his wedding finery. Let there be no light. Allow only shadows into this kingdom of man's making. See him alone in the room. See him free of a father's attention. See him step beyond the reach of elders and all who advise growing boys on the perils of weakness. Here is Kidane, shaking loose of unseen bindings. Here he is, gifting himself the freedom to tremble. All advice has been taken back and he is no longer the groom instructed to break flesh and draw blood and bring a girl to earthy cries.

See this man in the tender moment before he takes his wife. See him wrestle with the first blooms of untapped emotion. Let the minutes stretch. Remove the expectations of a father. Remove the admonishments to stand tall and stay strong. Eliminate the birthright, the privilege of nobility, the weight of ancestors and blood. Erase his father's name and that of his grandfather's father and that of the long line of men before them. Let him stand in the middle of that empty bedroom in his wedding tunic and trousers, in his gilded cape and gold ring, and then disappear his name, too. Make of him nothing and see what emerges willingly, without taint of duty or fear.

WHEN HIRUT AND Aklilu get back to the campfire, they pause, surprised by the exuberant scene in front of them. Men and women have formed a large circle and are dancing near the women's camp, a spontaneous celebration after Kidane's announcement that they will wage war against the Italians from here. They will not march into other territory. They will fight on familiar ground. The women leap, their figures caught in pale moonlight, illumined by the glowing campfire. Hirut puts a hand to her chest, made unsteady by this unexpected pleasure, her headache disappearing. Aklilu smiles down at her, then tugs her into the circle of dancers. He steps in front of her and settles his hands on his waist, and nods as Minim's *masinqo* starts beating out a gentle melody that is getting faster. Aklilu leans toward her and for a moment, she is breathless, captivated by his agility and the wide grin. He shakes his shoulders, the first moves of an expert *eskesta* dancer, then beckons her with his eyes to follow suit. Hirut steps forward, her chest near him, and lets herself go free, lets her shoulders move of their own accord, lets them shiver as if the weight of bones and blood did not exist. They dance, each leaping high, then higher, their bodies shivering and caught in the surge of cheers and shouts. Minim nods to her and begins to sing of the great warrior Aklilu and the woman who conquered his heart, and the two who move together to fight for mother Ethiopia.

A burst of ululations rises up as the singer's voice climbs, trembling with emotion, his pitch high and sweet. Hirut blinks back the tears to get a better look at those who have gathered around her, and encourage them on. This is happiness, she thinks, this is what it means to be free. As she dances with Aklilu, her rhythm bending his, his propelling her faster, she feels the tears climb into her eyes, and then she does not care when they roll down her cheek as she begins to sing and Aklilu sees and nods and smiles gently at her and draws closer. She leaps, her heart pounds erratically, her legs stay firm and strong. Only once, she searches for Aster but cannot see her, so Hirut loses herself in the group, dancing and cheering and singing beneath the thick beam of light filtering through the trees. This is where all the light in the world has settled, she thinks. This is where it has been while she was struggling in such darkness.

Aklilu throws his head back and laughs, nudging his chin toward Seifu, drawing him forward, jumping so high in front of the other man that the others pause and gape, and start to shout. Hirut steps back and gives Seifu room, and together they watch Aklilu. He is soaring, shoulders moving with the breathtaking speed of the greatest dancers, a body defying its own construction. Seifu cheers, thrilled by the dazzling display, the joy shifting his features, revealing his handsome smile. He waves his gun and lifts his arms, and his son, Tariku, darts into the circle next to his father. Tariku's mother, Marta, steps next to them and begins to dance. They are reflections of each other, one a younger version of his parents. Seifu mimes swift, cutting motions with his knife and Tariku mimics tilting the blade to gleam in moonlight. The crowd roars, the *azmari* launches into a new verse about twin lions roaming the fields in search of Italians. Hirut clasps her hands to her chest and lets the laughter loose. She begins to dance again, drawn into the center of the music and movement, her heart tumbling without reserve. They dance with abandon, finding ways to combine the body's awful capabilities into a fluid, unbroken rhythm.

Chorus

But you will feel a watchful presence even as you lie down to end the day. This is why you will tuck yourself into your blanket and clutch your hands as you try to fall asleep. You will pray a thousand prayers that you will count, one by one. You will pretend not to hear him when he approaches. You will close your eyes and clamp your mouth when he bends low. You will stiffen as he takes your shoulder and tugs to lead you away. You will not answer to your name. You will look up instead and say, Please. You will say, I am not a slave. You will say, I am Getey's daughter. You will say, I am the daughter of Fasil. You will say, again, because you do not think he heard the first time, Please. And you will say it until the word becomes a wall that you build around yourself as you are pulled out of your bed and into the blackest night of your life.

I know how he will do it. I know how he will say it. I know why Hirut will shut her eyes when she enters that terrifying sinkhole. She will imagine she can forget what she does not see, that all disappears when sunlight punctures the night. Hirut. I know that she will hear her name but she will not answer. She, too, will crouch and take shelter in her own arms and curse the powers that gave her to this fate. She will push her back against a wall and still hear that voice tap against her chest. He will tell her to say his name. He, a favored son of Ethiopia. She, no more than a space for him to fill. He will order her to hold him and mimic emotions she does not feel. He will forget what he breeds will burn forever, a hatred as pure as water, bendable and swift, small enough to fit into the tiniest crevices of a shrinking life.

VOICE III:

O blessed daughter, you who spin in slow circles. You who spread your arms and lift your face and follow the spiraling sway of the Earth. How long will you keep pace with its momentum? How long before you see that there is nowhere else to go? There is no escape but what you make on your own. Do not heed the other voices: Let it be, they will whisper. Who are you to resist, they will say. He is our leader, they will contend. Leave us to sleep, they will add. Let Aster be on this cursed night. Leave her to stumble on the narrow paths of her own making, cursing her husband's name. Daughter, you who think you are helpless and alone in your distress, stand in the fields and fight. Beg no more for mercy.

Chorus

Become the soldier you were meant to be. Arise, Hirut.

KIDANE IS ETCHED IN THE SAME HARD LIGHT THAT COATS THE ROCKY path between them.

He extends his arm in her direction and beckons. This is the move that begins the theft. It is this gesture that seals the night. The hand that stretches forth also violates a natural order. This is why Hirut shivers: she has just glimpsed what lurks in the newly ushered dark.

Hirut, come. Kidane makes of himself a looming figure, a hazy nightmare forming bones.

Hirut closes her eyes and wraps her arms around her knees. She holds herself tight, then she waits, a quaking figure pretending to sleep while listening to a man speak her name.

Hirut. He has found a level between silence and whisper, a tone that makes the distance between them shrink.

Hirut stares into the mouth of the forest. There are hours left in this night, so many unlit paths that lead only to greater darkness.

Little One, let's go.

Something is bending her toward obedience as if she were born only to serve.

I'm not going to make it through this war, he adds. I'm going to die. Do you understand what I'm saying?

There is a long, pregnant silence that stretches between them, a vast land that opens and she is sinking, helpless to stop the downward momentum.

Little One, you don't understand but you'll see. Get up.

When he says her name again, it comes to her as a warm, thick breath against the side of her face. It is a new obscenity crawling over her skin. He reaches for her arms and she looks up into the dark well of his eyes. It takes one minute, two minutes, three minutes for her to form the thought that they are face-to-face in an intimacy that makes her recoil but: a body capable of dying in war is also capable of injury, and what she knows of the body is its tender places, those areas incapable of complete protection, and of the many things Dawit has taught her, it is this that is her most important lesson: that men, too, can bleed in many ways. So when Hirut rams her forehead against Kidane's, she is just testing a theory, uncertain and unsure of what she is doing.

Wujigra, she whispers.

And when he blinks, surprised, but does not move away, she does it again with the force of a stone sprung loose of its slingshot. She hits Kidane's forehead with her own so hard, with such quickness and precision, that her ears ache from the deadening crunch. The impact shoots bright sparks behind her eyes and blinds her momentarily and she flounders in dizziness while he sinks against her for balance. Then Hirut, newly heroic and still afraid, finds her center, pushes him off, and stands to run.

That there is no sound is a fact she will remember only later. What she notes is the way night molds itself around her like a shield. She picks up speed and fills her chest with air and the darkness, too, moves aside and lets her go unhindered. Hirut sees the faintest of lights in the horizon, tucked into the trees, and she thinks: beacon, hope, shelter. She thinks: safety. She believes she will make it because she has left servitude behind and made of herself a weapon, like a bullet released and searching for its bloody rest. But he catches her by the legs and throws her down. Then he flips her over and flattens himself on top of her and even then, Hirut cannot grasp what is happening. She cannot understand why she is not still moving toward shelter. When Kidane pulls himself higher and pushes his groin into the space between her flailing legs, Hirut keeps searching the hills for that light.

And before Hirut can grasp what is happening, Kidane takes both her hands and holds them above her head and promises: Stop, stop, I'm not going to hurt you.

They are a great shifting mass draped in dull light, a thing both grotesque and familiar, made beastly by a girl's dazed anguish.

You have to knock a goat senseless so you can kill it, the cook once said to her. Slap your hand across its nose, hit that place just between the eyes. Hold it by the neck then throw it to its knees, it'll have no choice but obedience.

Hirut kicks and yanks and bites until she scrambles to her feet. She is so busy looking for her mother and the cook that she does not sense the hands flinging her back on the ground. Instead, she believes the sudden flight is proof of miraculous ascent. She imagines the separation between her feet and the earth as evidence of a greater feat. And as she rises in the air, held in a relentless man's grip, Hirut thinks of those men who turn into hyenas, she thinks of angels disguised as men, she thinks of Kidus Giorgis and his dragon-slaying sword and the saint's horse lifting its hooves to vanquish evil. Even when the ground rushes up to meet her back and Kidane's face looms above hers, Hirut still imagines flight. Soon, she will have to admit what is happening, but for now, her mind gifts her a small mercy: it leads her back into the cave where Dawit lies, his leg healed, the bandages off, his breaths back to normal. He extends her Wujigra and nods for her to take it. In the corner, Beniam holds his arms out for a warm embrace. O brave soldier, they say to her, past the ringing in her ears, past the cushion of blessed silence: Go ahead and shoot, make us proud.

Aster shouts into the night, a voice curdling with hatred and agony.

Hirut slides into herself again: the soft flesh, the slender bones, the tender crevices, and then she is just a girl struggling against oblivion. She says her mother's name, Getey, Getey, as he starts to move against her.

I tried to help Getey, Kidane says. It's because of me she could marry your father. I gave her that hut you lived in. I wouldn't let anyone take it. It's yours when we go back. Stop fighting, please.

Remember this on the day you die. Remember this and know why I killed you, Hirut says.

It is because some part of her still remains intact that Hirut is capable of speaking so boldly. It is because she has not yet been forcibly split that she is loud enough for the entire camp to hear. Because she is still whole, she is still sure of miracles, and this leaves no room to track the path of his hands. She numbs herself to the pressure of his pelvis while cursing the air he breathes. She grows deaf to his rapid sighs. She cannot hear Aster unleashing her husband's name in total and complete abandon. Nor can she imagine that Aklilu stands on the plateau above them, rigid with fury. Instead, she feels Kidane pause and believes, in that fleeting moment, in the power of her hatred.

Then Kidane spreads her legs with his knees and she watches her own spirit stand from her stained body, and walk away.

A BLACKBIRD PARTS the folds of darkness and flies against the sun. The soft lilt of women's voices tumbles down the hill. The tang of fresh injera coats the air above her head, and in the trampled grass at her feet, a mouse scurries from the frozen figure lying in its way. Hirut blinks, unsure of where she is and how she has come to be there. A light wind swirls dust across her face as she sits up and tries to move her legs. They are leaden, strange objects pinned to the earth. She tries again and fails, and tries again. She looks down. There is nothing to stop her from getting to her feet and walking away. There is no reason she cannot stand.

Let me help you. Aklilu stands off to the side and holds out a blanket and her Wujigra. I got it back for you, he says. He sets them down next to her and kneels, his eyes full of concern.

She turns her head. I'm fine.

I put food by the tree over there. He gazes into her eyes without embarrassment or judgment. I'm not leaving until you're on your feet, he says.

She has to bite her lip. To move will unravel her calm and throw her into shame. To give in to the shame will mean tears, and if she begins to cry, she will never be able to stop.

I'm okay, she says.

He shakes his head. I'll help you stand. We're moving out of here after we eat. And look, you finally have your gun. Aklilu looks down at her. There's no choice. Aster's waiting for you, you have to be strong.

She sent you?

No one sent me. He holds her gaze. I wanted to be here when you woke up.

Above her, the morning fog creeps low in the horizon. A cool band of wind lifts itself from the mountains and slides down to meet the shivering trees. What has changed is what is here, this girl struggling to flex her legs to move them. Over Aklilu's shoulder, a gray bird hops and pecks at the ground.

I can't move, she finally says, alarmed. She has taken it all for granted, she thinks. She once simply willed herself to enter rooms and climbs hills and wade into rivers and it was so. She once believed she belonged to herself.

Aklilu drapes the blanket over her and slips his arms beneath her armpits.

Hirut feels herself pulled upright. Balancing on unsteady legs, she squints into the dawning sky and swallows the tears that form a knot in the center of her chest. Aklilu hands her the rifle and she takes it, tracing the familiar lines her father made.

Can you walk?

She nods, made dizzy and ungainly by what is newly missing.

He wraps the edge of the blanket around her wrist and leads her to the tree, where an *agelgil* with food awaits.

Hirut shuffles behind him, staring at his hand, grateful for the material that guards her skin against human touch. She cannot think yet about this gesture. She is aware only of the compassion in the act. She does not question how he knows to turn his back and leave her be while he prepares a bite of injera. She does not ask how it is that he waits until she swallows her sobs before he turns around. He feeds her as if he is giving her *gursha*, as if this were a festive meal and his assistance were an act of affection and not pity. She eats the mouthful of food instinctively, guided by Aklilu's instructions to chew it all, and don't think about it, and you need your strength, and you must be brave, and I'll help you, and I'll watch over you, and eat, one more bite, do this one and we're done. He feeds her the *gursha* as if he is a host insisting a guest take one more bite because her presence is an honor, and she is loved.

KIDANE READS THE MESSAGE FROM FERRES: CARLO FUCELLI IS GOING to construct a new prison in the cliffs of Debark, it will not be built to hold prisoners and keep them alive, it will mimic the most deadly prison camps he commanded in Libya, move closer to him, do not let him start, destroy everything he does, the real war has just begun. Kidane tries to focus but there are bite marks on his hands and wrists. His neck stings from scratches that trail up to the small bruise in the center of his forehead. All he can think as he slips the note into his pocket is that it should not have happened as it did. Tired, he rubs his eyes then quickly drops his hands. Her smell sticks to his skin and drifts into his nose every time he moves. It is an assault. He has not been able to eat without that acrid scent drifting up and into his mouth. Every bite of dabo this morning reeked of old wood and rancid butter, of fright and youth.

Aklilu is waiting quietly outside of his tent for the day's instructions. The rest of his men are gathering their belongings and packing supplies onto donkeys. They have been working without their normal banter. No one has appeared from the women's camp to distribute the rest of the day's rations. Aster has not made her normal entry to inquire about new developments and new plans. A heavy pall has settled over his camp and the unease is another layer draped over the intensifying heat.

Should I come back later, Dejazmach?

Aklilu sounds tense, despite the politeness. Kidane knows the young man well enough to know he has not had his morning coffee or bread yet. He will wait until they are done arranging supplies and his men have finished their meal before he allows himself any food.

Stay there, Kidane says. He has to speak so the cut at the corner of his mouth doesn't bleed. I need two men to do some surveillance, he adds. Bring them here. Tell the camp we'll be moving higher into the hills, the march won't be as long. Tell the guards to secure the trail.

Seifu's been sending Tariku on scouts already, Aklilu says. He's good with surveillance.

Get Tariku and anyone else, Kidane says. Just do it. He reads the message from Ferres again.

No one has discovered that Ferres is a stunningly beautiful woman named Fifi, once known as Faven. Not even the emperor's best spies have managed to find out where she is located. Her messages come from nearly every corner of the country, and they are distributed to runners by her brother, Biruk, a blind weaver who travels from mercato to mercato selling his wares. The rumors say Biruk has never even heard this elusive Ferres's voice himself. The rumors contend that the weaver simply passes along written messages, all of them in a tight, neat script, every character of the *fidel* precise. The rumors hint that Ferres is an Italian, an officer of aristocratic blood with deep empathy for Ethiopia. They do not imagine that Ferres is a woman who provides special services for only the richest Italian men at an astonishing price. No one will ever know that once, before she was Ferres, Fifi also brought Kidane comfort and small joys in private moments.

Kidane wipes down the hem of his tunic and his trousers. He is dusty and disheveled. His hair clumps around his head. His eyes burn and they are surely bloodshot. Aklilu's sharp eye would not miss any of this.

And Worku? He needs to eat, Dejazmach.

On any other day, Aklilu would have obeyed in silence. This morning, he can't stop asking questions.

I said feed him! Kidane's voice trembles and he folds his arms across his chest to calm down, grateful for the shelter of his tent. He looks again at the scars on his hands. After it was done, he had let the girl go and sat beside her, prepared to comfort her, but she didn't cry. Instead, she scrambled away without a noise, pulling down the bottom of her dress as she flung herself into the night. She vanished without giving him a chance to let her know that he meant no cruelty. Kidane wipes his face and straightens. He holds himself tall, and gets ready to step out to meet his men.

Seifu and Tariku are molded from the same bones.

Tariku nods eagerly. I can do it, Dejazmach Kidane, he says. I've been a lookout for months. I even go by myself and check things sometimes. Tariku grins shyly at his father. I don't always tell him, he adds.

Seifu pulls his son into an embrace, beaming with such pure pride that Kidane smiles. On another day, he might have been jealous, but today there is a small sense of hope.

We're not sending you alone, Kidane says. He nods to the older man standing off to the side, his bright eyes blazing with focused intensity. He has not stopped looking up into the hills since the men approached Kidane's tent.

They're heading toward the cliffs, Seifu says.

Tariku nods. I saw some trucks with lumber yesterday, armed laborers too.

There's nothing there, Kidane says almost to himself. And as soon as he says it, he knows Ferres was right: that is where the new prison will be. We need to find exactly where they're starting construction. Stay away from the soldiers, look for the laborers, find their ammunition stacks and weapons. Be careful.

Never forget that they could be watching you, Seifu says. The worry is clear in his face.

Tariku grips his father's hand tightly. I've done this before, Abbaba, he says, pushing his long hair out of his eyes. He sports the outgrown curls of the *arbegnoch* and the length has become difficult to keep under control. On Tariku, the effect is a tall bloom of vivid black hair, like his father's. When he squints, he is made more frightening by the undiluted determination of youth.

Seifu settles a hand on Tariku's head. I told you to pull this back, he says. I'll braid it.

Tariku slides out from his hold. I like it like this, like all the fighters.

It's dangerous, Kidane says. They'll see it from a distance. It's good for the battlefield but not on this mission. Your father will braid it.

Tariku looks between Kidane and his father, momentarily shaken. Seifu pats his back and drapes his arm protectively around his shoulders and when they look at Kidane, comforted by each other's presence, Kidane sees everything he might never have.

⸺

HIRUT STEPS INTO the back of the line between the supplies and donkeys and the men serving as the rear guard. She can sense the way heads swivel as she gets into place. She focuses ahead, toward the front, where Aster and Nardos walk so close together they could be linking arms. None of the women have tried to speak to her since Kidane came for her. She has been left alone to get her belongings, pack bandages and powders, and find her own place in the march. She slips in line with the other servants, with the crates and pack animals and water gourds, with those objects other people need in order to survive. She is, she tells herself, where she belongs.

The woman in front of her turns around. She is a stranger whom Hirut has not seen before, one of the new recruits pushed out of a nearby village. You know, the woman says, I heard Aster didn't even go to his tent this morning. Nothing, not one word. A smile plays across the woman's lips before she grows serious. Now you just have to hope he doesn't get bored.

Hirut stays quiet, confused.

Anyway, the woman says, better him than a poor man.

Hirut speeds up until she finds a space in the line between two women. They look at her blankly, then keep going. She clutches her basket tighter and adjusts the Wujigra against her back. Instinctively, she looks for Aklilu, then moves farther up in line. New murmurs and stares pave her way. Hirut stares at her feet, careful not to trip over those in front. For several minutes, all shifts back to the normal boredom of a march. But then Aster spins around and the line stops abruptly. The women part as Aster strides toward her. She is wearing Kidane's old tunic and jodhpurs, the cape sags across her tight shoulders.

Enough of this, Aster shouts. I hear all of you talking. It's her fault. She points at Hirut. Hers.

Hirut stands alone in a growing circle of whispers and soft laughter. Then they are face-to-face. There are deep shadows beneath Aster's eyes. A vein thickens in the middle of her forehead. She has not slept either.

He's my husband. Do you understand? I know him better than anyone, Aster says. She is smoothing her tunic, flattening the wrinkles and arranging the folds. It is one of the signs of agitation that Hirut has learned to recognize. It is what Aster does when she tries to calm herself.

Between them in the quiet drops the whistle of curious birds, the caw of a distant raven, a donkey's tired bray.

So now you have your broken rifle and you think you can do anything. Aster grabs Hirut by the shoulders and shakes her hard, her voice made more frightening for how soft it is. I've seen the way you look at him.

Behind Aster, all the other women have stopped to stare. Nardos has come to stand closer, her arms helplessly at her sides. Hirut steps back and lets her basket go slack in her arms. Her rifle slides down against her arm. Thick shafts of sunlight spill onto the tops of trees, shining like gauze over Aster, deepening the delicate lines around the woman's mouth.

I'll kill him, Hirut says softly. Though her voice is steady, the words deflate her. She is speaking against a current.

The problem is you think you're the only one, Aster says quietly. You don't know how common you are. Then she wipes her eyes with the back of her hand. If you do anything to hurt my husband, I will kill you myself.

She turns her back to Hirut and pulls Nardos along, and the march begins again.

THERE ARE FOUR GUARDS LEADING THE SURVIVING ETHIOPIAN TO him, four grown men struggling to restrain a wily, rebellious captive who seems to believe he can escape though his compatriot was executed on the spot. Carlo takes another sip of his coffee as he watches the guards make their way up the short incline that separates the camp from this higher plateau. He has ordered his men to appear at the thick-rooted tree that stands at the edge of a footpath his workers will soon make into a road. It is a flat stretch of land at the top of the mountain they have secured as their own. Across the field, two tall boulders loom above a dizzying drop. Farther away gleams a patch of smooth ground he has had his men clear of stones for his new prison.

Carlo slips his binoculars around his neck and slides his sunglasses onto the top of his head, feeling a surge of pride. He checks the buttons on his shirt and wipes the dust off his boots. He feels for his pistol. There is one thing he has learned in Ethiopia: capturing an Abyssinian is never about capturing an Abyssinian: where there is one, there are two. Where there are two, there are multitudes. That he sees nothing in the hills is not proof they are not there.

Someone tell Navarra to meet us at the tree, Carlo says. Tell him the colonel needs him again. He smiles, thinking of this *soldato*, an earnest young Venetian who has come into his army with a camera. Then he motions the guards forward. This way, he says. And get Ibrahim, he throws over his shoulder.

The Ethiopian pulls against the ropes. He is younger than Carlo expects but old enough to be dangerous. He makes a handsome figure in his braids and white tunic: a Grecian statue from an ancient time. Dark marble sculpted by an expert hand. He has been beaten severely, but no bones have been broken, there are no stab wounds that Carlo can see. Only his swollen eye and bruised jaw speak to what the encounter with his men must have been like. He smiles as Ibrahim appears with the rest of the *ascari* and a rope. His *soldati* are moving quickly to get into formation. Navarra is jogging to get to his place beside him, his camera dangling from his neck. Carlo takes a deep breath. And so this begins.

Ibrahim salutes. The supply truck is coming soon, sir, he says. Your guest is also on her way.

The prisoner looks between the two of them, no longer struggling. His sharp eyes are moving from the rope to Carlo's face to the tree and then to Ibrahim. The young man swallows, and drops his head. He grows so still that the guards step closer to him, hold his arms tighter, suddenly more alert.

I'm ready, Colonel Fucelli. Ettore Navarra walks hurriedly to the tree, his camera already strapped over his shoulder, a fresh roll of film in his hand. Then he stops short, held breathless by the rope in Ibrahim's grip.

Carlo takes his time: the prisoner has a striking face with angular cheekbones and penetrating eyes. He stares at Carlo with the bristling, unpredictable air of a cornered boxer, a fighter ready to confront the final blow. Carlo steps close to the prisoner and pulls his sunglasses over his eyes. He stares, relishing the young man's discomfort and confusion; the prisoner is expecting noise and violence, he is not sure what to do with this silent, close scrutiny.

Navarra, Carlo says. You've been learning some Amharic with the *ascari*, practice your lessons, ask him what his name is. Remember what I told you, if you can't speak to them, you can't govern them.

Ettore Navarra has the air of a man just roused from sleep. He takes a deep breath, looks the captive over, then asks in Amharic, then Italian: What's your name? *Simih man new? Come ti chiami?*

Anbessa, the younger prisoner says without hesitation.

Anbessa, Ibrahim repeats. It means "lion." He might be part of the rebel group that calls themselves the Black Lion Resistance, he adds.

Carlo turns back to the prisoner. There is a deep gash on the side of his head. And still, he thinks this machismo will work. It's a pity, he says to Ibrahim. Some of them would make good *ascari*, wouldn't they?

The prisoner turns to Ibrahim and spits at the ground, saying a word that Carlo understands to mean "traitor." Or perhaps it means "slave." It is a common refrain amongst the Ethiopians when they see the *ascari*.

Well, let's get this over with, *fascisti*, Carlo says. Rome says the war is over, but we know better. This is why we're doing things my way, my rules. I'll show you how to win, really win, this war. He takes the rope from Ibrahim and settles it in his open palm. He pretends to weigh it, reveling in the prisoner's growing fear, then he flings it over a sturdy branch and watches it spin and drape down to the tall pile of extra rope on the ground. It is long, thick enough to hold a man, pliable enough to be knotted tightly and cinched around a slender neck. Carlo smiles as Ettore slides in to snap a photo then ducks out of the way. Nearby, the *soldati* and *ascari* wait, tense and silent. The dangling rope hangs in front of them all like a curious and skinny spectator.

When Navarra is done, Carlo resumes his stern expression. What you see is a thwarted ambush, Carlo says to his men. This means there's a whole unit somewhere nearby, he adds. If we let him go, we're inviting chaos. This is the stopgap. How much of this language of theirs have you picked up, Navarra? Carlo says to him. You walk around and talk to the natives when you photograph them?

I try, sir, but it's hard.

The Ethiopian is known for his reserve, do you know that?

They tend to be somewhat shy, Navarra says.

Blood drips from the cut on the prisoner's head and seeps into the shoulder of his shirt, spreading into a stain that looks like an insignia. He is shivering but trying not to show it. Navarra keeps looking at him, and the Ethiopian returns Navarra's stare and Carlo realizes that he is bleeding because part of one ear has been cut off. A warm sensation rises in Carlo's stomach.

Carlo nods to Ibrahim. Let's get started, he says.

Ibrahim and the guards push the prisoner to the rope. The Abyssinian's white clothing is a nice contrast to his men's uniforms. His injuries and that braided hair will be a subtle detail to draw the eye toward the savagery of these people. Navarra will make a tableau vivant, accented by bruises and blood, full of promise of what's to come. Carlo takes out his pistol and holds it in his hand.

The younger prisoner grasps audibly.

Do you know how to control these people, Navarra? Carlo asks. The clothes are an important clue, *soldato*, Carlo says. They don't care about dying, we've seen this in battle. They make themselves into targets, they think we'll eventually give up.

The younger captive throws back his head to emit an extended shout, his voice echoing and multiplying. Then he releases his full weight against the guards holding him, throwing them off balance. He yanks down on their arms as they stumble forward, then he raises his feet off the ground, and they are a tangle of bone and muscle, of desperation and confusion, of fear and obedience. They tumble toward Carlo.

Carlo jumps back, unnerved, and sweeps his pistol in front of him. He takes perfect aim at the prisoner's chest, his finger already on the trigger, his mouth open to give the order to shoot, sweat drenching the back of his neck.

Colonello! Ibrahim shakes his head.

Carlo takes a breath and steps back slowly, his grip still tight on the gun. It happened so fast, the reflex motivated by that old attack in Benghazi that left him with a knife scar in his chest. It is a terror that Carlo knows will never leave him. He smiles to ease the tension. You know what to do, Carlo says to Ibrahim, thankful for his presence of mind. It was Ibrahim's quick thinking that saved him in Benghazi, his unwavering loyalty in the face of dangerous intruders. This, Carlo will also never forget.

Ibrahim slips the rope around the prisoner's neck. The Ethiopian clamps his mouth shut, lifts his chin, and starts to breathe heavily through his nose. His chest contracts and expands rapidly. In his eyes, there is a frantic light, a surge of panic that is swallowing him up as Ibrahim makes a knot, working meticulously and quickly.

A soft, tender spray of sun filters through the leaves to fall across the prisoner's shoulders. The prisoner is younger than he first appeared. A young man still testing his courage.

A cry erupts from the *ascari*: *Una spia abissina!* An Abyssinian spy! They scream it like an oath. *Un abissino!* An Abyssinian! He's here to kill us!

Ettore braces himself against the noise and anger. He has managed to maintain a calm façade. It is getting harder to keep it up. In the cloudless light, the prisoner's stark terror lures the *soldati* closer to the spectacle. There is Mario, pushing through the crowd to get to the front. Fofi follows at his heels, mesmerized, his cheeks flushed. Giulio moves cautiously, his jaw clenched.

Colonel Carlo Fucelli pats down his face with a handkerchief before slipping it into his pocket. Navarra, take the picture now, the colonel says.

As if on cue, the prisoner shouts, his voice a surprising deep boom that ricochets across the hills. Ettore flinches, certain that he has just heard the unmistakable Amharic word for "Father": Abbaba.

Picture, Fucelli says. These boys won't wait long. He twists his mouth into a sardonic smile and folds his arms across his chest, pleased.

Ettore snaps the photo, aware that the prisoner is not looking at the camera. He is staring with derision at the shifting mass of men in uniform calling for his death.

Without warning, Fucelli thrusts his fist in the air. *Ragazzi*, he shouts. Forty years after Adua, the sons of the brave are back! He speaks louder. For times like this, *soldati*, Italiani, *bravi fascisti*, for times exactly like this, is why you are here!

Fucelli's eyes blaze with pride. This must be witnessed, he says to Ettore. He waits for a picture before slipping his pistol back into his holster. Fucelli takes the rope. Ibrahim, you have the stool? Carlo balances his cigarette in the corner of his mouth as Ettore takes another photo.

The prisoner bares his teeth, and the words he whispers are heavy with loathing.

Translate, Navarra, Fucelli says. Let's see how good you are.

He said he's going to kill you. Ettore is surprised at how the words fall into place in his head. These were the first words he learned in Amharic: "Soldier. I kill."

A useless gesture, Carlo says quietly. The last words of a dying, brave peasant, and he wastes them on me. Enough pictures, let's move on.

➤

FATHER: WHEN A BODY lifts of its own accord. When it stretches heavenward and flings its head back to catch the sun. When the wind aids in its ascent, and the gods of Olympus bend to cup the rebellious flight and hold it still. When we who are strong are held captive by the glories of resurrection. When neither cold nor heat nor human stench can shift our eyes away. When dark-winged birds carry a name and settle it in that burdened tree. When a body remembers its eternal grace and moves against invisible currents. When it rises out of its beaten shell, and returns our gaze still furious and proud. It is a miracle, Father.

N OW HERE THEY ARE IN THE BAR THAT FUCELLI RESERVED FOR THEM, a tiny *tej bet* in the center of Debark, nothing more than a single room with a corrugated tin roof. A series of chairs and a large unsteady table balance on a dirt floor covered with lemongrass and frayed rugs. It is the end of a long day. The prisoner still hangs from the tree. Ettore's camera still dangles from his neck. Two exposed rolls of film still poke in his pocket against his leg. There is ample evidence that he is here, outside of Gondar, in this *tej bet* far from home, and yet he cannot erase the image of his father stepping into the bar, a stack of photographs gripped in his hand while looking for answers.

Ettore rubs his head. He has had several beers and the waitress is bringing more, but it is only his father's voice that he hears. The cramped bar pulses with the commanding energy of Leo Navarra and his accented voice, the one he uses at home when there is no restraint in what he can say, when every word that comes from his mouth is exactly what he intends:

But have you answered my question, my son? Do you know what you would see if you sat in a dark, windowless bar in the middle of an African city and a girl were to walk toward you with a bottle of beer? What would you see, Ettore, if you turned in your seat to observe Mario and the others beckoning this waitress who is moving toward them in her native dress and lowered eyes. Is the body in shadow or in light? Remember, son, you are not home. There is no poetry in this place. There is no honorable stare that happens between these walls. Son, you who are here in this bar crammed full of soldiers drilling this girl with their eyes while a young man hangs, what do you have to say? I say the eye will hold in itself the image of a luminous body better than that of a shadowed object. I say, Father, the eye has the power to keep what it sees, the eye is greedy, the eye will always seek and devour that illumined figure made visible by predatory light.

Fofi says, Did you see him? Did you see the way he was smiling even when I pointed my gun at him from the ground?

Fofi says, Did you see the way he tried to act tough and stare at me even after they tightened the rope?

Fofi says, Did you get a picture of me next to his feet, Ettore? Can we call you Foto?

Everyone laughs, Mario the loudest, and Ettore nods and he laughs and raises his camera and points it at Fofi and he says, I'm going to shoot you now, and it is funny, Father, it is a joke, and so we laugh and we spend that night around that table telling jokes and miming faces so we do not hear the fresh cries coming from the villagers, their voices a ripple extending from the horizon to the ends of the earth. Because Father, this is war. Is this war? Fofi asks as Mario buys him another beer. This is not even war, Giulio says, but he is not laughing. And Ettore orders another beer and they watch the waitress balancing the tray of beers while dodging hands, and when she comes to their table she glances at the camera and says, No photo, and Fofi laughs again and points at Ettore and says, No Foto, and they drink their beer while Giulio keeps standing up and going to the door and checking outside, and I was glad on that day, Father, I was happy.

——

WHEN THEY MEET years later in Alexandria, Ettore will tell famed Egyptian journalist Khairallah Ali that each step away from Debark at the end of the long, bloody war was a relief. He will stare at the notebook sitting between them in a crowded café near the port and shake his head and shudder at the thought of that young prisoner hoisted up by rope. Khairallah will lean forward and say, But you haven't really told me much, my friend, and he will pick up his pen and wait. Ettore will begin again and repeat what he has said for years: The Ethiopian prisoner was frightening and there was no other choice. He was intent on killing us though we meant no one any harm. This was an incident that could have gone badly, but it didn't. It was larger than just one prisoner or our unit or Fucelli. We had to quell a rebellion moving from Gojjam into Gondar. It would have led to an ambush. Khairallah isn't writing down any of what he is saying, so Ettore will pause then say quietly: The prisoner was terrifying, those eyes. Khairallah will stare at him for a moment and ask: Is it true what they say about Fucelli? Did he make you photograph the Ethiopian while he fired those shots to make sure he was dead? And Khairallah will sink the tip of his pen into paper and draw slow circles as he keeps his head down and asks, Or perhaps what I've heard is true, that it was you who fired those final shots?

Photo

He is a body suspended in the mean play of light. A figure deformed by obedient shadows. There he hangs in a beam of dying sun, held up by a tree bowing from his weight. See his head and its bloom of curly hair, the shorn ear that appears like a dip on a narrow jaw. What is plain to see: a neck arching horribly, the spine distended, a mother's son pinned against a ripe afternoon sky. Behind him, the valley shrinks from the eager eyes of uniformed men. And what are they, after all, but the other sons of other mothers, and he the glorious proof of their mechanized ambitions? What we see: a boy pulled into manhood, a soaring body held back by gravitational laws. See him stretch against that terrifying rope, note the legs that kick against the downward tug: behold the rebellious silhouette spinning in a burning sun. And there, see him, too, at the edge of the frame, the taker of this photograph, the thief of this moment, there he is, almost out of view, made visible in the shadow stretching toward the elevated feet, a dark figure of a man firmly in focus, the camera pointed toward that defamation.

ETTORE STARES UP AT THE HANGING BODY AS THE OTHER MEN CONtinue their revelries into the next morning at the fire pit, this time in Colonel Fucelli's presence. Ettore points the lens toward the body's head and chest, hoping to catch that faint threshold between what lives defiantly and what is waiting to die. The prisoner's bloated face is slack. The neck strains against the unnatural angle. Blood has dried from the fresh stab wounds in his chest. His bare feet splay, twitching gently in the bottomless bend of earth. In the wind, it appears that he is pivoting, trying to spiral into the sky. There is nothing ferocious about him, yet as Ettore kneels and takes another picture his heart hammers so loudly that he cannot hear what Fucelli is shouting to the men above the clashing tunes from their guitars and harmonicas.

In the near distance, a rumbling sound grows. A truck. The music in the camp quiets.

Ettore stands, pauses to listen, then hurries back to the camp and finds the men staring at a Fiat truck rattling up the pathway that clings to the side of the mountain. It moves at an unhurried pace, almost lazily, an odd intrusion puncturing the heady chaos. Fucelli pushes through the gawkers to stand in front. He sweeps a look over his shoulder, his eyes bright, a smile spreading across his face. He is flushed, almost beaming. Fucelli salutes the Fiat as it gets close. There are two people in the front seat. The *camionista* returns the greeting from the driver's side, one sunburned arm shooting out from the open window.

The driver parks close to the *soldati*. There is a native woman sitting in the passenger seat. She is staring at the tree in the distance, looking at the hanging prisoner. Her distress is clear even through the glare in the window.

Fifi, you're late, Fucelli says. He goes to open the passenger door.

Every man arches toward Fifi as she slides one long leg to the ground, then the other. She leans gracefully on Fucelli's arm as she steps out in black leather heels. She kisses Fucelli three times on the cheek in the traditional native way, but she does not bow to him as Ettore has seen native civilians do. Her even features, carefully accented by kohl and red lipstick, seem to measure him up, a private assessment that ends in a small smile and a nod. Then her eyes rake past the colonel, past the gawking men, to rest again on the dead body. She is intelligent and alert. Even from Ettore's distance, her startling beauty is obvious.

You've lost weight, Carlo, she says. Her voice carries without effort, melodious. There was an ambush in Azezo, she adds, everything's slowed down.

Fucelli smiles. You'll feed me, get me fatter, won't you? He slips her hand onto his arm and closes the door behind her. He pauses at the truck, letting the men gaze.

Her dress is a flattering cut that hugs her waist and drapes gently against her hips then flares slightly at her legs. It is tasteful and elegant, the dress of a woman who is confident of her beauty but feels no need to show more than she wants. The color is a deep and rich red, vibrant without being crude. It is expensively made, perhaps even tailored for her, and the V-neck shows off one of those large gold crosses the natives wear and that every Italian soldier knows he could never afford.

Madonna. A voice comes from somewhere in the group. Until now, they have been staring in silent awe.

Fucelli saunters across the field with her, gallant and proud. He is leading her to his tent, away from the tree, and she matches his stride easily. Her manicured hand wraps around his arm in a manner both possessive and casual. The morning sun lies warm across her face, brushing against her sloping cheekbones and pointed chin. She has large eyes so luminous she appears on the verge of tears. In the red dress, looking at them with those eyes, she seems too alive to be in this place, too much of everything. She is the most beautiful woman Ettore has ever seen.

Soldato, una foto, Fucelli says, motioning for him. He is smiling broadly.

They have their backs almost directly in front of the tree when Fucelli calls him, but the couple does not seem to notice. Ettore will have to angle to avoid the feet that will appear as if they dangle almost over Fucelli and Fifi's heads.

Fifi leans into Fucelli's shoulder seductively, her mouth curving without revealing teeth. The colonel stands stiffly, his bent arm like a ledge for her slender hand. Ettore adjusts his camera for lighting and focus but even then, he knows she is too bright for a simple photograph. She is better suited for oil paintings on the largest canvas.

On three, Ettore says. He counts aloud, and just when he gets ready to press the shutter release, Fucelli replaces his smile with a stern, narrow-eyed stare. When Ettore is done, he looks up from the camera to see that a small frown plays across Fifi's mouth. She is serious now, angry even.

What's going on? she asks. Who is that? She looks toward Ibrahim and the other *ascari*, then back at Fucelli. Then she turns to stare at the prisoner. Her hand flies to her heart, then to her forehead.

Fucelli tilts his head to one side. You came alone?

An extended look passes between them. It is a challenge, Ettore thinks, a test on Fucelli's part, perhaps. Fifi looks down at her dress and smooths the skirt. She is regaining her composure with difficulty.

My maid's in the truck, Fifi says. She waves and the *camionista* goes to the back of the truck to let the woman down.

Fifi's maid is her opposite. She is heavyset, with a small, round head wrapped in a scarf. She steps down from the truck with effort, then turns and jerks back at the sight of the tree. She shifts from side to side, the movement swaying the skirt of her long dress, flattening then ballooning across her generous figure. She drops a burlap satchel at her feet. She is nodding but she cannot take her eyes off the corpse.

Where's she come from? Fucelli is looking down at the woman suspiciously.

I found her at the market not long ago. Fifi goes to the woman and hands her the satchel and takes her arm. She cups her chin to draw her attention away from the tree. Her hold is gentle, affectionate. She's an excellent cook, Fifi adds as she brings the woman to Fucelli. If you want me to stay with you, I can't eat your pasta every day.

Fifi's Italian is perfect, educated, with hardly a trace of an African accent. She speaks it with astonishing fluency. The servant stares at Fucelli but she cannot help her eyes straying back to the tree.

Tell her to look at him all she wants, Fucelli says quietly. In case she has any ideas, tell her what I do to spies.

She's just a peasant, an old slave, Fifi says.

They train them all, no matter what they are, Fucelli says. Peasant, slave, farmer, nobility, whore. He smiles cruelly. I've had your tent set up. She's not staying with you, I'll get another for her.

Then the two of them head toward the colonel's tent, the servant following several paces behind, turning periodically to stare at the corpse then at the *ascari*.

The light wind picks up, swirling clouds of dust around Ettore's feet. A chill is settling in the air. It will be only a matter of hours before dark starts to creep in and the Ethiopians have a chance to exact their revenge.

THE PRISONER HANGS THERE ALL AFTERNOON, AND AS THE SUN SETS into the horizon, a rough wind begins to blow a hollow moan through the hills. Ettore feels for his knife and loads a new roll of film into his camera. Fucelli has told him to photograph the changing light against the tree, and he has been assured of his safety. There are extra guards posted on the road down the hill. Additional sentries are keeping watch for any signs of an ambush. Aside from the eight at the tree, there are four more stationed a few paces away, serving as reinforcements. They are darkening figures in a landscape pulsing with the colors of a dying light. Ettore leans against a log he dragged from the campfire site and crosses his legs. He feels the poke of the blank sheet of paper folded neatly in his pocket, ready for a letter to his parents once it gets too dark to photograph. He will try to ask about events at home while evading the likelihood of censorship. Not every letter gets checked but enough do. He must find a way to ask if it is true that there were pamphlets distributed across the country asking if Jews are really Italian, if Jewish shopkeepers in Tripoli are being forced to work on Saturday or submit to flogging. Is it true, he wants to ask, that even after Mamma donated her wedding ring to the state in the name of Italy and empire, they are telling her that she is not good enough? And Mamma, he would write, what does this mean if we have never been observant, if Papa and I believe in nothing but what is evident before us? What are we, if not Italian?

He works for as long as the light allows. He uses the tree as a backdrop. He positions it in the foreground. He moves to accent the slumped body, then blurs it behind a sharply etched helmet set on a stone as a prop. He moves so close to the corpse that only the stiff hands are in focus. Then he frames the body so the callused feet dominate the picture. As he continues, he shifts from discomfort and reluctance to a quiet and certain confidence: these are some of the best photographs he's ever made. He is sure of this, and for a brief moment, that knowledge is enough to help him ignore the guards who keep looking in his direction, puzzled by his careful attention. Later, a bright moon will help him complete another set of photographs.

He is startled out of his reverie by Colonel Fucelli easing his way up the short hill while lighting a cigarette. The colonel takes a deep drag and air unwinds out of him in a long, smoky thread. He waves as he approaches.

Did you see this? Colonel Fucelli takes out a folded telegram from his pocket. They're trying to separate the Italians and the natives even outside of the major cities? No more living with our women in the mountains? So I can't commingle with any native women or I'll go to jail? He laughs. Let them try. Fucelli looks down at him and nods when Ettore scrambles to his feet.

I heard something about that, sir, Ettore says. He wipes the dirt from his uniform. This was the news from Asmara, rumor confirmed as fact by truck drivers. Shiploads of Italian prostitutes were arriving in Massawa. There was also this: the drivers, resting before driving on, debated about the expulsion of all foreign Jews from Italy. One of them even shook a newspaper clipping in front of the gathered soldiers. All appropriate officials, the article said, must record the ethnic and religious identities of every political refugee arriving from Germany and other parts of Europe. *Un ebreo, una spia*, the driver had shouted.

The news from Italy isn't good either, Ettore adds. He stops.

Fucelli looks at the telegram.

As soon as a country builds an empire, he says, it has to decide who is who.

The colonel stares at him for an uncomfortably long time.

You didn't take communion when the priest was here.

No, sir.

You don't take part in Mass, you don't pray before meals. The colonel smiles when he sees Ettore's surprise. I pay attention, *soldato*, especially to those who are important to the mission. Both parents Jewish?

Ettore looks at him, stunned. I'm not a believer, he says. Neither are my parents. We're Jewish, yes, but we're Italian.

Everybody believes in something, *soldato*. And I don't care what Rome decides to do in Italy, Fucelli says, we're here to win a war and I know how to do it. They begin with these natives, then they come for us, other Italians. The colonel taps the ash from his burning cigarette. You'll have to be smart about this. We have to stick together.

The sentries are pacing near the tree, slender shapes treading across a growing night.

I've got good soldiers, Fucelli says, but what you do is something else. He sweeps his arms in a gesture that feels rehearsed. Romans left us their texts and paintings, their statues. We'll leave our photographs and reels. He puts a hand on Ettore's shoulder and squeezes. Fucelli looks at the tree, then at the guards in the short distance. Go back to your tent, Navarra, he says. No need to do any more here. I've got to talk to the guards, you get some rest.

—

FOOTSTEPS. SLENDER BRANCHES snapping. There is no other sound. Carlo sinks lower into the grass, still hidden by the dark and shrubbery. He watches through his binoculars as three Ethiopians stare up at the body hanging on the tree. They are strong, slender men illuminated by the cloudy moon that shrouds the rest of the area and keeps him safe. The guards have taken breaks as he ordered them to do. The extra sentries he has kept posted were given the night off. There is no sign that anyone else is aware of this intrusion. It is only Colonel Carlo Fucelli who dares to sit alone on this stretch of land while outnumbered by his enemies. Carlo presses himself farther to the ground, tugging his mind away from Libyan battlefields, and Benghazi horsemen and the Senussi warriors' cries that sent a chill through every officer from Cyrenaica to Fezzan and Tripolitania.

One of the Ethiopian men holds the feet of the corpse while another climbs on the shoulder of the third to cut the rope. The knife swipes through the air cleanly, the long silver blade glinting in momentary moonlight. The corpse sags stiffly into the arms of the man with the knife. An audible grunt punctures the silence as he balances the body precariously, clutching it as if holding a child while the one beneath them both is staggered by the added weight, wavering then steadying himself with the help of his companion. They work efficiently, noise- lessly, until the body is on the ground, the neck still in its awful stretch. They kneel around the corpse, two of them bowing their heads. The other runs his hands over the dead man's face, kisses his neck, and lays a head on the still chest as if listening for a heartbeat. Then he cradles the prisoner, rocking back and forth until an anguished groan soon turns into the sound of a grown man weeping.

THANK YOU, CARLO. THEY NEEDED TO BE ABLE TO BURY HIM, FIFI says, sitting on a stool next to his cot. Her arms hug her knees, her head is hidden in the crook of her arms.

This is the first thing she has said since she turned her back on him at the tree on her arrival and walked into his tent, disobeying their long-standing agreement that she would never step into his workspace without him. She is rocking back and forth, her knee tapping against his leg each time she moves. Carlo shifts away and looks down at her. She is dressed in her traditional clothes. Her hair is braided in the way of native women. Her lipstick and the dark kohl around her eyes have been wiped off. He can see the peasant girl she used to be: Faven from Gondar, the ravishing beauty of the northern highlands. The young woman who fled to Asmara to remake herself into a *shermuta*, a *wishima*, a whore: Fifi, the stunningly beautiful madam loved by some of the smartest, bravest Italian officers Italy has ever known.

Carlo unlaces his boots, exhaustion washing over him in a deep and heavy wave. He groans with relief as he flexes his feet, then looks up when something moves at the corner of his eye. Her attendant: hunched under a blanket outside his tent, the silhouette of her figure an unnerving, ghostly presence.

Tell her to go to her tent, he says. And why doesn't she talk?

I'm not safe here, Fifi finally says. This—this prisoner you hanged means there are Ethiopians waiting to ambush you. You know what they'd do to me if they caught me. She wraps her arms around the top of her head as if to shield herself from a blow. You're breaking the law by having me with you. A native woman with an Italian . . . I can't stay, Carlo.

The men are singing outside as he untucks his shirt, and the servant still sits like a blanketed hulk, listening to every word.

You'll be guarded, he says, dropping his voice. I'll give you your own security. And Rome is too far from here to make a difference. He takes off his socks and starts to undo the buttons on his shirt. He slips it off and folds it neatly, smoothing the sleeves and collar. He flips the socks inside out and shakes them loose of dirt, then turns them back and puts them on top of his shirt. He pulls off his undershirt and pats it flat then folds it too. He finds comfort in this nightly routine, even though the clothes are filthy. It's not safe to bathe or wash at the river, and his men are trapped in the camp until he can make sure he has cleared the area.

You don't know these *arbegnoch*, Fifi says.

Oh, I know them, he says. And they're rebels on Italian soil, not patriots. He stares at her, upright on the edge of his cot, his palms flat on his legs, dressed in nothing but his trousers.

She rises to her feet slowly, taking in his desk, the messy pile of papers, the stack of bullets, his binoculars.

They're building my office, he says. I'll be moving in there soon.

Letting them bury the body isn't going to stop an attack. It just delays them, Fifi says. Her face is drawn and serious, her eyes red-rimmed and swollen.

He leans back on his arms. Tell that woman to get away from here, and look at me when I'm talking.

Her movements are laborious, reluctant, as she turns. She speaks to the woman in a voice more affectionate than he's heard her use before.

The older woman responds with a question, the tone flat and hinting at disapproval.

Fifi smiles and nods, then says "yes" in Amharic with that typical

Ethiopian inflection that makes it sound less like a word and more like a sharp intake of air.

The cook struggles to her feet and walks away. Then Fifi faces him, fatigue drawing her mouth down again, her hands balled into fists at her side.

You have your bodyguards, I have her, she says.

Even without her kohl and lipstick, her beauty radiates, but just behind those lovely eyes are the thoughts that she keeps carefully hidden. He imagines them in the hundreds, thousands, all volatile pieces of information that could help him unlock the native mind.

I don't think she would be good for much. Carlo tilts his head back and laughs. What's her name again? And nothing happens here without my knowing, he adds. I can keep you safe. He lies back and folds his arms beneath his head. A faint light quivers through the canvas, a stray star, he thinks, or the extended reach of the moon, but it is no enemy signal for an attack.

She says to just call her the cook, Fifi says. She runs a hand over her face and lets it rest on her cheek as she glances outside. It is a gesture he's seen many times in native women, this momentary pause before the troubled sigh.

I don't understand.

Il cuoco, Fifi says. The cook. I know, it's strange. She says she was stolen as a child, brought to work for a family. She refused to give them her name. So she's the cook.

You're Faven and now you're Fifi, he says. Every other waitress across Eritrea and Ethiopia is called Mimi. What is it with your people and their names?

I can't stay here after what you've done, Carlo. She stands between his legs, a slow, practiced smile erasing the worry out of her eyes. She kicks his boots aside and dips her head. She kisses the tip of his nose, and then settles her soft mouth on top of his. They're going to attack, I'm sure of it.

You'll stay, he says, wrapping his arms around her waist. He buries his head against her stomach. I'll keep you safe, I'll make all the arrangements for a bodyguard you choose yourself.

And this useless law says I go to jail if they catch us, not you. Only Italian men. He grins. You're safe. I'll get ten *ascari* to watch over you.

She gives a short, quick laugh. *Ascari?* Who? Your faithful Ibrahim? He looks up into her face. He'll do as I say.

She brings her face close to his again and he can smell the cinnamon on her breath, the tea she likes to drink. I'm leaving, she repeats. She focuses on a spot near her feet, her mouth settled in that same frown she had when he walked in. One hand is in her hair, loosening the ends of her braids absentmindedly. The silence stretches and starts to tug at them, drawing him closer to her. I can't stay here, she says.

Maybe it is the way she hunches into herself as she sits next to him on the bed. Or the way her braids are in disarray. It might be the way she crosses her arms and places one hand over each shoulder as if cold and frightened at the same time. Or maybe it is the strange, bright moon seeping through the canvas and exposing every detail to the night. Carlo can't explain what it is that makes him put an arm around her and press her against him. He is not prone to these acts of tenderness, but he does it without thinking, guided by nothing but the gesture itself. He doesn't know what he would say if she asked him to explain the warm feeling rising in his chest when she lays her head against his shoulder then moves her face so they are cheek-to-cheek, and heat travels to his face and rests in the center of his head, and there are no other memories of a night before this one.

She gets up slowly and steps away from him and lifts her dress above her head and drops it behind her. She does this in silence, as if they have come to an understanding. As if he knows exactly what to do when a woman who has just disobeyed him sheds her dress and stands as still as a graceful tree rooted in calm waters. Carlo picks up the dress and holds it tight against his chest. He breathes in the scents of her, the earthy musk, the hint of sweet perfume, and his stomach twists. Only then does he look up.

Even after nearly a year, when he first met her in an officers' club in Asmara and decided he would accept any price for her time, he is still jarred by the sight of her, the glow of brown and gold playing on her skin. He wants to lower his eyes as if this is nothing special, as if he is angry, as if she does not stand there naked, her slender body shaved clean of any hair except what is on her head. He should do the smart thing and refuse her until she says aloud that she will stay. He knows what she is doing, but it has been weeks, months, since he has looked at another woman. He has avoided the native brothels and turned down the new Italian prostitutes sent from Rome. He has waved aside those immaculate and stunning Ethiopians and Eritreans and Somali and Sudanese and Egyptians in the officers' clubs between Massawa and Addis Ababa. He has waited for Fifi because there is no one else like her, no one else who behaves as if she is not rendering a service, but bestowing a favor. There is no one else who will sit all night and talk to him in an Italian that rivals his own. There is no one else who dares to argue about the finer details of payment as if it were a diplomatic endeavor. Yet beyond the face and the curves and the supple muscles, there is also this: that sharp intellect that masks much more than it reveals.

She speaks in her language, saying something to him in that soft way that sounds like a song. He tries to concentrate on the words that he is beginning to learn in Amharic. He picks out only one: "home," *beyt, casa.*

You've gone somewhere, she says, smiling. She draws tiny circles across the back of his head with the tip of a finger and moves down to his neck and slides her hand up to massage the tender place at the base of his skull.

The sensation is immediate and intense: he feels tension rolling off of him, spiraling out of his head, drawing out every thought except the woman in front of him. He slides to the ground on his knees and traces the long line of her waist. He reaches behind her to feel the dimples in the small of her back, then he cups her buttocks. Slowly, he slides a hand between her legs, then works his finger into her. He gives into the illusion that this woman stands in the center of his palm, under his control. He looks up. Her head is thrown back, soft moans push from her throat.

One of my men will always watch over you, he says. I need you here.

He closes his eyes and imagines her guiding him toward Addis Ababa, pointing to the horizon, warning him about the signs of a coming ambush. He imagines her beneath him, giving away codes and secrets in that way that makes her words indecipherable to all but him. He imagines climbing steps in Rome, in Venice, in Brescia, in Calabria, cheered by adoring crowds. He imagines the flash of cameras, the microphones, the newsreels emblazoned with his picture. As she moves against him and pushes him deeper, his head spins and tips him into delirium. Soon, he will fall into a state of stupefied euphoria, aware of nothing but the sound of her voice saying his name, open to anything, including ambush.

He braces himself and clears his head. You'll stay with me, he says. He gets to his feet abruptly and presses her down by her shoulders, rougher than he needs to be.

She falls to her knees in front of him with a surprised gasp. He grips her hair and tugs her head closer to his stomach, then lower; feels her lips, the warmth. And as he pushes into her mouth, Carlo begins to feel that rush, the familiar surge of will and strength and force that is his. Unable to stop himself, he gives in to the pleasure, engulfed by awe and adoration and the ecstasy of it all, until he is collapsing against her and tumbling forward onto the bed, moving together.

Hirut is tending to one of the injured when the camp falls silent. She turns. Seifu, Aklilu, and Hailu stagger up the hill bearing their awful burden. Marta walks beside Seifu, pressing Tariku's hand against her stomach. They are all bowed by grief and tiredness. And when Kidane and Aster rush toward them, insisting they relieve the parents of this task, Hirut sets down the basket, ready to help, trying to steel herself against fatigue. She has been working without break to tend to the wounded in Hailu's absence. She has spent two sleepless nights cleaning and wrapping bandages and mixing powders. She has witnessed the final breaths of those too frightened to let go of her hand. She has held those who could not bear the agony of their ailment. All of it has stripped her clean of emotion, pushed her deep into a pit of debilitating fatigue. But none of this has prepared her for an inconsolable mother pressing a dead hand against her womb.

Farther away, a bomb rattles against the horizon, breaking into the looming night. As the group carries Tariku past her to Seifu and Marta's cave, Hirut turns back to the wound she is dressing. She must finish this before she joins them. She tries to shake free of a wave of dizziness. As she applies a fresh bandage, she swallows air to hold off the gnawing hunger. Her exhaustion is stupefying, but she works mechanically, numbly. When she is done, she stumbles to the mourners and wraps an arm around Marta's shoulder. She murmurs a short prayer for Tariku, then releases Marta back into Seifu's embrace before picking her way toward her bed to collapse into sleep then start her work again.

—

HIRUT IS STARTLED AWAKE by a touch on her arm, then a hand on her back.

Then his voice: Little One, come.

Kidane tugs at her until she has no choice but to stand. Hirut reaches for her Wujigra but he kicks it away. He clamps a hand over her mouth and whispers into her ear: I'm not going to hurt you. Be quiet, Hirut. Be quiet, shut your mouth. Shut it.

So this is why she stumbles into the forest silently and empty-handed. He races ahead with her in tow, turning one way then another, throwing her off balance while she does her best to yank herself away. She cannot see through the dark confusion, through the shrubbery, through the leaves that slap at her face. He does not stop until they come to a pile of leaves. He spins her toward him then draws her close in an embrace.

Little One, he says. You're shaking. Why so scared?

She cannot speak. Words have no weight, there is no language sturdy enough to save her. There is nothing she can do.

I'm not going to hurt you.

He presses on her shoulders, the weight steadily getting heavier until her legs are forced to bend, and then she is made to sit on the ground and look up at him.

You're all right. His voice balloons in the nightmarish well. You're all right, stop crying, it's okay. He kneels in front of her and takes her hands. I'm not hurting you, see? He kisses each wrist then he pushes her backward until she is flat on the ground, and he settles on top of her.

Her dress rises up, above her knees. His breathing quickens. An owl pivots to turn away. And then there is no sound to convince her she has not died. This is why she looks at his tightening features and opens her mouth: because there is nothing else to do, there is nothing left to be done. Even language has made its escape and freed itself from her. She has no body, no heart, no tongue, no breath. Only a fire bubbling inside, trembling like a tightening fist, pushing against her throat, climbing into her head, stretching inside of her until there is no past. There is no future. There is no time that is not here. This is why Hirut takes his face in her hands, to hold something that is not hers. To twist something in her direction. This is why she presses her palms into the side of his face and digs her nails into his head.

He pauses and says, Say my name, tell me my name, say it.

Instead, Hirut, empty of words, tries to drown herself in a wave of indifference. She does this because he leaves her no choice and no chance and no hope and no escape, and because she will never have the right words to make a path out of this moment. And because there is really nothing, nothing left to say, Hirut opens her mouth. At first it is a mockery of herself, of her emptiness, but then her mouth opens wider of its own accord, a bubble rises up from the back of her throat into her head. And then, she yawns. It is both absurd and luxurious. A shock and a relief. It is a fist uncoiling and expanding inside her body, a long, extended breath singed and shaped by hate.

He gasps as if stumbling. As if he has just broken and is now buckling in half. As if that open mouth and that bubble of air have begun to undo him. Hirut sees his surprise, sees the way it traces a path across his eyes. He is so startled that his mouth sags open and his breathing stops until all he can do is gasp again. Hirut blinks and squints, baffled. She purses her mouth, readies it, and then slowly opens it and watches him flinch as if repulsed. She shuts her mouth and opens it again: it is a loaded gun that she waves in front of him.

Stop that, he says, confusion rippling across his face. He closes his eyes but it is too late. He is growing limp.

She loosens her jaw and opens her mouth again. He shrinks and draws himself back but he cannot find a way to move around her. He is trapped by the compulsion that binds him to her, caught in the temporary shame of surprise.

She takes a deep breath and arches her neck back, privately stunned by her body's obedience, by its absolute servitude to any command.

Enough, he says, but it is a feeble order, unsure of itself.

Emboldened, Hirut tries to push him off but he is a dense, stubborn weight. He presses against her unsteadily, confident once more, and begins again. She looks at him, at the darting eyes, the slack mouth, the uncertainty creeping over the strong planes of his face. She is numb. She is terrified. She is helpless. She is furious. She is all these things that are finding a way to hollow out and become a bubble that starts to swell. She takes another deep breath and it is so easy, this time, to let the yawn tumble forward, round and robust. It pries her jaw apart. It pushes her eyes shut. It blooms, a sweet respite in the horror.

He tries to grind himself into her, but it is too late. He cannot escape the complete indifference stamped across her face, and Hirut refuses to look away. Because she sees it now: the fissures in the sternness, the crumbling ground giving way to reveal his weakness. It has been there all along, waiting for her discovery: all that he has ever wanted from her is a fight, another battle he can win.

Kidane jumps to his feet. He kicks her and curses while he pulls up his trousers. You'll be sorry you were ever born, he says.

Hirut sits up, waiting for her legs to stop their trembling, for her stomach to stop heaving, for her tears to dry and language to return. She begs herself to stand before him and declare herself a soldier, to find the words to shift herself onto stable ground. But she is frozen, helpless, mute, closemouthed while he gathers himself, wipes his face, curses once more at her, then storms away. She sits there in the filth of her body, frightened and angered at its insistence on survival. Then, finally, she stands up and finds the path back, stumbling and flailing beneath panic. There is no escape. There is no way out except through battle. There is no other choice but to be a soldier, to take her useless Wujigra, point it at the enemy, and hope for the mercy of her own death.

THEY WILL HAVE TO DO WITH TARIKU WHAT THEY'VE HAD TO DO WITH all the other corpses: they will have to bury him without ceremony, in the dark, on nondescript land. Churches have become easy targets for the planes. Cemeteries are deliberately bombed. There will be no gravesite, no burial on holy ground. Everything will have to be done as so many things in this war: quickly and efficiently.

They've given up, Kidane says, pointing to the latest village to refuse them a burial for Tariku. He puts an arm around Seifu's shoulders as Seifu grips his wife's hand. They sit around the campfire pit and watch Aklilu throw in a few fresh twigs. Kidane continues: They've decided it's better to hide and live like cowards. He flicks an eye at Hirut as he says this. I can't believe this. He drops his head into his hands. Where do we bury him?

Behind them, leaning against a large stone, Minim plucks a mournful tune on a *krar*. The gentle musician was the one to lead the procession to the burial site, and he marched ahead of them all as they returned back to camp, never letting his music falter.

They're scared, Aklilu says softly. They're afraid of reprisals. They're tired of burying family members or having them disappear because these Italians accuse them of hiding or feeding us. They're not safe and they're unarmed, and these Italians are paying them to turn against us. They need our protection, but we're the ones asking for their help.

Aklilu drops his eyes, avoiding Kidane's gaze. For a brief moment, Hirut thinks he's going to say something to her, but instead, he drops the remaining twigs into the fire and sits down next to her. Kidane looks between the two of them and frowns. She feels Aklilu's concern, the steadying force of his unspoken refusal to move away from her even though his place has always been closer to Kidane. Above all their heads, drifting in the cooling breeze, the steady thrum from Minim's *krar*. He is plucking at the strings so delicately that the sound comes to them like an aching whisper.

What did you just say to me? Kidane's voice is frighteningly soft. We're not protecting them like we should? You're saying this to me?

Let's kill this Fucelli and end it, Seifu says as he wipes his eyes and keeps his other hand gripped in Marta's. Why are we waiting?

Marta presses into him, her face contorted. His arm slips around her and draws her closer, and for a moment, they are so bound together by loss that they appear to Hirut like a single body grown thick with grief.

Kidane rises to his feet and looms over Aklilu.

In the distance, another series of planes approaches, growing louder before the sound starts to fade.

This is why Hirut takes no real notice of Kidane at first. But then he opens his arms and tilts his head and he becomes a figure tipping into a dark void, taking flight against a strong wind. She presses closer to Aklilu and feels him lean against her, a balance.

Tell me this, am I free? He turns in a circle then stops, looking at all of them. Why don't you tell me, brave Aklilu, am I free?

All eyes fall once more on Aklilu. Kidane raps on his chest with a hard knuckle and asks the question again. Though his face is still pointed up, she can feel the suggestion of his gaze, the accusation he is also hurling at her.

What makes me a slave to the *ferenj*? Kidane slaps his chest. How am I a servant to them in my own country? What makes you think giving up is acceptable? We are Ethiopians! He strides to Aklilu.

Aklilu doesn't flinch, and this, more than Kidane's anger, makes Hirut frightened.

The emperor's gone, Dejazmach Kidane, Aklilu begins calmly. For them, it's finished. They can't fight without their leader.

What's finished? What's finished when a man can't even bury his son as he should? When a mother has to leave her child without a proper blessing?

Aster sucks in her breath, a sharp hiss of air.

Kidane bends down and jabs his finger into Aklilu's chest. He spits the words into his face: What's over?

Kidane bristles with rage. He is preparing to unleash the full scope of his fury; he is unwinding the wrath he would have thrown at Hirut if not for his own humiliation. He hums with a deep-rooted revulsion that must leave its mark on the closest target.

Dejazmach, they're finished with dying and killing, Aklilu says. He is speaking with a stubborn insistence, and the closer Kidane leans, the more rigid Aklilu becomes. He is sitting up so straight that his back nearly arches. They did it when they believed in the fight, he continues quietly. But they don't believe in you. Or anyone else. Aklilu stares ahead, looking beyond the group, staring at a fog-covered horizon. They believe in the emperor. We've never fought a war without our leader.

Past Kidane's shoulder, Minim cradles the *krar* against his chest, listening spellbound to Aklilu. His ragged shamma is wrapped tight around his thin frame. He has stopped playing and in the descending quiet, a lone wolf's howl sweeps past the anxious group watching Kidane to see what he does next. Aklilu has thrown them all off balance.

The emperor's not here. Kidane kicks aside a twig then picks it up. He breaks it and twists it around his hand. A soft gray light lies over his features and blankets his concentrated stare. But I am. We are.

But we're not enough, Aklilu says.

Kidane turns toward Minim and stares at the distant hills, toward a place that has collapsed into the horizon's long line. Clouds separate in the wind, and for a moment a bright moon cups them all in a stark beam of light.

Well, you must know, right? Kidane says without turning to Aklilu. You must have read this, I'm sure.

He takes out an old newspaper from his satchel. He unfolds it and gently flattens the creased face of the emperor across his palm. He holds it out to Aklilu and Hirut knows right away which photo it is. She has seen Kidane staring at that same picture while seated in his office. It is the one he once kept on his desk beside his maps, laid open to reveal a solemn-faced Haile Selassie gazing at everything happening within those four walls.

Aklilu holds the picture closer to get a better look at the emperor's face. You know I can't read, Dejazmach, he says simply. I'm a fighter, it's what I was born to be.

Hirut leans in to take a look at the photo again. In Aklilu's hand, the emperor's head looks small and fragile, the creases in the paper prod his nose and mouth out of shape. She has seen this image so many times while cleaning the house that she feels she can draw each line and slope of Haile Selassie's face. He is a stranger but familiar, like a wandering relative come home.

Minim plays into the tense silence. The *krar* moves in slowly, tapping against Marta's voice whispering her son's name. The notes rise when her voice lifts, then tumble down when she drops her head against Seifu's shoulder. Hirut watches Minim, fascinated. He has turned their attention away from the brewing argument, this quiet man who rarely talks, who seems to carry an instrument as if it were his only companion. She stares at him, mesmerized by the tune, the slopes he makes the notes climb before letting them fall into a low moan. She has never truly noticed him before. He was simply just Minim, the soft-spoken man with the strange name that means Nothing.

She notes his slender, long nose and the bony elegance that makes him look both fragile and dignified. Beneath the long, thick locks of hair that fall across his forehead and around his ears, his face is narrow, the cheekbones broad, the chin tapered. He is someone she knows.

Known and unknown. She looks quickly at the newspaper image, then back at Minim.

He looks like him, Hirut whispers to Aklilu. Like Jan Hoy.

Like who? Aklilu glances around.

He looks like him, like Jan Hoy, like the emperor, she repeats and points to Minim. Then stops when Kidane pivots angrily toward them.

What's she saying? Aster leans forward, curious.

Kidane snatches the newspaper back and brings it to his face. He holds it out and squints again. He folds it so that only the emperor's face shows. He strides to the tree and leans down to look at Minim.

Minim scrambles to his feet clutching his *krar*. A nervous finger rakes across the stringed instrument and jarring tones drop like an injured animal.

Kidane flattens the newspaper clipping and holds it next to Minim's face. He looks from the picture to Minim, from Minim back to the picture.

What? Aster says getting to her feet. What's this?

Kidane leans into a frightened Minim, transfixed. Look up again, he says.

Aklilu stares at Minim intensely. I don't understand, he finally says. He, too, gets to his feet.

Meet at my cave, Kidane says. Bring him.

＝

MINIM, KIDANE SAYS, his tone as gentle as the time he told Hirut he needed her Wujigra. You look like the emperor, has anyone ever told you? Kidane looms over the slightly built man in the cave.

Hirut feels a surge of pity for Minim, and when he sinks onto his haunches, she rushes to him, guilty that her words have put him in this place. She settles a hand on his arm.

You're OK, she says.

Minim is working a finger through a hole in his ragged shirt. A candle flame plasters his silhouette against the wall behind him. When

Kidane steps forward to pull Minim to his feet, his own dark shadow molds into a hulking figure melting into Minim's.

He's scared, Dejazmach, Aklilu says softly.

Do you think I'm going to hurt him? Kidane's voice is startlingly loud in the cramped space.

But what can we do with this? Seifu asks. What's this have to do with Fucelli?

Kidane pushes Hirut aside and puts his arm around Minim. He starts to speak to the farmer in a soothing voice. My father and grandfather used to tell me stories of shadow kings, he says. Empress Zewditu even had her shadow queen when she led her armies. Our leaders couldn't be in two places at once, so they had their doubles.

Him? Aster says, pointing at Minim. He's just a peasant.

Minim is shaking his head. Can I go, please, Dejazmach?

Kidane holds him closer. You'll help us win this war, he adds. There'll be stories about you that generations will repeat. Kidane's face is alive with excitement, bright and eager. He is standing taller, the fury from earlier disappeared.

But what does he know? He's not even a soldier, Aster says. And you won't let the women fight? Her laugh is bitter.

Kidane nods to Seifu. We'll have to get clothes, weapons, anything we can find. Aster, you know someone who might have some of Jan Hoy's things. Get the clothes.

My God, you just do anything you want, Aster says. But she steps closer to Minim and runs a hand across his shoulders, then from one shoulder to his waist, then she gets on her knees and follows the line from his waist down to his ankle. She is quick and meticulous, mimicking the motions of a tailor. At Zenebwork's wedding, she says, the emperor was almost my height, maybe a little shorter. She nods. They're about the same.

Aklilu is staring at Hirut. He'll need a guard, he says. Someone trustworthy. Maybe even someone who can inspire some of the villagers to help us, especially the women. Weizero Aster, Aklilu continues, Hirut can stay with him from now on. We can't spare any of our men right now. He looks at Hirut then at Aster. She'll need to move to his area. It's a little further from the others but I'll be nearby.

A girl? Then Aster nods slowly. Of course, she says. Then she narrows her eyes and looks at Kidane. She'll stay with him. Then she looks once more at Minim and the newspaper. I don't believe it, she says softly. I can't believe it.

IT IS NOT YET DAWN WHEN A YOUNG BOY WAKES HIRUT AND MINIM TO take them up a narrow path to the new cave where Kidane says they must stay. Hirut struggles to keep pace. Her limbs feel disjointed, out of balance. She has not felt in command of herself since the first time Kidane came for her. Her body has not been her own, and she has found herself unsure at times of what it is that propels her forward from daylight to night. She tries to hurry now, embarrassed when Minim pauses to let her catch up.

In the cave, Aklilu, Aster, and Kidane are gazing down at a set of clothes at their feet. A short candle offers feeble light. In the tepid glow, Hirut can make out a red umbrella made of velvet with gold embroidery, its color vivid, almost touched by sunlight. A khaki military uniform is folded into a perfect flat square and lies on a stone next to a pair of leather shoes and a black felt hat. Kidane holds a black cape and a crisply ironed shirt. Even in the dim cave, the shirt is so white that Hirut's tired eyes cannot look without blinking rapidly. Its collar and cuffs are pressed into sharp triangular points, sleek as a knife.

An adviser of the emperor's in the area gave us these. Some things he left behind in Dessie, he must have expected to go back, Aklilu says. He picks up the military uniform and starts to unfold it. He holds it out to Minim.

Minim drops to his haunches and shakes his head, his attention glued to the large cape that sways on Kidane's arm as if from a ghostly pressure.

He can't sit like that, Aster says. Like a peasant. What emperor does that in public? Get him up. She motions to Minim. And doesn't he talk?

We have to do this before the others wake up, Kidane says. The girl will take him through Debark when we're ready. Then if it works, we'll move to Dabat and keep going. He speaks past Aster to Aklilu. His jaw is tense, his eyes narrow, and he is scrutinizing Aklilu, searching for something that makes the younger man stand taller. Make sure she doesn't ruin things.

Aklilu shakes out the uniform jacket and holds it against his chest. The shoulders are narrower than his own, slender and boyish in comparison. He puts down the jacket and picks up the trousers, calculating their measurements, then he hands it to Kidane. Everything will fit, he says. It's unbelievable, like a gift, he adds. And it was your idea, Hirut.

Aklilu nods to Hirut and stares at her with such intensity that Hirut has to drop her head.

Get him ready, Kidane says to Aster. You want to be a soldier, this is what it means. He throws the trousers in her direction and goes out, Aklilu following behind him.

Aster stares at Minim. Get him dressed, she says to Hirut. I'll wait outside.

Unsure of what to do, Hirut looks out of the cave to see blackbirds flapping into the ashen sky, the morning clouds thin as vapor. She feels the soft material of the trousers, the lightness of it, the way the seams lie flat, expertly sewn. It looks odd in her hands with their scars and dirty fingernails, the scrapes she cannot remember getting. The cape lies on the ground on a burlap sack, the stark-white shirt with its many buttons rests on top of it. She is afraid to touch anything, afraid to make a stain that will reveal both herself and Minim as impostors. Pushing the pair of trousers toward Minim, she half expects the emperor to stride in and order her jailed for treason.

Minim hugs the trousers to his chest, embracing them with a nervous glance. He caresses the khaki, awed by its fineness.

This isn't for me, he finally says. He shakes his head and looks at her, embarrassed. It's not for me to wear.

Outside the cave, she sees the fog seeping away from the horizon, lifting to reveal dew-drenched grass. Tall cacti and white-flowered shrubs form loose patterns through the field. A donkey brays just past a nearby hill and a young boy calls out greetings to his goats. The day is starting, and for a moment, it is as if nothing has changed.

It's for you, she says, and takes a step back. There's no one else who can do this. I'm sorry, she adds. It was my idea, but I didn't think—

But I can't do this, Minim says. I'll take the beating, whatever he does to me, I'll accept it. I can't do this. He taps his chest. I know who I am, he adds. I'm Minim.

We have to follow orders. She takes a deep breath and straightens. We're soldiers, she adds.

I know what happened, he blurts out. He took you near where I sleep. I know.

Her heart convulses.

We're soldiers, she repeats. Her mouth trembles.

I'm just a musician. My mother named me Nothing, Minim, do you know why? Because I had an older brother who died, and after him, what's left? I'm just a musician, I'm not anything else. Minim stops abruptly then, struggling to regain his composure. Then he motions to the scar on her neck. He did this? he asks softly.

She lowers her eyes. You have to get dressed. You have to, otherwise, I go back. She stops and stares into his eyes, at the gentleness and pity.

Finally, he nods and starts to put on the clothes.

━

MINIM SITS FROZEN on Kidane's horse, a red umbrella folded shut and resting across his ornate saddle. He is a breathtaking figure in uniform, his black cape dark as the dead of night, his polished shoes so shiny they seem almost wet. He is a replica of the faded picture, Emperor Haile

Selassie come to them with overgrown hair, a shaggy beard, and shoulders that slump into a concave chest. He is a battle-worn image come to life, creased and slightly faded, but held up by sturdy bone, guarded by two soldiers named Aster and Hirut who stand on either side of him, an example to all of Ethiopia's women.

You'll be all right, Hirut whispers, careful to keep her gaze ahead, where Aklilu and Kidane are in deep conversation, pointing from Minim to the valley below.

Tell him to sit straight, Aster says to Hirut. Remind him of who he is now.

Minim shifts in his seat and sighs. He is trembling so hard that the medals on his jacket sway.

All you have to do is sit on the horse, Hirut says to him. She has to stop herself from patting his arm. We will all stand in the shadow of your light, she adds, repeating what Aster told her: To be in the presence of our emperor is to stand before the sun. You must respect his power to give you life and burn you alive. Sit up, Minim.

—

KIDANE'S HORSE, ADUA, gallops from Debark to Dabat, from Dabat to Gondar, from Gondar to Azezo to Woreta and into Gojjam, a flash of white across a bombed and ravaged landscape. The rumor begins like this: with a secret message sent from Kidane to priests announcing the horse as a sign of the emperor's imminent arrival. From blasted doorways of churches, the news weaves through every mercato and home and gathers the strength of truth: the emperor is coming. The emperor never left us. He will appear before us soon to confirm that victory is near. Villagers step out of their huts every morning to search the horizon for a white horse. Shepherds and farmers point to flashes of sunlight and wisps of fog as proof of divine assistance. Crowds gather at wells dotting the highlands and whisper amongst themselves, waiting anxiously for the emperor's appearance.

HIRUT RUNS HER hand across Adua's braided mane, the horse's hair weighted with red velvet threads that dangle amber stones. The jewels catch the morning light as the animal shakes its head, reflecting warm color across Hirut's new uniform, mimicking a constellation of bright stars. Hirut looks down at herself and marvels once again at what she sees. She is dressed as a Kebur Zebegna, a member of the emperor's elite army. Her uniform, handed to her by Aster with unusual gentleness, have been perfectly sized to fit her. A rifle Aklilu took from an Italian is on her back, cleaned and polished. An ammunition belt is cinched at her waist. She is ready to join the procession that will present Minim to the villagers who have gathered in the Chennek valley surrounded by the Simien Mountains, the news relayed over the course of two days by messengers and *negarit* drums, the sky vibrating with the metered beats of frantic hands.

She touches her chest and feels her heart still thudding violently beneath the khaki jacket. She has moved through these last days trembling in fear, unable to sleep, so worried about her duties that she has spent an entire night marching while Aster slept. She has practiced the high-stepping gait of the emperor's guards until her feet ached. She has swung her arms stiffly with each step. She has learned to pivot her head crisply in one direction then the other, performing it again and again for a stern and relentless Aster until the woman finally nodded, satisfied. Aster has not left her side since this mission began, so intent on teaching her correct protocol and manners that even Aklilu and Seifu came by in the evenings to watch, fascinated by the many details she is required to learn.

All of this for one man? Aklilu said. But isn't he human like us? he whispered at one point before Aster's glare silenced him.

Rapturous ululations rise up and puncture the morning silence. Adua tugs against the reins, huffing loudly, trying to shake loose of Hirut's firm grip as she waits for Aklilu and Seifu to arrive, for the drummers and singers to get into place, for the march to the top of the hill to begin so she can lead the emperor while holding his red umbrella to shield him from the sun that is no equal to the man himself.

———

THIS IS WHAT's possible, Kidane thinks as he stares, stunned, at Minim sitting straight and tall on Adua. He has to remind himself it is not the emperor. Kidane bows deeply before the man and raises his head toward the sky. He shuts his eyes from the brilliance of the morning sun. For a moment, he thinks he sees the outline of his deceased son's face hovering just beyond his vision, a cloud disappearing in the early breeze. He wants to reach out and tell him: My son, my Tesfaye, I didn't know this was possible. I didn't know that we could tread that narrow passage between the living and the dead. I did not understand that we could make a man appear where there was once no more than empty space. Tesfaye, *lijé*, we can mend that breach between the mortal and the divine and find a way to make it whole.

On the hilltop where Aklilu and Seifu and Aster wait patiently behind him, Kidane wants to reach out and cup that small boy's face and beg forgiveness: I did not know, he whispers. Kidane takes his rifle and holds it in front of him. He salutes the King of Kings. He shouts all the names of the emperor, feeling the earth tremble beneath him as villagers in the valley below shift forward to get a better look. He says quietly to the ghost of his son: I thought all this time that I had lost you, that it was impossible to remake you in the form of another. I thought all this time that there was no more hope for me. Then Kidane turns to open his arms wide at the top of the hill, and in that gesture, he gathers his people together and holds them in his embrace.

He is here, our sun, our emperor, he says to them.

Kidane glances into the field as the villagers fall to their knees. The emperor comes forward on his white horse, led by his female guards.

Kidane takes in Hirut's uniform, her proud stance, her fierce defiance, and sees his redemption.

———

HIRUT'S GAZE CANNOT take in the crowds all at once. They spill over onto the surrounding hills, balancing on inclines, spread across other plateaus. Their soft prayers rise and fall in steady waves, a growing murmur drawn tight with anticipation, bursts of shouts punctuating it all. Aklilu and Seifu are beside her, striking figures in their uniforms, full ammunition belts draped across their chests. Kidane wears his headdress and cape, a ferocious expression on his face. Next to him, Aster nods to the spectacle, dressed in a uniform with a pistol holstered around her waist. They surround Minim, his bodyguards, and when Kidane moves aside to let the emperor step forward, the crowd gasps.

The valley grows silent.

They want us to believe our emperor has abandoned us, Kidane says. They want us to think they have killed all our fighters.

The morning light falls evenly across his features, revealing the fierce intensity in his eyes.

They want us to give up hope and give them our land. They want to think that you who are left, old men and able-bodied women, cannot face their armies with our help. Kidane turns and in the generous sweep of his arm, he seems to draw Hirut closer to him. Look at who is here to fight with you. Pay attention to his guards, these women who are also warriors, soldiers, daughters of our Empress Taitu who once led forty thousand against these *ferenjoch* the first time they invaded forty years ago. Have you forgotten your blessed leader, daughters of Ethiopia?

Hirut glances quickly at Minim and steadies the horse. Minim is uncomfortable, embarrassed, his head down. Up, she says, head up.

Minim takes a breath, his eyes close, and his back straightens. He lifts his chin and clears his throat and when he opens his eyes again,

Hirut finds herself staring at the emperor and she has to drop her head and turn around to avoid his royal gaze.

Hirut, Kidane says in a voice that carries through the valley. Show them who guards the emperor. Let them see that a woman will lead and fight, just like everyone else.

Hirut steps forward, refusing to meet Kidane's gaze. She looks down into the valley and says softly, I'm a soldier, a blessed daughter of Ethiopia, proud bodyguard of the King of Kings. She takes her rifle and lifts it above her head.

It is not horror but elation that shakes the trees that day. It is not a poisonous rain but unbearable awe that forces the cries from the emperor's people. As the emperor lifts his hand to bless his beloved subjects, they shout his many names: Jan Hoy, Negus Nagast, Abbatachin, Haile Selassie, Ras Teferi Mekonnen. They mold the sounds into the cadence of a joyous prayer while Minim gazes at them in the body of the King of Kings. Hirut steps back beside him, silent and stunned, feeling her chest swell, overcome by the display of loyalty and passion.

It was, she will later say, as if they loved me too.

CARLO REFILLS HIS CUP OF WINE AND SETTLES BACK ONTO HIS COT, A dull ache climbing up his spine and into his head. Strewn across the bed are new maps that indicate roads recently built or in progress. A train schedule lies on the crate next to him, and on top of it all, waiting for his immediate attention, is an alarming telegram asking him to verify rumors of Haile Selassie's return to Ethiopia, to these very hills where Carlo's camp is based.

Can I bring you coffee? Fifi calls to him from across the footpath that separates their tents.

From where he sits, he has a clear view of her and her servant drinking coffee. He can see the stack of wood that will soon become his new office, a space where he can work without intrusions.

He shakes his head and shifts back in case she can see him. I'm fine, he says, then continues watching them.

They are an unlikely pair: Fifi with her vibrant personality and lush beauty, and this sullen woman in a shapeless cotton dress with a rag on her head. Her face has that shiny, smooth patina of dark skin too long in the sun, the wrinkles almost invisible. Like so many natives, it is difficult to tell her age, only her eyes, wary and fatigued, give the years away.

He looks down at the telegram. Rome is paying attention to this peasant's tale of the emperor's return. Haile Selassie was just photographed in his English residence in Bath. There is no truth to these rumors. What is true, and what needs his attention, is the report of a

series of attacks on construction sites near Azezo. Railroad tracks leading to Addis Ababa have been ripped up again as far north as Axum.
All of this while there have been no actual sightings of rebels in any of
these areas. This is a country full of phantoms and he is being asked to
wage war on ghosts even as Rome keeps insisting publically that the
war is over.

Carlo wipes the sweat off the back of his neck. His hair is getting
unruly. He can feel the itchy beginnings of a beard. For the last two
days, the village women have not brought their usual gourds of water,
and he hasn't allowed his men to risk assault by bathing in the river.
The growing smells are starting to permeate the camp. He pulls out
the telegram and notices it is stuck with another, this one informing all
members of the armed forces that their great leader, Benito Mussolini,
wants a list of every officer with a Jewish surname. Carlo tosses that
one on his pillow, annoyed. Here in Africa, there are only two types of
people, the native and the Italian. Every other distinction just gets in the
way, and yet these bureaucrats want to complicate things with a directive that will only create discord for his troops.

ETTORE GETS TO the edge of the camp and keeps walking through the
ascari section, ignoring the curious stares, the sudden drop in conversation and laughter. He keeps going until he realizes he is heading toward
that dead place where the prisoner once hung. Ettore veers away from
the tree and sits down near the edge of the plateau, and waves to the
construction workers working on the foundation of the prison not far
away. Huge rolls of barbed wire sit in the crevice of two large boulders
overlooking a deep ravine. Planks of wood and piles of straw wait to
be turned into walls. He leans against a large rock to gather himself.
Colonel Fucelli has just told him of the order to provide Italy with the
names of all Jewish officers. They haven't started on those at your level
but they will, I can guarantee you, Fucelli had said. To me, you are Ital-

ian. Don't worry about what you hear, trust me, the colonel had added. Trust my love for this army and for every soldier who follows me.

He takes out his camera and sees there is one picture left, so he lifts it to look at the valley, then the hills. As he pivots, he spies Fifi's maid coming to sit at the tree, the deadly rope still dangling from the tall branch. She hunches over, her legs folded beneath her dress, as if aware of none of it, and starts to pick at grass and flowers and smell the strands. She is searching for something, staring at the roots of what she has pulled up, lost in her world. The light falls across her in a flat, gray sheet, smoothed of its edges by gentle fog, so he meters carefully, frames her figure against the tree, angles away from the rope, and draws in the grass around her and the rocky terrain just past her shoulders. He aims high enough to bring in the vast sky. Then he takes the photo and watches as her head comes up, perplexed by the nearly inaudible noise. He expects her to get to her feet and turn around to him, and when she doesn't, he breathes a sigh of relief and keeps watching. She pulls clumps of dirt and grass, sifting through it methodically, searching for something that makes her frown.

＞

SHE ONLY PRETENDS not to see him. She who has known what it means to be ignored and shrugged aside is well aware of the pressure of a stare, the sleek hand of observation. That she sits beneath the tree is no accident of fate. There is that fragment of rope that still hangs and swings in fog. She is aware of its former weight, of the burden it once carried: a name now moved into remembrance. She sits because she is slowly sinking into rage that knows itself to be helpless. Tariku, she whispers. Son of Seifu and Marta, may you live forever in memory. But she is also looking for roots and picking through dirt as she repeats those names because she knows, too, the needs of man and desire; knows what a woman can withstand of embraces and nightly visits before that body, too, must bear a new weight. She is aware of ratios and probability, of monthly cycles and inevitability. She understands the fickleness of chance. She knows precisely that to take from one day gives nothing to the other. That what the left hand hides, the right does not necessarily reveal. That blood can conspire to give life and to take it, to murder and to bless, to confirm a woman's place in the world every month, and deny it. And so she gathers and collects to give to Fifi, to end what grows inside of her and right the balance.

THE TWO ELDERLY WOMEN ARE DRESSED IN BLACK. THEY WEAR BLACK scarves around their heads, and they plod slowly into the camp, hunched by age and supported by their walking sticks.

Fucelli, we must see this Fucelli, one of them says in a wavering voice, her watery gray eyes searching the camp, the field, the *ascari* who are approaching. We saw a vision, and it involves a dead boy. Where is he?

Ettore pauses on his way to the canteen to pick up weekly rations. They are an odd sight, made stranger by their request to see the colonel. They look like twins, their features carved by identical wrinkles that weigh against gaunt cheeks and the same filmy eyes.

We've had dreams about Fucelli and a dead boy. He must do as we say to avoid the curses, the old woman repeats. She coughs and points a finger at one of the several *ascari* who are rushing toward them, curious and frightened.

Emama, a tall *ascaro* says as he bows in front of her. Our leader is coming, just wait. He motions for the rest of the men to move back, and even the *soldati* who have begun to make their way to the spectacle shift to make room. Why are you here? Are you a witch, *tenquay newot*?

The women are now in the center of a shrinking circle, the men leaning in, made breathless by fascination and fear.

We know his name is Tariku, this dead boy, the old woman says. She looks to her partner, who nods slowly. Tariku, who also calls himself *Anbessa*.

Ibrahim approaches, tense. Tariku, he repeats. They said Tariku?

The name is a ripple moving through the crowd.

A sharp glint pulses in Ibrahim's eyes. Ettore moves to stand beside him and eases his camera to the front of his chest. He can sense Ibrahim's confusion, something wavers in the creeping tension, something urgent and sharp that makes him flinch and turn his head, suspicious.

Ibrahim sweeps his hand in the direction they came. Go back to your people, we don't believe these things.

There was a boy who died here and he is restless. It was not right, the old woman says. She nods to her friend, who shakes her head and lifts the same pale eyes to Ibrahim.

Son of Ahmed, you know we are true, the second woman says. She reaches out to touch Ibrahim's cheek but he draws back, visibly shaken.

Who told them? Ibrahim looks at his *ascari*. Who told them my father's name? He steps away from them. Who told them?

We're here to see Fucelli, the first woman says again. Your *ferenj* leader took Tariku and he must find peace.

Several of the *ascari* laugh and translate for the others. Murmurs rise in a steady stream around Ettore and soon, more Italians are pushing into the circle, some breaking through to stand behind Ibrahim and take a better look. One of them shoves Ibrahim from behind and the *ascaro* spins around and stares directly at the grinning soldier, threatening and unafraid.

High up in the hills, Kidane watches through his binoculars. He is hiding along with Aklilu and watching as the Italians gather closer to the village women they have dressed in black to distract the camp. The women have all the information that other villagers have been able to provide: Fucelli stays in his tent in the mornings by himself, and his trusted *ascaro* is the son of a man from Keren named Ahmed, a good man with an honest son. Hirut and Aster are to keep their focus on the old women, waiting for them a few meters from the camp. They will rush in if there is any trouble. They will push their way into that growing circle and drag the women out, feigning surprise at two old and senile aunts who wandered away from market.

They have not counted on Ibrahim, though. His unwavering concentration is so intense that he will soon be able to discern every lie. He will only have to follow the stray thoughts in the women's heads to find himself looking over their shoulders, into the hills, toward Seifu and the other men.

What is it? Ibrahim shouts so loud that his voice echoes. Get out of here, he says, prodding the women away. Go!

The spell is broken as the women turn and hurry away. Then the earth swells with noise. The wind rises. And Ibrahim listens, stunned.

What is this? He puts his hands on top of his head. He turns toward Fucelli's tent, toward the single, piercing voice punching into the chaos: Ibrahim! Ibrahim!

—

THIS HAS ALWAYS BEEN at the center of his reckoning: that the beast is strongest in the quiet, that it gnaws first at its own throat, and all those men who search for its presence in treacherous sound will be destroyed by what rests mute in bright corners. It is not mayhem that births the creature. It is silence that plumps the meat on its bones then sends it off to kill. For years, Carlo has pressed his ear against the menace of his worst fears and told himself to listen. He has held every nightmare close. He has trained himself to expect the unexpected. He has bled his assumptions dry and turned them inside out. He has forced his phantoms to harden to bone and give the enemy form. This is how he has stayed alive. He has slipped past light and buckled into shadow both stupefying and dangerous.

So when an *ascaro* bursts into his tent without asking for permission, this is Carlo's first thought: the man must be punished. But then the *ascaro* doesn't stop and there is no apology. There is just that body barreling in at an ungodly momentum, colliding against him with a force that knocks him flat and leaves him breathless. He considers all the ways he can make this man pay, but a sharp blade flashes silver in the dimming tent and he hears his name crushed in the mouth of the intruder. It is shorn clean of respect, so empty of deference and discipline that he knows he is staring at an enemy Abyssinian. Carlo stares at the terrifying man. It is darkness itself that presses against him. It is vengeance dug up from the depths of the earth, rippling with muscle and noise. Time slows then speeds up. All memory tumbles backward.

A sharp knife scrapes the tender skin of his neck, slices into flesh and draws blood that warms the collar of his shirt.

That's all right, he says. It is a nonsensical phrase. A boyhood phrase. A series of words he has always used to fill that gap between terror and recognition: That's all right, Papa. Mamma, it's all right. That's all right, sir.

Carlo is pinned down on his back by strong arms and legs and there is that blade, searching for something it cannot seem to find on the stubbled skin of his bleeding neck. His mouth knows to open but every word has abandoned him except his name:

Carlo. It is a whisper, helpless and futile and it's all right, sir, it's all right.

A callused palm blocks his mouth, and air is replaced with stench and sweat. What was outside has crept inside. What was human has grown beastly. He who once led armies to victory is now alone staring at a thousand black nights wrapped in sinew and skin. It is a blackness that shrouds every thought. It bends time and thickens air until it is impossible to move his head. Impossible to do anything but listen to his name dropped from that hard mouth like a splintered bone sucked of marrow.

Fucelli, the intruder says. He stares down, almost bored. Eyes cold as stone, shiny as a river, rimmed in red, murderous.

Fucelli.

Carlo shuts his eyes. He opens them. Another person crawling into the tent, dressed in white, no bigger than a child. Rough hands pry his legs apart at the same time as his arms are spread wide and flattened to the ground. How many hands? How many men? He imagines wraiths and spirits, considers amorphous nightmares and unending dreams. But these are men, he reminds himself, thick with flesh and blood and bone, sharpened by hatred. They are savages bred from all that the world has ever rejected.

His belt is loosened, his trousers unbuttoned, his undershorts yanked down. He tries to jerk free and the knife pokes into his thigh, so quick it is cold as the tip of the blade comes out. The blade drags itself down the middle of his belly, curious, tests the soft meat above his hair. It glides down the tender crease of his pubis. It nuzzles the split curve of his buttocks then inches toward his anus. Carlo freezes, held hostage and trembling in anticipation. From a place inside his head where no words reside, in that space reserved for only the most special of muted horrors, he understands that a stranger's hand is reaching for the base of his penis, grasping it and tugging as another arm slips beneath his chin and forces his head back so he cannot see what is going to happen, so he cannot prepare himself for that brutal cut. Because it is sure to happen.

He struggles against that arm, brings his chin down so hard that he begins to choke himself. Flashes of a black curtain. Tears. Please. Please. *Aiutami.* Help me. He is begging and he doesn't care. Every word is meaningless. Every gesture futile. Every memory holds no sway in the face of this gargantuan, feverish disease eating through him, chewing its way out of every pore. That he has pissed on the hand circling that blade around the base of his penis, that his bowels contract and there is the stink of him, that he is rotting from the inside out, that he is quivering and pleading and wailing his own name, that it ricochets from that sweaty palm back into his throat, that he is forced to swallow his own pleas: all of this Carlo will choose to forget. All of this he will say happened to another man who was no man at all.

Then the Abyssinian slides off his chest and there is a momentary pause in the numbing terror, because what man would dare to do more than that?

Tariku, the man says.

The panic is a stray eyelash in Carlo's eye, a nagging warning that if he does not do something, he will be as he is: hands bound and legs splayed, his trousers at his knees, submerged in his own filth while held prisoner to a knife beginning its meticulous work. Behold the man, see him shrink and quiver, useless as a girl in the hands of an assailant.

A great and ancient weight sinks into his head. He smells blood. He smells his shame. He can sniff the coming carnage that will make him trophy and victim, spectacle and symbol, something else that is no longer a living man. And now there is that hard fist driving into his head again and again. See: blackbirds. See: dying light. If he wants he can end this. He can slip away and let them finish, leave them to their own wishes. But can I come back? He mouths this against that soiled palm and waits for an answer through the rushing in his head.

From somewhere: Fifi calls his name. But there is no Carlo, so there is no name, there is nothing that holds him firm in this fractured dark. She is an apparition; he, just a metaphor, the broken husk of a dying man. Stones drop from trees. Fruit sprouts from the ground. How easy it is to traipse across the valley of the sky. Right becomes left. Up plummets into soil. What makes a man can now unmake him. A pistol fires. A steady ache across his body. Heavy feet race past his head. A touch on his forehead. He will shut his eyes and sleep it away.

Carlo. She speaks in that terrifying language.

He hears: Faven?

He hears: Please, Seifu.

Then he opens his mouth, astonished at the freedom, and adjusts his eyes to a speckled world coated in tears and blood. Somehow, he manages to trace the path of horror to check himself: he is still intact.

He lets her say it again: Carlo. He lets her lean his body against her. He lets her hand pull up his trousers and hide his frailty, and press a cloth against his neck. She does everything except sweep aside his humiliation and in the half-life of his disintegration, it happens: terror snaps free and floats loose, unhinged. And as it uncoils inside of him to claim new territory, he begins to scream a name: Ibrahim! Ibrahim!

I LET HIM LIVE. THAT IS ALL SEIFU SAYS AS HE STANDS IN FRONT OF Kidane, tired and worn out. I let him go. His face is a twisted plane of emotions too frightening for Hirut to decipher.

Hirut shrinks back against the farthest wall next to Minim, unable to take her eyes off the men. Aklilu and his men are scattered through the hills, readying for the reprisals, helping to move the villagers into surrounding mountains. The women, the elderly, the children have begun their treks from their homes, carrying water and baskets with food, racing to avoid bombings and raids.

Kidane shakes his head again in disbelief. We'd killed all of his bodyguards, he says. We got rid of some of the other *banda*, there was no one left to stop you. You had the chance you were begging for. Because of you, Aklilu and the others are risking their lives right now. Even those old women did as they were told. This is the third time he has repeated the details of the ambush and Seifu's failure.

If I'd killed him they would have attacked by now, Seifu says.

Kidane picks up a whip that has been coiled and waiting at his feet. He slowly unwinds it and snaps it, testing its trajectory. The sound is crisp and cruel, a snake's hiss. Marta drops to her knees. Aster bends to pull her against her chest, shaking her head silently.

I don't care, Dejazmach, do it. What's worse than losing my son? Seifu takes off his shirt and flings it down. His chest is a series of scars that form hash marks from the sloping muscles of one shoulder to the

other. Close to his heart, unnaturally tight skin the size of a fist: a
healed burn.

Do it, Seifu says again. You're not the first rich man to try to teach
me my place.

Aster wipes her forehead with the edge of her shawl, then covers her
nose and mouth until only her eyes are visible. Stop, Kidu, she whispers. She takes a quick look at Hirut.

Hirut meets Aster's gaze, and she cannot help reaching up to feel the
scar that no uniform can ever erase. Aster flinches and turns away.

I'm not finished with Fucelli, Seifu says. He's useless to the army
now. He's too humiliated to tell what happened. That man soiled himself like a child, he begged. He's useless. Unfit for war.

Kidane rears back, angry, and cracks the whip. It cuts the air at an
angle and slides into Seifu's back.

Seifu inhales sharply and buckles. The whip arches back toward
Kidane, sprinkling drops of blood on its path.

Aster clasps her stomach. Enough, she says, he's one of our best
fighters.

Kidane stares at her, then throws down the whip and rubs his hands
in dirt. If you disobey me again, he says, his voice trembling, I'll finish
on you what you started with that Italian. On Tesfaye's grave, I swear it.

Aklilu appears at the mouth of the cave, wiping his blade. We
found a few more looking around, he says, I took some uniforms, so
did a few other men, we'll need them later. The collar of his Italian
uniform is smudged with blood. He makes a jarring, odd figure in
the enemy's clothes. He notes the whip and the blood creeping down
Seifu's back, and his look at Kidane holds none of his usual respect.

Hirut puts her head down to avoid the question in his glance.

Seifu stands and puts on his shirt. The blood seeps into his *ascaro*
uniform and spreads, branching like a deformed tree.

You've put us all in jeopardy, Kidane says. He smothers the quivering in his chin by pursing his mouth. Sweat rolls down his forehead.

Seifu puts a hand over his heart. I'm not afraid to die in this war, he says. To punish me is a waste. It's not enough to simply kill these *ferenj* dogs, he says. Some need to die slowly.

Kidane stares at the whip, stiffening gradually, then he leaves, rushing roughly past Aklilu.

—

IT HAS BEEN three days and Carlo still hasn't allowed anyone into his tent. He hasn't spoken since the attack except to tell Fifi to get out after he managed to revive himself. Fifi had watched him carefully, her heart hammering in her chest, the hatred in Seifu's eyes still a stinging wound. There was, in the paleness of Carlo's skin and the dark hollow of his eyes, the sign of something gone, a thread-thin fracture in the steadiness of his gaze. She had reached out to test him, to see how much he understood of her pleas to Seifu, but he had shrunk from her and stood up to place himself in front of his radio: the act of a man already in the solitude of his own thoughts. She had expected tears, some expression of anguish from a man so close to death. Instead, the sharp drone of radio static had climbed into the silence and surrounded them both as he flung off his soiled clothes to stand naked. A shapeless fear had sucked out the tent's rancid air.

Get your servant in here to clean this up, he had said, throwing on a clean uniform and kicking the dirty one toward her. It better look as if nothing happened when I get back. Then he looked at her, repulsed.

Fifi had stared at him as he left, surrounded by new bodyguards, truly afraid of the man for the first time.

Have some coffee, Fifi. It's the cook, holding up Carlo's cleaned uniform. Stains are all out, finally, she says, sniffing it. Your dress is drying, she adds. I had to soak everything a while.

Fifi stares at the pale blue chiffon dress she is wearing. The skirt's gold trim is garish, vulgar in the clear morning light. She wraps her shamma tighter around her shoulders and tucks it around her legs. If it's dry enough, I'll just wear it, she says. It's better than this.

You wear that with *ferenj* men?

Fifi smiles. You don't ask much about my work. She nods. They like it.

The cook shrugs. It's not my business. She pauses. But they know you're abesha. So why dress like a *ferenj*? Aren't they paying for an abesha woman?

Fifi looks at her quickly. They pay more when I imitate their women.

So you learned Italian, the cook says.

Not for them. Fifi takes Carlo's uniform from her and sets it on her lap. Why these questions now?

Who was it? The cook glances into the hills.

Fifi is careful to keep her face composed. I don't know, she says. So many groups make their own armies these days, they're everywhere in these mountains.

You're a traitor to them. These *arbegnoch* would kill you, too, if they could, the cook says. She speaks bluntly, without judgment.

Aren't you a traitor, then, working for me?

The older woman shakes her head, looking at her carefully. I'm nobody to Italians, and I'm nobody to them.

Ibrahim approaches, his hand on the holster. He is moving slowly, without the usual rigor. Dried bloodstains mark the front of his usually immaculate uniform.

He nods to the cook. He's still not out? He hasn't asked for food? Nothing?

The cook shakes her head. Isn't that office he's bulidng done?

Why don't you talk to him? Fifi asks. Maybe you can get him out.

Ibrahim nods to the cook. He's supposed to move in there. If he comes out, I'll be with the priest and imam for the burials, he says. He pauses and stares down at his feet then shakes his head. More Ethiopians managed to get in multiple attacks not far from here last night. I don't know where they're coming from, he says, sounding surprised.

It's a different group, Fifi says, or why would they leave Carlo alone?

It was the women, Ibrahim continues, looking at the cook. I thought they were villagers. Shock and regret are plain in his voice. We can't find them, the villages are empty.

Keep pretending I'm not here, Fifi interjects softly. As if you're so different from me.

Ibrahim stops and for a moment, his face contorts and all traces of remorse give way to spite. Tell him I need to see him, he says to the cook, then he strides away.

Fifi laughs, a short, bitter sound. Bright clouds slide overhead and for a moment, a cool wind rises and scatters dust. The cook stretches out her legs, drawn and tired; the liveliness that usually rests behind her intelligent eyes is a cautious stare. She is observing everything around her, turning at any sound.

Do you think it's true, Fifi says after awhile. That we'll be safe if we trust in God?

They've killed monks and nuns, haven't they? The cook dusts off her dress. What's God doing about that? She glances over her shoulder then squints up to the sky. I'm afraid for us when they come back for him, because they will.

Where are you from? You've never said. Fifi is careful to keep her gaze ahead, away from the cook.

The cook brushes a fly aside. She watches the hills with an alert wariness. The village doesn't exist anymore, she finally says to Fifi. Everything's gone.

You were there when it happened?

A hardness slides across the cook's face. She nods. Then they took me to Yifag and sold me.

Fifi reaches to touch the woman's arm but the cook pulls away and adjusts the scarf on her head. Tiny gray curls are visible around her ears but when hidden beneath her scarf, she appears ageless.

Quietly the cook adds: You should be careful.

Farther ahead, a burial procession marches down the hill, led by an imam and a priest, followed by Ibrahim and other *ascari*. Four black-clad women trail beside them on either side. They are professional mourners, expressive faces upturned, their fists pounding on their chests.

He's going to be worse from now on, the cook says. He's going to be crueler to everyone, especially you. Get away from here, let's leave now.

Fifi rubs her forehead and wipes her eyes. I can't leave, she says. She puts a hand on the cook's arm and rests it there when the woman does not resist. Go, you go and find a safer place.

The cook shakes her head. Where's there to go in this country? What place is for me?

ETTORE WAITS OUTSIDE COLONEL FUCELLI'S TENT, CLUTCHING THE camera he was ordered to bring. He clears his throat and glances at the six new bodyguards that stare at him. They are formidable-looking soldiers, all Italian, all in Blackshirt uniforms, men he has never seen until they came by truck three days ago and quietly posted themselves outside Fucelli's tent. Rumors say they are mercenaries from Asmara, that they hail from Massawa, that they are in fact former Blackshirts much too ruthless for even that most vicious arm of the military. They have the strong-jawed meanness of movie villains, one has a long scar down the side of his neck, and another has a tattoo of a woman's leg peeking from his sleeve.

Navarra, are you just standing there? Fucelli's voice comes through the canvas, sharp-edged and gruff.

Ettore steps inside, aware of the guards shifting ever so slightly in his direction, observing his entrance. He draws back at the smell that greets him: as pungent as curdled milk. It hangs, thick as another body, in the warm and humid tent. Fucelli sits upright on his cot, rifling through a stack of papers. His jacket is buttoned all the way, and a sweat stain spreads along the wilted collar. A thick bandage around his throat is stained with iodine and a pink line of blood. It is a dampened light that casts the space in pale yellow.

The colonel glances up at Ettore and nods. It's not as if I didn't expect this, he says. Maybe it was inevitable. Fucelli nudges the stool beside him. Sit, Navarra, we have some things to discuss. His eyes are blood-shot, swollen. There's something I want you to see.

Fucelli slips a photograph out from a stack of papers. The strong scent of cologne wafts past as the man shoves the picture at Ettore. Take your time, he says. Above Fucelli's lip is a thin sheen of sweat.

It is a close-up of an elderly native man, his wrinkles carving deep ridges and draping his filmy eyes. A series of tiny moles form a circu-lar pattern on one cheek. On the other side is a birthmark the size of a thumbnail, a dark moon floating in the gaunt recesses of his thin face.

At some point, Fucelli says, you understand you're not trying to kill anyone. You're not trying to defend land or a fort or whatever they tell you to go out there and fight for. You're just trying to survive until it's over. Because it will be.

Fucelli points to the photograph. They're types, all of them. Easily categorized. The colonel's breath is tinged with coffee and cigarettes.

Ettore nods. Yes, sir.

You're studying their language and you don't know? Fucelli grabs the photo. Come on, look at him. A typical Tigray, he says. You see the nose, the eyes? Fucelli tosses the photo onto Ettore's lap. Look at this one here, he says, pulling another picture from the same pile of papers. Afar, quite distinct by the hairstyle. He takes another out of the pile. This one, he continues, shaking it in front of Ettore, this one's magnificent, isn't it? Fucelli speaks rapidly, taking out photo after photo, discarding them on the ground, not caring if Ettore can see them.

Finally, the colonel stops and stares at the disarray at his feet. He kicks aside the photos and stands. They call you Foto, don't they? Fucelli asks. Very clever. But tell me what we're missing. Fucelli pulls out a loose cigarette from his pocket and slips it into his mouth. They move like rats, they're too hard to catch, he says. This is the only way to hold one still. A picture. Understand? He gestures toward the photo of the elderly man.

Yes, sir, Ettore says. He glances down at the image still on his lap, looking for distinguishing characteristics.

Fucelli picks up a picture from the floor. In it, a young woman stares angrily into the camera.

This one, Fucelli says. Rome keeps bragging about the new colony but we can hardly keep Addis Ababa intact. It's still a war zone everywhere else, and these people seem to fight even though their emperor's run away. Though I'm sure you've heard the rumors too.

Ettore leans back though the colonel has not moved toward him.

Fucelli exhales a long thread of smoke and watches it fan and disappear in front of him. I've got reinforcements coming, he says slowly. We're building this prison a little further away, higher up in the mountains, and we're going to do it right. We're going to suffer more attacks, but we're ready. We'll have prisoners soon enough, and you're the photographer, not me. Am I making myself clear or do I need to spell this out for you?

I think I understand, sir, Ettore says.

Go meet my convoy when it arrives. We'll start documenting this new prison from the beginning. We'll record everything. They'll remember what we did to build this empire. You're dismissed.

Yes, sir. Ettore stands and salutes.

Be at the bottom of the hill first thing tomorrow, Fucelli says. There's only one road leading here from Axum, you can't possibly miss it.

———

TO OLD JEMBERE, the *soldato* perched at the top of a nearby hill and pointing his camera toward the road below is just another strange sight in a country straining from confusion. The *soldato*, breathless from exertion, arrived just after sunrise, zigzagging down the narrow path where he, Jembere Kefyalew, was waiting once again to thwart the enemy. Jembere had to drag his bike out of the way so the *ferenj* could pass, quietly insulted by the Italian's lack of response when Jembere saluted with all the proper etiquette of a victorious military man. What does he know of what it takes to win a war, the old man thinks now as he watches the *soldato* lean forward and aim his camera at an empty road. If he looks, he would see nothing but an aged man standing next to his flimsy bike. The *ferenj* is as most *ferenjoch* are: too arrogant and ignorant to know that he is Jembere Kefyalew, loyal servant to the late Emperor Menelik, trusted soldier to the late Empress Taitu, proud warrior come to fulfill his lifelong promise to never let Ethiopia fall into foreign hands.

Every day since Mussoloni's invasion, Jembere has put on his best clothes and come out to stop the *ferenj* advance. He waits for convoys in the dark and witnesses the sun spill across the valley. He positions himself at the top of the highest hill so he can see the Italians approach and gauge their distance. Many mornings, he has waited in vain, but he knows this, too, is the course of war. Some days, there are planes that dip close to trees and hover over hills and huts. At first, he mistook them for dragons and fell to his knees to pray the evil away. But even then, Jembere Kefyalew, loyal servant to Emperor Menelik, trusted soldier to Empress Taitu, proud warrior of Ethiopia, did not fail in his promise to keep his country safe. He stood straight and rigid while the planes performed slow circles around his land. He refused to flinch. He moved not a muscle when they barreled toward him, gleeful in their spite. He did not even bow his head to avoid a treacherous, dipping wing. He simply loaded one of his bullets and aimed, then he let them rattle away, fearful of his diligent might.

Today, the convoys will come, he is sure now of the pattern that has emerged: first those planes, then the trucks, then the *soldati* in their cumbersome leather boots trampling this road that was once part of the land that was his son's birthright. One follows the other like an awkward dance and he, once more, will be ready.

—

THE CONVOY IS at a standstill. The marching columns have stopped. It is difficult to see past the settling dust but that old man in the tattered

suit and rusted bike is plain to see. He stands in front of the halted row
of trucks that unfurl in front of him like sheet metal stretched across the
land. It is a silent spectacle in the valley. Ettore cranes his neck to get a
better look ahead. Angry *camionisti* lean out of their windows. A few of
them begin to honk.

Come on, move it! Get out of here! *Vai via!* Jembere, get the hell out
of the way!

There is a steady heat filtering back, choked with fumes and dust
and noise.

Ettore glances around, tensed for the signs of another assault, but
there is no movement or sound coming from the surrounding hills. The
thick patches of greenery in the near distance are undisturbed. The trees
sit peaceful and picturesque. Only a lone bird soars high above the undulating landscape, a graceful kite sliding through rays of early morning
sun. It is tranquil except for the unfolding, baffling scene below him.

The old man is a startling sight. He is dressed in a tailcoat and wool
trousers faded to a dingy gray. His well-tailored shirt has a high collar
that once stood neat against his slender neck. All but one button is missing. The shirt has yellowed with age, and where a bow tie would have
been there hangs a thin black ribbon. A rope at his waist keeps his trousers at the perfect length, grazing his ankles and stopping just above his
bare feet. He is an apparition from a forgotten era, a lovely ghost on the
verge of disappearing. Just in front of him, a solidly built man in shorts
and a sagging T-shirt steps out of his truck, his boots unlaced, his socks
bunching at his ankles. Several others climb down from the backs of
other trucks, the marching columns collapse into groups of men getting
closer to the front to see what is the matter. A large circle is forming
around the old man.

Ettore lifts his camera to take a picture then pauses. It is not the old
man that his eyes are dragged toward, however. It's the women on
the periphery who are watching everything. White-clad and rigid as
guards, they are a neat row several paces above the chaos. Their unde-

tected arrival on the hill feels almost like a gift, this chance to capture what Fucelli was trying to explain in his tent. Ettore takes a picture then notices the driver who first stepped out of his truck turn in his direction and salute.

He waves to Ettore. Come meet my old friend, Jembere! He grins and digs a handkerchief out of his pocket to wipe his forehead.

Ettore slides down the hill to the road and approaches.

I've met most of the journalists in the area, the driver says. He has kind eyes, a gentle mouth. Anyway, take a picture if you want before I move him along.

The old man is one of those natives who hides their years behind tiny wrinkles and bright eyes. There is a papery softness to his skin, fine creases draping over his delicate bones. Ettore takes a step forward and lifts his camera. The old man narrows his eyes and glares at him. He squares his shoulders and puts his feet together. The hand gripping the handle of his old rusty bike tightens. He is impervious to the rippling menace surrounding him.

Jembere, *amico mio*, don't scare the man! The driver chuckles.

The sun is a gentle sheet of light falling across the native's shoulders, leaving touches of silver sparking off his unruly white hair. Ettore nods as he winds the film. Jembere doesn't respond, he doesn't blink. Taking a step closer, trying to imitate one of Fucelli's photos, Ettore sees the rage that simmers beneath that stern expression. There is nothing here that speaks of feebleness and placid old age. Anything could happen. The native might charge. Then a thought: What if this old man is just a distraction set up by the Ethiopians?

He turns to the driver. You're not afraid of an attack?

The driver laughs. His gun doesn't even work. He takes out his handkerchief again and wipes his face. He turns to the old man. Jembere, *ibakot*, he says, then continues haltingly in the native tongue. He puts an arm around Jembere's shoulder. Once I had to carry him off the road, he adds. Light as a child. The driver pats Jembere's chest. Come on, *amico mio*. There's tenderness in the man's voice. They're like children, he adds, just remember that. He takes the bike from Jembere and pushes it toward the side of the road.

Ettore stops to watch them, then looks around and sees the women walking away to disappear on the other side of the hill, as quiet as they arrived.

Jembere stares one last time at the soldiers and trucks then he gets off the road to take his bike back from the driver, the tails of his jacket flapping in the wind, his back straight.

COLONEL FUCELLI DIRECTS ETTORE TO WALK WITH HIM UP AN INCLINE and closer to the large boulders overlooking the edge of the cliff where the new prison is being built. The colonel steps delicately into the center of the V-shaped gap, looks down, and then turns around. Behind him, there is barely enough room for one more step. There is nothing but soil the width of a child's foot, then the plummeting fall.

They're going to ambush our trucks, Fucelli says. What we build, they intend to bring down. What we lift, they will collapse. Rome wants me to treat them as simple bandits, but they're going to fight like dark sons of Apollo. Memnon was shielded by Zeus, why doesn't Rome understand this? He pulls down his sunglasses.

Clouds gather overhead as a chill sinks against the mountains. Blackbirds shiver and caw from the flat tops of squat trees.

Ettore tries not to stare at Fucelli. His uniform reveals an unnatural girth. His jacket bulges slightly in the middle. Rumors have been circulating that he now wears two belts. That the ambush has made him so paranoid that he no longer sleeps at night. Some of the *ascari* have begun to whisper that he is mobilizing a secret army, mercenary bandits that terrorize Ethiopian and Italian alike. They have now begun to say that his *madama* is trained to kill with poisons that mimic the taste of beer and wine. That her cook knows how to mix it into foods. That together, they are waiting for Fucelli's orders to test it on army rations, selecting those Fucelli feels most likely to betray him.

Navarra, take a look over here. Fucelli places a hand on one of the boulders. He stretches his other arm to try to touch the opposite side. Can you get a shot like this?

The light behind him is pale and even, bleached by the clouds and altitude.

It's quite dramatic, Ettore says. He takes several steps back. Colonel Fucelli is a tiny figure dwarfed by an imposing landscape. The V that opens reveals the undulating mountain ranges, the horizon disappearing in stark clouds. The top of the V expands until the space between those great, hulking stones lets the sky pour in. Just above it all, two birds soar majestically through the wind.

Now, *soldato*, really take a look, the colonel says after a few pictures.

Ettore moves next to the man, aware of the breeze slapping against his face, a threatening force that could push him over if he turned at just the right angle. There is a magnetic quality to the edge, a suctioning force coming from the gorge below. He puts his hands against a boulder to stop the sensation of tumbling forward. He dares to raise his eyes: the landscape has no end, it stretches far beyond what he can see, one sharp peak giving way to another. That it is impossible to see how far the drop below is, is a thought that makes him weak at the knees. He is sweating again, even in this cold.

How long do you think it takes for an average Ethiopian to reach the bottom, Navarra?

There are only sharp, jutting stones that lead to the deep gorge below. There are no easy paths.

They're good climbers, sir, Ettore says. They're fast and they know how to handle this terrain, but still, I think it would take some time.

Fucelli puts an arm around his shoulder and tugs Ettore closer, his fingers dig into his arm painfully. Think, Navarra. If we pushed, how long? How many men could we do in a day? That's the question. Your father taught you how to estimate, I'm sure. Does he still have his job, by the way? You know what's happening back home. Terrible, terrible thing.

Sir? News has come from Italy about increased restrictions on Jews, about a coming purge of Jewish professors from universities, about the establishment of a government office to deal with the country's "Jewish problem," but his parents have said nothing to him. He has received no letters at all.

The wind flattens Fucelli's hair back, gives him a sleek look that transforms his narrowed eyes into a hateful squint. He wipes his hands on his shirt then shoves them in his pockets. Think you could get a picture mid-fall? the colonel asks.

⇒

LEO NAVARRA TO HIS SON, Ettore Navarra, on the day of his departure for war:

King Minos says, Daedalus, my faithful servant, build a labyrinth impossible to escape. O great solver of riddles, fashion it so we can capture and hold what is both man and beast. Great Daedalus, you of the spiraling mind, work yourself into this winding maze. Let no one see your solution for escape. Keep it secret from all, even that boy who sits beside you and watches, arms itching to stretch across a span of wings and leap into the sun.

And when Daedalus built the labyrinth, Ettore, how could he have imagined his own imprisonment? What we raise up, my son, will follow us down. Build what is good in Africa, son of mine. Build what you want to carry with you always in here: and his father taps Ettore's uniformed chest as the *Cleopatra*'s horn blares and the cheering crowds roar and wave goodbye to their departing soldiers. Did I really raise a son to be a soldier? Leo Navarra asks as he embraces Ettore quickly then turns his face.

⇒

HOW MANY YEARS has it been since that day? Ettore keeps his head turned away from the prison site and presses his back against the tree that grows like a lone soldier on the opposite side of the plateau. On a footpath just beyond him, a group of villagers stare in quiet confusion at the activities of the construction workers. He tries to focus on writing a letter to his parents instead, ignoring the pressure of his camera against his leg, that steady reminder of all the photographs he has not taken today, the photographs that Colonel Fucelli expects of him. Papa, they are making a prison that will hold no prisoners. They are going to fling men into the sky who have no wings. They are going to test the laws of gravity and terror and order me to photograph the ascent and fall. We are going to make Icarus and hurl him into the sun.

Ettore pauses to watch two laborers balance a wooden plank up the last steps of the incline to the plateau. A swath of land has been cleared for the foundation, and a pile of stones and rolls of barbed wire for a fortified wall sit next to the patch of ground unnatural in its evenness. He should be reporting to Fucelli each night with a roll of film for the colonel to send to Asmara to develop. But today, the fourth day of this task, is also his father's birthday and he has waited with growing anxiety for any news from home. None has arrived.

A sharp whistle sails above his head and Ettore looks up. One of the truck drivers is pointing to the ridge where the Ethiopians were standing. He is gesturing frantically. There is no one there anymore. Ettore stands and grabs his camera, tucks his notebook into his bag, and rushes to the *camionista*. They have been too lax, even the guards that Fucelli sends to watch the site have been sitting in whatever shade they can find, bored from the monotony after so many days.

They just left, just like that, the driver says, snapping his fingers and wiping his face with the edge of his dirty T-shirt. The man looks around, worried. Should we leave? He slaps his hat on his head then takes it off and shoves it in his back pocket. Did you hear what happened in Addis Ababa?

It is all that anyone can talk about: the relentless reprisals for the assassination attempt on Viceroy Rodolfo Graziani. The suspects have all but vanished. Thousands have been arrested. Blazing fires have raged in Addis Ababa and even towns across the highlands, some for as long as three days. Civilians and *soldati* alike have been given free rein to do what they want with any Ethiopian found on the street. Jan Meda and other fields around Addis Ababa are filling with mass graves. Rivers are flowing with burned bodies. The prisons are beyond capacity and the requests to take some of the captives and expedite their death sentences have been sent out to every military base across the country. Truckloads of prisoners: men, women, and children are crisscrossing the highlands, heading toward prison camps in Danane and other sites not put on maps.

Fear and paranoia are thick in every military base. Graziani's brutal retaliations have been embarrassing for Rome. The details of the massacres are being retold in newspapers, in whispers around campfires, in bars across East Africa and Libya. And now, the newest rumor: the guerrillas are getting stronger. They are increasing in number due to these reprisals. Villagers report seeing their emperor. They have seen him in the northern highlands, gathering more troops.

Ettore shakes his head, trying to calm the driver. Colonel Fucelli wasn't worried about it, he says. And he's usually very aware of every possibility, he adds.

This is true: Fucelli, on hearing of Graziani's light injuries and the ruthless response, merely laughed. And if he'd been in my position when these savages attacked me? he'd asked Ettore. That man's a coward, always has been, Fucelli added. And this is like killing a fly with a cannon ball.

This place, the driver continues, shaking his head. This place, I can't wait to go home. They just disappeared, he repeats. Then he stops, shakes his head again as if befuddled by a riddle, and walks toward a group of laborers staring at them in the clearing, watching for signs of alarm.

Interlude

The emperor lights a match and lifts his head to the cloudy sky above his new home in Bath, England. He closes his hand around the flame. He tries to hold it there as the heat licks against his palm and shoots waves of pain down his spine. He murmurs a chant to smother the growing agony. But then: he cannot help it and he snatches his hand away, defeated. He shakes his head, grateful for this private moment. What does it mean to burn an entire human being? This is the question that shook him awake in this pre-dawn hour of a new day. What does it mean to listen to the cries from a flame-engulfed home and stand with a rifle to shoot any who escape? And is it really possible that these Italians are throwing children into those same burning huts and houses? What kind of god fashions men like these? What miracle can stop this evil and send these foreigners back to their wretched homes?

His house in Bath is large and made of stone and wood, rich with the smells of rust and dying flowers. It is many-roomed with paneled walls and a staircase leading to his sleeping family. In the large front lawn where he stands now and gazes at the hills that resemble the rolling landscape in Harar, it is still difficult to convince himself that he is here, in England, and so very far from home.

His city is burning. His country is crumbling. His people are being butchered mercilessly by Italian civilians and military alike. He thinks he can smell the smoke even from this distance. He can hear the trucks that are dragging living bodies bound by rope until they are dead.

Just behind him on a ledge at the window, his small English dictionary flutters between the words he has tried to find to best convey this horror: paralyzing, terrorizing, mortifying, shocking, stupefying. To kill: to make dead, to extinguish life, to murder. Ghostly apparitions have been trudging past him since the night before, motioning him back to Ethiopia: Haile Selassie, Jan Hoy, Teferi, we're waiting. Where have you gone? Teferi, Haile Selassie, come home.

The hills that return his stare in Bath show him no mercy. Home is everywhere. And every morning in this country has been like the first, an unending spiral into dejection, sunlight a timid spray behind stubborn clouds. He wakes in a large bed at one end of the gulf that separates him from his wife. He stands up, careful not to wake her, and looks around the spare room. He reads his Bible and says his prayers, then gets dressed and shrugs a shamma across his shoulders to ease the persistent cold. He walks into each day knowing what he will face: the same chill, the same feeble light, the same heavy raindrops that flatten on him like an accusatory finger.

His fighters have moved deeper into the mountains. Carlo Fucelli is building a strange, new prison in Debark, his camp bloated with excess artillery and reinforcements. Kidane is based near the site. His men will continue to fight as hard as ever, but they need weapons, they need your help. They are wondering where you are, Your Majesty, Haile Selassie, Teferi, where are you?

This is where he is: hunched in front of his speaker as Radio London announces the massacres in Addis Ababa. This is also where he is: crouched in plumes of smoke and screams, readying to charge at the advancing enemy. He is here, too, in his smoldering city, picking his way through the destroyed homes and mass graves left behind by those butchers. In Bath, in his home named Fairfield, Emperor Haile Selassie needs no help in imagining fire-ravaged huts and buildings, trees splintered by bombs, the teff and sorghum fields poisoned and burned by gaseous fumes. But he cannot imagine what the Italians are doing to human beings, his people, his subjects, the children of a generation born to lift his country up. Soon, the empress, his children, and his advisers will gather around this same radio and tilt toward the news and listen as if their bodies can soak up every hissing detail. But he, the emperor, Jan Hoy, Haile Selassie, Teferi Mekonnen, all he wants to do is stand up, then walk into another room to cross an ocean and enter his port and sneak through the highlands to tell his people he has returned to fight. Instead, he is here, where there is no sun, where all that breathes survives in shadow.

Mɪɴɪᴍ'ꜱ ᴛʀᴀɪɴɪɴɢ ɪɴᴛᴇɴꜱɪꜰɪᴇꜱ: ᴋɪᴅᴀɴᴇ ᴍᴀᴋᴇꜱ ʜɪᴍ ꜱᴛᴀɴᴅ ᴀɴᴅ ꜱɪᴛ, walk and pivot. He settles Minim's arms at his sides and his hands in front of him and brings his index fingers and thumbs together in a subtle triangle. Aster watches closely, making adjustments, bowing to Minim and waiting for his signal to lift her head. Together, the couple holds his chin and pulls back his shoulders, and stops his quick glances backward to Hirut. They monitor his smiles, lecture him on the right demeanor with young subjects and injured soldiers, remind him again and again how to respond to soldiers and peasants and nobility.

You are our father, Kidane and Aster say to Minim. The country is full of your children. You are the sun and we walk in the light of your grace. Don't forget this, don't become less than you are. Don't you hear what's happening in your country? You must be our every hope.

Minim begins to walk straighter, to take more measured and even steps. He squares his back and raises his chin and learns to blink as if he has always stood in the glare of the sun. Minim wakes now in the mornings and solemnly waits for Hirut to serve his coffee. He turns his head as she approaches and gives only a nod to convey his approval. They start to move together, one tethered to the silent orders of the other, one following as the other hints at the direction they want to lead. By the time Kidane and Aster return to their routines, Hirut and Minim require no words to be understood, no sound to make known what the one who leads is asking of the one who guards.

And as Worku and other runners crisscross the country with reports of more reprisals and bodies left to rot on Italian gallows, Hirut and the men and women move higher into the hills to train at night. They swing their knives while sprinting and aiming for the enemy's throat. Hirut balances her rifle while galloping on Kidane's horse. She angles her spear as Adua speeds down the field, and when Aklilu rushes to pull her down, she kicks so close to his jaw that he exclaims in surprise. They continue night after night after night until Hirut finds that her fear has lost its edge. The routine dulls the terror. She becomes so accustomed to the lean-and-swing of the knife exercises that she finds herself practicing the moves in daylight: while collecting firewood and hauling water, while serving coffee and bringing the emperor his food. Her body molds to its requirements, her mind shapes itself around new loyalties, and it happens almost naturally, until it is nothing to imagine a figure stumbling and falling. She is new and unstained, free of blood and unafraid. She is made whole. She pictures Kidane's face illumined by a sliver of light in the dark. She imagines him imprisoned by a hundred shifting shadows, and she is the king of that dark dominion. She balances her knife in an expert hand as he pleads to be released. She slides it in an arch across his throat, and when he rises, due to a miracle, due to poor aim, due to lack of strength, Hirut no longer falters but does it again and again and again, striving for perfect vengeance.

BOOK
3
RETURNS

Photo

The prison: a shrunken wooden box of a building surrounded by a barbed-wire fence: one small widow, virtually airless, without the mercy of light. There, between two hulking stones, beyond a short footpath leading toward oblivion, Fucelli points to a dark form in the sky, his mouth open, his eyes wide, that pale face twisted in gleeful cruelty. Above his head, a startled bird arrows up, into the sun. The *soldati* and *ascari*, menacing figures sculpted in shadow, lean toward the plummeting form of a prisoner made heavier by despair. Two trucks frame the vision like guard posts, windshields and tires splattered in mud, canvas dropped to reveal two more men, bound by rope and frozen by terror, waiting for flight.

Photo

A young boy, bony shoulders and large-headed, shivering in the bright sun. Lips chapped, mouth parted, eyes stark in a gaunt and hungry face. A slender finger raised to the sky, a gesture for patience, for time, for mercy, for hope.

Photo

A woman slumped against a walking stick, paralyzed leg dangling beneath her long dress. A row of braids that fan out to thick, dark curls. Tattoos gracing the line of her throat to her jaw. Bruises near her eyes, at her mouth, a thread of blood dried against her ear. She is mid-sentence, her tongue against her teeth, curving around a word lost forever.

Photo

A young man, furious and proud, uncombed hair blowing freely in the wind. Sharp cheekbones, a slender chin, narrow eyes unafraid to glare at the photographer. A finger pointed, an accusation, an eternal damning.

Photo

Two. A young woman clasping an older man to her chest. Delicate features twisted in fear, swollen from fists. A mouth that dips to one side from a blow that has drawn blood and caked on a lock of hair. A stained dress. The older man: a masculine version of her, face darkened by sun, features stiff, shocked, a slender cut that follows the back of his neck, blood dripping into his worn T-shirt long past clean.

An Album of the Dead

Twins, bound back to back. A young man caught mid-movement, features a blur except for that open mouth. A boy, lanky and broad shouldered, hands clasped together to beg. An old woman, defiant, immobile, chin up, eyes blazing. A man, face beaten beyond recognition, a series of swollen, broken features. A couple, wife clinging to husband, face buried in his shoulder, his ripped shirt exposing a long, angry cut. Two young men, wild curls thick against their necks, gripping hands, face-to-face, eyes only for each other. A young man, rigid as a soldier, a bloom of dark curls framing a furious and handsome face. A young man, bookish, eyeglasses, trembling, shaking head forcing a sweep of blurry features. A young man, hands bound behind his back, shoulders protruding painfully, a slender neck jutting forward, mouth pursed to spit. A girl. A young woman. A nun. Two slack-mouthed beggars. Three young deacons, steady eyes. A girl. Another. A young man, his brother, his father, identical faces reshaped by blows, equally swollen. A girl buckling from fear, the top of her head, the face twisted in anguish and confusion. A girl, a woman, a young man, an elderly man, a man and his wife, a family of three, a defiant old man, a brother and sister refusing to let go of each other, a bent-backed woman, a tall, lithe boy. A blind man, opaque eyes. Twins, again, bound back to back.

Signature: Ettore Navarra, soldato e fotografo
Signature: Colonello Carlo Fucelli, Ricordi d'Africa

IT TAKES NOTHING MORE THAN A SLIDE OUT OF LINE AND A STEP AWAY from the mail truck for Ettore to imagine himself back home at the kitchen table with his father, the two of them bent over a blank sheet of paper while his mother cooks, his father's hand wrapped around his, both of theirs around a newly sharpened pencil, his heart beating rapidly, fearful of making a mistake. Let me see your handwriting, *figliolo*, my dear son, let me see how you write your alphabet. Ettore's father takes his hand and guides it over the page, placing each letter between the markers, the lines slender and straight, the curves plump like inflated balloons. Imagine the shape of a word mimicking the shape of a thought, Ettore. Let your hand follow, like water follows itself in a river. Don't give up. You will learn to keep pace with your thinking, you will chase your ideas in handwriting that is clear and always strong.

Ettore stares down at the envelope. All the years of waiting push against him. His knees are weak. He is sweating even in the cooling breeze. He cannot focus though he keeps wiping his eyes until they hurt. He looks down at his hand again, his palm is open: this is the first letter he has received from his father since embarking on the *Cleopatra* and heading to war. Every message before now was filtered through his mother: Your father misses you, your father has bought a map of Ethiopia, your father says he loves you, your father asks if the reports about renewed attacks are true, he says your name every night before sleeping.

Ettore hurries to the canteen and sinks against the building, the idling mail truck a grating noise in his head, the petrol fumes dizzying. He glances around but no one is paying attention. Everyone else is stretched toward the postman and the large canvas bag from which he withdraws handfuls of envelopes while shouting names. Ettore hunches over the letter: his mother's name is in the upper-left corner but this is his father's hand. No one else makes letters shaped as if they were racing for the other side of the paper. The speed of Leo Navarra's writing has always been a wondrous confirmation of his astounding intelligence. And here is his own name, in bold letters in the perfect center of the envelope, *TO: my son Ettore Navarra*. There is no censor's stamp; this letter has managed to slip past them.

He feels along the edges of the envelope and traces the firm, solid marks that make his name. Ettore opens the envelope carefully, tearing it on the long side. Then he unfolds the letter, afraid to straighten the crisp creases, and he reads:

My dear son, there is one thing you must keep in mind as you read this: I have never been a stranger to myself. I know clearly the costs of my decisions, and I understand well who has suffered my consequences. I hope one day we will sit together and I will have the courage to explain it all. For now, I write to finally tell you this: I was another man before you knew me. I had a family before you, another son and wife. You are my second-born, your mother's first. I have never told you about my former life because I have taught myself to believe that what exists is what matters. What is visible is what counts. But you don't even know my name, my son. My first wife, Anya, would have wanted me to tell you. My second wife, your mother, Gabriella, understands my caution. She knows how much can be contained in a word.

I can tell you this: one night in Odessa, under a light so soft you could have photographed the shadows of ghosts, my old life ended. After I lost my first son, I did not know what I was. What do you call a sonless father? If I had found that name I would have exchanged it for Leo. When I was close to your age, I stepped out of the town of my birth, in Ukraine, and moved to Odessa for love. Then I was forced to turn my back on it because of everything that city destroyed. I left Odessa a Jew and entered Venice an atheist. When I escaped, all I tried to do was get as far away as possible on land, by foot. Alone. I forced my body to bear every pain and deprivation it could withstand. It was my attempt at penance. I sought my own forgiveness for being alive. You might have heard your mother whisper of the pogroms of 1905. Is it important to give you details? What do I tell you about them except they are coming again and I have failed to protect you?

There are those who are meant for distance, my Ettore. I am one of them and I fear so are you. We are seekers of boundaries. If we are lucky, we will chance upon those generous enough to be drawn into our fold. Your mother has done this for me. She allows me to take her hand in the dark every night. She holds me until I fall asleep. She stays awake until I am sure there is no smoke seeping into our home. Is there a greater gesture of love than this? Is there a greater act of selfishness than what I force on her every day?

I have said this to you before: every visible body is surrounded by light and shade. We move through this world always pulled between the two. I know that you have never understood me. You have found my instructions harsh and unforgiving, full of questions and irreducible. But you have lived without fear so you have always felt you had the right to judge. I have taken this as proof that I have done something right. Your father built a family and a new life without bowing his head. He raised a son to imagine a better future. That has been enough.

Ettore, bear witness to what is happening. Make living your act of defiance. Record it all. Do it relentlessly, with that stubbornness and precision that is so very much like your father. This is why I gave you your first camera. Do not let these people forget what they have become. Do not let them turn away from their own reflections—

—why am I telling you this? These are not a father's dying words. What do you understand of what I have said?

My dear son, your mother sits in the kitchen while I am in my study.

She, too, is writing you a letter she will put into a box we are saving for you.
We write separately because you have now become the holder of our secrets.
Your mother and I know too much about each other. We can no longer be
safekeepers of new knowledge. We cannot take another truth. She cannot
bear to look at me if she thinks I have one more layer she has not seen. I
am telling you this because you will not see us again. As surely as my light
burns in this office, I will not see my second-born, brother to a ghost, son to a
phantom. Do not come back, Ettore. No matter what you hear, do not repeat
your father's history in the place he once called home. Stay in Abyssinia.
Find the man you will become. This will not be my last letter but it will be
the most truthful. I have always loved you. —your father, Leo

➤

HIS CHEST ACHES. His head spins. He is shaking uncontrollably, the
rhythm both ugly and pitiless. Ettore stares at his father's signature,
the letters are abrupt and jagged, hurried and slanted. He goes back
to the beginning of the letter: My dear son. My dear son. He leans
against the wall of the canteen, presses his head on the firm surface.
He tries to trace the logic of his father's thoughts, the implications
behind his questions: *What do you understand of what I have said? Is*
it important to give you details? What do you call a sonless father? Ettore
goes back again to the letter, forces himself to read it, forces himself to
let the weight of it press down on every memory of his father, of his
father's relentless instructions and unending disapproval, until his life
sinks beneath every fact and assumption he took for granted. Because
he cannot escape this uncompromising detail: he was not the son his
father wanted, and perhaps he never will be.

➤

AND SO THIS IS WHY he stays at the canteen and waits for the daily
truckload of prisoners. He wants to be amongst those who will give of
themselves then spin like ash into oblivion. He will photograph them as

they are suddenly made aware of their boundaries. He will search for himself in their twisted figures flailing and breaking in the plummet. Ettore pauses at the threshold of the road that climbs to the cliffs, waiting for the truck to inch its way up. The vehicle has rolled to a stop. It is idling, its engine protesting. The driver leans out and waves ahead of him, then tucks his head lazily back inside. It is only then that Ettore notices Fifi's servant. She is blocking the truck's advance and motioning with a basket in her hand as she walks forward. She ambles slowly, confidently, and nods to the driver. She slips a hand into the open window, then she goes to the back and settles the round, flat *agelgil* the natives carry onto the bumper.

She takes out a bundle of leaves and distributes it quickly to the prisoners. She glances over her shoulder and when she sees Ettore, she angles to obstruct his view of her arm reaching again into the basket then into the tarp-covered truck bed. She moves so fast, it is difficult to tell exactly what she is doing. She pauses and looks around again, then turns and speaks urgently. She listens to something the prisoners are telling her. She nods. Then she walks away with her basket tucked in her arms. She does not look at Ettore. It is easy to assume she has said a prayer for them and let them say their confessions. But today, Ettore knows it's something else, another breach in the natural order of things.

———

THE COOK SLIPS a small pouch of powder wrapped in khat leaves to each of the prisoners. Get ready to be in constant touch with death, she says. You will die but do not give them your fear, she adds. Do not beg.

The prisoners' hands and legs are bound, but they press toward her as best as they can and stare terrified into the sunlit valley that expands past her shoulders. Every other day, there are at least five who arrive. They come between two and three in the afternoon. They're driven up to the prison near the cliffs at precisely 3:30 p.m. They are photographed in front of the prison by 4:00 p.m. They are re-bound and cumbersome clothing is cut loose. They wait in the newly built prison until they are pushed off the cliff between five o'clock and five thirty, providing that *sol-dato*, Navarra, with the best light. All of this synchronized by the watches the *ferenjoch* love to obey. She has begun trying to prepare each truckload, hoping to move them away from naïve hope and into steady conviction.

Eat this right away, she tells the new prisoners now. Chew it well and swallow so you become angels and learn to fly. She refuses to speak in a whisper even though she knows Navarra is watching; Fifi has bribed the driver and other guards.

What she sees, peering into the back of that truck: men and boys, women and girls, all of them confused, all of them frightened, all of them unprepared to leap into the air when thrown.

There is no escape, the cook says to them. But you can make a way to the other side. Take this, it's *astefaris* and something else to take your mind far away. And she shoves an extra bundle toward them, biting her lip to stop the trembling.

I'm dying for Ethiopia, one of the young men says.

I did nothing wrong, why am I here? a girl adds.

Tell my mother you saw me, they all plead.

The cook shakes her head and stretches out a hand to settle it on the leg of the closest one, an elderly man quivering in his worn T-shirt. You'll die needlessly, Abbaba, she says. You'll die for no cause, because you are innocent, and they will not remember your name.

She looks to the rest of them. But tell me who you are, she says. Tell me slowly and repeat it three times, and I will make sure you are known. I will make of you a remembrance worthy of this fall. Say your name to me now. Say your name as you are photographed. Say it as you leap into the air and learn to fly. Do not let them forget who they have killed.

Then she ducks away and takes those names to Fifi, who will transcribe them into a ledger she has taken from Carlo Fucelli, and together, they will bury it in the ground in Fifi's tent and slide the cot back on top and when the war ends, they will bring it out and speak the names, one by one.

—

ETTORE WAITS UNTIL the cook disappears, then strides to the back of the truck. He raps his knuckle against the bumper to get the *camionista*'s attention. I'm just taking a look, he says.

He sticks his head inside the canvas-covered bed, flinching at the sudden darkness, momentarily overwhelmed by the stench of sweat and wood, of dirt and dried blood. Ettore turns away: he has never looked directly at these prisoners. He has seen them only through the lens, and only for the purposes of arranging them in perfect light: their worth measurable in the balance of shadow and sharpness. He has found ways not to hear their pleas and curses as they pivot, poised like a dancer, on the edge of the cliff for that last picture, the final image very likely the only one they have ever taken in their life. Every photograph has become a broken oath with himself, a breach in the defenses he set up to ignore what he really is: an archivist of obscenities, a collector of terror, a witness to all that breaks skin and punctures resolve and leaves human beings dead.

Staring into the truck with his father's letter burning through his shirt pocket and into his heart, Ettore sees that thing that must give of itself, that bounded thing forced to acknowledge its own feeble existence. He feels a surge of pity for the prisoners looking back at him in confusion and despair. He wants to reach out and grasp the hand of the elderly man closest to him and find a way to explain that he means no real harm. The body is contained by its extremities, he wants to remind the old man. We are all made finite by our own nature. What will happen to you today is what happens to all of us in the end. You will break and fall but then you will owe no more to this world.

My own rupture, he would add if he could be understood, has been a slow progressive fall to the bottom. It has been an endless descent that began with these words: Take a picture, *soldato*.

Instead, Ettore stays quiet and wipes his brow, the heat bearing down as heavily as ever. He lets his eyes adjust: they are no different from all the others, men and women in a range of ages and a young boy clinging to his father's hand. A hard kernel of light falls across the young boy's shirt: it is covered in grass stains, as if he fell while running, as if he tripped on something and tumbled at full speed before his father could catch him. All of them are chewing something, mouths moving in slow synchronicity, teeth grinding down thoroughly before swallowing in healthy gulps.

What's that? he asks. He is surprised at the roughness in his voice, the way he so easily becomes that *soldato* that Fucelli wants. How natural it has been to swerve into cruelty. How effortless to be splintered by the headlines that declare every Jew an enemy and a spy. How easy it has been to read those booklets defending the prohibition against Jews owning businesses and even working in photography, then to unleash his helpless anger on those prisoners who trembled in front of him. How simple it has been for Colonel Carlo Fucelli to suggest that he does not belong here. That he might not be Italian. That obedience is his only hope.

The father of the young boy points to his mouth and shrugs, eyes narrowing and starting to glaze. It's medicine, he says.

One of the women drops her head and smiles.

The boy points to Ettore and shouts, *Viva l'Italia!* And his shoulders shake from suppressed laughter and the other prisoners join in.

It is a sound that cuts into Ettore. He steps back, staggered by the indecency of it, by its vulgar ease. The prisoners wait for him to respond, watching in mockery and disdain, these pathetic creatures unaware yet of their destiny. What is the miracle of man if not this dark resolve in the face of horror? It would be simple to turn around and go back to his tent until it was time to climb up the hill and take their photographs. It would be simple to pretend today was a day like any other. But Ettore looks at the placid expressions, lets his eyes trail over their sluggish features, their dirty clothes, their unkempt hair, and what he sees is a confirmation of something his father said long ago: There is no way but forward, my son. That is the only true escape.

Photo

A boy in a stained shirt rests his cheek against a tall boulder as if it were a father's chest. He stares at the camera, doe-eyed and curious, his lips folded around a mouthful of food, a stream of words, a cry for help, a burst of laughter. One palm balances against the hard surface of stone, his finger raised and pointed ahead, the gesture an accusation and a plea for patience. His small heels dip over the plateau's edge, his broad toes cling desperately to earth. What expands behind him is majestic and stupefying: a vast landscape of tall mountains and merciless rocks, a gaping ravine that drops out of view, breathtaking even in this frozen glimpse. His face: a blur of tender features: the shaking head moving faster than shutter speed, swinging left then right then left again in defiance and horror.

What cannot be captured: that he repeats his name until that final free fall, Zerihun, Zerihun, Zerihun, and the ricochet of his voice is the earth's mournful lament, land tempering its cruelty.

—

THEY SAY THEIR NAMES and demand to know his. They drag themselves toward the threshold then collapse to the ground in mindless laughter. Light wavers around their sluggish figures: unsteady bodies sinking into haze. Ettore leans in, arches close, orders *ascari* to keep them still, but it is impossible to get a steady shot. The last push is desperate. It is a plea for normalcy, a return to control and command. The prisoners tip over the edge with soft bones, relieved and graceless, and all Ettore can photograph are awkward figures buckling into empty space, shouting their names into a gulf that multiplies their voices, a repetitive, deafening chorus. They spill over the edge as if gliding underwater, drowning and surging up for air, spinning between a rapturous dream and a paralyzing nightmare: ghastly shapes of unspeakable words: dark marks against the sky.

Years from now, in that port city café in Alexandria, Ettore will explain to Khairallah Ali that nothing of his father's life was really exposed in the letter that Ettore received. He will force himself to admit, when Khairallah Ali asks him about Leonardo Navarra, that he still does not know enough about him. My father was always a stranger to me, he will say. I knew him through his questions, not his answers. Ettore will also confess, after a tense pause, that he sometimes wonders if there were more letters that never arrived to him, other letters from his father that were lost in transit. My father was a man of few words and many meanings, Ettore will also add. But I am sure there were other letters that would have told me more. He would not have asked so few questions.

Ettore is partially correct: Leo Navarra did indeed write everything about himself to his son in many letters. In fact, Leo surprised himself and broke his silence to reveal every aspect of his existence to Ettore. He wrote himself into being. Both the past he had chosen to leave unspoken, and that other past left for dead. Leo wrote furiously. And in those moments when he wanted to shrink away and leave it all behind again, he kept on writing. When he was finished and could say no more without repetition, he packed those many letters into a box. Then he and Gabriella put it away and waited for Ettore's return. It is this box that Khairallah Ali hands to Ettore in Alexandria so long after the war. It was delivered by a friend from Venice instructed to find the Egyptian journalist who might know the famed Italian photographer whose parents were taken by the Germans and sent first to Risiera di San Sabba and then on to Auschwitz. It is this box that Ettore opens and searches repeatedly for the other letters.

Yet on the night that Leo was certain that it was indeed smoke that he smelled rising in his adopted country of Italy, he got out of bed, crept into Ettore's room, and took out all of his letters from the box. He moved into the kitchen and pulled out a pair of scissors from a drawer. He waited until he could control his trembling. Then he held each piece of paper between the sharp silver blades and began to cut. He destroyed every last letter, thoroughly and meticulously, then swept the floor clean. He worked for hours, aware that Gabriella was in the doorway in her nightgown, crushed by grief. The next morning, he sat down and started a new letter. It was much simpler, more concise, more fitting of the man he now was. Then he put that letter addressed to his son into the mailbox and went to sleep until his dinner.

This is why when Ettore sees his father's letter in Ethiopia some part of him realizes he is looking at a broken man. He sees the evidence in the small, perfectly even script: Leo Navarra has tried to strip his handwriting of its usual flourishes and erase any emotion that might give too much of himself away. He has tried to rub himself out of his past again and leave only what is necessary inside the lines. Leo has also, in fact, left a final challenge for his son. He has hidden himself between the words, tucked in every space and margin, and he has written in such a way that he still manages to beg: to be found, to be rescued, and to be held up—for once—in the soft glow of tender light.

A Brief History of Leonardo Navarra

It was not that he knew all the things he could not say. It was not that he understood with ringing clarity those facts to be transmitted through inference, and those details that could only be shaped into sound. Leo Navarra, born Lev Naiman on 19 April of an indeterminate and quite ordinary year, was not ever sure that what he left unsaid deserved the honor of that treatment. Neither could he be certain that those things he chose to utter were better served by their vocalization. He had always been profoundly aware of the infinite distance between those two poles of expression. He had witnessed too many errors of omission and tactless inclusion in the talks between his parents. Their words, all those trapped in muted gestures and those hurled out of shouting mouths, hovered just at the periphery of his vision as a boy, waiting for him to stumble.

On the day that Leo, born Lev Naiman to two exhausted parents in a tilted wooden house, learned to speak, his mother said his first words did not produce the usual noises of a new tongue practicing language. She insisted to friends that her young but intensely alert son, balanced on her left hip, looked into her face one bright day and simply said: We must all suffer our consequences.

When Lev's tired father, Maksim, came home one night to behold his son repeating those words, he sat down at their table, put his head in his hands, and mumbled: He was born in Izyum but it was once called Izyumchik and before that it was something else lost to his gen-

eration. He does not see that soil by another name is the same soil. He
imagines that a word can alter a shape. But you must teach him, my
beloved, that it is the land that carries our suffering when we die. It
is the land that remains the same, no matter what we call ourselves.
And what he meant, Lev would later learn, was this: that only soil will
remember who we are, nothing but earth is strong enough to withstand the burden of memory. To become unknown, it is not enough to
shift a name, one must go where the land has always been a stranger to
those who share your blood.

Lev Naiman; see also: Leonid Novsky; see also: Leonardo Navarra,
husband to the lovely Anya (21 March 1881–19 October 1905), father
to little Boris (25 November 1902–19 October 1905) whose last full day
of life was spent sleeping in his terrified mother's embrace while his
father stumbled home from work, shouting for them through the fiery
streets of Odessa, careening up the smoke-filled staircase until neither
air nor word could escape from his mouth. Leo, father to Ettore, husband to Gabriella, proud Italian, eternal atheist, firm believer in facts
and details, and holder of the unshakeable conviction that what is seen
must also necessarily be true, wrote a letter to his only living son and
pinned a half-hidden life on the page. He did so with a zealot's assur-
ance that it would be decoded and discovered. But that would not necessarily be the case, as Khairallah Ali realized sitting in that café in
Alexandria with Ettore.

THE ACT ITSELF IS MEANINGLESS, SUCH A SMALL THING, LIKE A FATHER setting a little boy on a tall stack of firewood and pulling out the bottom log. There is no sentimentality to the order Carlo Fucelli gives to Ibrahim: Get me that letter Navarra can't seem to stop reading after two solid weeks. Get it immediately and let me look at it before he knows it's gone. It is what men do to those they command: they push and bend and wait to see how long before the boy finally breaks. They do it because they can. They do it because it makes the distracted boy malleable again, and impressively obedient. The photographs of the prisoners have not been coming in as regularly as they should. Ettore Navarra is not taking as many as he used to. The *ascari* are reporting that he spends his time leaning beside the thick-rooted tree that is some distance from the cliffs while they push the prisoners.

Ibrahim delivers the letter to him in the middle of the night, thrusting it into his hand then waiting for him to finish reading. Carlo does not ask how he went into the Italian section without being detected. He trusts in Ibrahim's skills, in his complete allegiance to every order. Carlo forces Ibrahim to wait as he reads it again and the effect is still the same: the sentences are clear, but the emotion slips out of his hold at each full stop, every new thought disintegrates by the time he arrives at the next comma. There is nothing here he can hold still and pin down to scrutinize. This is a letter where meaning rises to the surface in dim light, then disappears, an intimate message from a father to a son, from a father to himself.

Carlo Fucelli sits down at his desk and pushes the letter aside. He picks up the urgent telegram announcing that a Luce News crew is arriving at the same time that intercepted messages reveal that Haile Selassie has ordered Kidane to ambush his camp. The Ethiopians will attack tomorrow, he is to allow the camera crew to film it all. Carlo rubs his eyes, deliberating on his next steps, astonished by his good luck. Finally, when Ibrahim coughs discreetly, he stops and hands Navarra's letter back. Staring at the telegram again, Carlo finds himself strangely depleted of language, fatigued, as he nods to the man and hears him spin away, no more than a swoosh in the night.

Carlo strides out of his office the next day to meet with the crew from Luce News. The orders from Rome are to give them full access to his men, to let them film the confrontation while ensuring their safety. Italy should not still be fighting these rebels. This war was declared a victory for Il Duce. The northern front should be subdued by now. Let the cameras see Italian might. Carlo checks the buttons on his jacket, straightens the helmet on his head, wipes his sunglasses clean, and slips a cigarette into his mouth. Every detail must be considered, from his appearance to his performance: he must act the part he has wanted all his life, that essence of leadership that he has worked to exhibit in Ethiopia. He must be the heroic leader, the ruthless enemy, the fearless commander at the helm of an undefeatable army.

But something in Leo Navarra's letter has nudged against memory. As if the man had been writing to him, the ghost-son he lost, a man now risen from the flames and ashes to fight against his opponents. Leo Navarra has introduced him to something new: a paternal affection that does not include even a hint of mockery or disappointment.

Today, this detail strikes him as breathtakingly potent, perhaps even fatal prior to battle: there are some things he has never known about grown men, about those who watch over the small boys who grow into men. This ignorance feels like a quiet disease discovered too late, an infectious wound that was gnawing deeper while he thought he simply had an itch. His father was a difficult man, trapped by his own competitive inclinations, but Carlo Fucelli had assumed this was the way of most fathers. To see the aching reserve in Leo Navarra's reminders to his son was to see a love and adoration too large to be contained in mere words. It is to see what he has lacked his entire life.

This is why Carlo insists that the camera crew take long, lingering shots of him in full uniform, proud and unafraid in front of his prison. It is for those men like his deceased father who confused fear with cowardice, mistook tears for weakness, and blamed a soft heart for the unspoken hatred that a son learned to nurture until it was time to leave home and sail to Tripolitania. It is for them, *ragazzi*, Carlo wants to say to the camera crew, it is for all those who doubt the legends we will make on this day, for all those who refuse to believe that simple men can be gifted a hero's remembrance. Today is for all those who do not think it is possible to rise up from total collapse and still walk on one's own two feet.

Focus in close, Carlo Fucelli says to the cameraman as his men set up their barricades. Pan up slowly. Get wide shots of the prison and swoop right to capture the cliffs. Shoot from the rebels' perspective. Get your stills of the landscape before the attack. The Abyssinians are on their way and we'll defend our country as you have never seen. I will give you a battle worthy of the Roman Empire, worthy of the great Trojan conflict. I won't send the tanks or cannons to destroy them before they approach. I won't bring the planes to spray them with poison while they're still getting dressed to fight. We will do this as our fathers did and win for Italy with bayoneted rifles and bare hands. Focus and zoom and steady the shots. Prepare for wondrous displays of bravery. Look! Behold the enemy now in the dust rising on the horizon. See their might but do not be deceived: they will come as Memnon came for Achilles. And they will die just the same.

THIS IS HOW THE AMBUSH BEGINS: WITH THE SLOW RISE OF A MONarch's shadow from a tall mountain peak. With the emperor's faint image caught in the whir and snap of a camera, reflected in the glint of a lens to ricochet against fog and hill. As Kidane's army, new recruits and seasoned fighters, prepares to separate into groups that will surround the Italians, the Shadow King and his female guard step forward onto that highest crest and gaze below. The army looks up and grows silent, awed by the presence of Emperor Haile Selassie, thrown into speechlessness by the sight of the guard who steps forward, resplendent in her uniform.

The whispers: He has come back. He is here. Jan Hoy will free his people. He will charge with us and kill the enemy and reclaim his throne. He is here!

They do not fear the growing rumble sliding through the valley from the Italian camp. The noises do not matter. Instead, they look toward Hirut, their new image of Mother Ethiopia, the one who represents all the women who have survived the war to raise their guns and fight or rush onto the battlefield to carry the wounded. The army falls prostrate. They press their foreheads into dirt. They curse those rumors that claim the emperor has fled to a foreign land. They thank the Almighty that their great leader has come to lead them in battle. And they vow to fight until they win or die.

Hirut glances at Minim as he slowly slips back out of view, behind the hill, and away from the line that will lead the charge. The army has dispersed into their positions, and no one is aware that the emperor has disappeared from sight. It is nearly impossible to distinguish his slender figure from the soft plume of dust that fans like a cape at his back. Hirut shivers as she watches him leave and sees Aster a few steps away doing the same. It is almost too much to bear: the thrill and the terror, the call and the risk, the honor and the obligation. She looks at Aklilu beside her and she feels herself steady and grow calm beneath his unwavering gaze. She nods to him, and he smiles back, then together, they look toward the fighters below and she finds Kidane. He is gripping Seifu's hand, nodding to Amha, glancing up at Aklilu, then over to Aster. Most of the other women who will fight alongside them are in dresses. Hirut imagines she can decipher what Kidane says to Seifu then signals to Aster, and what Aster in turn relays to the other women waiting for her command, it is what messengers warned them about already: The Italians are prepared. This will be no ambush but a real battle.

Get ready, Aklilu whispers. Follow me and stay close, he adds. He squeezes Hirut's arm, the pressure reassuring against her trembling. You've got a new gun now, the Wujigra is safe, you've been training.

When Kidane gives the signal, they will charge at the Italians while another group, led by Amha and Hailu, will swerve around the hill toward the construction workers' camp to puncture tires, steal tools and weapons, and cut communication lines. They will burn tents and kill those who get in their way. They will set fire to that awful prison and hurl the barbed wire off the cliff.

Hirut braces herself. The valley expands. Her ears begin to ring. She is sweating. They must run into the valley and then climb the next hill in order to begin their assault. There is a vast stretch of land they must cross where anything can happen, where everything is possible.

Steady, steady. Aklilu's voice is a brush of cool wind. Be strong, brave soldier, I'm right next to you.

And then: the darting light, a fallen star, a beam playing on water.

Kidane spins and arches toward the enemy, then flings himself down the hill, graceful and effortless, feet like wings, his long curls whipping in the wind, a dark and murderous crown. The army pivots in his direction, leans forward, and charges behind him without one sound, the valley below still trembling in anticipation.

Aklilu pulls her, and soon she is thrown into the sweep of dust clouds, other figures pushing beside her, against her, around her, to make their way to the enemy. She feels like she runs alone, a solitary figure balancing on slippery rocks. Then she trips over grass and finds herself helplessly caught in her own momentum. She falters then rights herself. She is shoved aside and forward and backward and she cannot see Aklilu. She stretches her hand as she barrels down the hill but he is nowhere.

Wait, she says softly. Wait for me.

She cannot see anything but the ground in front of her, and her legs moving her forward. She knows she is running, she knows she is quiet, but she cannot fathom how she is managing to do all this while paralyzed inside. She tries to call Aklilu's name, tries to lift her voice and puncture the silence, puncture this strange numbness, this uncontrollable momentum, but the sound is a soft buzz thrumming through her head, coursing down her spine and leaving her breathless as everything of this world unfolds in slow motion. Shoot, she tells herself. Shoot at the enemy. But she is blinded and deafened by that strange, internal cacophony, the world a dim outline pulsing in dust.

Hirut runs toward the noise. She runs away from it. She propels herself into the smoke and twirls out from it. She hears her name, then hears nothing at all. She jumps into the line of gunfire and swerves around it. She smells the tang of spilled blood and the suffocating aroma of new flowers. She spins in the chaos, pushed by instinct, guided by something else not her own. I stood up inside myself, *Emama*, she hears herself say, I stood up and I rushed against the enemy like a soldier and I saw that there was no one there, I saw that I had already killed them all without a shot. Then Hirut is spiraling in a whirlwind all her own, compelled by fury and fear, a singular figure stumbling across a now-empty hill, away from the action, further from her army, moving toward a separate, different battle.

—

SHE NEARLY CAREENS INTO HIM, moving so fast that she has to wheel her arms to stop herself. She imagines a knotted twig, then a pile of hardened dung left to bleach in the sun. The round-faced *ferenj* jerks his head back to look up at her, so stunned by her sudden appearance that he has no time to stand and pull up his trousers. His gun lies at his feet like a discarded shirt, a mound of leaves clutched in his hand. He delicately balances on his toes over a stink that hangs all around him, the odor so sharp that Hirut has to cover her mouth.

She takes small steps backwards, her rifle slanted across her back while he watches with his mouth sagging open, incapable of anything except the expulsion he has already started, helpless in the midst of this bodily function.

I'll go, she mumbles, but she cannot stop staring. She has never understood the *ferenj* to be real. These foreigners are mysterious killing beasts drained of goodwill and compassion, heartless and blood-less, machines.

He drops his leaves and grabs his rifle, the actions slow and blurry. He shouts and his soft, pink mouth sags open, his tonsils wiggle in the panic of his words.

She has done this many times before in her dreams: She has swung her rifle from her back and aimed and shot at Kidane. She has buried a single bullet into his chest then bent down to make sure he was dead. She has killed him many times, day after day, night after night, while walking and sleeping and eating and caring for the wounded. She has trained her-self to brace for the blunt force of discharge. She has carved a single line into the barrel for a new enemy down. She has practiced it so many times with Aklilu during training, and in her sleep, and as she dreamt, that her body knows just what to do. She imagines Kidane and pulls the trigger.

Boom, she says alongside the crack of the bullet spinning free. Boom.

Then she steps back to avoid his jerking legs, the splatter of blood pooling in the leaves, the new stink of urine, the soiled uniform and boots. Boom. And she picks up his rifle and shoulders it across her back, and runs.

Hirut hurls herself toward the noise, toward the grunts of pain. She pushes until she has no sensation and can only keep pace with that obedient body speeding back across the hill, aching for a final resolution. The closer she gets to the curtain of dust, the louder the clash of the rifles on her back. They flop against her spine, knocking into each other, forming a clamor that ricochets through the hills.

Hirut! This way, this way. Watch out!

Aklilu stands at the threshold of the cacophony, motioning her to one side, bloodstains streaked across the front of his shirt. He is waving his arms, drawing a dirty sleeve across his forehead to swipe aside the hair falling into his eyes, plastered down by a bleeding wound near his ear. The look he gives her is one of panic shielded by a hard glaze of cruelty, the emotions colliding in his open-throated scream of her name. He steps away from the tangle of bodies: uniformed and white-clothed, helmeted and bareheaded, and Hirut thinks for a moment he is opening his arms to her, calling to hold her tight and keep her from harm. Then she catches sight of Aster in the tangled group, weighted with dirt and blood, swinging her hand up and down, up and down, the gleam of a blade flashing with a terrifying quickness.

Help me! Aster is fury and fear woven into one simple body, a knot of rage bent over a limp and broken man.

Aklilu is motioning her away from the fight, Aster is beckoning her forward. Hirut feels the tug of safety but one of her rifles slides off her back, lands in the crook of her arm, and she who has nothing left that is really hers understands there is no other way. She nods to Aster, throws down the extra rifle, and charges into the huddle of bodies, screaming with her eyes shut.

She trips over a pair of legs, sinks onto her elbows, and scrapes her chin against a dirty boot. An elbow connects with her jaw and she jerks her head, blinded by the impact. She reaches out, tries to guess where she is, how far she has fallen. It is impossible to distinguish whole bodies. There are legs and arms, torsos and knees. She tries to stand but Aster flings her full weight against her back as she struggles to wrest a rifle away from an *ascaro*. Aster shouts curses at the soldier, making sound into a wall, and Hirut feels herself pressed down and flattened, and she knows she will die like this: trapped beneath legs. She swings her rifle up, tries to slide out, then she cannot breathe and starts to gasp, the sensation stifling and familiar: of being held in place in a dark night with Kidane's heavy weight across her. Hirut panics. Her chest tightens and she elbows and shoves and kicks until a hand takes hers and pulls her out and keeps pulling and she lets herself be dragged because what do girls like her know about rebellion, what do girls like her know about resistance, what do girls like her know but how to live and obey and keep quiet until it is time to die? And so it is not at all a surprise when she finally lifts her head to stare at Kidane in a sweat-stained uniform. He draws her closer to his chest while gripping her arm in that familiar way. Hirut pushes back, notes his confusion.

And when he takes her arm again and points away from the fighting bodies and says, And what if you are with child? You must keep yourself safe. Hirut feels herself bloom with a fresh and untapped terror and she imagines herself wholly destructible and worthy of death all at once.

There is no language but this:

Boom, she says. She picks up the rifle at her feet, taps her chest and mimes pulling the trigger. Boom. Kill me. She wipes the tears from her cheeks and says it: Shoot me. Boom.

Already, relief is washing over her. The hard knot that formed long ago inside her stomach is starting to unravel. The feeling is so sweet that she cannot help smiling and then she starts to laugh, spinning away from Kidane, watching him jump back into the fray. Boom, boom, please, shoot me. She is close enough to see his flushed cheeks, the scarred hands, the sweat on his neck, the dark curls that mat at his forehead. She does not know where Aster has gone. She cannot think. She is here, where she should be, at the center of the world, spinning free, finally.

~

SHELTERED BEHIND THE BARRICADE, his rifle aimed at an empty hill across from the narrow strip of land in front of him, Ettore sees an Ethiopian moving toward them at a fast sprint. Startled by the sight, he glances toward the rest of the *soldati*, all of them waiting to charge into the valley below. Fucelli has been sending them in waves, lengthening the battle for the cameraman, prolonging the attack and clumping groups across the field, spreading the points of contact. The colonel has been warned that Ethiopian reinforcements will come from behind the central fray, and Ettore can see now that they will provide a cinematic backdrop to the series of skirmishes dotting the valley.

Ettore settles into his weapon, trains the sights on the rebel. He considers this unnerving lone figure rushing at them, the impossibility of it. He must surely be an actor sent by Fucelli for the camera, a symbolic reminder of Italian strength.

Mario presses himself into his rifle, the veins in his arms bulging from the effort to hold his weapon steady. Then slowly, he lifts his head. My God, he says, my God.

A group of Abyssinians are astride horses in brightly colored saddles at the top of the hill across the valley. They are galloping down at full speed, a burst of light and color: a dozen warriors with wild hair, their cries like a discordant Greek chorus. Far ahead of them, that improbable figure, his chest exposed to the *soldati*, leaping over stone and grass, incomprehensible. Beautiful, even.

Then a dozen more on horses soaring down from that hill, close to engulfing that slender rebel, leaving the lonely soldier to scramble out of the way.

Is this real? Mario asks. Or is this for the camera? The face he turns to Ettore before swiveling back around is astounded and scared.

The *thuk* of spear: and a *soldato* toward the end of the line, behind the barricade, screams in pain. The soldiers shift forward, tense, and wait for Fucelli's order to shoot. They aim at the hill, at the soldier stumbling through the horsemen, confused and confusing.

But the Abyssinians keep rising from the other side of the valley, several now on foot and charging toward them and still: no order from Fucelli, no order to shoot, no order to do anything but wait for these men, a hundred bolts of lightning bound into human form.

Hold fire! The order comes from down the line. Let them get closer.

Fofi shifts his rifle from left to right, right to left, his head low. Giulio is breathing through his teeth, the hissing sound a current sliding through their row. The *soldati* lean against the rising cloud of dust and the crescendo of hooves. They flinch at the Ethiopian war cry, rising slowly, ballooning in the echoes slamming against their ears. Ettore balances on his toes. Every muscle stretches taut. His mouth is dry. Waves of noise sink against his head and he blinks to clear his vision: but what he sees is real.

No firing! Hold fire!

What's this? Ettore looks up so fast his helmet tips backward. Who's she?

The lone soldier is a delicate-featured girl in uniform: a solitary Abyssinian floating above grass, moving effortlessly between the horsemen, captivating and surreal.

Fofi drops his gun and presses both hands on his helmet, pushing thick wrinkles across his forehead. Santa Maria, she's crazy.

The sky has opened above the awkward vision and a pool of light heralds her descent. Behind her, the horsemen have backed away. They are arranged now in a straight row, splendid in their white, their rifles and spears pointed up as they stare at the young woman.

The *soldati* hold their breath as she carves an uneasy silence into the valley. Over the hill, in the next valley, there is the faint rumble of a fight, of shouts, of gunfire, but in this place where the earth lies flat and grassy between two jagged peaks, there is nothing but the isolated figure slowing her steps until she is walking, bewildered. Until she is standing meters in front of them, directly in front of Ettore, pointing at her chest and saying, Boom.

She taps her chest again. There is a reckless abandon in her movements, a skittishness that makes it seem as if she will leap across the barricade and reach for his throat.

Go, Ettore says, because he does not know what else to say. Go. *Vatene.* Hurry before they catch you. He makes a motion as if he is shooing a stray dog, as if there is a thought he is trying to disregard. He does it again and shakes his head, lost.

➤

SHE STANDS THERE like a gift from the gods, like a sunlit path that has opened just beneath his feet, begging Carlo Fucelli to take that step toward true and eternal greatness. From his position above his men, Carlo smiles and waves at the cameraman, who is strategically positioned to get a view of the valley and barricades. I told you, he shouts down at him proudly. I told you we would show you something new. Then he gives the order: Get her and bring her here.

Chorus

Sing, daughters, of one woman and one thousand, of those multitudes who rushed like wind to free a country from poisonous beasts. Sing, children, of those who came before you, of those who laid the path on which you tread toward warmer suns. Sing, men, of valiant Aster and furious Hirut and their blinding light across a shadowed land.

Sing of those who are no more,
Sing of the giants still amongst you,
Sing of those yet to be born.
Sing.

Hirut stumbles through the wasteland, spinning further and further from any place she has ever known until she becomes a stranger to herself, until she is an unknown figure wandering across endless burnt land, charred remains of a distant former life. She only pauses when a rope hits the bridge of her nose then drops down to her collarbone. Hirut stares at it, confused, as it begins to tighten. Before she can turn around hard boots kick her legs from beneath her. She falls, the descent awkward, ugly. A pale, sweating Italian hovers over her, bridging the space between where she is and the hills where she should be. He is slender-faced with dark stubble and eyes as small as points. A burst vein splashes one eye with red. He laughs as he looks at her. Other voices rise behind him, guttural and male.

Hirut curls into herself. She tucks her chin into her neck, squeezes her legs together, and shuts her eyes. If she fights, they will kill her. If she stays like this, they will kill her. There are horrible things that Italians do to girls, but no one has warned her about the interlude between discovery and death, between recognition and assault, that stretch of time when anything and everything is possible and all the frailties of the body are exposed to merciless light.

Another man bends over her, deathly pale with shadows beneath his blue eyes. The bottom half of his face lifts in a slow smile. He grabs her arm, a handkerchief in his hand, and yanks it hard. Get up, *teneshi*, he says in Amharic. He speaks calmly but it is deceptive. He is barely contained, ready to explode.

Hirut drags herself to her feet, frightened, and looks down for her gun but it's gone. She glances at the men crowded around her, smiling and eager, curious and cruel. She hunches, drops her head, and shuts her eyes. There is nothing new here. What looms in front of Hirut has always been there: the grand valley, the green hills and rocky plateaus, the trampled white flowers she feels like stuffing into her mouth and chewing for food.

Bella soldata, he says. His voice is soft, strangely pitched. He slides a finger down the side of her face and angles her chin to one side. He peels open one of her eyes, forcing her to look at him.

I'm Carlo Fucelli. Do you know my name? he asks in Amharic. Then he pauses and calls over his shoulder: Ibrahim!

Hirut turns her head to hide the jolting fear the name causes. This is the officer who killed Tariku and the one Seifu left alive. Fucelli, the Butcher of Benghazi. The man throwing Ethiopians off of mountains.

A tall *ascaro* approaches and salutes. Fucelli speaks to him and Ibrahim nods, sliding his eyes in her direction before focusing back on the Italian.

We have your friend, Ibrahim says to her. Where's Kidane's camp?

She looks at Ibrahim, shocked, and shakes her head. That is answer enough for Fucelli. He nods to Ibrahim, and the *ascaro* takes her arm and drags her quickly through the crowd of Italians pressing themselves against her, touching her hair, her back, her arm, her waist, all those parts that belong to a prisoner and not a soldier. He leads her past the rows of tents where *ferenjoch* rise to their feet at her approach. She notes the way they stare and nod while stepping behind her to follow. The procession grows, one Italian at a time, until they are a long, winding row moving serpentine toward another series of tents where *ascari* watch with amused expressions before joining the line that stretches like a second rope around her, shoving her higher up a steep hill as

she feels Ibrahim tighten his grip on her arm, as behind her, in a pun-
ishing Amharic seeps the unspeakable word for what she has become
in a matter of hours, something else that is less than a prisoner, less
than Hirut, something stripped of context, a thing without language or
nation or family or love, something from an in-between place, neither
fully human nor wholly animal, a thing that is only folded flesh to be
forced apart and used and disposed of at will.

—

SHE STARES AT the barbed wire that encircles the small square building
like an ugly scar. She looks from the gate with the padlock to the dizzying cliff a little further away. She feels herself swaying, caught in the
breathtaking suspension of that V-shaped gap, head spinning even as
her feet are firmly planted on the ground.

Fucelli snaps his fingers and the soldiers around her step aside and
what appears is a breach in logic: Aster. But she is removed from herself, taken out of uniform and made so naked that she is unrecognizable.
She is nothing. She is no one. She has become unmoored and unraveled,
and belongs to no family, to no name, to no lineage. She is drained of
noble blood, twirling in the dirt, surrounded by uniformed men wearing leather boots that pound a steady rhythm into dead grass.

Hirut covers her face but Fucelli shouts and Ibrahim yanks her
hands down.

Prisoner, *prigioniera*, Fucelli says, and points to Aster. He points to
Hirut: *Prigioniera*, he repeats.

A *soldato* pushes his way out of the gaping crowd and dances awkwardly next to Aster. He mimics a ghastly, cruel version of *eskesta*, thin
shoulder blades poking through his sweaty shirt. The men whistle and
cheer. He is eager, his thin mouth pursed, those pale and narrow features etched in a sharp hunger. Aster spins, feet alighting on tiptoe then
heel, lurching as another soldier jumps into the circle and drapes an
arm around her waist. His movements are sloppy and ugly. He squeezes

Aster's breast and forces her head up. Aster's eyes are swollen shut, her mouth hangs slack and along the graceful curve of her collarbone are deep purple bruises. The soldier lifts one of her hands and waves it at Hirut and the laughter spills over their heads and tumbles past the cliffs and multiplies in echoes.

Aster! Hirut lunges toward her, toward that sea of men howling into an abyss and the rope around her neck snaps and tightens beneath her chin, chokes her of breath and sound. She coughs, gasping for air. Let me go, she says. Let me go to her.

Because: there are mercies in this world that must be granted to those who have remained unmarked all their lives. There are unspoken rules for those who were born to carry rich histories and noble blood. There are ways the world must move in order to keep everything intact, and girls with scars must recognize their place amongst those who make those scars. Hirut leans forward, incoherent with shock and revulsion and a deeper emotion that cuts through her like sharp glass. Because if this can happen to Aster, wife of Kidane, beloved daughter of Ethiopia, then what more is waiting its turn with her?

Aster: Hirut throws out the word like a name attached to a secret. I am here, she wants to say. I am here and we are alive, she wants to add, but she is no longer sure what it means to live. She is not sure this is not another form of dying.

Hirut stretches her arms but Ibrahim snaps the rope against her neck so hard that it burns.

Stop moving, he whispers. Stop it or he'll get worse.

She lowers her head as best she can. Just beyond Aster is a civilian with a strange-looking camera peering through a lens. Past him, a group of *ascari* watch quietly. Past their shoulders, down the incline, are their tents. Hirut searches for signs of Kidane or Aklilu, looks for that flicker of light that will announce their coming, but there is nothing.

Chorus

We try to step in front of Aster. We try to speak so she can hear: Daughter of Ethiopia, blessed soldier, take the hand we offer and learn to live. But she is still a girl, still that young bride left alone in her new husband's bedroom with her back pressed against a wall. And so when they tell her, Go on, Aster, and dance for us, what can Aster do but dance? We see her. We see that woman who has become that young bride stepping out of her wedding dress. We see how she tries to stand, battered face and all, with her fists raised and trembling in fury. Look as she sweeps those knotted hands through the darkness, throwing her head back in defiance while shouting Kidane's name. Watch as she stares down at herself, confused by what she has become. Listen as she curses what has brought her here, as she curses names long forgotten. As she peers into the great cavernous hall where her father prepares another wedding toast, and she curses him too. There she sees her mother and the other women bend into one another, arms gently pressed against stomachs, and she hears their whispers like blasphemous oaths:

She will get used to this like we did.

She will learn to love him like we have had to learn.

She will learn obedience as a way to survive.

She sees the cook glance up from the plate of food she is setting down on the table. She sees the cook turn her way and shake her head and say: There is no way but through it. There is no escape but what you make on your own. And the bride, once a soldier, turns back to the stairwell, walks up the stairs, enters her husband's bedroom, and lies on the bed and opens her legs and tells herself she will know what to do and there is nothing to do, and she lets herself disappear until all that remains on that bloodstained bed is a girl remolding herself out of a rage.

Interlude

Haile Selassie looks at the picture again, holding it up to the light. He should be packing for the family's trip to Brighton, but he is facing an impossibility outside of any known language. He lays aside the shirt he was slipping into his small travel bag. It is all there but he cannot believe it: a bound figure splayed against the sun, a mortal man struggling with angelic flight, doomed by earthly sinew and muscle, betrayed by bone and flesh, held in place by tough rope and merciless wind. It is a new cruelty that drags itself up and settles heavily upon him, a second skin that traps him in a thick and pungent rot. Haile Selassie sets the bag on the floor then walks out of his bedroom into the hallway and down the stairs, uncertain of where he is going.

At the bottom of the stairs, he veers through the drawing room, into his morning room, then out to the garden. He stands beneath a soft drizzle that feels like a weeping sky. He inhales, fills his lungs with damp air, and looks up. Some men are inclined toward flight, he thinks. Some men are angels that yearn for expansive skies. Some ache to free themselves from the gravitational bondage of Earth. Didn't Icarus yearn for the same? Didn't his father, that great Daedalus, make him wings to push him into his truest form? Wasn't it only hubris that felled Icarus, and not the unnatural inclination toward flight? But it is useless to pretend: his men are falling from the sky. They are being pushed and thrown and they are breaking themselves on the terrain below.

And then there is also this small, startling detail in the latest message from this Ferres, a repetition of an earlier message from two weeks ago that he shrugged off as inconsequential a nagging rumor that he must deal with today in his meeting: the prisoners claim they have seen the emperor preparing for a great ambush. They shout his many names in addition to their own as they fall. Villagers refuse to believe Haile Selassie has left his people and gone to a foreign land. We have seen him, they insist. We have seen him with our eyes and our enemies will die. The damp chill soaks through his sweater, plasters his shirt against his chest, and for a moment, Haile Selassie feels the cold like a hand pressing against his sternum, trying to split him apart.

When he arrives in his office, his advisers have readied an Italian newsreel from that propaganda machine, Luce. They have positioned his chair in front of the screen and their own seats in a half-circle behind him. They stand when he enters and bow perfunctorily, all of them clearly disturbed. Your Majesty, they say, and he hears in their voices the slightest inflection of uncertainty, as if they are asking whether he is really himself. He sits and nods and someone shuts off the lights and he finds himself staring into a vivid square of white as the reel begins. He lets his eyes blur over the familiar images of the rocky landscape and the Nile, of his soldiers raising their old rifles, of Italian ships and marching columns, of churches illuminated in bright sun. Then. It is as if he is staring into a slowly rising river, his reflection snapping and pulling, distorted then familiar.

What is this? he asks, but he is speaking into the hollow of his chest and there is no sound in this suffocating room except the snap of the reel sliding his own image onto the wall. The emperor bends in. There he is. He sees a face shaped like his, a forehead as high as his own, his beard. That is his uniform, his cape. He is staring at himself standing atop a hill where he has never been, raising his hand in the way he was taught to raise it when addressing subjects. It is a distant shot, but it is distinctly him. But what is this? he asks again.

Then his bodyguard steps forward, on the right side of his duplicate self, and the camera zooms in, the picture is grainy, unsteady, as if the earth is sliding off its axis. The emperor blinks and rubs his eyes. It cannot be: A woman? We are being guarded by a woman? Then the reel ends and slides to black. Start it again from the beginning, he says.

Emperor Haile Selassie sits rooted in place, afraid to move, afraid to gaze once more at the broken light roaming over his walls. But there he is, the parts of him that have come in the form of a distorted twin. And he begins to wonder what is real, and if it is in fact true that he is actually in Ethiopia and the imposter emperor that the Italians love to mock is the one sitting in this chair right now, in a room that is a duplicate of another that thrums with authenticity in Ethiopia. And behind the fake walls of this office and those fake curtains, the emperor also wonders if the sun outside has been duplicated, if the world has been made false, if all truths have been turned inside out. Even in this office that is truly his, he feels it: he's already starting to disappear, moved offstage by fake men who pretend to be his allies.

Haile Selassie reaches into his pocket and pulls out the key to his office in Addis. He presses it into his palm, reassured by its firmness, the molded edges that dig into his flesh. At night, he lays the set by his bedside table next to his Psalms and his English dictionary. He keeps spare clothes packed in his trunks. There are briefcases filled with duplicate documents. He has prepared himself for immediate departure, but nothing he does can erase what he has done and remake it into something else. Flight. To fly. To flee. To leap away from solid ground and let the wind take hold.

Haile Selassie has to fight against the surge of loneliness that wells inside him. He stands up and the office lights flick on, and he walks to his window to look out and confirm where he really is. He flattens his palm against the foggy glass. He lifts it. Inside the delicate shape of his hand, he makes a cross. Once, it was said that the emperor of Ethiopia was like a sun to his people. But these days have proven that we live and die in the shadows, the emperor thinks. We do nothing but hold dominion over all that rests in shade and fog. All else is an illusion, a falsified appearance, a ghostly twin that trails behind us, hungering after our every breath.

SHE IS NOT SURE HOW LONG THEY HAVE BEEN IN THIS SINGLE-ROOMED jail. She has lost track of the stretch of a minute, of how it seeps into hours and blends into night. It is so dark and cold and her eyes have grown weak at a frightening pace. It is difficult to make out Aster's hunched shape. It is hard to know if she herself is breathing, or if they are both even alive. Hirut blinks slowly, waiting for her eyes to adjust. Aster is draped in the dirty abesha chemise that was thrown inside for each of them, crouched at the edge of the pale beam of sun that falls through the tiny window above their heads. She is crouched, a bent figure burdened by the receding light.

Aster, it's me, she says. Hirut knows better than to touch her. She sits near the door instead. I'm here too. They caught me too. They took our uniforms. She crosses her legs and leans on her arms. The pressure is reassuring. She is afraid of crumbling and disappearing, of being taken and being left behind at the same time: a body tumbling between hands while dying inside.

Aster?

But Aster does not move, not even when the beam of light crawls across her curved back on its way out.

HIRUT IS STILL AWAKE when the sun rises. The guards are changing shifts outside, their murmurings and greetings intimate and friendly.

One of them rattles the sheet of corrugated aluminum that makes the gate. It is where Fucelli ordered the *soldato* named Navarra to take her picture. The gate is attached to two thick metal posts and secured with a padlock. Around the perimeter is a wooden fence, the four rungs wrapped in a double layer of barbed wire. There is no way to escape. She has tried already. She has dug into the dirt floor of the prison only to find a concrete foundation beneath. She has stood up and walked around this cramped room, testing for soft slats of wood, for breaks in structure, for secrets, but still: nothing.

Hirut lays her head back against the wall. She has been sitting in the same place by the door the whole night, afraid she might be sleeping when Aster gets up. The woman is curled into herself, her breaths so quiet that several times Hirut leaned closer to make sure she was alive.

One of the guards whistles and taps against the gate. There's food, he says. Coffee. There's enough for both of you. His Amharic is fluid, natural.

She lets him walk away. She wants to starve herself, she wants to fade away and seep into the dirt and slip out of this place. She rubs her eyes. She cannot remember the last time she slept and she is dizzy. Her stomach hurts and her throat is dry.

Kidane, Aster mumbles. Kidane. She moans, her feet kicking, caught in a dream of momentum. The feeble dawn light is streaming in, still blanketed in night. It spills a soft haze over her shivering figure.

Aster, Hirut whispers. You're here with me.

She clasps Aster's hands. She knows the places the mind roams in the dark. She knows how easy it is to spiral away when given too much time in those corners. She traces the ridges of the scar on her own neck, feels the rough skin that sinks against her collarbone. She did not know until days ago that there were different kinds of nakedness. She did not understand until seeing Aster that there is a different kind of exposure, one that is indecent and upsetting. That some bodies were not meant to bend, and that this makes them weaker rather than stronger, unable to withstand what those like her can walk through their days locking into pockets and ignoring.

Aster raises her head. A thread of panic shakes her voice. Kidane? Aster sits up slowly. I'll lead. She feels around her, groping in the dark. Where's my gun, you stupid girl?

We're in prison, Hirut says. We got caught, I don't know where anyone is. Her chin trembles, tears spring to her eyes: speaking the words again solidifies them as true.

Aster props her back against the wall and looks around, then glances down at herself and gasps. She crosses her arms over her chest, tugging the dress around her. The necklace, didn't he put it on me? Then she presses her ear to the wall. They're listening, aren't they? Please take me home.

We're in an Italian jail.

Aster holds her face between two trembling hands. The dress slips to the ground. She touches her bare shoulders, her bruised face, and feels along the inside of her thighs. What they did. It happened? She presses herself straighter against the wall. It was me? That was me?

Her hands fly up in the air, then collapse into her lap. She stares at them, blinking away the shock. Where's my husband?

The face Aster raises to the crude ceiling is a canvas of cuts illuminated by the early sun. She makes the sign of the cross and then takes a deep breath and does it again, and the last exhalation saps her of strength. She folds into the ground. Where's my Kidane?

Hirut looks away. Put on the dress. There's food outside, she says, getting to her feet. I'll ask for blankets. She lifts the hem of her own dress, once belonging to someone taller. The collar hangs lower on her chest and she has to pull it back to hide her scar.

They can't keep us here. Why are we here? Aster turns her face to the wall and begins to cry softly.

Hirut stands at the door, her hands at her sides. She is afraid to open it and let the sun crash in. She does not want to see what sits in front of her, reflecting something that she has always been. Carefully, she turns the knob and slips out, eyes stinging and tearing in the sudden light. She sways on her feet, unsteady and disoriented, until a guard points to the tray of food just inside the fence: chunks of dry bread and two cups of cold coffee. The other two guards are standing behind him, aiming their rifles in her direction.

Hirut glances farther behind the trio: there are more guards pacing in front of the path that leads to the camp down the hill. And just steps away, those two large boulders that open like pleading hands toward the sky.

—

INSIDE THE COOK'S TENT: an extraordinary and vocal trembling. Fifi watches her through the opening in the flaps. The woman paces back and forth in that cramped space, her trusted spoon slapping against her leg, her murmurings unwinding and drifting through the canvas as an extended, agitated question. Fifi taps from the outside again, waiting for the cook to notice her and let her in, uncertain what has come over the woman who is usually so punctual with her daily routines that even one missed meal is cause for alarm.

Today, the cook did not come out to bring her coffee. She did not serve injera or bread or offer to sit with her and eat before they started their day. She has not come out of her tent since they finished dinner the night before, hunched quietly over the tray in Fifi's tent, barely speaking, always alert to noises coming from the prison and the newly arrived prisoners.

Last night, Fifi had dared to ask her: Do you know those women they captured?

The cook had stared down at her food. Then after a long silence, she said, Don't let him hurt them. Her mouth had been trembling. He'll be cruel, but you can stop it.

Who are they? Fifi asked.

The cook shook her head. I know what he does, she said. I know the kind of man he is. Enough, she had added. Enough is enough.

Let me in, Fifi says now, knocking against the tent flaps.

The cook motions her in. They stand, facing each other in the small tent, unsure of what to do.

What did they do to the older one? Why was she naked? The cook looks down at the spoon in her hand and, as if realizing how hard she is clutching it, sets it down gently on her cot. She rubs her hands against her legs, the gesture quick and vigorous, angry. I saw them dragging her to the prison, she continues. What happened?

Fifi shakes her head and sits down on the bed. You know, she says. I don't have to tell you, do I? And I haven't seen Carlo since they came, she adds. He won't speak to me. I know he's taken their uniforms, he's given them abesha chemises to wear now. That's all I know.

It is hot in the tent and the scents of turmeric and cinnamon are thick in the space. The cook looks down next to Fifi's feet and drags a small basket out from beneath the cot. Give this to them, she says. Give it to the girl, she'll know what to do with it.

Fifi shakes her head. I can't get close to them, she says softly. You know them. She waits for the cook to say something, to deny it, to confirm, but the cook straightens and waits for her to continue. There's nothing I can do, Fifi adds. Trying to say anything to Carlo will make it worse.

There's always something you can do. The cook is sweating and behind her eyes, a startled and frantic light. You do so many things, she says, the sarcasm thick.

Fifi folds her arms across her chest and steps close to the woman. She is tall enough that the cook is forced to look up. I'm not afraid of you, she says. I'm not afraid and I'm not ashamed. You think what you do is beneath you, she continues. I know my place.

The cook takes a step back and stares at her hands. I didn't mean that, she says. I mean that you can do whatever you want. You're beautiful.

And the look that the woman gives Fifi is filled with that wary jealousy that wants to assert and deny its existence, and it is now Fifi's turn to step back, to prepare for the envy that is certain to follow, the resentments that lead to dissolving trust and camaraderie. Because it has happened so many times before, since childhood, and she curses herself silently for thinking the cook would be any different.

The cook continues: You're free and you can talk to him like no one can. He'll act like he's not listening, but he'll listen.

Fifi shakes her head and drops her arms. She smooths her dress and walks toward the exit. She pauses at the threshold. You mistake my powers with that man.

He loves you, the cook says softly.

Fifi laughs. You don't know what love is, then.

And immediately, she regrets it, regrets the jagged pain those words invoke in the cook, the flash of anger and resentment that settle fully in her round face.

Without a word, the cook bends to put the basket she pulled out from beneath the bed back in its place. When she stands, her face is a mask. Do something, she says.

FIFI POURS HER COFFEE AND SETS THE *DJEBENA* ON THE FLOOR NEXT to her feet. She does not need to look at Carlo to know he is again wearing his two belts. He is pacing slowly in the small new building that is now his office, his steps awkward because of the tiny knife he has bound to one ankle. There are deep circles under his eyes, red lines that trace the curve of his thick eyelashes.

When did you eat last? she asks. She looks around. There is only one window behind his desk and she can make out the two body-guards in front of it outside, so tall that they nearly block the sun. When he sits, he is staring directly at the door. A chair is propped on its back legs against the wall, as if he uses it to jam the door shut when he is inside. Another small door to his right leads to what could be a storage space.

He reaches into his pocket for a cigarette and lights it. You're tense, he says as he smiles through smoke. The curtains of his office are still closed, but a soft, warm light filters past the bodyguards and into the room. It drapes his face, smooths the sharp lines of his new gauntness.

Your soldiers are excited about the new prisoners. She sets her cup on the tray and spoons a tiny bit of sugar into the coffee. It's hard to sleep sometimes, she adds.

The noises in the camp have ballooned since the prisoners were cap-tured. The men are louder. Their laughs have gotten more robust and jarring, and even the way they walk has become more pronounced, more forceful. The camp has shifted to accommodate the new prisoners, loosened restraints on everyday behavior.

They were in Italian uniforms, Carlo says. And armed. He leans into her. What women are these? What do you breed in this country?

He opens the storage door and pulls her into a second room. Inside, there is a cot, a short bookshelf with stacks of his files, a squat lamp, and a metal chair. It is a windowless, cramped space, no larger than a closet. There is a T-shirt crumpled at the foot of the bed, a pair of dirty socks are on the floor. A newspaper lies folded over the back of his chair.

He pulls back the thin blanket on the cot and sits down. He tugs her closer to him and presses her hands to his mouth. He kisses her palm. Do you want to know how many your people killed in the last week, only kilometers from here?

Fifi looks at the pistol protruding from his jacket. She is sure that beneath his pillow is the knife he sleeps with. The other is strapped around his ankle. He has at least seven bodyguards outside. I haven't seen you in days, she says. She pulls her hand back and rubs his head.

He buries his face in her stomach. You've missed me? He looks up. Or you're curious? He sits back.

He reaches for the newspaper hanging over the chair. He opens it carefully and lays it in her lap. There is a tiny article sandwiched between two stories of new phone lines connecting military posts: *Haile Selassie Returns?* Then below that headline is a brief account of excited villagers claiming to have seen the emperor, *il Negus*. Carlo reaches under his bed and pulls out the flat steel box that he uses for storage. Its latch is undone, the lock sprung open. He wipes the bottom before setting it on the blanket, between them. He takes out a leather-bound Bible, written in Ge'ez, illuminated by drawings of angels with large, soulful eyes. It takes her a moment to recognize it: a gift from her brother, Biruk. Carlo flips the book open. Inside is her name, her birth name in her brother's handwriting, followed by her own tight script. He turns the page, then another, his actions deliberate, all his agitated energy channeled into the steady palm balancing the book.

She knows where she has kept the book hidden since her arrival. She knows it has been in the bottom of the bag with her European clothes and perfume. It is a personal reminder of her former life, a way back, on difficult days, to who she used to be: Faven from Gondar, the beautiful daughter of a merchant, the sister to an earnest artist slowly going blind.

You can read. You can write, he says. He sets down the Bible on the floor and pushes the newspaper aside. You primitive people, he continues, his lips quivering. You think you're so civilized, but you can't get rid of your superstitions and hysterical visions. You get your witches to predict we'll only last five years in this country. He pauses to laugh. And now you say you've seen the man who was just photographed in England, in Brighton. Stupid, savage, ignorant slaves, all of you. He is trembling. He hands her the book, then he chuckles, the lines around his mouth deepening.

She sits up. Ever since you were attacked . . . She stops. I was the one who saved you. Not one of your faithful guards or soldiers. Me. If it weren't for me, she says, that Ethiopian would have killed you.

So your people think Haile Selassie was part of Kidane's ambush? Is that so? He can just miraculously enter the country and go back to England between meetings? The tiny muscle near his right eye is twitching. All those books you own in Asmara and you've never once said anything about them, he says. You've never once talked to me about what you read. You want to pretend you're just a simple whore. You must think I'm stupid or that I love you.

She stiffens. What do you know about love, Carlo? She watches him glance over her shoulder, unable to meet her gaze. She traces the outline of the top belt around his waist, notices the way he jerks away then forces himself to stay still. She taps on it. Nothing but me kept you alive, she whispers into his ear. What's wrong with you?

She unbuttons the first few buttons of his shirt. She runs a finger along the scar on his chest, feels the tiny hairs around the wound. He is wearing a small wooden Coptic cross that she didn't know he owned, similar to the one she wears, similar to the one the cook also has. She drops her hand.

You don't know as much as you think, he says.

Fifi clasps her hands together and waits for what's next. Outside, she hears loud voices and whistles; the men are starting again with the prisoners. Soon, they will gather around the jail and badger the women with lewd shouts. She has heard it from her tent, prevented from leaving by a guard's ever-watchful gaze. It is the cook who has taken to stationing herself as close as she can to the prison, hiding and watching the men then reporting back to her, trembling with an uncommon fear.

He takes hold of her face, his palms warm and damp on her cheeks. He brings his forehead close to hers. He blinks slowly. I know what my men are doing. And you know how the prisoners react? They stare at them with faces like stone. All you people are the same. Inscrutable.

Carlo slides his hand under her dress and rubs her thigh. Take it off.

Fifi pulls the dress over her head.

He flings it aside then presses his palm against her breast. He holds still and watches her carefully. Your heart's beating so fast, he says.

He bends his ear to her heart. She can feel it picking up speed, pounding loudly. The body reveals our every deception, it finds ways to see everything: her brother told her this on the day he confessed he had gone completely blind.

Fifi pushes Carlo's head away. I can read, but you know that, you've always known that. I wasn't trying to hide what's right in front of your face. You're looking in the wrong place for whatever you're looking for. It was me who saved you. Your men would have let you die. You think they're protecting you out of goodwill? You think Ibrahim cares anything about you? Yes, I've read every book you've seen on my shelf. Dante, Aristotle, Psalms, Dumas. I like them all, but who do I have to talk to about them now that you've bought all my time? You? She laughs. My cook? She shakes her head. I gave up so much to be here.

He grabs hold of her jaw and sinks his thumb into the tender place where her jawline meets her ear. It is so painful it makes her head spin.

You hide everything, just like your people, jumping out of hills and grass and God-knows-where. Coming at us from every direction, your witches cursing us and casting spells. Your emperor appearing and disappearing. He wipes the back of his neck, his face is flushed. You're a people of lies, full of lies and myths.

Fifi nods. So you had someone come into my tent while I slept, she says slowly. Who was it? Your faithful Ibrahim? She turns to him and pushes her face close to his. And why wouldn't some of us read, Carlo? Why not? You can find an Ethiope in the earliest books. We are older than this Roman culture you're so proud of. We existed before you, when you were all just peasants, not even a people.

He licks his lips and blinks slowly. I could put you in prison right now. He grabs her wrists and squeezes.

Carlo, she says softly, Carlo, why fight? She pulls out of his hold, still naked, her hands flat at her sides. She stands in front of him. Is this really what's going to be in your next report to Rome, that you think your Abyssinian whore can read? You don't think some of those who read your reports are old clients of mine? You're going to tell them the emperor attacked your camp and that you want to put me in prison? She makes her laugh brittle and thin. For what? You're the one breaking the law by sleeping with a native. And every book in my home that you've seen, I've read, some twice. I can read Italian and I can read Amharic. I've been reading since I was a girl and one of your kindhearted priests gave me books in exchange for some affection. Lonely men, all of you. You're no different from any of the others, Carlo. Show me something they haven't done.

He spins her around and drops to his knees, then settles his mouth between the dimples just above her buttocks, his lips dry as sandpaper. He kisses along the curve of her waist then his thumbs rest on either side of her lower back. His fingers grip the curve of her waist, digging into her stomach.

Before she knows what he is doing, he digs his thumbs into the tender flesh of her lower back. It is an agony so ripe and cutting that a red blaze shoots through her back, up her head, and into her stomach. She cries out as he wraps an arm around her waist to keep her close and pushes again. The pain is dizzying, and she cannot breathe.

In all your readings, you never figured this out? An old Roman trick to immobilize the enemy. He cups his mouth over the places he touched. None of your clever little books or lonely men taught you about this? He kneads into her with his fist.

Her legs buckle. She slumps against him but he shoves her upright, refusing to let her go.

Stop, she says. Her face is bloated with pain, her head throbs from an ache deeper than bone. It is a primal sensation.

He lets her go and sits again on the bed. He pulls her to him. His fingers intertwine with hers. He kisses her wrists then pulls her head down and kisses her on the cheek. He taps her nose, a playful gesture suddenly frightening.

I'll always know more than you, he says, then he lies back on the bed and waits for her.

ETTORE SHUTS THE DOOR SOFTLY BEHIND HIM AND SALUTES COLONEL Fucelli. You asked for me, sir?

There is a charge in the room, a low, pulsing current that makes Ettore nervous. Fucelli is staring out the window, his back to Ettore. Two of his bodyguards stand at attention on either side of his desk. Two more are stationed at the door. Ettore knows that there are also *ascari* at each corner of the building, but it still does not explain the tension he feels stepping before the colonel.

Fucelli spins around and motions for Ettore to sit; dark stubble shades his jawline and crawls down his neck. One side of his face is red, as if he has just woken up. Ettore sinks into the cold metal seat.

The colonel slides a folder across the table. Look at this, he says.

The folder is full of photographs of nude and seminude women. Italians and Turks. Greeks and French. Some others of unknown nationality made to look Arab. All the women are gazing into the camera suggestively. Their names are imprinted on the front: Belle, Giulietta, Divina, Nadia, Marie. Ettore stares at the small, crisp photos. They are studio photos, the chaise is the same in two and soft lighting gives some of the shots a dreamy quality. On the back of each is a tiny inscription: *carte de visite*.

As a boy, I thought all women were the same, Colonel Fucelli says. He rests his chin in his hand. What a man knows about a woman is a sign of his maturity, don't you think? I imagine your father didn't teach you much about the subject. Am I right? he asks, staring steadily at Ettore.

No sir, Ettore says, feeling color rise to his face. He shifts the strap of his bag higher on his shoulder.

Fucelli takes the folder from him. He places the photographs four across and three down. He holds up one of a woman in a chaise wearing filmy white undergarments. Are the men still talking about Haile Selassie? he asks.

They are, sir. Ettore nods.

Go on.

Some are afraid the two prisoners are part of an army of women. They say Haile Selassie even has female bodyguards. Ettore shakes his head, imitating Colonel Fucelli's own expression of disbelief. They call them Amazons, sir. They think they've come to seduce and kill us and the *ascari*. They're exaggerated stories, he adds. There's no proof this is true. Then Ettore sits up straight and places his hands on his knees. He clears his throat.

Fucelli holds his gaze. Most of these men are illiterate, soldato. They're bound to believe in superstition. They're scared of many things. He pauses. It's interesting, you know, Fucelli continues. We fight other men, but we're frightened of women.

He pushes another photo toward Ettore. A bare-breasted woman lies back on a chaise with her hands behind her head. A silky sheet drapes over her stomach, discreetly covering her lower half. Does she scare you? the colonel asks.

No, sir. Ettore smiles, but the tension has returned to the room.

The men are starting to believe anything they hear about these Abyssinians. Fucelli folds his hands in front of him and leans forward. You know the story of Penthesilea. You're more educated than most of them. He waves a hand toward the door.

Ettore shifts in his seat and looks down at the picture. The one who fought against Achilles? But she was killed.

But she fought well, and do any of these men think they're Achilles? The colonel taps his forehead.

But Achilles died later too, sir.

What do you understand of what I've just said?

Ettore shifts again, made uncomfortable by the echo of his father's question. Our men are frightened of these Abyssinian women, he says slowly. They make up stories about them and believe them, he adds.

Color is spreading across Fucelli's cheeks. His ears are bright red. Go on.

We think they're so different from our women because we don't know anything about them, he continues. This makes us scared, sir. Ettore pauses, unnerved by the colonel's eagerness, his obvious interest in every word Ettore is saying.

The men have to find a way to believe something else, Ettore says slowly. They have to believe they're Achilles, the Achilles who lived to defeat his enemies.

The colonel nods. They have to believe they're Achilles, he repeats. His face is flushed, sweat has collected above his lip. Get your camera and get to work, Foto. Start with the prisoners, the younger one. You're not photographing women, you're creating Achilles. He begins putting the photos back into the envelope.

Yes, sir. Ettore stands to leave.

Oh, Navarra? The census is coming, arriving soon. When you complete yours, bring it to me. Understood? The colonel's eyes are probing. I'm sure your father is having to do the same thing right now. He shakes his head and adds, A shame.

Ettore nods quickly, too quickly, and can barely manage a salute before he turns and hurries out the door, gulping mouthfuls of air.

—

ETTORE LEANS BACK against the tree on the outskirts of the plateau and stares at Hirut. He gazes across the flat spread of land leading to the prison and tries to comprehend what it means to wake every day behind barbed wire that knots around a sturdy fence. He unbuttons his shirt and untucks it, aching to take it off and strip himself free of this uniform, of its betrayals. He takes a breath, another, to calm himself. Just beyond the prison is the path to those treacherous cliffs, and he tries to imagine the first instant after the leap, that suspended moment before free fall. He shakes his legs to loosen their stiffness, to still the shivers he feels climbing up his chest and into his jaw. He wants to shout to Hirut and ask her how she does it, how she manages to stay in that jail, leaning against that wall as if it were the most natural thing in the world to be trapped.

She has been staring listlessly toward the horizon, toward the wide crevice between the large boulders. She has not moved in the hours he has been there. Fucelli's orders are to observe and document her for several days, but it is now midafternoon and there is still nothing to write. Overhead, the sun beams down from a merciless sky and makes it difficult to keep still and concentrate. Twice already, he has taken out his father's letter to reread it. Ettore gets to his feet and shrugs his bag across his back. He drapes his camera around his neck to that Hirut will see it and be ready. A foul taste settles in his throat. He understands now why his father had been so angry when he enlisted in the army: Leo knew the true worth of a uniform, he had learned long ago how little it really protected. He knew that only those things most evident were seen: blood and birth and homeland.

He walks toward her slowly, curving his mouth into a small smile. The guards draw in as he reaches the barbed-wire fence. He is a magnet tugging at the center of their orbit. They angle their rifles at Hirut's chest and begin to take turns pivoting between the prison and the hills, newly alert. It happens without a word, choreographed to such an impeccable precision that Ettore feels a renewed awe for all that Colonel Fucelli has managed to achieve with his troops and all that he is promising to do for him.

Indeminesh, Ettore says to her. He sits down and crosses his legs directly in front of Hirut. How are you? *Indeminesh?*

The question is nonsensical. The *ferenj* repeats himself again, then speaks a series of words that is an incomprehensible list, without context or introduction. Then his voice trails off, awkward and flat. Hirut stares at the horizon, rigid and upright. She has come out every morning since their capture to sit in this place against this wall and search for signs of Aklilu. She has forced herself not to move, not even to wipe sweat or wave aside a fly. There is nothing to do here, she has said to Aster each day, but be a soldier and continue training. And though Aster has only raised her head then laid back down again, still asking for Kidane, Hirut knows that to plan an escape means first understanding where to go.

What she has learned: The *ascari* work in pairs and speak only in signals. They rotate every two days and have shifts of six hours each. They stagger their breaks and no two ever leave at the same time. They do not speak to the soldiers and laborers who trudge up and down the hill while they extend the road below. The two who guard the prison are men comfortable with killing, men who are made bored by the absence of violence. The other four find ways to sneak looks at her, sometimes curious and most often repulsed. All of them are cruel. All of them would shoot her if ordered to do so. She and Aster are not safe. The monotony of these days is temporary, a period of deceptive calm before a new terror takes its place. She must find a way to escape.

Indeminesh? How are you? The *ferenj* tries again to pull her attention back to him.

Hirut refuses to turn her head, refuses to do anything but stay vigilant in her search for a signal from Aklilu. The thought of him now forces her to sit straighter, she imagines he is beside her, urging her to stay strong. And she knows that with him is Seifu and somewhere, Kidane strides across those hills finding ways to come to Aster and set them free. There is Hailu and his quest to keep all the injured alive. There are Nardos and Abebech and all those women who ran beside her while charging down a hill. There is Minim and the emperor, those two held together in the body of one gentle man. There is Beniam and Dawit and Tariku and those countless others buried in unmarked graves. She can feel them gather around her and build a wall of themselves that keeps this *ferenj*'s bastardized Amharic and his dull gaze away from her. These Italians are machines draped in skin, devoid of emotion, of any intelligence that allows them to move through Ethiopia with anything but beastly cunning. Hyenas, Aster once called them, they move in packs and kill through deceit and one day they will eat themselves.

This is why Hirut does not turn her head in the *ferenj*'s direction even when he says her name. She does not flinch when one of the *ascari* storms to the barbed-wire fence and threatens to beat her if she does not speak to the Italian. She does not change her breathing or stiffen her body or flail helplessly when that same *ascaro* yanks open the gate and bends into her face and shouts her name until it is a hard and painful blast in her ear. Instead, she looks up at his face, bloated with futile anger, and calmly waits for whatever comes next. Because this is one thing that neither the *ascari* nor Fucelli nor this stupid *soldato* staring at her with a gaping mouth will ever know: that she is Hirut, daughter of Fasil and Getey, feared guard of the Shadow King, and she is no longer afraid of what men can do to women like her.

—

HE REPORTS EVERY MINUTE of his interaction to Fucelli and when the colonel says, Go back, Ettore goes back the next day and the next, and when he returns to tell Fucelli what is happening, the colonel nods as if he is not surprised and tells him to do it again.

Keep talking, don't stop just because she can't fathom what you're doing, Fucelli says. Imagine her like a beast to tame, a dumb and frightened dog. And then the colonel adds, The census has arrived in Africa, notice has come from Asmara.

It is the fourth day and Hirut is still unresponsive. Aster is still inside the prison. His camera still hangs, unused and useless on his neck and the rolls of film that Colonel Fucelli has been expecting remain in his bag, unexposed. He knows the *ascari* have begun to mock him in their silent ways. He can feel their anger with Hirut shift to bafflement then frustration with him. He knows he is expected to force her into compliance, that he is to punish her insolence with greater force and more brutality than they ever could. He knows the *soldati* have heard of his hours spent in front of the girl testing his Amharic phrases, laying them before her like tender objects eager for her attention. He has learned different verbs to set in front of her, waiting for the one to make her move.

To be. To sleep. To eat. To stand. To awaken. To serve. To cook. To clean.

The list grows longer. The mockery behind him intensifies. The jokes around the campfire become more pointed. They do not understand how much changes as the eye grows accustomed to a thing. How the unfamiliar contours of a face can become a path into an inscrutable mind. What the mouth says has nothing to do with what someone means. It is the face that speaks. That he has not managed to see more than a resolute and stubborn girl is proof of the Ethiopian native's unfamiliarity with all that he finds commonplace. She has no reference points that intersect with his: no myths or fables, no ideas on science or philosophy. She is unlearned and unschooled, illiterate and limited. Unknowing and thus, unknowable. She lacks the imaginative capacity to consider an existence beyond her frames of reference: these mountains, her village, the hut where she was born. What rests behind that face and in that mind are sturdy, thick thoughts of survival and routine, and nothing else.

—

TO DIE, he finally thinks to say on the eighth day. He repeats the word again in Amharic then Italian. To die: *memot*: *morire*. He notices her hands tremble slightly in her lap. He goes on: I die. You die. We die. They die. Hirut, he says: They die, he repeats. They will die. *Yimotalew*. He feels his chest constrict.

A space flickers open between them and even though she still refuses to turn in his direction, he sees how the words unwind something inside her that she struggles to keep contained. He sits straighter, tries to keep focused, to keep thoughts of the census away: Mail is arriving in a few days. Ettore raises his camera, leans back, and snaps a picture of her profile, those wet eyes, the sun glowing in a lush horizon that will be faded to black and white on film. He waits for her to move, to wave him aside so she can be left alone. He marvels momentarily at her discipline, that military rigidity that could rival any soldier's. She blinks her eyes dry. She presses her back more firmly against the wall. She brings her knees to her chest and wraps her arms around them. Then she goes back to that unnerving, stubborn stillness.

He is not sure why he takes out the photograph of his parents on their wedding day. He keeps it next to Leo's letter as if one offers a clue into the other. In the picture, his father is stern and somber in his black suit and crisp white shirt. He looks as if he is on his way to university, as if his time in the photo studio is a temporary pause in an otherwise busy day. Gabriella is dressed in a delicate white dress, the lace trim around her neck and wrists a tender spray across slender bones. Her dress drops elegantly at her waist and stops low on her slim frame. She is seated in a chair, back straight, chin ducked demurely, her eyes trailing to the side to catch a glimpse of her new husband. Leo leans one hand on the back of the chair as if it is support that he needs. As if he has come from a long journey and even on this day, his wedding day, he is tired. His father, Ettore notices for the first time, is much older than the four years they have always claimed stood between them. Looking at it now, he also sees his mother as a slightly startled, eager young woman, somewhat in love but more perplexed. His father is stoic and dutiful, and there is a haggardness around his eyes that lends him the air of a tortured poet.

Ettore repeats the words again, softly almost to himself: To die. *Memot*. She looks down at the picture, then at him, then she grips her hands together and stares at the photo again. He feels the tension in her, how she coils into herself, so he points at his father and decides to confess in Italian the most truthful thing he can, because she will never understand: This is how I hold my father still. This is how I stare at him without having to answer his questions. Ettore wants to add in Amharic: My parents could be dead. They might not be dead. But he is stopped short by vocabulary, by the conditional tense, by that way of speaking that shifts everything into the hypothetical, into an imagined existence that could or could not be true. Everything is possible at once. I could die. He could be dead. She might have died. We might die together.

She knows that he is pointing to his dead father and asking her to feel pity for him. He is repeating the words in order to make her react, as if it is so simple. As if dying were not ordinary, as if a dead father were something only he has suffered in this world. She thinks of Beniam and Dawit and Tariku, and all those that this *ferenj* has helped to kill and leave orphaned and make childless. She thinks of her father and her mother and the Wujigra and Aster curled like a child inside the prison. She thinks of Kidane and those ways she would still be whole if only this war hadn't started. If only these *ferenj* invaders hadn't come. And as she counts the many ways so much has died and been split and been ruptured because of Italians like him, Hirut feels the fury rising in her, the taste so sour in her mouth that she is certain he will know how much she wants to reach through the barbed-wire fence and steal his rifle and point it at his arrogant and dulled heart. *Innateinna abbate motewal*, she whispers. My mother and father have died. She drops her head and has to blink away the tears. She stiffens to calm herself. She wraps her arms around her knees to shove the anger back inside of her until she can become immobile again: a soldier on guard, watching for a signal from her army.

To die, he says. Except he does not know the correct way to say "I die." He mispronounces "he dies," and when he gets to "we die," Hirut listens to him and she turns and says softly: We won't die. And she watches him blink stupidly as if moved by the sound of her voice. Then she turns her head once more and gazes out into the horizon, searching for flashes of light as his camera clicks: tiny glass teeth chewing into the side of her face.

—

THAT NIGHT, ETTORE DREAMS: Leo is dressed in his wedding suit and holds a census form to his chest. He is trying to get home before his heart bursts through the page. Inside he can feel he is shrinking. His skin is loosening and soon he will be stepping out of himself, his bones moving faster than he, pushing past vein and flesh and ligament and muscle to leave it all behind again. He must find a corner. He must stand between stones and pull himself together. But he is too slow. He is too methodical. He has forgotten the haste of childhood, the dream of flight. He hides in a crevice between two buildings near Santa Maria Formosa, searching for Gabriella. He gives in to the hinged darkness and takes off his suit. For a moment he is long and lean and whole. Then Leo sheds his skin and folds it neatly. It is a perfect square in a spinning world. He is nothing now but muscle and bone, veins exploding like supernovas. He presses the form to his chest again. He is trying to hold what must be held. He reads the page and his heart slides out. It tumbles and collects at his feet. He reads some more and his lungs collapse. He gets to the end and his stomach churns. It begins to chew him up. And Leo utters his beloved wife's name and holds out his hand. Then he goes home, bone scraping on bone.

IT IS HIS BIRTHDAY AND COLONEL CARLO FUCELLI SALUTES HIS reflection in the mirror to begin his private celebrations. He opens his jacket and flattens his hand across the two belts he has taken to wearing since that horrifying assault. All along, he has assumed that the attack diminished him as a man. He has always believed that there is no true defense or recovery from any assault that exposes a man to his ultimate frailties. He has not known how to pivot away from the crippling humiliation that changed how he walked through his days and ended his nights. What those Abyssinians put on display for Carlo Fucelli, son of Domenico Fucelli, to witness about himself involved much more than his most intimate parts. They unzipped his trousers and tore out his very spirit and ever since then, he has been moving through his routines with a numbness that only disappeared in the most deliberate acts of power and revenge. His prisoners have also taught him this: It is possible to wipe dust and ash from one's feet and step forward, wholly remade. Anything is possible. And with that, Carlo slips off his extra belt, buttons his jacket, and steps out of his office to reintroduce himself to his men.

His men wait for him on the flat stretch of land between the prison and the cliffs. They have done as he has ordered and arrived at dawn, ready for battle. There is no sound besides the rustle of wind through tall grass and trees, and all that heralds this new beginning stands in breathless anticipation of his arrival. Carlo feels his heart swell. He will give them a show on this anniversary of his birth. He will teach them how a strong man can be made without the use of his fists. And as he approaches the prison, Colonel Carlo Fucelli, son of Italy, conqueror of Benghazi, breathes in the fragrant scent of a fresh new morning, and waits for his moment to begin. Anything is possible, he says to himself, moved by the quiet obedience of his men standing at attention in neat rows before him. Anything is possible because today, I am possible.

Off to the side, Fifi and her servant are a silent chorus of two looking on worriedly. He nods to Fifi, who turns her head, disturbed but powerless to disobey his orders to be present. Overhead, the sky is slowly blossoming into blue, the sun a distant spray that holds no firm shape in the brightening expanse. A string of clouds disrupts the clean line of the distant horizon. Fog clings to rough mountaintops and flows between hills. All else is grass and rock and farmland: open terrain waiting to be claimed. There is enough room for all of Italy in this vast and empty country, he will point out to his men in another moment. Carlo shuts his eyes and nods. He slips a cigarette into his mouth and unbuttons the bottom of his jacket so the rumors can be dispelled for good: he no longer wears his double belts. He will never do so again. He has no need for symbolic protection. He has overcome his demons and today, he will bring them to their knees.

Carlo Fucelli presses his hand against his chest. He leans toward his men and shouts loudly and clearly in Italian, then Amharic, Arabic, Tigrinya, and Somali: There are those who are meant for distance, and those who were born to fall!

Ettore Navarra glances at his friends beside him then turns to Carlo, baffled, as Carlo knew he would. Carlo wants to remind him: Our fathers do not make us, Navarra. We are born with our own possibilities. There are those meant for distance and those who must bear the consequences of our choices. What he means to say to the young soldier is this: Today, I can be a witness to my own rebirth and bury the man those intruders attacked.

Carlo pivots to Fifi instead. Aida, young maiden governed by the laws of love, slave to her desire for her father's enemy, *faccetta nera*, come here, he says. Take my hand.

While Fifi approaches slowly, he opens his arms wide in a gesture of goodwill toward his men and for a moment, he is overcome by affection and gratitude for their allegiance, their dedication to his ambitions.

They have been breaking rocks and moving stones and dynamiting tunnels into mountains. They have been working in scorching heat and sleeping through cold nights. They have had no respite except for the breaks when new prisoners arrive and then tumble over the cliffs. The racial segregation laws forbid their mingling with native women but he has not stopped them the times they have risked ambush in order to go to a local bar. He has felt pity for them, in fact, and he has ordered his *ascari* to safeguard their trips each time. There has been nothing else to keep these young men preoccupied. So when Carlo puts out his hand and motions for Fifi to step forward, he is well aware of what he is unleashing. He knows the form of this beast he is nudging awake.

Faccetta nera, cara Aida, vieni qua. Come to me, my black-faced darling. Come here, dear Aida. Carlo puts an arm around Fifi's shoulder and draws her close. She is trembling, gripping her hands in front of her, her body rigid.

Stop it, she says to him.

Carlo leans into her ear, makes sure that his teeth brush against her cheek when he says to her: Pay attention to how a man is made. Then he pushes her away. *Carissima* Fifi, Faven from Gondar, how many names does a person need? He nods to Ibrahim.

Ibrahim shouts over his shoulder in Arabic and two *ascari* rush forward.

Carlo smiles again and points to the prison where the two female prisoners sit inside, quiet and unaware. Carlo grips Fifi's hand and refuses to let go. Go on, Navarra, he says. Get them out so we can begin.

Me, sir? Ettore turns to Colonel Fucelli. He is shaking.

Fucelli slips on his sunglasses. He stands with his hands on his waist and only his mouth, a firm line across his face, gives away the slow-building tension nestling between them. How much of what I have said do you understand? the colonel says. Then he laughs. Get the prisoner out, Navarra, the younger one. Unless you're afraid of a girl.

Ettore hears soft laughter ripple through the line. He glances at the men, then at the colonel's beaming face, and anger seeps out of his belly as shame rises to beat against him, and because there is nothing he can do and there is so much he does not know and there are things he is afraid will never be explained or discovered, Ettore spins toward that barbed-wire fence and shouts for an *ascaro* to open it. He jerks at the door until someone unlocks it. Then he barrels his way in, searching for that seam in the earth that has come undone to expose his humiliating weaknesses.

Hirut shoots to her feet, desperate for a place to hide. She is knocked breathless by Navarra's intrusion. She stretches a hand to Aster and calls out her name, but there is only this *soldato* waving his gun in her face while telling her in stilted Amharic to go outside. He is a body quivering with cruel resentments as he drags her out.

—

HIRUT BLINKS WILDLY in the new morning sun. There is an entire army looking at her eagerly but all she can do is stare at Fucelli and his woman. And the cook. Hirut stumbles backward, made dizzy by the sight of this woman whose disappearance she has learned to accept as a certain fact in a confusing world. She presses her back against the prison wall and sinks down. She is clothed but she is naked. She is a spectacle but she is invisible. She is a girl who has been split, and what stands here is both flesh and shadow, bone and silhouette, no more than air filled with smoke. And the cook. The cook. The cook.

Hirut looks at the woman but the cook shakes her head and her mouth trembles and there are no words needed for what she is telling

Hirut: Do not act like you know me, do not look this way, you must find your own escape.

Navarra is inside the barbed-wire fence, his camera held up like a shield. Somewhere next to her, Beniam tugs at her feet. Kidane hefts her into the air and slams her back to the ground. Aster raises the whip and lets it slice through her thoughts. Time melts and spins her senseless in this broken place where the cook can stand on the other side of a prison fence and watch her without offering to help. Hirut shuts her eyes and tucks her head. She extends a hand to an imaginary Aklilu, lets Beniam grip her ankles, lets her Wujigra rest across her back, and she waits.

Ettore stares at Hirut crouched and shivering violently against the prison wall and feels his anger fading, giving way to remorse and pity. She is, after all, no more than a native, no more than a girl accustomed to harshness. This is a body unbroken by servitude and orders. This is a girl buoyed by the endless calls to serve. Here she is before me, Father, slumped low like a dying beast, waiting for me to offer her relief.

Ascari! Fucelli says as he points to two guards. Make her stand up. Navarra, get ready!

But Hirut refuses to be moved, even when the *ascari* pry her head up and her shoulders down. She is still bent so far into her chest that Ettore can see the ridges of her spine.

If she doesn't get up, tell her I'll throw her over the cliff myself, Ibrahim, Colonel Fucelli says. Then he snaps his fingers and turns. Fifi, *bell' abissina*, come. Bring your slave. Ibrahim, you know what to do now.

Fifi and the servant step forward slowly. Ettore notices that Hirut is so troubled by the sight of the two of them that she barely protests when Ibrahim approaches, tugs at the top of her dress by its shoulders, then pulls it down to her waist. The material rips. Hirut looks down at herself, dazed, then at the two women, and whatever it is that engulfs her becomes too much to bear. Ibrahim steps back, his face like stone, as Hirut begins to mutter then speak loudly in an Amharic that is too fast for Ettore to understand.

What's she saying? Fucelli asks Fifi, his arms folded over his chest.

Names, Fifi says. Just the names of people, maybe her family. Then she turns to Fucelli and puts a hand on his arm. Please, Carlo, she says. Let her be.

Fifi steals a glance at Ettore, and for a brief moment they lock eyes and what he sees reflected back fills him with renewed shame. Ettore takes another step away from Hirut. He doesn't want to look at her anymore. He doesn't want to be inside this barbed-wire fence listening to the mutterings of this terrified girl. He looks at the colonel, the calibrated glee, the hardened features, the pride, and the barbed wire rises like a border between them.

Shouts and claps erupt from the *soldati* and *ascari*: *Il Duce! Viva l'Italia! Faccetta nera!* Their voices hang overhead like low-flying planes, the rumble an endless ricochet through the hills. Ettore stands inside the fence with the girl, spinning in his own universe, horrifyingly alone with this native.

Groups of soldiers gather closer. The colonel's madama and her servant hunch into themselves, their arms crossed identically in front of them. Neither of the women can look at the girl. It is the girl who cannot stop staring now. She is fixated on the two women, her trembling growing more pronounced as her mouth opens to form a word she cannot push into sound.

The colonel moves next to Ettore, a hand on his pistol. Navarra, he begins. Last week, a unit in Kossoye was nearly wiped out in an ambush. We know Kidane's rebels are hiding in these hills. We know some of them are women. Take the picture, *soldato*.

The girl is swaying, her face lifted to the sky, the scar on her collarbone rising up in her deep, heaving breaths.

Tell her to keep still, the colonel says. Aren't you an Italian? He pivots toward Fifi. Watch this, both of you, or it gets worse for her.

Fifi straightens, agitated and uncomfortable, and smooths the skirt of her long dress. She taps her servant on the shoulder and pushes her upright. They grip hands and, together, they look at Ettore, their disgust evident.

Navarra, do your job.

This is what Ettore sees when he looks at the girl: That there is a dying-away that happens in a breathing body. There is a tumble into oblivion that occurs while we are still inclined toward movement. Hirut cannot stop blinking and mouthing an inaudible word. She is swaying and bending to the ground. One arm lifts slowly, motioning toward Fifi before dropping heavily to her side. She is giving up.

Ragazza, ti prego, stand still, raise your head. Ettore lifts his own chin, and an emotion like pain surges inside his chest. He holds his hand out to the girl but she will not look at him, and for the first time he wonders if he is worthy. Ettore raises the camera to his eye and finds relief. Through the viewfinder, she is just a small, lonely figure, parts misaligned until he focuses and puts her back together.

Ascaro, the colonel points to Ibrahim standing with the other *ascari* several paces away. Tell her what happens to those who don't obey. Tell her, if you want, what I've taught you to do.

The clear morning sky washes a pale light across Ibrahim as he steps to the fence, fearsome and splendid in his uniform. He pauses. His mouth wavers from its usual sternness. He whispers something to her so softly that it sounds like a rush of breath.

A smile plays across Fucelli's lips. In Libya it wasn't so hard, was it?

Hirut's defiance slips away. She gets to her feet and places both her hands behind her back and plants a foot up against the wall. She stares at Ettore, her eyes full of spite. She wants to launch herself from there, he thinks, she wants to become a bullet spinning toward him and into his chest.

He takes a photograph and advances the film. He readies the camera again. She doesn't move so he takes another photo. Then he waits and Ibrahim mutters under his breath. And behind him a solid, thick wall of silence pushes out of the soil, so impenetrable that the sun cannot shine and he is on the precipice of a cliff, staring down at an endless fall. When she still doesn't move, he snaps another picture, identical to the one before, and another and one more. Then he stops, unsure of what to do, a slow panic building inside him.

Carlo, this is pointless, Fifi says. She is clutching her servant, holding the woman's hand to her chest.

Keep your mouth shut, Fucelli says. He rests a hand on his belt, tapping on the buckle while his head lowers and his breathing grows jagged. He appears to coil inside himself, a cornered animal ready to fight to the death, to leap forward and attack the girl.

Then Fifi steps in front of him and shouts: Hirut! She stands upright, tall, and when Hirut looks at her, Fifi salutes, holding the stance of an Ethiopian soldier.

The *soldati* gasp. The *ascari* lean forward. Fucelli blinks quickly. The girl raises her chin. She drops her hands to her side. She blinks away every expression in her eyes until they are flat and dark and cold. She stands straight and steps away from the wall. She brings her feet together. She lifts her hand to her forehead in one crisp, graceful swoop. She stands at attention, a soldier.

Colonel Fucelli strides past Ibrahim and goes into the gate. He pushes Ettore aside. He pulls her away from the wall and walks around her in a circle that shrinks until he looms close to her, glaring into her face.

Hirut stares past him as if he is invisible, as if he does not matter.

They stand like that for so long, that Ettore moves in and photographs Hirut. He kneels and frames her dusty feet and slender ankles. He stands and captures the slope of her neck and the well-formed head that refuses to bow. He frames her face and shoots again and again and again.

He does not know when Fucelli comes beside him but the man's fists are knotted, and he is swinging in the direction of Hirut, who stands immobile and impassive, the slide of her eyes toward Fifi and the servant the only hint at what might be pride, but might also be mockery.

Ettore steps closer, propelled by Fucelli's shoves. He knows the lens cannot focus at the short distance that the man has pushed him, but Ettore takes photos of Hirut's eyes anyway, knowing only he will ever see the way hatred sways so easily between shame and fear. I am doing as I've been ordered, Father. I am the beast bound by obedience. I am the creature buoyed by calls to serve.

Then it is Aster's turn. Where Hirut was quiet and defiant, the older woman is movement and noise. She is a body crashing through restraining hands, spinning so wildly that Ettore cannot take a photograph. When the top of her dress is pulled down, she pulls it up. When she is pushed against the wall, she slides down to the ground. When the colonel comes to yank her upright, she grabs his legs to throw him down. She screams a name that makes Ibrahim flinch and the *ascari* pause, and even Fucelli says: Now I have solid proof that they work for that rebel leader, Kidane.

Hirut leans exhausted against the doorway, watching Aster with a trembling mouth, her hands on her face. The more the woman refuses to be stilled, the more Hirut begins to move. She opens her arms and swings her hands. She spins out of an imaginary hold. She is beautiful movement reduced to its most essential parts. Ettore angles away from Aster and leans toward Hirut. He adjusts the shutter and darkens shadows. He makes her a slender figure trying to find her rhythm, caught in a stunted pirouette: graceful and sad.

WHEN THE CENSUS FORMS ARRIVE, COLONEL FUCELLI SIMPLY HANDS Ettore the envelope and says, Navarra, make sure every Italian soldier fills this out. Return them to me in two days. He puts a finger to his lips. Fill out yours too, of course, though we do things differently here. Then Fucelli shakes his head to silence any questions and gives him a salute. You may leave, *soldato*.

Ettore walks out of the office uncertain of where to begin. He stands at the edge of the wide road leading to the other *soldati*. It is afternoon and mail has arrived and most of them will be in their tents reading their letters and crafting responses, trading gossip of home or relationships or sharing memories of homecooked meals. They will talk as they have always talked, without him or with him as an often-silent figure listening and nodding, laughing when appropriate, absent of stories to exchange in the name of friendship and camaraderie. He has always been there, but not there. Cautious of ways that a story can lead to a question he might not be able to answer: Where did you say your father's from? What about your grandparents?

The men come from every part of Italy, from Milan and Turin, from the rustic, rolling villages nestled near Florence and Siena, from the ports and rocky hills surrounding Palermo and Calabria. Despite the years away from home, despite their post in this place where boredom is interspersed with moments of intense fear and paranoia, they are hopeful and devoted to the empire they are creating. Some are educated, like

Ettore, though many more gave up schooling for the demands of the fields or family-run businesses. But nothing speaks of their differences more than their language.

A staccatoed Italian rolls off the tongues of the Milanese. A rippling, elegant version of the language, peppered with breathy *h*'s slides out of the mouths of the Florentines. And from the Sicilians, an Italian that seems to twist rebelliously in the mouth before released, at once forceful and fragmented, its grace resting on the fine balance between utterance and song. *Every Italian has an accent, my love,* Gabriella once said to Leo, unaware that Ettore was listening to them argue from his bedroom. *We are many countries in one, what is there to hide?*

He goes from tent to tent, counting the men and counting the forms. He distributes them in stacks, nods and drops them in open palms, leaves them on top of blankets, turns away before the questions and the knowing stares. The narrowed eyes that stare at him and seem to scrutinize him malevolently. At the construction site, a worker he does not know shrugs and says to him, *The sooner we get rid of these antifascisti ebrei,* the better, and he smiles at Ettore as if relieved. Certain other men grow silent. Others burst into laughter. Some take the form from his hand and go to sit in groups around the fire pit, new rumors and gossip starting already. He finds Fofi and Mario together, waiting for him at Mario's tent. He feels the accusation in their glances, the hostility in the question that bursts from Fofi: *And what's Fucelli going to do for his Foto now?* Ettore stays quiet and keeps moving on, then he holds the last form against his chest and goes to find the darkest corner.

Name: Ettore Navarra. Place of birth: Venice, Italy. Date of birth: 20 July 1913. Father's name: Leonardo Navarra. Mother's name: Gabriella Rachele Bassi Navarra. Father's place of birth: Unknown. Father's date of birth: Unknown. Name of maternal grandmother: Rachele Bassi. Name of maternal grandfather: Mauro Bassi. Name of paternal grandmother: Unknown. Name of paternal grandfather: Unknown. Religion: None. *Where was your father born, Ettore? Can you tell the class a bit* about your family, let's practice how to spell the words. I don't know, Maestro. Go home and ask him and tell us tomorrow. Papa, where were you born? My life began when you were born, my son.

━

YOU'VE GOT THE FORMS? Fucelli asks, bending to adjust the knob on his radio. He looks at his watch as a faint static hum threads through the room. Certain days, you can almost get Radio London, he says softly. He turns quickly. But we won't tell Rome, will we? He smiles and shakes his head. It's the only way to know what's really going on, he adds. He straightens and holds out his hand. Give it here. He nods approvingly. You got it done in record time.

Ettore opens his bag and gives him the envelope.

The colonel opens the envelope and takes the census forms out. Where's yours?

Ettore points to the one at the bottom.

Fucelli pulls it out and reads it, his eyes flitting across the page, pausing periodically. You know nothing about your father, he says as he folds Ettore's form in half and slips it into one of the files on his desk. Why's that?

I don't know, sir. Ettore shakes his head. I don't know, he repeats. What will happen to my parents, sir? His voice cracks, weakened by the thought.

Colonel Fucelli shakes his head. The trucks arrive in three days to collect our Jewish soldiers and workers. You need to be elsewhere when that happens. In the meantime, do you have those rolls of film for me? I'll send them off to a studio. His eyes fill momentarily with uncommon kindness. This is war, *soldato*, he says. No one survives fully intact.

They can't write me letters anymore can they, sir?

The colonel drops his head and thinks for a moment. Why don't you go to the bar tomorrow, some *ascari* will take you there, they'll let you know when you can come back. He fishes in his pocket and pulls out a folded envelope. Here, he says, handing it to him. I was saving it for another time, but take it, ask for Mimi. If there are two or three, look for the tallest one. She'll know what to do. He smiles, boyish suddenly. These are orders. You're dismissed, *soldato.*

ETTORE SITS ALONE in the tiny, crowded bar and waits for the waitress. Outside, the *ascari* who followed him are near the door, drinking their beers, waiting patiently for him to do as Fucelli ordered. There is only one waitress and she is gliding through the dark bar, glancing at him while spinning from table to table. The other men, mostly Italian laborers, some with their native companions, surge in her direction but the waitress wades through the noise and sways easily past the hands and craned necks. And then here she is almost in front of him with a smile frozen on her full lips, her eyes flat and observant, knowing. Ettore holds his breath. She is graceful motion in this place not meant for such tenderness.

She slows. She pauses in the center of the room as if she knows he has been waiting. As if she knows it was he who took the photographs of Hirut and Aster, of that hanging prisoner, of those falling bodies. As the bartender beckons her to collect another order, she arches her neck and lifts her chin. Light washes over the slope of her throat and flares at her collarbone. Ettore leans forward and for a moment, there is no sound, there are no voices, and he has never been made to fill out a census that will split open his life. She pivots in his direction as if she can hear his thoughts above the calls for more beer, more wine, more cigarettes. Her mouth trembles. Then she nods to him and brings his beer. She dips her mouth close to his ear and says, I'm Mimi, wait for me and we leave together.

THERE IS THE trick of light in the room and the shuffle of stirring dust. There is the creak of the bed when I settle next to the waitress. We lay back and the scrape of the metal frame against the wall is the only sound I hear besides your voice reading to me from that other Leonardo: The boundaries of bodies are the least of all things. There is more Father: there is also a rifle rolled up in one of those scarves these women use. It is leaning in the corner of the small room, and not even the soft glow of the sun that filters in can make me forget this is war. What I'm telling you is that you do not belong here, none of this is for you, but I am afraid to let you go.

She mistakes his silence for hesitation. It's okay, she says. *Va bene.* She guides his palm to her waist then down to her stomach and his fingers brush the smoothness of the flesh just below.

He can feel his own rough breaths when she presses herself against him. Wait, he says. He plants his hand over his eyes: he needs to steady himself. Just give me a minute.

It is all right, she whispers, don't be afraid. She speaks mechanically, enunciates carefully, as if her mouth must conform to the words, as if Italian were unnatural.

She may know nothing more than the sentences she's been repeating, she may know nothing more than what she practices alone, in front of the mirror, at night. Or she may know everything. She may know why they call him Foto, a shooter of photographs, a collector of ghostly images, an archivist of the dead. She may guess why Fucelli paid for her services for him.

I don't do this, he says. But this is war. He feels the shadows in the room, the bristling rage of phantom voices. It is so hard to breathe next to this body.

She smiles, recognizing the word. War, she nods. *Paterazm. Guerre. Pólemos.* She trails a finger across his chin. She flattens her palm over his heart. She holds it there for so long the room seems to swing around them and shift the shadows closer until all the prisoners he has ever photographed stand at the foot of the bed, staring down at him: the girls, the brothers, the twins, the fathers, the elderly, the women, the boys, the young men. Ettore shuts his eyes and holds his breath. His hands have clenched to fists and he wants to bolt out of the shrinking room.

Tomorrow you go. Tonight, you stay with me. They say I can call you Foto?

I'm Ettore. I'm a soldier, he adds, I'm Italian. He stares once more at the tiny room. He is so far from home. I just turned in my census form, he says, testing her comprehension. That's why I came to the bar. He waits for something to happen, for the door to burst open and men to drag him out and ship him back to Rome. I gave it to the colonel. That's why I'm here, he wanted me to have this. You're a prize. You're a bribe to make sure I stay obedient, he adds softly, bitterly.

She nods and smiles blankly and presses closer to him until they are as still as new sweethearts, side by side, hands clasped, their nudity only a minor detail. The gesture is so innocent, he lets his head touch hers and allows his hand to relax in her palm. There is a warm pocket of pressure in his stomach.

I'm Italian, he says again, drifting on the steadiness of her breathing. When she does not respond, he lets himself say what he's been wanting to confess: My father had another life, a son and a wife. He was some-one else before I knew him. There is another side of him that he says he erased but I don't believe him. It's why he's tried to cram my head with information, so I don't realize what's missing. So I don't realize how much he wishes I were someone else. I've always been a disappointment.

Her hand caresses his leg, his stomach, then his chest and he feels the softness of her breasts as she slides on top and buries her face in his neck, her legs wrapped around his. He lifts her face and stares into it, at her liquid eyes and high cheekbones, at her full mouth and the curve of her chin. From the corner: a faint shuffle, like leaves, like a curtain, like a thought taking form.

I know why your people are always crying, he says. I know why you kept looking at the door when I came into the bar. I know why the bar-tender stared at me. I know many things. I know you hate me. I know

I am an enemy. I know you can't trust me. I know wherever I go, your people die. Then he cannot speak because there is that patch of shadow again, vibrating at the edge of light. He closes his eyes. This is war, he tells himself. This is what it means.

She shifts so the softest parts of her press closer, so flesh molds against flesh, without resistance, every bend wrapping into him, around him, and he pushes against her, relieved by her gentle insistence, then he is rising into her, letting go, and they stretch on the bed and move together, all sound crumbling away until there is nothing but the warmth of her and the illusionary safety of a firm embrace. They find their rhythm, slowly, gradually and in the swelling urgency, Ettore senses the solidity of his heart, the strength of his arms and legs, the broad span of his back. He is sturdy: bone and flesh, strong muscle and cartilage, a full-bodied man, a soldier. Blood rushes through him, races him toward euphoria, and yet, even in those final moments, Ettore's eyes open briefly, cautiously, before closing again.

When they are finished, he presses his mouth against her ear to say something, to admit it is not over, that it has just started, that he will never speak of her to anyone, that he will hide it from his father when he goes home, that now he, too, has a secret. But there is a discreet knock at the door and a bell and when she slides out from the thin blanket and stands, her face is remote. Her dark skin rises like a wall between them.

It's time to go, she says, and tosses him his clothes. She turns her back to dress and when she looks at him again, she is in her white dress. Good luck.

T HE PHOTOGRAPHS OF HIRUT AND ASTER ARE DEVELOPED. THEY ARE made into postcards and passed out to Fucelli's men. They are sent to newspapers and used by journalists. They are kept as souvenirs and discussed in administrative meetings. The photographs of the women are distributed to shops in Asmara and Addis Ababa, in Rome and Calabria, in officers' clubs in Tripoli and Cairo. Hirut and Aster are called many things: Angry Amazon, Woman Warrior, African Giuliette. They are handled and ripped and framed and pasted into albums and from everywhere come the requests: Can we put them in front of huts with their rifles? Can we stage an attack with a few of your men? Put on your cleanest uniform, Fucelli. Put on your most ravaged uniform, Fucelli. Put on your helmet. Put on this medal. Put on these sunglasses. Stand in profile. Stand between them, Colonel, and tell us what you've learned about the native.

IS THIS HER? Kidane holds the photograph up to the light. It is Aster's face and her body, but it does not look like her. He is aware of the men watching him, of Nardos standing in front of him with her hands over her face, rocking back and forth while speaking words he cannot quite hear.

Kidane drops the photograph to the ground and wipes his hands on his shamma. He knows he is in his cave surrounded by two of his men and Aster's closest friend, but he is also alone in that bedroom on that first night, looking at a frightened girl holding her anger like a shield.

There are more pictures with Seifu and Aklilu but he will not look at them.

Did Ferres say anything else except we should wait? Aklilu asks.

Seifu is hunched over a photo of a pair of legs dangling off the ground, the bottom of the uniform trousers soaked in blood. This is Tariku, Seifu says, lifting his head, his eyes wide. This is my son, look at him. He kisses the image and holds it to his chest. Why aren't we killing this Fucelli right now? Why aren't we running down this mountain and slitting his throat in his sleep?

Aklilu puts an arm around Seifu's shoulders and draws him close. In that tender gesture, Kidane can feel the accusations they are throwing at him. There have been many days since the women were taken when he has sensed Seifu's anger and Aklilu's frustration. They want to attack and yet Ferres keeps begging for their patience. And now the spy has sent them pictures that include Seifu's son, Tariku. It is only Kidane's status that keeps him safe from the man's violent grief.

Aklilu takes the photo out of Seifu's hand and lays it on top of the others. In the stack are pictures of Hirut that Aklilu has been careful to place at the bottom of the pile. He has tensed, visibly defiant, each time Kidane reached to pick one up.

They're making them into postcards and passing them around, Aklilu says.

They've always done that, Kidane says. There's nothing different now, except we know the women.

He looks beyond the cave entrance to the row of tall trees flanking a footpath. The sky outside is a pale blue, early morning fog still lingers as midday approaches. The wind is gaining strength outside, blowing through the haze that has helped shield them. It is getting harder to decipher sounds beyond the cave, every tumbling leaf mimics an approaching intruder. They are not so far from Fucelli's camp, and more than once, they have spotted an *ascaro* in the hills below, scouting the land.

I'll go back and finish what I started, Seifu says. He stares at Kidane, his jaw set, a manic glint in his eyes. I'll kill him slowly.

They have been having the same conversation for days, weeks, hours now. Seifu pressing his point relentlessly while Kidane repeats his orders, increasingly more antagonistic toward the man. There was a time when he felt that same loss as a father, but he can no longer understand what drives the man.

Women's voices and the clang of metal pots drift up from below. The villagers have come with food. They will leave it with Nardos and the other women who have been hiding in an abandoned village, making use of the few huts that have not been burned or bombed. There are no more inhabitants in this once well-tended patch of farmland, and the name of the tiny village is unknown. The nearest church has been destroyed and there is no sign of those who would have tended to its restoration. When Kidane's army leaves, it will crumble and disappear, and it is like this across the country: entire communities erased, sometimes in a day.

We have the emperor, Kidane says. We have a shadow king that everyone believes is real. Kidane pauses, waits for a new idea to form. He has rolled these two facts around in his head for weeks but nothing else has come from it. He sits upright, his hands on his crossed legs. He leans forward, following the path of his words, seeing where they will lead. They lead him back to the pictures, to the obscenity of his wife's body displayed for strangers' eyes.

Then: Imagine if the emperor came into the Italian camp, he says. Imagine if he led an ambush to rescue them.

Cut off the head, Seifu says, and you kill the body. We should go after Fucelli, throw him off those cliffs piece by piece and let his men watch before we kill them too.

Fucelli's guarded better now than before, Aklilu says. We need a full assault on his soldiers. He's expecting you to come back, he says to Seifu. He's waiting for it.

They speak well into the afternoon. Every new plan has a dead end. Every reason for hope is outweighed by risk. It has been like this since Aster and Hirut were captured. They fall asleep in Kidane's cave and wake again to the same limited choices, the same limitless dangers. Days bleed away while the Italians continue building roads and bull-dozing mountains and throwing innocent people off high cliffs. They have been destroying villages and demolishing huts while construct-ing square homes with sharp corners and installing Italian families and merchants. While Kidane's army has waited for Ferres's mes-sage to attack Fucelli, they have joined other patriots to demolish rail-road tracks and cut telephone wires. They have attacked laborers and destroyed supply trucks. They have poisoned water wells and stolen radio transmitters.

Across the country, guerrilla fighters have ambushed at night and walked peacefully through streets during the day, waving at Italian merchants and shopkeepers. The patriots have learned to attack in unex-pected places: officers' clubs in the early morning, in brothels reserved for Italians, in hotel rooms used by high-ranking officers. They have crept behind dozing guards and sleepy administrators and left noth-ing but slumped figures. They are everywhere and nowhere, men and women of a shadow world where a different king rules.

And yet, here are Kidane and his army today, hiding in caves, wait-ing for a spy's instructions before making a move. But his army has continued to grow. Soon it will be twice as large as at the start of the war. He has used Aklilu, Seifu, Nardos, and Amha to stay the fighters' impatience. He has brought Emperor Haile Selassie into secret meet-ings and urged the patriots to wait, God's time is coming, but wait. All of this while new messages from Ferres arrive with the same warning: Stay clear, he expects you, they are safe. So Kidane waits some more, crouched silently in the hills above the Italians.

⸺

THERE ARE THINGS that no longer frighten her: the barbed wire and the *ascari* guards, the sudden jangle of the padlock, the unexpected intrusion of Fucelli and Ibrahim asking about Kidane. Hirut no longer flinches when a stone is thrown at their tiny window, nor does she stand up when footsteps stomp past the gate in the middle of the night. Since the photographs were taken weeks ago, a thick fog surrounds her every thought. She wakes up daily and goes outside as ordered, cushioned by a warm, invisible palm. Some days, she imagines a shield has fallen over her heart. Other days, she imagines her parents standing guard. Light-headed and oddly heavy-boned, she moves through her days and nights grateful for the respite from stark terror.

So when Fucelli hammers on the gate and tells her and Aster to come out, there is nothing different on this day for Hirut to feel. This day, too, she thinks, will begin and end in the mouth of the dark. They will be taken outside and made to stand until the sun goes down. They will be forced to undress or put on a uniform or salute in their abesha chemise for newspapers and cameras, for those newly arrived *ferenj* settlers who have never seen a female soldier up close. Maybe today, too, a new captive will be brought out from the place where he was found and made to stand still for pictures. He will refuse salutes and poses as always. He will not speak a word of Italian. He will do nothing but stand in a way that manages to both displease and entertain Fucelli. Maybe today, journalists will once again nod and smile and applaud while they keep on snapping their pictures. They will call the new captive an Ethiopian lion, and at least one or two will do their strange salute and shout "Anbessa." They will shake hands with Fucelli and some will hug him, thrilled to meet the great conqueror of Benghazi. Then they will leave and Hirut and Aster will go back into their jail, exhausted and dusty, and sleep.

But today, Fucelli has two new prisoners, elderly priests roped tightly together by the leg. They walk in awkward steps between Ibrahim and the *ferenj*, hunched beneath their long robes, old men struggling to maintain a cruel momentum. Fucelli's thick leather boots leave a plume of dust that rises into Navarra's indifferent, pale face. Both Fucelli and Navarra wear identical large sunglasses, Ibrahim has his propped on top of his head. All three soldiers walk in long strides with purpose. As they get closer, an unspoken threat seeps from Fucelli, a vindictive malice that has not been there for some time, since that first set of photographs was taken. It is so strong that Hirut braces herself against the wall, the sharp breath she takes a needle puncturing her usual reserve. Startled, she puts her head down to avoid falling into the black hole of his covered eyes.

Aster exclaims and moves closer to her. Priests? Old men? she whispers. She makes the sign of the cross and shuts her eyes.

Hirut waits for the usual onlookers to make their procession, but there are no other spectators besides Navarra and Ibrahim. Fifi does not follow behind them. There is no eager audience of soldati or *ascari*. The cook has not been forced to climb up the hill. Even the guards have moved on toward the cliffs. A vulture hops near the cliff's edge, pushing the guards away. It is all so out of the ordinary, so new, that Hirut senses the first threads of horror wrapping around her chest and climbing to her throat. She looks toward the landscape, toward the familiar, and waits for the numbness to return.

I know as long as these women are alive, Kidane will come, Fucelli begins. And because they are here, we have no room for more prisoners in the jail. He slides his sunglasses from his face. He pats one of the elderly priests on the back. Which is bad luck for you, I'm afraid, he adds. But if they tell us where he's hiding, then, maybe, you've got a chance. You want to live, don't you?

He looks at Aster as he speaks. These priests were praying over fresh graves in rebel territory, he adds. They claim there are innocent children buried there. I claim they're lying. He clears his throat and slips his sunglasses on again.

Ibrahim's voice trails behind his, rapidly translating, the menace apparent in both languages. The priests grasp each other's hands, their eyes closed. The glance Navarra gives Fucelli exposes the surprise that Ibrahim has shoved behind lowered lids and a pursed mouth.

You think some are too old to die, Navarra? Fucelli smiles.

It is Ibrahim's voice, cracking at the last words, that pushes Hirut toward the fence and brings her hands around the barbed wire. The numbness returns and so she tightens her grip around the metal spokes, ignoring the soft tear of flesh.

Abba, she calls out to the priests, Abba, tell them I'm here. Tell my mother to find me when you die. Tell her where I am. Tell my father I'm sorry.

Ibrahim blinks rapidly and steps back.

Fucelli frowns. Navarra, why aren't you getting this? He takes out a handkerchief and wipes his forehead and neck.

But Navarra is not paying attention to Fucelli. He takes off his sunglasses and steps toward her to clasp a hand around each of her wrists. His hold is tender, his touch is almost comforting, non-threatening. It is warm skin brushing against skin, bone steady against bone: a human being seeking firmer ground. Hirut squeezes so hard on the barbs that she can feel the puncture wound in the soft skin between her fingers. A thread of blood sits waiting to flow down her wrist. It is not until she feels an ache in her jaw that she realizes she is grinding her teeth. Hirut looks at Navarra's bewildered face. She looks at his hands still hanging on to her wrists. She glances down at herself, at that clothed body pressed against that evil fence, and she tries to remember her name, but what comes to mind is the lone word that points to the singular mistake that led her here and to the end of her life: Wujigra.

She shakes her head as Navarra begins trying to pry her hands off the fence. No, she says. Wujigra, she adds, speaking to the priests, throwing her voice across the space between them. Tell Abbaba I'm sorry about my Wujigra.

And Navarra says: Abbaba, Papa, Mamma, *carissima* Gabriella.

Behind her, Aster: My child, what's happened to you.

Navarra, let go of her. What's going on? Fucelli asks, peering at her through his sunglasses, throwing her reflection back to her, forcing one Hirut to step away from the other until there is enough space between them to breathe fully.

Ibrahim translates carefully, his voice caught in emotions that force him to stop and look at the ground. Colonello, he says, Colonello Fucelli.

They think she is lost. They think she cannot see herself, double-bodied and split, clothed and naked, young and old, bending toward the priests who reach through the fence and put a hand on both her heads and give her solemn blessings. They think she has found a way to escape while standing still, but Hirut, daughter of Getey and Fasil, born in the year of a blessed harvest, knows that this is also a way to fight.

Wujigra, she says to Fucelli, because that is the only word for the language of hatred she now speaks.

Wujigra, she says to Ettore Navarra, because it contains the full range of the disgust that she feels for him.

Wujigra, she says to Ibrahim, because he must surely have a father who once had a Wujigra, because he must know the loss she means.

Hirut says the word even as the priests are led away, making the sign of the cross in her direction, then turning to bless and pray for each other. Hirut says the word even as they are lined up, side by side, legs bound together, between the tall boulders. Hirut says it as the vulture pads down the field then launches off the edge to wait below. Hirut says it even as the priests link arms and throw their heads back and shout a word that echoes back as *anbessa*, lion, and Ethiopia. She repeats her private prayer while Navarra lets go of her wrists and whispers her name as an absolution she will never give him. She repeats the word while Navarra obeys Fucelli's orders and staggers toward those old priests and photographs their final flight.

Chorus

We tip toward her in the dark well so she can hear: Make of this anguish something dangerous enough to throw, tender Hirut. Turn remembrance into a sly weapon you draw out and hurl in battle. You who are doubly bound to seek vengeance without retreat, rise up and walk toward your mothers and sisters who wait to strengthen your resolve. Stand, Hirut.

But the girl cannot hear us through the smothering blanket of her rage. She is focused on her balance on that soft precipice she mistakes for firm ground, her arms extended like wings, her face lifted to harsh sun. When Aster comes behind her to hold her close, maternal and pitying, Hirut shoves her away and calls out a name that falls like a boulder between them: Kidane. And then this girl, senses attuned to every secret in Aster's face, asks the question she has not known until now how to ask: What happened to my mother? What did Kidane's father do to her?

Aster says to her: We do not have to follow our mothers' stories. We do not have to walk in the path they give us.

So Hirut asks again, the sharp wire digging once more into her hands: Tell me about my mother.

There is this: a young woman named Getey attached to a young bride named Aster like an appendage. Aster, full-bodied and treasured, bound like a gift to a new husband who is also a stranger. Getey is taken to Aster's new house by Kidane's father. Getey, the father says. I will miss you, but my son's new wife needs assistance. You will be in a home with my son, who loves you like a sister. This Aster might be difficult, but you are a gift, don't forget. You will always be my treasure, and I will come for you as I need. And Getey, taken from Kidane's old home and left at Aster and Kidane's new doorstep, stares at Kidane's father's retreating back. She is too stripped of language to say: Get away and leave me alone, and Don't ever come back here, and Next time I'll kill you. She steps across the threshold into the house through the back door, through the kitchen nestled next to the servants' quarters where she will sleep and, she hopes, forget about her old nightly terrors. She will reach true womanhood in this home where Aster, too, will learn the ways of wives and women and all those who tread the difficult path in between. When Kidane's father, prone to roaming his land in search of the enemy, comes looking for Getey, it is Aster who blocks the door and tells the old man: This is not your place anymore. It is Aster who holds Getey, and says, I'll give you my gun and a bullet. It is Aster who forces Kidane to step in front of Getey and her love, Fasil, and say to them both: Run, hurry, and I will find a way for you two to be free.

Aster tells all of this to Hirut, who listens while staring into that bottomless well, suffocating in the dense fumes of revenge. And when Hirut turns to her, as Aster has always known she would when this day came, and asks: And why did you do nothing to help me? Are you so jealous that you have no heart? All Aster can say is: Your mother was both beloved and brave. Your mother knew how to fight.

HE REPEATS HER NAME LIKE A LAMENT, LIKE A SORROWFUL REFRAIN that is both a warning and a plea. Hirut presses her back against the jail wall as Navarra approaches, shocked by the fact of his appearance. It is too early in the morning. It is not time for new prisoners to arrive. There are no others with him ready to watch another spectacle. She lowers her head, trying to hide her fear when he gets to the fence and says her name again. He waits for her to respond, dropping to sit cross-legged, both arms leaning on his knees, his face twisted in emotion. He starts to speak rapidly, words bursting out of him, while he shakes his head. Deeply frightened now, she stares at this *ferenj*. He is at eye level. He is out of breath. His cheeks are flushed and sweat rolls freely down his neck. He is an unusual sight on a normal waking day. He has broken protocol. What was, is no more.

He reaches into the bag he never leaves behind and takes out a photograph. He holds it up in front of her, his hand trembling, and says: I die. You die. We die.

Hirut jerks her head away from that humiliation. It is a picture of her, one of those she knows the *soldati* and *ascari* pass around like a new fascination and an unending joke. They have come often to the prison waving the photos of her and Aster, laughing and shouting at the full-bodied women while caressing the flattened copies in their hands. Their arrival sends Aster sliding back into the building while Hirut chooses to stay outside and practice resilience, testing her strength in the face of their ridicule. She has managed, somehow, to keep the tears away and her head up, her back straight, her gaze locked on the horizon for long enough to watch them return to their camp, finally bored. She has counted each retreat as a triumph, another mark on an imaginary rifle.

But Navarra: he is an abnormality, a distortion without his camera.

Go away, she tells him, surprised by the firmness in her voice, pleased by the way it makes him flinch and shake his head and reach into his bag, desperately searching for something else.

He takes out his parents' photo and points. They die, he says in Amharic that is more fluid, more sure than she has heard him use before. They died. They are dying. I die. *Irgitegna negn. Sono sicuro.* I am sure.

He knows the words and their meaning well enough to express their urgency, well enough to let each vowel stretch itself across varying shades of grief. Hirut cannot see past the shifting paleness of his skin to really look at him, but she can interpret the longing and anguish resting in each phrase. He takes out a letter she has seen him read repeatedly and opens it. He points to the handwriting, to the strange-looking characters, and then jabs a finger into his chest.

Son, *lij, figlio,* he says the words then rattles the letter and adds, Abbaba. He points behind him toward the horizon and the hills, his hand sweeping across those two ravenous boulders and the cliffs.

It is a letter from his father, she understands. His most treasured possession. Abbaba, she says softly, correcting his pronunciation. Abbaba, she says, calling out to her own father, a coiled fear settling in her stomach. Every cruelty has its methods, but this one she does not know.

Hirut braces herself, brings her knees to her chest, tucks the skirt of her long dress under her toes. She waits. She imagines herself as a camera's eye chewing through space to gnaw at his jawline and sink against that distant place where these *ferenjoch* keep their feelings and memories. Click: she blinks to capture his cautious pause when one of the guards ambles past him, curious and confused. Click: she focuses onto that paper he hunches over as if it is a secret treasure, as if it is an object he must protect at all cost.

He points to another word and then jabs his finger toward the mountains and says, *Hagere*, my country, *il mio paese*. It is not my country.

Aster peeks out of the door. She stares at Navarra, her eyes narrowing. What's he doing? she asks. She pushes the empty tray of food toward Hirut. This morning, as usual, it was Hirut who got their bread and coffee from the gate and she will hand it back to the *ascari*.

Navarra lifts his head and waits for Hirut to answer. Hirut stares back, caught in the uncertainty of his gaze. She has grown so numb that it no longer matters whether he might strike her or not. She does not care if he takes out his camera to push it in her face. She is not afraid of him anymore. She is a soldier trapped inside a barbed-wire fence, but she is still at war and the battlefield is her own body, and perhaps, she has come to realize as a prisoner, that is where it has always been.

Navarra! Navarra! It is Fucelli, his long steps leading him from the road onto the plateau.

He is a propulsive object aiming at the jail, a weapon turned in their direction, preparing to explode. His arms swing in stiff rhythm, his feet raise clouds of dust behind him. A silence falls across the field, the sky behind him dims and all that pulses in the hidden bends and caves of the hills leans forward to watch his crashing momentum.

Ettore draws back from her, unsettled but not surprised. He mumbles and purses his lips. There is a tightening in his features.

Aster slowly closes the door to the prison.

Hirut watches Ettore, the way he stuffs the letter back into his bag and slips the photo into his pocket, the way he secures the bag shut then slings it over his shoulder as if it has always been there. She recognizes that panic, that whiff of childish terror that also hints at debilitating obedience. She knows the impulse riding through him right now, that instinct to avoid confrontation through humiliating subservience. She looks at Fucelli striding toward them, the assuredness that can exist only if there is no resistance. He waves a piece of paper in his hand as if it were a flag.

No, she says to Ettore. Be a soldier, *soldato*.

Ettore jumps to his feet, fumbling with his camera. His smile is too broad, too effusive, and as Fucelli gets closer, he shoves his hands in his pockets. He slumps his shoulders, dips his head, his eyes gaze down then look up through lowered lids. This is the cook: You have to know how to stand so they see you but do not see you. You have to look at them as if you are not looking. Be invisible but helpful. Be useful but absent. Be like air, like nothing. Hirut crosses her legs. She rubs her hands across her dress, she keeps busy, pretends to be distracted. That she is not leaving him alone to go inside the prison with Aster is a detail she will not allow herself to consider for many, many years. He is a child, she says to herself now, he is just a cruel, frightened child.

One of the *ascari* guards walking past the prison glances at her, then at the two Italians, then pauses at the fence, leans in, and shakes his head.

That one, he says softly in Amharic, sliding his eyes toward Fucelli, who's now motioning Ettore to him. He's not good.

Hirut looks up, startled. The *ascaro* is one of the older guards, one of those who has seemed the most hardened and cruel. He's not good either, she says, pointing toward Ettore as he stands in front of Fucelli and salutes.

The *ascaro* shrugs. He's just obeying orders, he says. He holds her gaze. That's what soldiers do, he adds. Then he continues pacing.

The two men are in the middle of the field, several meters away from where Hirut watches. They are speaking too softly for her to hear, but it's clear to see when Fucelli claps Ettore on the back. Ettore grips the straps of his bag to hold it in place. And when Fucelli pushes the piece of paper into his chest, Ettore steps back to let it float to the ground. Fucelli picks it up and holds it out and waits. Ettore shakes his head. He taps his chest, looks behind him at Hirut, turns again to Fucelli, and shakes his head once more. Fucelli grabs Ettore's hand and pushes the paper into it. He folds his arms across his chest. He spreads his legs apart and lifts his chin. He speaks in a voice that glides easily across grass and barbed wire. He is speaking in Italian but it is coated in another language, one of urgency and demand. She watches Ettore collapse into himself. She sees the hand that trembles as it shakes open the paper. And she expects the colonel to take it away, because those who have are always seeking more.

Instead, Fucelli slips his sunglasses on top of his head and clears his throat. He angles to spit at the ground. Then he begins to speak, his voice so loud and clear, so crisp, that the hills tug at the words, elongate them and fill them with air until they float and multiply and filter back over Hirut, a cascade of sounds she can only translate by watching the way that Ettore holds his head and shakes. He turns to look at her, and in that space something tremulous and tender rises between them, an understanding absent of any language that might give it form, give it boundaries, and give it an end.

Then Fucelli finishes. He salutes. He waits. When Ettore finally salutes, Fucelli turns and strides back down the hill, as purposeful as ever.

THE HUMILIATION IS A WOUND SO PAINFUL THAT ETTORE REFUSES TO acknowledge its depth. There is no way but forward, he thinks as he sits on his cot, still shaken. There is nothing to do but return to Italy like the telegram orders and face the consequences of his insubordination. He has been found out, likely reported by someone in the camp, and there is nothing the colonel can do to stop whatever that will happen next. Fucelli will petition on his behalf but he will leave when the mail truck arrives next week. The colonel will not place him under arrest as the telegram orders; a soldier's work is not done until he is dismissed. Ettore looks around at his neatly made bed, the crate topped with only a kerosene lamp and an outdated newspaper. He spills the contents of his bag onto the bed and picks up the photo of Hirut. She would not look at it. She could not bear witness to herself, even as a seminude figure draped in wondrous light. That was what he had wanted to show her: his ability to turn a starkly hideous moment into something else.

Ettore reaches beneath his cot and pulls out a flat metal box. It is one of those that nearly every soldier and even the colonel owns. A standard metal box easily found in Asmara or in a *tabacchi* in Gondar. It is a way to protect letters and postcards, small objects to save for the journey home. Inside are the letters he has written to his parents that he knows will not pass the censors, a record of his days in Africa, a memento he has kept as much for himself as for them. He sifts through the photographs, stacks labeled neatly by year and placed in chronological order.

He has included newspaper clippings and notices of events that will become shorthand for other memories when he has one of those conversations he has always wished he could have with his father. There are photos that he has exchanged with other photographers in the area. There are pictures of strangers that he will never know, images he has not even looked at yet. He collected them simply to have them as proof that once, he, too, had been an Italian in Africa. He will bury this box somewhere safe and dig it out when he is free of this war and the census and its constrictions. He thinks back to his frantic rush toward the prison when he heard Fucelli was looking for him and a message from Rome was involved. He cannot explain his need to be in the presence of Hirut, to feel her disdain and let it roll over him while hoping to feel its ebb and the gradual push of something else kinder, gentler, and forgiving.

≈

HIRUT PEEKS THROUGH the crack in the door, pressing herself against the frame, motioning for Aster to be quiet behind her. There is a tugging in her chest as she observes Ettore, a slow loosening of the knot she has gotten used to. He is at the tree, holding a square object and turning in slow circles to take in the horizon and the cliffs, then the prison and the road. He does it again as if memorizing the landscape, as if looking for something held in the crevice of light slipping over the hills as the sun sets. He drops to his knees. He crawls to the thick roots that push out of dirt and intertwine to grow as sturdy and large as human limbs. Her hand settles on her throat as he pulls up a short-handled shovel, the tool hovering in his hand as the horizon flares a burnished orange steeped in blue. He is molding into a silhouette, a dark form moving silently on a grand stage.

Hirut wants to ask aloud what he is doing as he digs, but she already knows. Her heart twists in her chest as she realizes that she is watching an old version of herself, that girl who was a keeper of things she should not have claimed as her own. He is doing as she once did, in the naïve belief that what is buried stays that way, that what is hidden will stay unseen, that what is yours will remain always in your possession. He is being foolish.

Aster stands next to her and nudges her out the door. Then they are sitting cross-legged and against the wall, tipping forward, watching as he shovels dirt to one side, sheltered by the same darkening sky that serves to make them difficult to see. The *ascari* are starting their usual patrol of the hills, moving quickly in the opposite direction while leaving one bored guard to stand at the cliffs. Ettore pauses to let them disappear into the trees. He stands, whistles, coughs, and when none of them looks his way, he continues to work. As he digs, neither Hirut nor Aster speak, held rapt by the *soldato*'s urgency, so engulfed in his secrecy and despair, that they do not pause to ask what could be in that box. They watch him as he buries it. Then he stands and stares down at the mound, kicking debris and twigs on top of it until the rocks that camouflage his efforts are no more than useless stones.

Ettore pats the covered hole into shape. He has buried everything except his father's letter. He has given up to the earth all the letters his mother has written, all those he can never send, and all the photos he will gather strength to show his parents later. There is no other choice. It is as close to destroying them as he can get, as close to saving them as he can manage. He is afraid that the authorities will order him to turn everything over. He is worried that there is no longer any safe place for his private thoughts.

When he is finished, Ettore dusts off his trousers. He sneaks a glance toward the prison and sees a silhouetted Hirut get to her feet. He turns to her, hesitating before walking closer. She points to him. He moves toward her, drawn by the hand reaching through the fence, drawn by the voice that is no more than a whisper, propelled by this night that has wrapped itself around his secrets. He feels protected and exposed, cautious and brazen.

So when Hirut points to the mound that looks as innocent as it did this morning, Ettore nods, surprised and freed by the gesture. And when she says the Amharic word for "to bury": *meqiber*, he repeats it back in Italian: *seppellire*. When she whispers, "secret": *meestir*, he answers back, *yene meestir*, my secret, *il mio segreto*. When she pauses and looks at him and says, *il mio segreto*, he is forced to stop and approach her and they stare at each other through that fence that has become a border between two countries.

Il mio segreto, he says, pointing to his chest.

Il mio segreto, she says, pointing to his chest.

He shakes his head and points to her: *Anche il tuo segreto*.

But she shakes her head and smiles, a somber light in her eyes, and says, *Yene meestir aydellim*. It's not my secret.

And for a moment, it is he who is in the prison and they both know it. It is he who is captive to a force larger than himself. Ettore spins on his heels, his heart beating rapidly, sweat drenching his back, and he believes he can hear her as he makes his way to the camp: *Yene meestir aydellim*.

OF COURSE CARLO HAD TO DELIVER THE TELEGRAM TO ETTORE HIM-self, to have let him find out any other way would have crushed the man beyond repair. He reassured Navarra as much as possible but he still cannot get rid of his uneasy feeling. It is a nagging guilt that he cannot shake loose. A sense that he is responsible even though the opposite is true: he has done as much as he could. This is why he invites Fifi to his room and lets her hold him longer than usual. He speaks to her as he has not done before: about victory and its costs, about loyalty and its burdens. He takes her hand and raises it to his lips as he talks, pressing her palm against his teeth, reveling in her caresses.

He waits until she is asleep before he slips out of bed and turns on the kerosene lamp. He taps a cigarette out of his case. He lights it and inhales deeply. He has grown to like Ettore Navarra, he realizes. He has come to feel paternal toward him. Thanks to Navarra, he now questions what it means to walk through gradients of shadow and seek brighter lights. It is not fair that the *soldato* will be punished for disobedience that Carlo himself encouraged, but that is an unsentimental consequence of war and law. Conflict tests the limits that make a man, even that beloved son of Leo Navarra. The order to stand trial in Rome is no more than an effort to reinstill the most fundamental task of a soldier: obedience. All will eventually return to normal.

There was nothing to worry about, he told Fifi. But it was, in fact, Fifi herself who suggested he take action tonight. It was she who told him to remove the *soldato* and send him to Asmara then to Massawa immediately. To put him on the next ship back to Italy. Give his camera to someone else who can take his place right away. You need the photos for your reports and records, without those, what does Rome know of what you're accomplishing? What will he tell them of what you did with his census? Even I have to admit this, Carlo: You must reassert your authority and do it now. Protect yourself. But Carlo shook his head and told her no, and he shakes his head now as he extinguishes his cigarette and crawls back into bed.

Leo, he whispers in the tiny room as he draws Fifi close and pulls her arms around him, she wants me to strip your son of the only thing he has at the moment when he needs it most. He presses himself against Fifi as he continues. She wants me to take that camera away as if he can be so easily replaced. Carlo taps his heart. I'm not a cruel man, he says softly against Fifi's neck. He feels her stir and kiss his cheek. I have kindnesses yet to bestow to my men. No, I'll wait for Rome to do its work. Then he draws her nearer and falls asleep.

Chorus

The woman who cradles a sleeping man in her arms: this is not what she was meant to do. She was not born to soothe troubled men and ease their worries. She did not learn to read and speak foreign languages in order to brush Carlo's hair from his eyes. She has always known her fate to be more than this. She has always known it to be bigger than any man. Though she embraces as if she were meant to hold children, she has never wanted those things that make a woman's stomach into a home. She was born, she has always claimed, to be free, to roam across borders and find refuge in books and seek new loves unhindered by the rules of a villager's life.

Here is the woman staring at the colonel as he sleeps, looking at him as he stumbles into a dream, his face a patchwork of feelings. Faven: she whispers her own name, then stops. Then: Ferres, because it is an oath and a name she has made into a wall. Does her childhood friend Seifu know this of her? Does he know of the loyalties that even now she is balancing against a young girl's ambitions? See the hand that slides to rest against Fucelli's throat. Feel the air that catches in his chest even as he remains asleep when she repeats: Ferres. See Fifi shrug aside his arms, stand from the bed, and turn her face so he cannot see her twisting expressions if he awakens. See Ferres slip out of the room to return to her tent and wake the cook.

THE MESSAGE TO KIDANE FROM FERRES IS SIMPLE AND DIRECT:
Now, immediately. Do it now.

—

ETTORE KNEELS AT the spot where he hid the box. He wants to dig it
up and bury Leo's last letter. He wants to keep the letter and swear that
he will die before he gives it up. Ettore wipes his eyes and swallows the
ache in his throat. He feels as if he has broken a promise he never knew
he made. He has betrayed his father's words, disrespected the lessons
of the man, all in the name of obedience. And now it is he who has
been betrayed. Ettore sits down and settles his back against the tree and
stares at the moon, waiting as a guard walks by, his faint whistle flitting across a halfhearted melody. He opens his bag and takes out one of
the pictures of Hirut that Fucelli developed recently, one of those that
shows her defiance and hatred while standing at attention. He flips it
over and starts to write:

What are you holding in your hand, Papa, the shaded body or reflected
light? Mamma, we call her *donna abisinna* but her name is Hirut and she
is a soldier and a prisoner. He shrinks his handwriting and puts down
what he knows to be both true and false at the same time. Papa, your
name is Leo and it is not. You are an atheist and something else I have
come to understand as light. What is reflected from you, to me? What is
illumined by your life, Mamma? What does it mean to be Leo's wife and

my mother? As Ettore writes furiously, bent close to the pen, other noises seep in: the tender snap of grass, rustling leaves, a bird's sad sweep, then whispers: urgent words spoken low. He looks up. The sentry is no longer pacing, the whistling has stopped. The silence is ominous and complete.

Ettore scrambles to his feet. He swings his rifle in front of him and for a fleeting moment, he hopes for an ambush, an attack that will shred this photo and his note and that telegram and send it to the wind and into forgetfulness. He leaves the tree and creeps closer to the jail. The voices again. For a moment, he imagines that boy hanging on the tree, twirling in that awful breeze. In how many ways can we fall, he will ask his father when they meet. Tell me so I can prepare. He steps out of the dark, into a spray of moonlight. He is near enough to the fence to see the shape of two figures, startled, step back from the gate.

Ibrahim? He keeps his own voice low.

A cold pressure falls on his shoulder. A blade slides gently across his throat. A fleshy hand covers his mouth. Ettore shuts his eyes as his rifle is ripped from his hands. His bag is taken and a kick at the back of his legs forces him to his knees. He puts his hand behind his head when the knifepoint settles against his jugular vein. He braces himself and waits. So this is how it will end, in darkness. He is the shaded object. He should have known. He sees Hirut step out of the dark in front of him. She puts a finger to her lips and shakes her head. She is handed his rifle from someone who still holds that blade to his neck. He understands the command: Hirut, kill him. Ettore swallows. He will keep his eyes open. He will look at how it all ends. He will seek that body trapped in both light and shadow. Hirut raises the gun to her chest. She points the barrel in his direction and she whispers to him:

To die. *Morire. Memot.* You deserve to die. Then she raises the gun high, grabs it by the barrel, and brings it down on his head.

He plummets, caught in shafts of light, an object blotted and bloated, reflecting only what it has retained. He falls, free, reveling in the thrill. What Ettore will remember as he swims through oblivion toward the sharp moon are the uniformed legs and the swish of skirts across tall grass. The soft whispers will come to him blurred of language and distinction, and what remains will be Hirut's face peering down at him, checking his pulse, before she grabs her photo and his father's letter, then takes Aster's hand and runs.

~

HIRUT STARES AT THE PHOTO that she takes from his possession: her own image frozen and flattened, drained of color and blood, filled with his handwriting on the back. Then Hirut makes her escape with Aster. She races through the hills and toward the caves. She rushes into the comfort of the damp and dank cave that was once hers, and sinks against Aklilu's embrace. She holds the picture to candlelight. She narrows her world to its perimeters then presses herself to the ground and stares at the frightened girl. They are twin images: one begging for assistance while the other pleads silently for forgiveness. One alone within the folds of barbed wire, and the other catapulted into history, doomed to roam through borders and homes, never more than the object imprisoned by the eye.

~

THE ULULATIONS. The tears and hugs. The shouts of joy and grateful weeping. The large meal and tej. The prayers. The curses on their enemies. The dancing. Hirut stands in the middle of the large circle with Aster, gripping her hand, afraid to let it go, the two of them dressed again in uniforms, soldiers once more. Behind the revelers and the other fighters, behind the women wearing dresses and waving knives, behind the uniformed troops jumping and shivering in ecstatic *eskesta*, Aklilu stands with Minim, their emperor. Hirut stares at Aklilu, held in the tenderness of his gaze, unwilling to break away as he nods and touches a hand to his heart then his lips, then nods to her. She begins to understand even as she is swept up in embraces and kisses, that these moments, too, hold a power beyond simple words. These gestures, too, can puncture a night and set it aglow in unspoken promises. As Hirut nods to Aklilu and touches her heart, as she presses her own fingers to her lips and says his name, she feels her chest expand with forgotten warmth. She brings her feet together and straightens her back and she smiles when he does the same and in unison, as one, they salute.

THE STORY THE *ASCARO* GUARD TELLS FUCELLI IS THIS: THE PRISON-
ers changed to jackals then helped the ambushing Ethiopians in the
attack. They leapt past the cliffs and flew away. All of this happened
before we could react. It was the work of the devil, outside of human
capability to stop it, even for a man as great as Ibrahim. He rushed to
help and did all he could, I am sure of it because I was there. He doesn't
deserve the whip, Colonello Fucelli. *Per favore*, he is our beloved leader,
our *sciumbasci*.

But this is what Fucelli says as he ties Ibrahim's hands around the
tree: *Fascisti*, we are fighting the army of Memnon, but we are the brave
sons of Italy, offspring of those who fell in Adua nearly forty years ago.
Didn't the sons of Troy rise from the ashes to build the glorious empire
of Rome? We don't run, and every coward will be punished.

Sons of Rome! *Viva l'Italia!* The shouts ricochet through the mountains.
The *ascari* stay quiet.

Fucelli shakes the horsewhip to test its pliancy. The echoes die away
and a quiet anticipation sits on top of the suffocating heat. News of the
ambush last night had traveled faster than Ettore could get to Fucelli's
office. He had not been sure how to explain to the colonel why the Ethiopians had left him inexplicably alive. But the colonel was ready for him.

You fought them off, Fucelli said after he listened to Ettore's account.
They put the knife to your throat and tried to overpower you but you
resisted and they knocked you unconscious and fled. They left the

camera? The colonel had tensed at his confession that he lost his father's letter. That's a shame, Navarra, Colonel Fucelli said.

They knocked me out, sir, he explained. I couldn't stop them. How could Ettore have known what he was starting when he said, We searched all over for it.

We? Fucelli stood from his chair.

Ibrahim made sure I got here safely. He found me.

And he didn't fight them off? Fucelli asked. He let them come into my camp and let my prisoners escape? Just like he let those savages into my tent to attack me?

We punish cowards, *ragazzi*, Fucelli says now, dragging the horsewhip in the dirt. An Italian is not a coward, an Italian fights and inspires others to do the same. You are an Italian, Navarra. Let's show Rome and remind the others. This will go into your defense. Then he holds the whip for Ettore. Go on, Navarra, here's the *ascaro* who let them attack you.

A murmur grows, rolls into a fist-sized stone of noise that sinks into his head. Ettore grips his camera and automatically lifts it to his face. He is less than three meters from the colonel, almost the perfect distance to focus on him clearly. It would take a few steps backward then he could capture the lines of his arm, his shoulder, and blur everything else against a dizzying background.

Sir?

Fucelli shoves the whip into Ettore's chest. He smiles, a muscle twitching in his eye. Prove which of you is Italian.

Ettore glances nonsensically behind him as Fucelli slowly unbuttons his jacket, taking his time, aware of the dramatic performance that it is. The colonel then undoes the buttons of his shirt. He exposes the scar that extends from his shoulder and across his chest. It is thick, keloid. Skin has grafted back to itself. It is paler where it meets the old wound.

Fucelli spreads his arms and turns to the other men. You've heard what happened to me in Libya, he says. There was a savage who came into my room and tried to kill me. I fought him off, *soldati*. I never gave up and I have the scars to prove it. Fucelli grabs Ettore's wrist and pulls him forward, toward Ibrahim's naked back and says, Do it, for your own sake.

It is muscle that draws tight around the whip and keeps Ettore's grip firm around it. It is the same set of ligaments that da Vinci illustrated with a series of threads. What is inside the body can be re-created outside of it. So when his arm moves up and still maintains its hold on that slender whip, Ettore looks and sees just a body in motion, obedient to its natural inclinations, separate from the man whose blood supports that rise and bend.

Ettore follows the path of the whip as it sails through the air to sink into Ibrahim's quivering back. He feels the impact of leather on skin and the tender slide into uncarved space. It is not his will that propels the graceful tool to lift and dig itself into tendon and muscle. It is the body in agreement with itself, splendidly engineered, tipping toward increased momentum and force. And he raises his arm again and the army roars and there is no word to express the exhilaration coursing through him and I hear them so clearly it could be your voice against my cheek, Father: Good, good, and what is broken is not skin, tendons have not been split, and muscles are not damaged, it is not bone that peeks through all that holds a human form together and makes us what we are. This is the miracle of man, Leo, you whom I will never know. It is there in Colonel Fucelli's arms thrown open as if to embrace me while he speaks my name in repetition: Navarra, Navarra, well done, well done. Rome will be pleased.

That is the miracle.

Then Fucelli says, Tell the *ascari* to help you take him down, *soldato*. And the morning light becomes an unforgiving glare across Ibrahim's torn back, exposing the tremulous space that separates the living from the dying.

Ettore drops the whip and looks down at his clothes, splattered with drops of blood, evidence of that deed that deserves no name. His wrists are sore. His arms ache. He is sweating and short of breath. He feels his weakness in these small signs, and so it is no surprise that when he tells the *ascari* to untie Ibrahim and take him away, the native soldiers stand at attention and stare ahead. They do not even give him the courtesy of a salute. They do not yell the customary *Abet*, to acknowledge they received an order. Fucelli lights a cigarette and watches him through narrowed eyes. Ibrahim is slumped against the tree, his head bent low. His breaths are labored, dragged from someplace that rubs against torn flesh.

Tell them again, Navarra. Fucelli lets the cigarette burn down between his lips, the red glow turning black then ashen before falling. Rome will hear of this and let you go.

Ettore repeats his order while Fucelli taps the pistol at his waist, traces the line of the single belt there. The colonel shifts between Ibrahim and the *ascari*, between the *ascari* and his *soldati*, between his bodyguards on one side of him and Ettore on the other.

He'll stay there until one of you decides to get him down, Fucelli says to the *ascari*. He spits on the ground. Navarra, you don't leave until he does. Then he walks back into his office and lets the bodyguards shut the door behind him.

———

WHAT IS IT that unites men of extraordinary strength, Papa? What immortal breath sweeps through taut muscle and dense bone to fill a chest with a god's sacred power? There is no rational law, Father, for what I am seeing. There is no sensible rule to explain what beats beneath Ibrahim's stubborn heart as his *ascari* gather in silent support. Ettore watches, transfixed. Ibrahim has refused to allow his *ascari* to untie him. Now, he collapses completely against the tree, his body sagging, so elastic that it is only his painfully angled head that balances his full weight. He presses so hard against the tree that bark has scraped the skin off his cheeks. His eyes are swollen from the pressure.

The crook of his neck is covered in bruises and cuts. His men drop to their knees to plead. They shout to get his attention, but he rejects their assistance with a grunt, too weak to do more than work an unsteady finger under the rope binding his hands, a short fingernail scratching feebly at the surface.

——

IBRAHIM IS A SORROWFUL FIGURE propped on a stool forced beneath his knees for support. His men have not left him alone since the day before, and a new day is about to start. They have taken turns holding him up to keep him from choking. They have laid large leaves across his back and spoken gentle words that sounded like prayer. They have done the best that they could, some weeping, broken by this dogged determination that is at once stunning and agonizing. A small boy in a ragged T-shirt whom he has never seen, one that they call Abdul, has kept his own vigil next to the man.

Ettore raises the camera to his face, leaning against a rock that is several paces away. It is impossible to photograph what is unfolding. There are only the increasingly pronounced movements of Ibrahim's right arm, his greater mobility: a bird preparing to climb through the air then soar. Through the viewfinder it is nothing, but Ettore takes the picture anyway and keeps shooting as the *ascari* bend and heads bow and hands lift in benedictions. He keeps taking photos as Ibrahim releases a long, painful moan before his hands hang to the ground. He tumbles sideways and his men rush around him, visibly shaken, unafraid to reveal what no words can possibly express: that something greater than they know has been killed. That something they do not understand yet has taken its place.

——

THIS: A HUMAN FORM staring down from the hilltop, a slender figure sheltered by trees and fog. There is a hand, not impossible to discern from such a distance, stretching forward as if to cup the rays of an early sun. It is a gesture both imperial and merciful, arrogant and generous: to hold the heaven-sent beams of light, to suspend them before they tumble down and add new punishment on an anguished man's bleeding back. Below the hilltop, *ascari* surround Ibrahim. They are grim, so trapped in righteous fury and stubborn obedience that it is only Ibrahim himself, with a quivering finger raised in pain, who signals toward the hilltop and that human form: a shadow of a king, and the ruler of his own invisible kingdom.

No one else but Ibrahim, still struggling with that knotted rope, spies Hirut and Aster in uniform, standing and watching his humiliation below while a spark of light freezes then skims across the sloping valley. It is only Ibrahim who will later tell his men: I saw the emperor in the hills, and it is he who freed the women. It is only Ibrahim who understands the warning behind that advent of light and a fog-shrouded form. Only Ibrahim who chooses not to give Fucelli time to prepare. Only Ibrahim who alerts his *ascari* instead and says to them: Leave me here and go when I loosen my ropes, run to the hills and wait for me.

B Y THE TIME ETTORE HEARS HIS NAME, IT IS TOO LATE. THERE IS NO chance to do anything but look at the other *soldati* hunched over their coffee outside their tents and call out, Did you hear that?

He sets his cup down and turns on his stool slowly, raking his eyes across the field of tents. He listens, his heart beating loudly. His name comes again, followed by the colonel's: Navarra. Fucelli. And when the names ricochet once more through the hills and light skips across the valley, all Ettore has time to do is rise to his feet and confirm to himself an awful truth: The Ethiopians have come for us. And they come for us in daylight.

And even after Ettore grabs his rifle and helmet, even after he recognizes that it is, indeed, his name tumbling and snapping above his head, even after he races with the other *soldati* to get into position behind stone barricades, he still cannot comprehend what exactly is happening. There is something so strangely amiss that even a valley shifting with frantic *soldati* looks unnaturally empty. He is certain of something both hidden and illuminated by sunlight: a photographic negative that reveals everything and nothing at once.

Ettore crouches behind the barricade. As the men wait for Colonel Fucelli's orders, the urgent whispers begin to settle around him: The prisoners are looking for Ettore and Fucelli, then they'll kill the rest of us. He looks up into the hills. Rebels are rushing toward them, armed. And then above them all, flanked by two soldiers Ettore is certain are

Hirut and Aster: the emperor. Haile Selassie sweeps into view on a sun-lit horse, the jewels braided into the animal's mane flashing like a thousand eyes. It is only the sight of Fucelli running toward them in full uniform, throwing himself in front of the barricade, in front of them all, and aiming his rifle at the enemy that keeps Ettore and the rest of the *soldati* rooted in place, held firm by loyalty and training.

The colonel shakes his head and gives the order to wait. He is alone, unprotected, but he does not seem to care. Don't shoot until I tell you, he shouts to them. Don't let them scare you like this, *ragazzi*! Your leader is here!

And then from behind them all, from the hills that the *ascari* should be guarding, a new set of voices and war cries, a thousand Abyssinians and a thousand more rushing undeterred directly toward them. Ettore realizes at the same time as the rest of the Italians what has been a blindingly plain fact all along: the *ascari* are gone. They have simply disappeared.

And then the enemy is rushing down to Carlo and the rest of his men, led by that man whose name he refuses to utter. Carlo watches their approach through binoculars, as calm as he has ever been. He will fight to the last man. He will fight even if every *soldato* gives up.

My place is here, Fucelli says softly to himself. Then they will bury me at home and I will live again as a hero.

He feels the ground give as the Abyssinians get closer. Then the splatter of rocks and snapped twigs as the enemy splits into two and then three, then begins to separate some more. Right flank. Left flank. A rear guard is surely pushing through forest and brush to leap on his men from behind. Not long from now, they will be completely surrounded.

There is no way but through it, Fucelli shouts to his men. There's no escape but forward!

He turns briefly to look at them, these boys who have grown into men under his command, who stare back at him now while sunk low behind their barricade. He knows that Kidane will divide his army into smaller groups. They will spread themselves across the Italian lines and attack from multiple positions. Unimpeded by an *ascari* army that has vanished, they will try to force his men to scatter, to disintegrate into frightened mayhem, and then simply surrender. Carlo steels himself for the clash and looks into the hills, ready.

And then there he is: the ghostly figure of that runaway emperor, a spirit solidified into human form: Haile Selassie, charging down at them on a vivid white horse, a chorus of women's voices whipping at his back like a thick, royal cape. He is moving deftly, flanked by female soldiers that Carlo Fucelli identifies immediately as Hirut and Aster. The rest of the emperor's troops are racing alongside the two women, swift and astonishingly agile. The emperor: It is him. He has returned. He never left. He is here. The King of Kings. The miracle of all miracles. The impossible made flesh.

Colonel Fucelli rises from his position and steps in front of the charging army, in front of the emperor on that splendid horse. The colonel strides forward, a solitary figure, foolhardy and brave. At the base of the hill, in the gaping mouth of the rushing beast, Colonel Carlo Fucelli, famed conqueror of Benghazi, son of Italy, kneels and aims his rifle at the emperor's chest. He lifts a hand to stay any urge by his *soldati* to protect him from the approaching Ethiopians. He knows the figure he makes: A lone man framed against a bleached morning sun. An irrepressible soldier silhouetted against a vast, unforgiving land. We can remake ourselves anew, Carlo Fucelli whispers as he taps his heart beating loud beneath his jacket. This, too, is another way. This, too, is a resurrection.

Carlo turns to his men staring stark-eyed and shocked at him. Tell them about this, he shouts. Tell them what I did. Then he turns to find himself facing Aster, her rifle aimed perfectly not for his heart, but for the tender flesh of his stomach. She races toward him, pauses, and for a moment, they are locked together in her spiteful gaze. She pulls the trigger, shouting a name like a command: Seifu. The bullet is a fist in his gut. He gasps, uncertain of her generosity, of this gift of life she is offering him, until he sees another man further behind her, holding a picture while screaming a name like a benediction: Tariku, the man shouts, Tariku.

◆

THEY MOVE WITH the effortless grace of an oncoming storm, a growing rumble in the morning light. Hirut's new uniform tugs as she runs, the shirt pulling across her shoulders as she takes a deep breath, then another, and sprints ahead. She folds herself into the driving momentum of the soldiers around her, all of them surging forward in leaps, one foot flying in front of the other. If you turn to your side during battle, Aklilu told her, if you look at just the right time, you'll see angels running beside you, flicking bullets away with their wings. She steals a quick glance and sees only the emperor galloping ahead on the horse, Adua. She sees Marta and in front, Aster is throwing herself down the hill, charging toward the singular figure of Fucelli kneeling with his rifle aimed at Minim. On the other side of her, Seifu and Kidane, Abebech and Nardos push the others faster, their arms rising and falling in synchronized signals, keeping rhythm with the flashes of light skidding across the valley, playing across Italian helmets, pausing on the opposite hill where another unit of men and women, led by Hailu and Amha, waits for the order to rise and then attack.

Hirut lifts her face to the sky, no longer afraid of warplanes. Behind her, the army roars, the shouts like the knotted end of a whip slicing through the wind, cracking against the hills, the blast so full of rage that her chest gives under the pressure.

We'll protect each other, Aklilu said to her as they prepared for the ambush. Together we'll stand up and fight. You'll lead with me, and they'll never forget your name. The children of Ethiopia won't forget that you fought when it was hardest. This is our war for our country. Your leader is the man who fights beside you, the woman who will die next to you, the patriot who sings of Ethiopia. Take my hand, Hirut, my love, *yene fikir*, stand with me and we'll fight, and win.

Above them all, Worku's trumpet is a relentless wail across the valley. Around Hirut are men she has known and strangers recruited from regions distant and near. There are women in dresses and uniform, carrying knives and raising their arms to swing down in the method taught to her long ago in that other life by the cook. There are priests who have emerged out of their caves, their Bibles tucked against their chests like added armor. And as the army runs with Hirut, she feels their strength. She feels the spirits of the dead seep into her bones and steady her like steel. And for a moment, she looks away from the valley in front of her and gazes, transfixed, at the hills in the horizon, as if she can see Fifi rushing away from the camp, helping the cook carry Ibrahim farther from Fucelli's army and closer to his waiting *ascari*. She stares as if she knows exactly what it is that the cook will whisper to Ibrahim once the women reunite him with his men, as if she comprehends the many meanings in the older woman's words: They'll try to make us useful, and we must be free of them. We must find our own way to live. Hirut gazes ahead, her body moving of its own accord, until she slowly comes back to herself. And here is Hirut: wondrous soldier in the great Ethiopian army, daughter of Getey and Fasil, born in a blessed year of harvest, racing toward the enemy, unafraid.

CARLO'S *SOLDATI* ARE OVERWHELMED. They have been pushed out from the barricades and then trapped from all sides. They have been forced to retreat so far from any protection that Carlo orders his remaining soldiers to scatter and fight to the last man. The slaughter is relentless without the assistance of *ascari* and planes, and he can be no help to them with a bullet lodged in his stomach. Lying alone on the field, he clutches his side to stop the blood. He glances up, gauging the distance to safety. It is too far, he is too weak.

Coraggio soldati! Retreat! Carlo screams to his men. He lets the force of his voice substitute for a splintering heart. Go to the hills! Retreat!

From above the whir of spinning bullets, between the grunts of wounded men, forms this thought: He will die on this forsaken mountain he made into a military outpost, his corpse will be left amidst the debris and the forgotten tents. There will be nothing to mark his demise except his blood soaked into this wretched soil. No one will weep for him. No one will save his flesh from vultures. He will watch himself rot from above, the sun warm again, while his men collect their belongings and sail back home. Honor is no mortal thing, he reminds himself, hoping he can believe it. It lives in creation. It is everlasting.

Colonel! It is Ettore, running at a low crouch toward him, his eyes frantic, his mouth a grim line. They've broken all of our lines, he says, breathing heavily. Let's go toward the hills behind us, they're moving the other way.

Navarra slides his arm beneath Carlo's waist to lift him up. The pain is so severe that Carlo cries out. He puts a hand on Ettore's shoulders. Leave, he says. Get out of here, *soldato*. He looks at him for a long moment. He does not know what to say next, but this much has to be spoken. Well done, *soldato*. But it's finished. I'm finished. Don't let them take you back to Italy. Do as your father said, he loved you.

There is a low-pitched whistle behind them. An Ethiopian signal to attack. Ettore looks over his shoulder and there is a strong-jawed man racing furiously toward Fucelli, holding a photograph in front of him while shouting a name: Tariku! Tariku!

This stopped being your war a long time ago, *soldato*. Get out of here before he kills you too. Save yourself.

It is too far to see it clearly, but Ettore knows the photograph the Ethiopian is holding. He knows this man is Tariku's father, he knows that as surely as there is a bullet for Fucelli from this man, he deserves one too. He gets to his feet and turns around to face him. He holds up his hands and waits.

The man pounds his chest as he gets closer: Seifu, he says. Seifu. He screams his name like a declaration while he pushes Ettore aside and pulls out his knife and bends to grasp Fucelli's head and arch his neck.

Carlo blinks slowly, his eyes seeking Ettore's, trying to feign calmness. Survive, he whispers. Then he adds softly: Don't leave any part of me in this place.

—

HIRUT STUMBLES THROUGH the smoldering ashes of the burned field and finds Carlo Fucelli's dead body, a tattered handkerchief draped over his swollen face and neck, his belt and bloody trousers gaping open, his legs spread wide. She kneels down and lifts the handkerchief. On his eyes lay two Italian coins. His collar is drenched in dark blood. Hirut undoes the shirt to check his heart and confirm that this monster of a man is truly dead. She presses her palm against his still chest. She takes the coins from his eyes and throws them aside. She slides off his shoes and pulls off his socks and reaches for the small knife strapped to his ankle. She says a prayer over the man, asks God to damn this one to eternal fire, to scorch the bottoms of his feet with poison rain. She makes the sign of the cross and takes one last look at Fucelli, then she makes her way to the other side of the field where she last saw Kidane fall, wounded and alone.

The sound is like a sparrow winding out of the mayhem, a pure note so sweetly pitched that not even a cannon's boom could drown it out. Ettore pauses in his rush away from the field where he covered Fucelli's body as best he could. He knows that voice. It is Hirut caught somewhere between a song and a cry, a wail so painful and free it rises above the trees and fades into clouds. Without realizing it, he begins to run to her.

She is across the field from where he left Fucelli, tucked just beyond some burned tents and the curve of the hill. Her back is to him, and she is on her knees hunched over the body of the man Ettore knows to be Kidane. The man is still alive, breathing heavily and loudly, reaching up for her face as she draws back then slaps his hand down. They are two figures floating in a dark river, one holding the other on her lap, bending to cradle him and whisper into his ear. She is embracing him gently, rocking back and forth, her head close to his, her arms tucked beneath and around his neck. Ettore wants to say, But he cannot breathe like that. He wants to say, Sit up, Hirut and give him air. But Hirut is rocking and murmuring, her grip tightening on the man.

Kidu, she says, Kidu. Then she lifts her face to the sky and as Kidane tries to reach for her face to draw her near or push her away, Hirut stares down at the dying man, her eyes narrowing. I am a soldier, she says. I am Getey's daughter. They will forget you and remember me. She clears her throat, wipes her cheeks, and says it again as Kidane groans and breathes his last, his hand falling on his chest, grasping for nothing: They will forget you and remember me.

It is Aklilu who shouts first, a ruptured voice ricocheting into the hills: Kidane. Kidane: anguish in the form of a name.

Aster follows behind him, screaming for her husband.

Hirut blinks quickly, startled, and looks down then over at Ettore. They are several paces apart, but close enough to speak. She shakes her head, Go, she says. It's finished. Go back to your country. Get out of here.

He points toward the old prison. My letters, the box, my secret. Your secret. I have to go.

She understands and offers no resistance to his suggestion. She is quiet, staring down at Kidane's body with a horrified expression. Slowly she nods. Yes, she says. My secret.

Ettore spins and runs toward safety, toward a place he will make into a home until he finds her again.

5 May 1941

IT IS A LONGER JOURNEY BACK THAN THE EMPEROR REMEMBERS, THE road an endless dark ribbon stretching farther and farther into the horizon. Haile Selassie opens the window of his Rolls-Royce and hears the smooth metallic purr of the caravan behind him. They are all returning with him, his ministers and advisers, his family and his body-guards. His army is marching in front of him, those fearsome men who never gave up. He touches his chest, nudges aside his many medals and feels the outline of his sternum, the rapid beating of his heart. He has left nothing in England. He has taken even the hurried scraps of notes he made to himself in the days before departure, picking them up one by one from his rubbish bin, saving them in his pockets, in the corners of his suitcases, in his briefcase, until he is certain he has gotten each one. If he could, he would have scraped up every thread, every piece of hair, every drop of water that rolled off his skin onto English ground and brought it back. He wants to walk into his city a whole man, miss-ing nothing, complete.

He hears a strangled sound pushing its way into his reverie and he pulls his head back inside the car, into the warmth of the supple leather seats. His wife, Menen, sits next to him sobbing softly into the handker-chief she clutches as if it were his hand. He touches her leg and closes his eyes, hears the steady drone of tires spinning over rocks and pot-holes, feels the gentle weight of her head on his shoulder. He takes a deep breath then another, wills his mind still, urges his thoughts to settle here in this country, on this road. Exactly five years ago to the day, he was forced to leave Ethiopia in a locomotive racing for the border, his staff staring at the shrinking city behind them, the soft cries of his wife soaking once again into the handkerchief in her hand. He can smell the acrid tinge of smoke hovering just beyond his face. It is a tarry, pungent mix of burning rubber and rotting carcass lingering above the trees, falling in wisps driven by the wind. The Italians have left so much of their violence behind. How many generations will it take to erase it all? To forgive it all? And yet, he must speak to his people of divine love. As if the heart can withstand so much destruction. As if it is not too much to remember.

On the side of the road, a row of his soldiers calls out his name, proud in their worn and stained uniforms. Haile Selassie leans his head out, and then he sees her: Kidane's wife, the Aster that Menen has spoken of while shaking her head with both admiration and disbelief: She took her husband's rifle and led his army, Menen told him. She put her own women in the front and left no Italian alive on that hill in Debark. Then his wife touched her chest with her fist and nodded, Who says we can't do as the men?

Slow down, he tells his driver, not caring that the procession in front of him is moving along while those marching behind him have to stop. He leans farther out the window and Aster steps forward. She is dressed in uniform, with a cape that hangs across her shoulders perfectly. She keeps her eyes lowered, but she raises her rifle and salutes sharply, and behind her and all around, soldiers mimic her action. A young woman beside her steps forward too, eyes blazing, mouth set, and dares to look him in the eye. Dares to test the power of his gaze. Haile Selassie salutes back, looking past that insolent young woman, refusing to let himself think of all it can mean.

Forward now, he tells the driver. Keep going until we must switch cars and meet the general and the British. For now, let us be alone. Then he looks at his wife and holds her hand to his cheek: We're finally home, he says. Home.

As Emperor Haile Selassie rides in the back of the car purring through the hills into Addis Ababa, the weight of his absence settles like stone on his shoulders, pressing him down until his chest aches. He tries to convince himself that he has been given another chance to hold open his arms and beg forgiveness from his daughter Zenebwork, from his people, from those living and lost. This is what it means, he thinks now as they enter his city. This is what it means to be haunted by the dead.

━

MINIM KNEELS at the steps of St. Giorgis Church, praying with a heavy heart he cannot seem to push toward joy. He came to this church to be alone but he is surrounded by a crowd of worshipers giving thanks for the return of their king. Jostled and pushed amidst the rows of white-clad believers, Minim is dressed like the poor peasant he is, his long hair held back by a strip of Hirut's old netela. His heart is a hollow weight sitting in the pocket of his chest. He shifts away from the crowd and leaves a space next to him for another man his size.

Your Majesty, he says to himself silently. Yes, he answers, and holds a hand out to himself. Let us go together to our throne.

He tells himself the tears that fall to the ground from his eyes are not his alone. They are what Haile Selassie would have shed if they were both allowed to cry.

Your Majesty, he says. Who will remember me?

There is no answer, only his own silent breathing. He is trapped by his own skin, swallowed by the marching feet, suffocated by the purring procession and the satisfied cheers of Addis Ababa's people. In villages and small towns across the rest of the country, in the mountains and caves, the people are still waiting for him, eager to bow to their leader, the proud warrior king who galloped into battle on his horse to fight for them against the enemy.

Your Majesty, I am alone.

Minim waits, and in the tender breeze rustling through the open church doors, he hears what it is that his emperor wants to say: Every sun creates a shadow and not all are blest to stand in the light.

We have returned, he tells himself.

Minim looks down at his slender fingers, the nails still neatly filed and short. He glances down at his feet, and lays a hand on the beard he learned to trim as well as any royal barber. Every day, he will grow back into himself until he can be who he is: a man who was once everything to everyone, then was reborn again to be nothing.

EPILOGUE
REUNIONS

1974

THEY HAVE BEEN COMING IN FOR WEEKS TO STAND IN FRONT OF Ettore in their faded uniforms. These men who slip off their shoes and tighten their empty ammunition belts and tell him to take their picture. In every face, he looks for Aklilu. He begs the door never to open and usher in Seifu. They call him The Ferenj, sometimes Tal-yan, once in a while they use Foto but nobody uses Ettore anymore, not even the Italians who still live in Addis Ababa. To them he is *lo straniero*, though Ettore knows they know his name, they have seen it on the postcards they preserve in envelopes and albums, those images of a young soldier named Hirut and her officer, Aster.

He wonders if some of these *arbegnoch* know of those pictures too. If that is why some of them come in and stare at him then walk out. Others stand at attention with flames for eyes and declare they would still kill him on orders. Most of them surely know that he will photograph *arbegnoch* for free, but these patriots insist on paying. Lately, they have been coming into his studio in increasing numbers, these aging, proud men whose bones he once thought were made of steel. Every day, his studio blazes in sunlight as the door opens and opens and opens and he is thrown further and further into those years he has wanted so much to forget. They tell him their *ferres sim*, their nom de guerre, often they refuse any other introduction. Some say that this grumbling revolt of the youth is part of the war that began in 1935. What war ever really ends, one white-bearded man once said to him, near tears.

He sleeps in the back of his studio in a flat he rents in Piassa. He has been here for nearly fifteen years, moving from Asmara to Alexandria to Gondar, where he spent decades searching for Hirut in the regions around old battle sites, in villages large and small. He traveled long distances, a portrait of her face in his pocket, and always he asked, Do you know this girl who once fought with the great Aster? He searched in convents, in churches, in the caves between Gojjam and Axum, in the villages tucked inside the Simien Mountains, in every place he thought she might be. Finally, he gave up and found his way to Addis Ababa, this city that still acknowledges and mocks his defeat, hoping that somehow she would hear of his search and come to find his studio. He used to sit at Enrico's Café, hunched into his cappuccino, listening to conversations, waiting for them to veer toward that long-ago war and those women who knew so well the breaking points of fragile men. He waited to hear about Aster, the great wife of the great Kidane. But there was nothing. Only stories of the other proud warriors, those valiant men who were coming now into his studio, demanding proof of their greatness.

Two days ago, he stepped outside to find the scrawls on the walls of his building: *Ferenj* get out! Down with imperialism! Mussoloni out! Ettore wants to say that the protests on the streets have revived old memories of that other war—his war—but he knows it is something else that it has resurrected, something sharper than a memory, something alive that was waiting all this time to come back. In the studio, the old men are surprised that he doesn't flinch when they point their rifles at him as he peers through his camera. There are times when he wishes they would do what they threaten. Times when he wants to step from behind the lens and press his chest into the barrel and say, What right do I have to remain? It is what he still says to himself at night, in those moments when his brain has emptied itself of work and there is nothing to block those years from hurtling back. He lies in his small bed in the cramped room crowded with boxes of negatives and photos, and finds himself repeating, I photographed the dead and dying. I helped kill the innocent. I left my parents to their fate. What right do I have to remain?

—

HE IS REPEATING this quietly one morning when the door opens again and he flinches as always before looking up, dreading Seifu's appearance. One day, he knows, the man will find him. For a moment, he stares at this tall, elegant man with a shock of white hair, dressed in a well-tailored suit, and says nothing. Then he recognizes those eyes, that face. Dr. Hailu: the famed physician from Black Lion Hospital, the man who once fought beside the great Kidane, the man who refused, for over a decade, every effort by Ettore to speak to him. Ettore puts down the loupe he is using. He pushes aside the stack of contact sheets and fumbles with the cloth to wipe his hands. Neither of them speaks as he stumbles toward Hailu still standing at the door in his dark-gray suit and a shirt that seems impossibly white against a light-blue tie.

Dr. Hailu, he finds the voice to say. *Lei è dottore Hailu? È giusto? Likinegn?* Am I right? He is speaking in a halting Italian, a slow Amharic, as if they are both aware that language will never trudge the distance between them.

Hailu glances around the messy studio, looks long and hard at the backdrop of the Simien Mountains still hanging from the last shoot. You should leave this country, he says. This is not a place for foreigners.

There is no room for formalities, for falsehoods that would drape the harshness of the memories they share. He knows what Hailu is saying to him in the way he is speaking these words. He is addressing him as a familiar, refusing him the courtesy of formal address, of the respect that language bestows on those who are older or of higher rank or esteemed. They are simply two men standing in front of each other, one still regal and commanding, the other more wrinkled, more disheveled, more bowed by the years—a foreigner, a *ferenj*, Tal-yan.

Ettore steps forward so they both stand in the shaft of light flowing through the open door. I've received an official notice of eviction from my landlord, he says.

He looks around at his studio, tries not to let the man see the fear and sadness of it all, the relief that also floods in.

I have until the end of this month, he adds. Then he looks at Hailu and hopes this man can see what he himself has not been able to say. I've been searching for Hirut, he says. I gave her something, letters from my parents that I'd like to get back.

But Hailu is already turning away, stepping out of the door, and Ettore wants nothing more than to keep him here, to ask him: Surely you did not come here just to tell me what you know I already know?

I can photograph you if you wait, Ettore adds. It is a silly thought but he cannot stop himself. I can take your photograph and have it ready by tomorrow, for your children, for family. It's free, he lets drop.

Hailu shakes his head but he pauses as if he, too, has something to say. Framed by the door, backlit by sunlight, that glorious white hair gleams.

Your Amharic is good, Hailu says over his shoulder. You've learned a lot being here, haven't you? Then he turns back around and those eyes tremble with a fury that Ettore should know by now, but he draws back into himself nevertheless and lowers his eyes briefly before lifting them again.

You don't think you've taken enough? Hailu's voice quivers. What gives you people the right to act as if this is your home? Did you bleed for it? Yesterday, I operated on a boy—

Ettore flinches.

I operated on a boy, Hailu repeats. He is controlling himself with difficulty. Just a child. One of these protesters who wants to pretend he's a soldier. Who will keep our children safe in this country? People like you? he scoffs. You've done enough. Get out. All of you, and leave us alone.

I can't leave until I see Hirut, Ettore says. I know you fought with her, Dr. Hailu. Inside, he is roiling, shrinking beneath this man's disgust. He takes a breath to steady his voice. Once, before this place, he was someone, too, he wants to say. I have nothing else left of my mother and father except what I gave her, Ettore says instead. It is a double grief to lose someone when you are far away, he adds. And it is Ettore who now swallows the growing anger, the helpless rage that chews into his throat and takes away his words. I gave her their letters, I had letters for them I never sent. Dr. Hailu, I was afraid of the Italians too. I am Jewish. My parents . . . they were taken away, I never found them. If I could just find Hirut—

I don't know where she is.

Why did you come here? You must know I've been looking for her.

Hailu pauses and looks down at his hands. Ettore follows his gaze and notes the slender fingers with their tapered nails, the smooth skin. They are the hands of an educated man. How long ago it has been since they faced each other in a war that eventually counted them both as the enemy.

A messenger will come to you in two days. Send a letter to her through him, he will know her. That's all I can do.

You didn't have to come here, Ettore says. His heart is pounding so loud he can hardly hear his own voice. Thank you, Dr. Hailu. He bows deeply.

The man looks away then gazes at the backdrop again. I don't understand what I'm seeing these days, Hailu says. Back then, we knew immediately who to hate.

There is the silence again. Standing in a bolt of shifting light, he can see now that Hailu's eyes are red-rimmed, swollen from lack of sleep, but they still hold an unmistakeable fierceness tempered by a deep sorrow. We are old, Ettore thinks, we were young then, I was young, I was foolish, I was afraid of dying. But what words are enough now?

Would you like to take some photographs I shot of the Simien Mountains? Of some of you? You might recognize some of the *arbegnoch*. I have them. Ettore is speaking quickly as he goes to his desk and begins to pull out a box of photographs. Please, let me give you something. They're all here, some of my photos from those days. He is desperate to keep Hailu there, find a way to apologize, but Hailu has already walked out the door, leaving it open so sunlight streams in, a bold intruder in the somber studio that once felt like shelter.

Alone again, Ettore looks around, willing himself to focus on the messy pile of photographs in front of him. He used to be much neater. His photos used to be arranged by date, newspaper clippings kept in strict chronological order. The box he gave to Hirut a lifetime ago was carefully organized and labeled. Since leaving the army, he has come to care less about the sequence of things. Has come to understand that it is impossible to connect what happened to what will. What he knows is this: there is no past, there is no "what happened," there is only the moment that unfolds into the next, dragging everything with it, constantly renewing. Everything is happening at once.

—

SOMETIMES HE DREAMS of her, imagines her stepping into his room as if she belongs there, as if she has been waiting all these years for Ettore to catch that elusive corner of light and see that she was just a girl, just a frightened girl learning to be a soldier. On some nights when he aches for female company and finds someone to bring home, Ettore startles awake and is certain he sees Hirut, and that she has found him herself. Then his companion moves and moonlight stutters and Ettore stares into the empty dark and silently repeats his father's words: The boundaries of bodies are the least of all things. He wants to add, I'm sorry, I was not a good son, I was not a good man, I did many things wrong. He wants to shout that he had to do what he was ordered, that he was terrified, that all of them were at the mercy of war. But all Ettore can do is lie back and draw a stranger's body closer to his and try to fall asleep to the familiar ache of old regret.

Interlude: 1974

Protesters have gathered in squares and schools across the city, calling for his ouster, but Haile Selassie sits in his office winding his gramophone, waiting for the final act to push Aida and Radames into the cave and toward the last song. In his nearly eighty years on this Earth, almost half of them have been spent with Aida and her father, Amonasro, with Radames and the Egyptians, and today, he needs their reassuring presence to push him toward those glorious days in 1941 when he returned triumphant from exile. Haile Selassie settles the needle in place and leans back on his sofa to let the melody flood the room and drown the chaos. He stares into the corner of the room, into the golden haze of the afternoon light seeping through his curtains, and he looks for so long that he thinks he sees the curtains shift. Then Amonasro steps out of the shadows and extends a hand.

Haile Selassie, Teferi Mekonnen, Amonasro says to him. Are you just going to sit there?

Haile Selassie blinks and rubs his eyes, and Amonasro is no more. The emperor sits perfectly still, bewildered. Then when he looks again, Amonasro has returned.

Teferi, Aida's father says.

Yes? The emperor pats his chest to calm his leaping heart. He knows Amonasro is not there, but he cannot convince himself that what he sees and hears is not real.

We must hurry, Amonasro says. We are fathers and kings.

Amonasro wears a simple shamma, finely woven and draped expertly. His head is a wild bloom of curls: a warrior's hairstyle. Across his handsome face, a slender scar traces the line above his brow.

Haile Selassie looks through the window. It is late afternoon and the demonstrators have not gone home. Dust continues to rise from their marching feet. A brick thrown over the gate with alarming strength almost hits one of his tense guards. What he sees is what exists, so what is it that has just stepped into his private office?

Help me save my daughter, Amonasro says. She has gone to meet the enemy of my people and we must stop her. Help me save my Aida. He points behind him, beyond the emperor's office, out of the palace, to that place where a woman sits on the edge of a precipice and waits.

Amonasro looks nothing like those awful drawings and pictures sent back from Europe's opera houses. The man standing before him is proudly Ethiopian. That he has not bothered to bow before Haile Selassie is a small detail that the emperor will allow, since he is refusing to bow himself.

Not now, old friend, the emperor says, shaking his head. Do you not see that we must save Ethiopia? Haile Selassie taps the window next to the sofa, taking comfort in the reliable sound. Do you not see that our people are in pain?

Help me before it's too late and we are no more, Amonasro insists.

Haile Selassie says what he has been thinking, what he has thought for decades: But the girl, your daughter, this Aida, was foolish to fall in love with the enemy. She was stupid to forget her own royal birth and lead with her heart. This is doom she brought on herself. Why didn't you teach her better?

Amonasro bows and drops his head in his hands. I fought a war with Egypt and she was captured, he says. It was my fault. Surely you know what I mean, King of Ethiopia, father of a dead daughter.

Abbaba. Abbaba. And this time, it is Zenebwork quivering in the gentle glow of sunlight rippling through the curtains from the window on the other side of the room. Abbaba, did you forget me?

The emperor ignores his daughter and turns to Amonasro. He hears his name rise above splintered screams from beyond the palace compound, then a word rings clear above the cacophony: *Leyba! Leyba! Thief! Thief!*

The emperor peeks through the curtain then shuts it. Nearly forty years ago, the same people were falling to their knees at his return, overjoyed to have their country back after it had been stolen by invaders. He shakes his head and turns his attention back to Amonasro.

You fought a war that they started, Haile Selassie says. He thinks of the invasion, of those treacherous Italians, and the fury from so long ago rises again and burns his chest. You were forced to do as you did, he says to Amonasro, tipping into that shimmering space between them. But their songs will never tell the entire truth, Haile Selassie adds. They will never sing of their own corruptions.

He sees Zenebwork moving closer to Amonasro. On any other day, he would greet her and offer her consolation as he has done since he sent her off to be married to that terrible man. He would apologize and let her anger tear through him, knowing that this is also what it means to love. But today, she is too much. Today, everything feels like too much.

Abbaba, he wants to find his daughter, Zenebwork says. We must help him.

To leave a daughter to die alone is a father's greatest failure, Amonasro says.

Haile Selassie stares at Amonasro and squares his shoulders. He puts his feet together and shifts from side to side. He pats his medals and stiffens his back. He juts out his chin and clenches his jaw. Even after all these decades, his body remembers these movements, it has not forgotten what it means to be at war.

Abbaba, did you forget me?

Outside: his name shouted like a curse. Inside: guilt crashing against him and suffocating him of air. So Haile Selassie settles the needle toward the end of the record on the gramophone. He tries to focus on that final act in *Aida*, waits for Radames to discover that confused girl who has entered the cave to die needlessly with him. And as he listens, the emperor shakes his head in the empty room because he has come to discern the realness of those things not seen. This is why, perhaps, he is not surprised when Simonides steps out from behind the curtain and slides next to Zenebwork. The emperor watches as the old philosopher puts an arm around her shoulder and draws her close.

Teferi, did you forget? the Greek poet asks. Which room in your memory did you leave us? Then he looks back at the emperor and shakes his head too.

How many times must I bear witness to my daughter dying? This is Amonasro, still clutching his face in his hands.

And then the three of them—Zenebwork, Simonides, Amonasro—pivot toward Haile Selassie and before any of them can speak, Haile Selassie clears his throat and taps his sternum and he says, We have placed everything here for safekeeping. He flattens his palms on top of his head and repeats again: We placed everything here as well. We will hold this country together in this way.

Teferi, Simonides says. Surely you remember where you belong. Surely you know how to put everything in its rightful place. We taught you well, did we not?

This is what he remembers: taking a weeping Zenebwork and a sorrowful Menen to the train station to return Zenebwork back to that terrible man, leaving his daughter in the care of escorts and waving to her as the train sped away.

Your place was not with him, my daughter, Haile Selassie says now. It has always been here, with us. I'm sorry, *lijé*, I'm so sorry I let you get on the train.

Then he waits for Zenebwork to leave as she has always done, but this time, she does not. A shot rings from the distance, followed by a series of rapid gunfire. The emperor flinches.

There is another who wants to take our place again, Haile Selassie admits. There is another who wants our throne.

Zenebwork holds out her hand and crosses the threshold between shadow and light, between night and a new day, between his old life and this one bursting to break free.

But you remember, don't you? Simonides asks. You recall the life you left behind in the rubble? Step into those rooms and find your place. Do not leave the dead unclaimed.

But Amonasro shakes his head and says, Let's go. And he says, We are kings. And he adds, We must save our daughters from those dangers of our own making.

And Haile Selassie feels Zenebwork leaning into the shadow descending on him. She is listening, waiting for his response, her anger like a solid wind slapping against his face, stinging his eyes and bringing tears down his cheeks. He taps his sternum again and Aida's voice balloons in the room. She is calling for Radames, working her way toward becoming a ghost.

My people looked for me when they could no longer identify their dead, Simonides continues above Radames's voice soaring toward his last breath. When the dead are lost, those who carry their memory will find you, Teferi. And what will you remember to tell them?

We are kings of Ethiopia, Amonasro says again. We must save our children from the dangers of our own making. And Amonasro points to the emperor's uniform: You must become someone else so you are not recognized, as I did when I was captured. You must become a shadow of yourself and bear witness to your own demise, like me. Come, Teferi, let's go.

So Haile Selassie reaches into the bottom drawer of his desk where, tucked in the back, is a neatly tied parcel he has kept hidden for nearly forty years. He takes out a threadbare shirt and sagging trousers. He holds the items up: it is what one of his men brought for him to wear as he left his country in 1936, a feeble disguise in case he needed to leave as someone other than an emperor. He feels a shiver course through him and he turns to look from Amonasro to Simonides. He avoids his daughter's stubborn gaze. He slips out of his clothes and puts on the peasant's costume.

When he is finished, he turns to look at himself, the shock a cold splash against his face. What he sees reflected in the mirror is that other image of himself, that other one who once moved in his shadow and led armies against his old enemies with a girl for a guard: the Shadow King. He touches his cheeks, his brow, the gray hair that now graces his burdened head.

Is the king dead? Zenebwork asks. Is my father gone?

We are here, *lijé*, the emperor says. It is us.

Long live the king, Amonasro and Simonides say as they look at him and nod.

The king is dead, he says.

Long live Ethiopia, they all say.

Abbaba, Zenebwork says, Are you sending me away again on that train? She slides next to his ear, pressing against his cheek.

Haile Selassie shakes his head. Zenebwork, my daughter, I will go get you and you will stay with me, the emperor says, reaching out to take his lost daughter's hand. You will stay with me till the end of my days. Don't let go, he whispers. Don't leave me.

Then Haile Selassie and Zenebwork walk out of his palace together. He feels the warmth of her seeping into the cool breeze. Beside him, Simonides the aged poet, and Amonasro the grieving father of Aida, move together through Piassa, past Ettore's shuttered studio, and toward Addis Ababa's train station.

THE AIR THAT SWEEPS THROUGH THE TRAIN STATION WHEN ETTORE STEPS in is thick, heavy with old dust and sharp fumes, and a pungent scent that brings tears to Hirut's eyes. Hirut lowers the cover back on the box and presses it into her lap. She tucks the letter inside her dress. She feels the corner of the envelope, softened by age, poke into her chest like a cautionary finger. She is supposed to give him everything. She has wanted to rid herself of every memory of him and those years, but she knows the value of that letter and though she may not know what the words say, she has learned how to decipher the movement of the hand: its tightness or sprawling openness, its generosity or selfishness. She has seen the small, perfect script crammed onto the single page and she imagines a frugal, strict father: her father with his own precise lines on the old Wujigra that she still polishes every day, the evenness of the row with the five marks, the symmetry of it all.

She understands what this letter is, and so she knows that Ettore has no right to it because of all that they have lost since he invaded her country, because of all she has lost, because she is a thief, and she has had to take in order to correct an unnatural balance. Because Aster was right: girls like her were born to fit into the world, the world was not built to mold around her. Because there are those born to own things, and those brought forth to keep those things in their rightful place. Hirut takes a deep breath, slides the closed box from her lap onto the ground, flattens the letter close against her skin, and adjusts her dress to hide her scar as best as she can. Then she waits.

Ettore bursts through the door and stands at the threshold, searching, while draped in dying afternoon light. He is older and more worn,
his face creased with lines brought by both years and worry, and Hirut
might have felt a softness for him then, might have understood the way
time carves its way steadily across the body, but she sees him standing
rigid, with a military bearing that he has not forgotten: as if he still has
a rifle and that camera slung around him. And that is when she knows
for sure that he will not get that letter.

Hirut turns, uncertain of why she is trembling.

Then when Ettore walks into the station with his shoulders slightly
raised from the memory of a camera he was wise not to bring with him,
Hirut stands. For a moment, she has to feel her dress to make sure it is
on, that she is not naked before him, shaking in loathing and humiliation as Fucelli orders, Again, *soldato*, take another picture.

Hirut straightens. She lifts her chin and stares at Ettore as he pauses
and looks at her, recognition and shame rippling through light and
shadow to shrink the space between them. And when he takes a step in
her direction, nervous and bewildered, Hirut salutes.

He pauses, nearly stumbles, and between them the valley expands
and gunpowder rises in the breeze to choke them both, but he keeps
moving forward as if he has been expecting this, as if he has prepared
himself for this moment, has been getting ready for it since the last time
they faced each other on the battlefield. Ettore walks toward her as if
the path to forgiveness lay between them, as if years erase scars and
photographs and history, as if that hand stretching out to grasp Hirut's
can raise the dead and return all he has stolen.

He expects pity, this much she can see through the haze of old battles
and the unearthly silence. He expects the years not to have hardened
her fury. He expects to walk toward her as if he has never worn a uniform, as if he did not mold himself to fit its contours. Here is the truth he
wants to ignore: that what is forged into memory tucks itself into bone
and muscle. It will always be there and it will follow us to the grave.

Ettore has to look around to make sure that Seifu is not there when Hirut stands up and salutes. What he feels is a steady pressure at his back, a knife's blade poking between his shoulder blades. Because when she gets to her feet and raises herself tall and gives him that Ethiopian salute, he thinks he sees her face transformed by hatred and revulsion before it shifts into something else he cannot describe, a recognition of something just over his shoulder. If he had brought his camera with him, he could have captured it to study later. He sees the box next to her feet, the same one filled with his letters and old photographs, the same one that must surely contain that last letter from his father that he hopes—knows—she must have taken in the ambush, along with that terrible picture of her.

He has brought with him another photograph to give Hirut, something to exchange for the box, and the letter, and everything he has taken from her. It is a photograph he took of her in a quiet moment between her and Aster. They are unaware of his presence just beyond the prison, oblivious to everything but their own urgent conversation. Hirut is drenched in bright sunlight, the rays scalloping radiant beams around her head. She is angling toward the other woman, hands clasped around that barbed-wire fence, tipping against it without concern for comfort, impervious to the sharp metal digging into her palms: a soldier determined to continue despite pain. He had stared at Hirut then, really looked at her without the filter of a lens. You and I, he had said to himself in that moment, are not so different after all. A steady tightness had wound itself around his chest until he lifted his camera to take the shot.

He had misunderstood himself until it was too late. He had mistaken the gentle certainty he felt with her as an inspired inclination toward the camera. He had confused his heart for his eye. He had become his father's son, the son of a man who was a ghost, caught between what could be expressed and what needed to be kept silent, slowly disappearing.

Hirut, he says, speaking her name to himself in the train station. He stretches out his hand, her photograph in his shirt pocket, sweat collecting at the back of his neck. Hirut, he repeats. It is a name and a call for forgiveness, a sound falling at his feet to clear a path for him to walk.

Ettore sees Hirut still standing at attention, her mouth a firm and hard line on a beautiful face. He trembles, unable to stop his knees from buckling. He knows that she sees his outstretched hand and still, Hirut refuses to shift out of her salute. Refuses to be anything other than the soldier she has always been, even when a prisoner. The boundaries of bodies are the least of all things: the words from so long ago come back to him.

Hirut, he says again, certain that this is how he will become undone. This is how a name exposes a breach in the earth. Hirut, he repeats, and lets himself slide forward. He takes out the photograph and extends it to her. Look, he says. Look. Please.

Look, he says to her. I'm sorry, he adds, as if that is an apology, as if those are words strong enough to pull the ripped seams of her together and hold her intact.

Hirut shakes her head, still straight-backed in her salute, and takes a step away from him. Stay there, she says, don't get any closer.

She is not looking at him, though. She is staring at the improbable figure who has come through the heavy doors into the station. It looks like Minim, but he is at home, her neighbor, far away. So she is certain it is the emperor. Haile Selassie, also called Jan Hoy, also called Ras Teferi Mekonnen, also called the sun unto his people. It is him. Hirut freezes in that salute. There is no logic that can balance this vision.

Outside, the voices of protesters meld with the prayers of the devout and all that sways between cruelty and devotion lays itself bare before her: manifest in an aging king dressed as a peasant, and a former enemy soldier repeating her name.

Minim, she says, letting her confusion wash over her and take control. Minim. Then she corrects herself, because she knows who it is. Jan Hoy, Emperor Haile Selassie, Your Majesty, how have you come here?

A crack in the world has been revealed and the emperor stands at its center, hearing this woman point to him in shock and call him a word like it is a name. Minim: Nothing.

Minim, she says again, as if it is an oath and a plea, as if this utterance will absolve his people of their past and future deeds. Those same people who have been raising their fists and shouting outside as if they want to hammer a dent into the heavens.

He turns to look for Amonasro, to ask him: Is this the child you were trying to save? But Amonasro is no longer there. He looks for Simonides, but the Greek poet has also disappeared. The only one who remains is Zenebwork, who is vibrating in this other woman's rage, melting into it, finding comfort in its sharp contours.

Haile Selassie turns to look at this woman again. She is stuck in her stiff salute, pivoting between him and an Italian that the emperor is just noticing.

Are you waiting for your father? he asks her, because he is not sure of anything. He is uncertain, even, of who he really is, dressed in the clothes of a peasant while a woman who is starting to look vaguely familiar tells him he is nothing, then addresses him by his many names. He has forgotten her, he decides. He has left her out of one of the many rooms in his head and she is floundering, desperate for recognition, for a way to step out of the world of the dead and into the living who carry names.

Do we remember you? he continues. We must, he adds. We are sure of it. Give us your name so we can bring you forth.

She tilts her head: My name is Hirut, daughter of Fasil and Getey, proud wife of the great Aklilu, grateful mother of two strong daughters, closest friend and neighbor to the powerful Aster. Then she points to the shocked Italian bowing nervously to him. He is an invader, she says. Tell him to leave, if you are really the emperor.

The Italian flinches and stares at him, then lowers his eyes.

And who are you to tell us this, Haile Selassie says to Hirut.

I am a soldier, Hirut replies. I was the brave guard of the Shadow King.

Haile Selassie nods slowly. And others are trying to replace us again, did you know that?

Hirut, Ettore says. I don't understand what's happening but please, take this picture and give me what's mine.

The emperor turns from the stunned foreigner speaking in perfect Amharic and grips his own empty hand.

Hirut drops her head and folds her arms across her chest. Go away, she says to Ettore. Leave my country now. Take this, she adds, shoving the box toward him with her foot. Get out of here. *Vatene*, she whispers. You're not welcome in this place.

She speaks those words through a growing chasm that has swallowed that thing her heart cannot contain. Standing before him, Hirut recognizes him as something both startling and familiar. A new truth and an age-old deception.

Hirut, he says, I'm sorry. I did things I shouldn't have, he adds. I followed orders, and I did much more. My father's letter, is it in the box? Do you have it?

Ettore swallows and wipes his eyes and she sees a fleeting glimpse of the young man he once was. The young man she both hated and pitied and understood and something else unnameable.

I have nothing left but what's in there, he adds, pointing to the box. Nothing else has any meaning to me except what's in this room, right now, but I must leave. Let me take something with me, please. And he says her name with the familiarity that has always existed between them, marred by years and war, but still intact: Hirut.

Hirut feels the emperor's eyes on her. He is shaking his head, looking from the box to Ettore, from Ettore to her, from her to his own tattered clothing and his hand grasping air.

The dead will shelter the living, Haile Selassie says quietly. They will find us once we have named them one by one. Isn't that so, my daughter? And he nods to his empty hand.

Hirut feels something rise to the surface, an emotion that has always been there, waiting. She lets it roll over her and press into her chest then blossom in her head. And in the broad band of light creeping through the windows of the train station, Hirut takes out the letter and extends it to Ettore as she begins to speak:

Getey, Fasil, Aster, Nardos, Zenebwork, Siti, Tesfaye, Dawit, Beniam, Tariku, Girum, Amha, Bekafa, Bisrat, Desta, Befekadu, Saleh, Ililta, Meaza, Lakew, Ahmed, Eskinder, Biruk, Genet, Gabriel, Matteos, Leul, Hoda, Birtukan, Mulumabet, Estifanos, Hewan, Lukas, Habte, Mimi, Kiros, Mohamed, Wongel, Atnaf, Jembere, Imru, Senait, Yosef, Mahlet, Alem, Girma, Gelila, Birtukan, Freiwot, Tiruneh, Marta, Harya, Hayalnesh, Mengiste, Zinash, Petros, Anketse, Sergut, Mikael, Mogus, Teodros, Checole, Kidane, Lidia, Fifi and Ferres, and the cook, the cook, the cook, and as she says their names, she feels them gather around her and urge her on: Tell them, Hirut, we were the Shadow King. We were those who stepped into a country left dark by an invading plague and gave new hope to Ethiopia's people.

Hirut turns from Ettore, now folded into his grief while clutching his father's letter. She lifts her head to the sounds of gunfire and shouting. Then she steps toward the emperor as the calls for his demise spiral up like windblown clouds.

I'll walk you home, she says. I'll protect you from those outside, Your Majesty. I'll be your guard. She takes his hand and grips it tight. She watches as he extends his other hand beside him, grasping air and time.

And as the door closes behind them, Hirut stands tall and repeats the names of those who came before her, of those who fell as she rose to her feet in choking fumes and continued to run, and she lets memory lie across her shoulders like a cape while she salutes the Shadow Kings, every single one, and raises her Wujigra, a brave and fearsome soldier once more. Then Hirut and the emperor walk to the palace together.

Photo

Look at the two of them: those women pressed against the barbed-wire fence while one clutches it in her hands as if it were knotted silk. Look at the flicker of light that will soon consume the enemy camp and announce a man who will race down the hill, his legs sturdy and sure, his arms swinging with fury while he cries his son's name. What is seen cannot explain what exists: Hirut and Aster pressed against the barbed-wire fence while Hirut clutches it in her hands and the other woman says to her: They're coming to get us tonight, they will kill every guard and set us free and you must be ready, the cook has let me know. And when Hirut turns her head so that rays scallop around her like a brilliant flame, what can the eye see but just a young woman seeking comfort in the warmth of an afternoon sun? What does the eye know of her only request: Let me kill the photographer myself. What can the camera see of her later mercy and that lifelong rage she will finally release in the surrender of a father's letter to his son? What can Ettore know, after all, of the distances crossed and promises kept, of those unworded emotions that she has left unbound by futile vocabulary? What can he know except what he sees while staring at that young woman grasping knotted silk as if she were born to be draped in it: a beauty incomprehensible and ferocious, strong enough to break through bone and settle into a heart and split it forever.

AUTHOR'S NOTE

The first stories I heard of the war between fascist Italy and Ethiopia came from my grandfather. His tales focused on the heroic but poorly equipped Ethiopian fighters who struggled against a modern European army. Growing up, I imagined these men, stoic and regal like my grandfather, facing tanks and sophisticated artillery with outdated guns, and winning. It wasn't until much later that I discovered the story of my great-grandmother, Getey.

She was just a girl, married but too young to live with an adult husband. When Emperor Haile Selassie ordered families to send their eldest son to the army, she volunteered to go as the eldest child; her brothers were not old enough. Her father disagreed and when he gave his gun to her new husband to represent the family, she sued to get the weapon. She won the case, and in front of the judges, she took her father's rifle and began to sing the boastful songs of Ethiopian soldiers as they recounted their many strengths and courage. She enlisted, and went to war.

My great-grandmother represents one of the many gaps in European and African history. *The Shadow King* tells the story of those Ethiopian women who fought alongside men, who even today have remained no more than errant lines in faded documents. What I have come to understand is this: The story of war has always been a masculine story, but this was not true for Ethiopia and it has never been that way in any form of struggle. Women have been there, we are here now.

ACKNOWLEDGMENTS

This book is a work of fiction. Historical events and timelines have been altered or compressed for the purposes of the narrative. The many years spent writing this novel have led me to stories that I had not known existed, and that I did not know were mine. I have many to thank for each step of the way. This list will not do them justice, but it is my humble attempt.

My first introduction to this history came from stories told by my parents and relatives, by all those Ethiopians who refused to let this story die, and in the retelling kept the dead alive. The earliest pages were written at a residency at The Santa Maddalena Foundation at the invitation of Beatrice Monti della Corte. Thank you, Beatrice, for sharing your memories. The Fulbright Scholar Program and the entire Fulbright staff in Rome opened doors and provided life-changing opportunities while answering my most tedious questions. My research advisor in Italy, Sandro Triulzi, and his wife, Paola Splendore, led me to new discoveries, introduced me to those who could answer more questions, and invited me over for meals rich with stories and laughter. The Emily Harvey Foundation was a gift in the early days of this book. Shaul Bassi and Università Ca'Foscari in Venice made that beautiful city feel like home and gave me the time and space to research and write. The Puycelsi Writers Retreat gave me blessed isolation and breathtaking views from which to begin edits. Tarekegn Gebreyesus, Debrework Zewdie, Ruth Iyob, Gabriel Tzeggai, Ruth Ben-Ghiat, Shiferaw Bekele, the late

Abiye Ford, and many others provided invaluable advice and resources. Two incredible women, Deb Willis and Ellyn Toscano, supported and listened and pushed me toward new ways of seeing images and talking about them, and never let me forget the true joy of research. My fantastic colleagues in the Queens College MFA Program in Creative Writing & Literary Translation provided immeasurable support and understanding during this entire process and alleviated so much stress.

To those who never said, Aren't you done yet? Thank you. To those who did, it's okay.

To my readers who dropped everything when I rushed in with a draft, and kindly offered invaluable feedback—Laila Lalami, Maud Newton, Sabina Murray—I owe you. Special thanks to those who have given me encouragement and no-bullshit advice over the long years of this book, and opened their homes and shared many meals: Mylitta Chaplain, Sarida Scott Montgomery, Tedros Mengiste, Anketse Debebe, Jennifer Gilmore, Elif Batuman, Mona Eltahawy, Emmanual Iduma, Chiké Frankie Edozien, Robert Rutledge, Cheryl Moskowitz, Diana Matar, Molly Roden Winter, Alessandra di Maio, Harya Tarekegn, Hayalnesh Tarekegn, Genet Lakew, Hiwote Kenfe, Awam Ampka, Gunja Sengupta, Jeff Marowits, Yasmine El-Rashid, Alberto Manguel, Craig Stephenson, Gregory Pardlo, Jeff Pearce. To Juan and Nelly Navarro, for your generosity and kindness over the years. To my love, Marco, who was all of this and so much more, who believed in me through endless drafts and long nights and stayed up just to talk: we did it.

My deepest gratitude to my editor, Jill Bialosky, who waited patiently and read carefully and edited brilliantly. And to my agent, Lynn Nesbit, who was there and believed and pushed when sometimes I faltered.

To those women and girls of Ethiopia who would not let themselves be completely erased by history, who stood up when I was looking for them and made themselves known. I see you. I will always see you.

THE SHADOW KING

Maaza Mengiste

DISCUSSION QUESTIONS

1. *The Shadow King* highlights the previously lesser-known role of female soldiers fighting in the Second Italo-Ethiopian War (and in world conflicts more generally). To what extent do you think art is the most useful means of changing existing historical narratives? What are the advantages of using fiction to showcase new aspects of historical experience, versus nonfiction?

2. Characters in *The Shadow King* are anchored by objects that carry great significance for them: Hirut's rifle, Aster's necklace, Ettore's letters. What do you think accounts for the power of these physical objects? Are there any objects in your life that hold a similar kind of strong personal significance?

3. What do you think about Kidane's use of the nickname "Little One" for Hirut and, in a flashback, Aster (p. 48)? What do you think he intends to convey by using this phrase, and how do Hirut and Aster respond to it?

4. What do we learn about the story of the cook's life through her scenes with Hirut and Aster? Why is the cook the only character in the novel to remain unnamed?

5. The ethics of Ettore's work are ambiguous. On one hand, his photographs help him "bear witness" (p. 287) to the violence of war, but on the other hand, Ettore feels increasingly uncomfortable with his work and feels that "every photograph has become a broken oath with himself" (p. 291). To what extent are Ettore's war photographs important records of violence perpetrated, and to what extent are they acts of violence?

6. Minim becomes a shadow king for Emperor Haile Selassie, but the novel is full of characters who act as doubles or shadow versions of one another. How many characters in *The Shadow King* function as the shadow of another character? What do you think comprises or defines a shadow king?

7. Why does Emperor Haile Selassie flee Ethiopia? How did the sections from his perspective influence the narrative? Did you feel sympathy for him, anger, some other emotion?

8. Aster, Kidane, Leo Navarra, and Haile Selassie have all lost children, and Hirut has lost both of her parents. How does the loss reverberate through their lives, and how do those losses explicitly shape their actions and choices in relation to other characters?

9. Inside Hirut's box of photographs are "the many dead that insist on resurrection" (p. 3). How does the theme of resurrection function throughout the novel? To what extent does the novel suggest that resurrection is possible? To what extent is resurrection of memories or secrets in fact inevitable?

10. *The Shadow King* includes many narrative descriptions of and questions about the ethicality of war photographs. Which do you think is a more faithful record of historical experience, photographs or writing? How does the novel influence your feelings about this choice?

11. What role do Getey and Fasil, Hirut's parents, play in the narrative of *The Shadow King*? How does their memory influence Hirut and Aster?

12. What do you conceive of the relationship between Carlo Fucelli and Fifi? Do you think they loved each other? What are the dynamics of their relationship?

13. What was the effect of learning about characters from both the Ethiopian and the Italian sides? How do you think the novel would have been different if it were told solely from Hirut's perspective?

14. The chorus says of Aster's relationship to Kidane, "She will learn obedience as a way to survive" (p. 316). Is this true in the end of Aster? Is this true of Ettore, who calls himself "the beast bound by obedience" (p. 351)? How does Hirut subvert the idea of obedience as a survival strategy throughout the novel?

15. After learning that Aster helped Hirut's parents escape, Hirut asks Aster, "And why did you do nothing to help me? Are you so jealous that you have no heart?" (p. 368). What do you think informed Aster and Hirut's relationship at the beginning of the novel? How has their relationship changed by the novel's end?

16. Why do you think Hirut returns forty years later to give Ettore the letters?

SELECTED NORTON BOOKS WITH
READING GROUP GUIDES AVAILABLE

For a complete list of Norton's works with reading group guides,
please go to wwnorton.com/reading-guides.

Diana Abu-Jaber	*Life Without a Recipe*
Diane Ackerman	*The Zookeeper's Wife*
Michelle Adelman	*Piece of Mind*
Molly Antopol	*The UnAmericans*
Andrea Barrett	*Archangel*
Rowan Hisayo Buchanan	*Harmless Like You*
Ada Calhoun	*Wedding Toasts I'll Never Give*
Bonnie Jo Campbell	*Mothers, Tell Your Daughters*
	Once Upon a River
Lan Samantha Chang	*Inheritance*
Ann Cherian	*A Good Indian Wife*
Evgenia Citkowitz	*The Shades*
Amanda Coe	*The Love She Left Behind*
Michael Cox	*The Meaning of Night*
Jeremy Dauber	*Jewish Comedy*
Jared Diamond	*Guns, Germs, and Steel*
Caitlin Doughty	*From Here to Eternity*
Andre Dubus III	*House of Sand and Fog*
	Townie: A Memoir
Anne Enright	*The Forgotten Waltz*
	The Green Road
Amanda Filipacchi	*The Unfortunate Importance of Beauty*
Beth Ann Fennelly	*Heating & Cooling*
Betty Friedan	*The Feminine Mystique*
Maureen Gibbon	*Paris Red*
Stephen Greenblatt	*The Swerve*
Lawrence Hill	*The Illegal*
	Someone Knows My Name
Ann Hood	*The Book That Matters Most*
	The Obituary Writer
Dara Horn	*A Guide for the Perplexed*
Blair Hurley	*The Devoted*

Meghan Kenny	*The Driest Season*
Nicole Krauss	*The History of Love*
Don Lee	*The Collective*
Amy Liptrot	*The Outrun: A Memoir*
Donna M. Lucey	*Sargent's Women*
Bernard MacLaverty	*Midwinter Break*
Maaza Mengiste	*Beneath the Lion's Gaze*
Claire Messud	*The Burning Girl*
	When the World Was Steady
Liz Moore	*Heft*
	The Unseen World
Neel Mukherjee	*The Lives of Others*
	A State of Freedom
Janice P. Nimura	*Daughters of the Samurai*
Rachel Pearson	*No Apparent Distress*
Richard Powers	*Orfeo*
Kirstin Valdez Quade	*Night at the Fiestas*
Jean Rhys	*Wide Sargasso Sea*
Mary Roach	*Packing for Mars*
Somini Sengupta	*The End of Karma*
Akhil Sharma	*Family Life*
	A Life of Adventure and Delight
Joan Silber	*Fools*
Johanna Skibsrud	*Quartet for the End of Time*
Mark Slouka	*Brewster*
Kate Southwood	*Evensong*
Manil Suri	*The City of Devi*
	The Age of Shiva
Madeleine Thien	*Do Not Say We Have Nothing*
	Dogs at the Perimeter
Vu Tran	*Dragonfish*
Rose Tremain	*The American Lover*
	The Gustav Sonata
Brady Udall	*The Lonely Polygamist*
Brad Watson	*Miss Jane*
Constance Fenimore Woolson	*Miss Grief and Other Stories*